"BRANN, YARO IS TRAPPED!"

Brann looked questioningly at the change child Jaril. "Trapped?"

"I was round a bend about twenty feet behind when the thing closed round her." Jaril shuddered in his peculiar way, his outline melting and reforming, his hands growing transparent, then solid. "I tried to get to her. There was a barrier. I couldn't see it, I couldn't feel it either, not really, I just couldn't get to her. I tried going over it. Around it. Under it. I went into the mountain itself, I slid through stone. That's dangerous, it's so easy to get confused so you don't know up from down, but I did it. No good. It was a sphere, Brann, it was all around her. I couldn't reach her. I couldn't even feel her there. Do you understand? My sister. The only being in this place who's LIKE me. If I lost her, I'd be alone. I went wired for a while, I don't know how long." He shuddered again, the pulses of fleshmelt moving swiftly along his body.

"When I knew what I was doing again, I was eagleshape, driving south as fast as I could fly. I couldn't think why for the longest, I wasn't capable of thinking, Brann, but I kept flying. After a while, I decided I was coming for you. Brann, we need you. . . ."

A GATHERING OF STONES

JO CLAYTON

DAW BOOKS, INC.
DONALD A. WOLLHEIM, PUBLISHER

1633 Broadway, New York, NY 10019

DAW Book Collectors No. 776.

First Printing, April 1989

1 2 3 4 5 6 7 8 9

PRINTED IN THE U.S.A.

IMPETUS:
The drive toward Rebirth begins:

The Chained God looked at h/itself and found little to like in what h/it saw. Even as h/it watched, cells died and h/its intelligence diminished by that much. H/its LIFE diminished. Time is, h/it thought. The harvest is due. Bring forth the Tools. Draw in the Catalysts. Let the Rebirthing commence.

BRING FORTH THE TOOLS:

COME THE GENIOD
  THEY—
(plural in the limited sense that there were many discrete
units and in the fuzzier sense that there were a number of
agglomerations of these units with varying degrees of
self-awareness)
  THEY—
were hunger and desire in a self-created void. They were
fierce with life but already beginning to die, turning in a
frenzy on each other, the stronger devouring stray units and
smaller agglomerations. They had been too greedy here,
had eaten life with an appetite never satisfied, breeding and
breeding, splitting and joining until the reality they occupied
was filled with them, the geniod, a name they'd swallowed
with some long-forgotten life-form and adopted along with
the knowledge of NAMING.
  THEY—
knew despair as their numbers dwindled.

A LIGHT appeared in the darkness, a pinpoint, then a
fire.

  THEY—
drew back, frightened; density increased, desire rose and
drowned fear.

A VOICE called: COME AND FEED.

  THEY—
hesitated. They had been stung before, their units, their
ogienowad, were trapped and consumed by the creatures
they were grazing on, food rebelling against its destined
role.

The LIGHT expanded to a shimmering oval.
IT screamed: LIFE! ENERGY! COME AND TAKE.

6

THEY—
milled about a second longer, then the largest geniod leapt for the GATE and swept through it, the rest swept along behind it, exploding into a new reality—dropping into a forceweb that closed around them, the trap they'd feared.

I HAVE A BARGAIN FOR YOU, GENIOD: AGREE AND LIVE: REFUSE AND DIE.

We agree. We agree. We agree.
What do you want?
We serve better when we work for ourselves as well.
What do you want?

LISTEN.

We hear. We hear. We hear.

ASSEMBLE. COLLECT. DELIVER.

What do we deliver?

THE STONES.

What do we get for doing this?

FREEDOM. FOOD. A WORLD TO GRAZE ON.

You can promise this?

I CAN.

We accept.

##

These assemblages of ogienowad merged and grew larger, took the forms of men and women and traveled about the World, dining on the sly, their greed constrained by fear—fear of the GOD who'd summoned them. He told them where to go and what to do, he found them a place to rest and ruminate, a cavern of crystals like the inside of an immense geode where they could hover and glimmer and wake in those crystals fantasies of light and color.

These are the tools the Chained God used to break the stonebearers loose and send them out to acquire the Stones, these are the geniod

   —First among the assemblages, the strongest in will and skill and power:

PALAMI KUMINDRI geniod   Who took the form of a
                          Jorpashil courtesan

—Her servant and Housemaster:
CAMMAN CALLAN geniod   Who took the form of a
                            Temueng wrestler

—Another Courtesan, not so intelligent or powerful as the
Kumindri:
TRITHIL ESMOON geniod   Who took the form of a
                            Phrasi courtesan

—The last of the named geniod (unimportant, except for
his effect on Settsimaksimin):
MUSTEBA XA geniod   Who took the form of
                            Settsimaksimin's teacher
                            and master

—Numerous others, unnamed but very busy at the Chained
God's work.

DRAW IN THE STONEBEARERS:
They are the chosen—by the God and by the Stones themselves.

1. BRANN
2. YARIL and JARIL
3. SETTSIMAKSIMIN
4. KORIMENEI
5. TRAGO
6. DANNY BLUE

1. BRANN, THE DRINKER OF SOULS, affinity: Massulit Called (by friends and those fond of her), Bramble, Bramble-all-thorns, Thornlet.

She was born in the mountain valley called Arth Slya, her father a potter of genius, her mother a weaver of tapestries. When Slya Fireheart thought up a plot to get at some Kadda witches who were too powerful for her to touch directly, the god reached into the realities and plucked forth two juvenile energy beings, JARIL and YARIL; Brann was *changed* so she could feed them and in that *changing* became DRINKER OF SOULS and effectively immortal. In the course of Slya's plot, she rescued her people from slavery, opened a Gate for Slya who came stomping in and destroyed her enemies. Then she was turned loose to live how she could, an eleven-year-old girl in the body of a woman in her twenties.

She wandered about the world for a hundred years, settled for another hundred years as the Potter at Shaynamoshu. At the end of that time another God—the Chained God—meddled in her life and drew her into his scheme to acquire the Great Talisman BinYAHtii, using as instruments KORI PIYOLSS and the sorceror/king SETTSIMAKSIMIN along with the sorceror Ahzurdan and the out-reality starman Daniel Akamarino. In the final battle between Brann and Settsimaksimin, the God acquired the Talisman, Settsimaksimin's heart gave out and he nearly died. Because she'd found much that was admirable in her enemy—disregarding

9

a little thing like repeated attempts to kill her—Brann healed the wounds BinYAHtii had inflicted on him and the weakness in his heart; having saved his life, she carried him off to a lovely island (Jal Virri) in the heart of the Myk'tat Tukery where they spent the next ten years in friendship and peace.

2. JARIL AND YARIL, THE CHANGERS, affinity: Churrikyoo
Petnames: Jaril called Jay; Yaril called Yaro

Juvenile energy forms drawn from one of the layered realities.

Their base forms were lightspheres (at first just big enough to fit within a man's circled arms, later larger), Yaril's slightly paler than Jaril's, but they could take many shapes and appear convincingly solid in them though the eyes they saw from were clear crystal and marked them as demon. At first they were completely dependent on Brann; she drained life energy from men and beasts and fed it to them to keep them from starving. In the course of the action against Settsimaksimin, Brann won their freedom from the Chained God; he changed the Changers so they could once more feed directly on sunlight and similar energy sources. They were still linked to Brann by strong ties of affection, but they were no longer her nurslings. The two hundred years on the World have brought other changes; they passed through their equivalent of puberty and acquired sexual drives and needs that they could not satisfy without others of their kind and age. After Brann took Settsimaksimin to the island Jal Virri, Jaril and Yaril ranged restlessly about the World, trying to work off the energies that threatened to destroy them.

3. SETTSIMAKSIMIN, affinity: Shaddalakh
Called (by friends and those fond of him): Maksim, Maksi, Maks.

He was born in Silagamatys the chief city of Cheonea, sold into slavery at the age of six, a child-whore until he was ten, bought out of the pleasurehouse by the Sorceror Prime Musteba Xa who wanted to use the boy's Talent to enhance his own.

After releasing himself from his apprenticeship by killing his Master, he studied and practiced and became one of the four Primes among the sorcerors of the World. Around this time he came upon the Talisman BinYAHtii; this sparked his ambitions for his homeplace. He returned to Cheonea, kicked the corrupt and feeble king off his throne and took the reins of power into his own hands. It was a long struggle, but he broke the power of the Parastes (the local lords), put the land into the hands of the folk who worked it, outlawed slavery, hung some slavedealers, burned the ships of some slavetraders and began setting up a new sort of government where the peasants and the so-called lower orders would have some say in the circumstances of their lives. To do this he had to keep BihYAHtii fed (the life of a child a month was the price for access to the Talisman's power) and alternately cajole and compel the god Amortis to act against his enemies. Being warned (as part of the Chained God's scheming) that Brann Drinker of Souls would be drawn into the fight against him, he struck first and sent Tigermen demons to kill her. The Changers arrived just in time to save her and the battle was on—a battle Settsimaksimin lost after a hard struggle that cost him much, including his hold on Cheonea.

At the end of ten years on Jal Virri he was growing restless, tired of living without ambition or effort.

4. KORIMENEI PIYOLSS, affinity: Frunzacoache
Originally her name was simply Kori (which could mean either Maiden or Heart), but when Settsimaksimin put her in school and compelled her to remain there for ten years, she took the name Korimenei (which meant Heart-in-Waiting).

The Finger Vales of Cheonea had served the Chained God since the time when the Wounded Moon was whole, which meant essentially forever, but when Kori was thirteen-going-on-fourteen, the soldier-priests of Amortis came to Owlyn Vale, tied the Chained God's priest to a stake and lit a fire under him. Then they declared the folk on Owlyn Vale must serve Amortis instead. A few months later Kori's youngest brother (the closest to her of all her kin) came to her with the Chained God's mark on him, chosen for the new priest. Once that was out her brother would be burned also. She was the several times great-granddaughter of Harra Hazani who carried a promise from the Drinker of Souls: She or any of her descendants could call on Brann in time of trouble and Brann would come to give whatever help she could. Kori looked into Harra's Eye, located Brann and sent a cousin to summon the Drinker of Souls to fight Settsimaksimin and help her keep her brother alive.

Some months later she was in Silagamatys for the Lot (where three children were chosen, a girl to serve in the Temple as teacher or priestess, a boy to serve as a priest or soldier and another—either boy or girl—to be fed to Bin-YAHtii, though only Settsimaksimin knew this, the people thought the third child was sent to Havi Kudush to serve in the Great Temple of Amortis); during this time, Settsimaksimin became aware of the strong Talent she had in her, plucked her from her people and sent her off to school in Silili, half a continent away from Cheonea, getting her out of his hair and keeping her safe at the same time; he liked her and was proud of her spirit. To keep her in school he imprisoned her brother in crystal and informed her only she could set him free. All she had to do was go to the Chained God's altar in the mountain cavern where she'd found Harra's Eye and set her hand on the crystal. No one else could wake her brother; if she got herself killed, he'd sleep forever in that spell-crystal. At the end of the ten years, when her training was finished, she could leave with his blessing; if she tried to leave before that the Mistress, one Shahntien Shere, was instructed to punish her at the first attempt and kill her at the second.

The ten years passed pleasurably enough, she enjoyed her schooling after she'd got used to the constraints on her and she'd proved an excellent student, beyond even Settsimaksimin's expectations (he kept an eye on her from Jal Virri, sent his eidolon to talk to her every few months), but as the time for her passing-out ordeal approached she was getting more and more anxious about her brother, more and more eager to go release him from his enchanted sleep.

5. TRAGO PIYOLSS, affinity: Harra's Eye
Called Tré by friends and family.

A six-year-old boy used as a pawn, by the Chained God first to bring Brann into play against Settsimaksimin, then by Settsimaksimin to keep his hold on Kori Piyolss, he slept under enchantment in the Altar Cave of the Chained God.

6. DANNY BLUE, affinity: Klukesharna

Danny Blue was one man, two men, three men. One man, because he had a single body. Two men because he was made from two men and their memories and personalities lingered within him. Three men, because Danny Blue had developed a life of his own, a personality that was both more and less than a blend of his two half-sires with memories that belonged to him alone.

He was born in the body of the Chained God (an ancient starship) where the flesh of his two sires was merged into one man by the power of the God, where Brann Drinker of Souls was midwife to the birth of his personhood as well as his fleshbody.

AHZURDAN was once a student/apprentice of Settsimaksimin's. When he met Brann and was drawn into the Chained God's scheme, he was a second rank sorceror of considerable ability but regrettable habits, being addicted to dreamdust and in flight from reality. He was born into a Phrasi merchant family of considerable wealth and social ambition; his mother belonged to the minor nobility and impressed into her son all her attitudes toward lesser beings. He was a momma's boy and didn't get on with his older half-siblings at all well, though that was not entirely his fault, they were an intolerant lot. He was also an unsatisfactory son, being totally uninterested in the family business. When his talent came on him, he nearly burned down the house and did singe a spiteful older brother. By this time his father was quite happy to pay the fees and bond him to Settsimaksimin's service for the usual seven years. He worked hard and learned fast, but he never managed to match his Master and left his service at the end of those seven years resenting Settsimaksimin, jealous of other apprentices, angry and unhappy.

DANIEL AKAMARINO was born in a reality where magic was fraud and wishful thinking; he made his living on assorted starships as Communications Officer, Propulsion Engineer or Cargo Superintendent/Buyer, having a Masters Rating in all three. He was a man not bothered by much, seldom felt the need to prove anything about himself or his beliefs; impatient with routine, he drifted from job to job, quitting when he felt like it or because some nit tried to make him do things that bored him like wearing boots instead of sandals and a uniform instead of the ancient shirts and trousers he got secondhand whenever the ones he had were reduced to patches and threads. He had no plans for settling down; there was always something to see another hop away and he never had trouble finding a place on a ship when he was done with groundside living. The Chained God snatched him in mid-stride and transferred him to the World, landing him in a road in Cheonea.

He joined the Owlyn Valers as they went to Silagamatys for the Lot, met Kori, through her linked up with Brann and Ahzurdan and went with them into the Chained God's pocket reality, where he and Ahzurdan became DANNY BLUE and went with Brann to fight the final battle with Settsimaksimin. When that battle was finished and Brann was concentrating on healing the sorceror, he picked up the Talisman BinYAHtii—and was snatched back to the Chained God's body.

That was how the Chained God acquired BinYAHtii.

Danny Blue roamed about the ancient rotting starship and struggled to relearn Ahzurdan's magic; all the sorceror's WORDS and mindsets had to be reconfigured to suit the new personality. When he felt strong enough, he tried to attack the God, but was seized and slammed into a coldsleep pod where he spent the next ten years in stasis.

DRAW IN THE CATALYSTS:
These are the stones of power, the great talismans:

BinYAHtii   Held by the Chained God.
Manifests as a rough circle of reddish stone pendant on a massive gold chain, set in a heavy ring of beaten gold.

Churrikyoo   Held by the Servants of Amortis in her Temple in Havi Kudush, the holy city in central Phras.
Manifests as a small glass frog, battered, chipped, filled with thready cracks.

Frunzacoache   Held in the essence pouch of a shaman of the Rushgaramuv Temuengs.
Manifests as a never-withering berry leaf pressed between two thin round layers of crystal set in a ring of tarnished silver cable, pendant from a silver chain.

Harra's Eye   Held in the secret, sacred Cavern of the Chained God.
Manifests as a sphere of crystal about the size of a large grapefruit. Not known as one of the stones of power because it is a new focus; it has lain dormant in the Cavern, waiting. None of the first rank sorcerors has learned of it or used the power locked in it.

Klukesharna   Held by Wokolinka of Lewinkob in the Henanolee Heart, in the island city Hennkensikee.
Manifests as a small rod of black iron melted off a meteor, cooled in the shape of a clumsy key.

Massulit	Held by the Geniod in the chamber of crystals sunk within the white cliffs of the Lake Pikma ka Vyamm, the inland sea in the heart of the Jana Sarise. Manifests as a star sapphire the size of a man's fist, the color of the sky at the zenith on a clear spring day.
Shaddalakh	Held by Magus of Tok Kinsa in the holy city of the Rukka Nagh. Manifests as a spotted sand dollar made of porcelain.

THE REBIRTHING: PHASE ONE
The stonebearers are set in motion

I: BRANN THE DRINKER OF SOULS

Jal Virri in the Myk-tat Tukery
Brann and Settsimaksimin
In the tenth year of their hab-
itation within the Tukery, they
are restless.

1

The wide bed creaked as Brann rolled onto her side. Maksim
muttered a few shapeless sounds without waking enough to
know what he was protesting. She finished her turn and lay
on her back, staring at a ceiling swimming in green-tinted
light. The sun was barely above the horizon, shining directly
in through the tight profusion of vines Maksim had coaxed
across the windows. Given his choice he would come grudg-
ing out of bed sometime past noon and would have hung
thick black curtains over the windows, but Brann needed a
free flow of air and a feeling that the outside penetrated the
room, that she wasn't shut into something she couldn't
escape from. The vines were a compromise. She smiled at
the shifting leaf-shadows; the light that came through in the
very early morning was such a lovely green.

Maksim was sleeping soundly again now the nights were
cooler and Brann was once more sharing the bed with him.
Solid, meaty, comforting to sleep against once he settled
down, he was a furnace that got hotter as the night went on,
a blessing in winter but impossible when the nights heated
up. When the hot season arrived, Brann moved into the
other bedroom and Maksim was once again tormented by

17

the bad dreams that wracked his sleep when she wasn't
there to chase them off; he'd lived a long time and done
things he refused to remember; he had reasons he considered adequate at the moment but they didn't ease his mind
when he looked back at them. During the day he pottered
contentedly enough about Jal Virri, reading, working in the
many gardens beside the sprites who tended the place, but
when night came, he dreamed.

Brann and Maksim slept together for the comfort they
took from each other, body touching body. They shared a
deep affection. One might have called it love, if the word
hadn't so many resonances that had nothing to do with
them. Maksim found his loves in Kukurul, young men who
stayed a night or two, then left, others who loved him a
longer time but also left.

Brann went through a short but difficult period during the
first days they spent on Jal Virri; she wanted him, but had
to recognize the futility of that particular passion. It was a
brief agony, but an agony nonetheless, a scouring of her
soul. His voice stirred her to the marrow of her bones, he
was bigger than life, a passionate dominating complex man;
she'd never met his equal anywhere anytime in all her long
life. She shared his disdain for inherited privilege, his sardonic, sympathetic view of ordinary men; her mind marched
with his, they enjoyed the same things, laughed at the same
things, deplored the same things, were content to be quiet
at the same time. Anything more, though, was simply not
there. She too went prowling the night in Kukurul, though
it was more distraction than passion she was seeking.

There was enough of a nip in the air to make her snuggle
closer to Maksim. He grumbled in his sleep, but again he
didn't wake. She scratched at her thigh, worked her toes,
flexed and unflexed her knees. It was impossible; how did
he do it, sleep like that, on and on? She never could stay
still once she was awake. Her mouth tasted foul, like something had died in it and was growing moss. Her bladder was
overfull; if she moved she'd slosh. She pressed her thighs
together; it didn't help. That's it, she thought. That's all I
need. She slid out of bed and scurried for the watercloset.

When she came back, Maksim had turned onto his stomach. He was snoring a little. His heavy braid had come
undone and his long, coarse hair was spread like gray weeds
over his shoulders; a strand of it had dropped across his face
and was moving with his breath, tickling at his nose. She

smiled tenderly at him and lifted the hair back, taking care
not to wake him. Lazy old lion. She shaped the words with
her lips but didn't speak them. Big fat cat sleeping in the
sun. She touched the tangled mass of hair. I'll have a time
combing this out. Sorceror Prime tying granny knots, it's a
disgrace, that's what it is. She patted a yawn, crossed to the
vanity he'd bought for her in Kukurul a few years back.

The vanity was a low table of polished ebony with matching silver-mounted chests at both ends and a mage-made
mirror, its glass smooth as silk and more faithful than she
liked this autumn morning. Maybe it was the green light,
but she looked ten years older than she had last night. She
leaned closer to the mirror, pushed her fingers hard along
her cheekbones, tautening and lifting the skin. She sighed.
Drinker of Souls. Not any more. I don't have to feed my
nurslings now. They're free of me. She stepped back and
kicked the hassock closer, sat down and began brushing at
her hair. There was no reason now for the Drinker of Souls
to walk the night streets and take life from predators preying
on the weak. The changechildren could feed themselves;
they weren't even children any more. They came flying back
once or twice a year to say hello and tell her the odd things
they'd seen, but they never stayed long. Jal Virri is boring;
Jay said that once. She paused, then finished the stroke. It's
true. I'm petrified with boredom. I've outlived my useful-
ness. There's no point to my life.

She set the brush down and gazed into the mirror, examining her face with clinical objectivity, considering its planes
and hollows as if she were planning a self-portrait. She
hadn't been a pretty child and she wasn't pretty now. She
frowned at her image. If I'd been someone else looking at
me, I'd have said the woman has interesting bones and I'd
like to paint her. Or I would have liked to paint her before
she started to droop. Discontent. It did disgusting things to
one's face, made everything sag and put sour lines around
the mouth and between the brows. Her breasts were firm
and full, that was all right, but she had a small pot when she
sat; she put her hands round it, lifted and pressed it in, then
sighed and reached for the brush. It won't be long before I
have to pay someone to climb into bed with me. She pulled
the bristles through the soft white strands. Old nag put out
to pasture, no one wants her anymore.

She made a face at herself and laughed, but her eyes were
sad and the laughter faded quickly. Might as well be dead.

She rubbed the back of her hand beneath her chin and felt the loosening muscle there. Death? Illusion. Give me one man's lifeforce and I'm young again. Twenty-four/five, back where I was when Slya finished with me. No dying for me. Not even a real aging, only an endless going on and on. No rest for me. No lying down in the earth and letting slip the burden of life. How odd to realize what a blessing death was. Not a curse. Well . . . once the dying was finished with, anyway. Dying was the problem, not death. I wonder if they'd let me? She got to her feet, looked over her shoulder at Maksim. One massive arm had dropped off the bed; it hung down so the backs of his fingers trailed on the grass mat that covered the floor.

She went out, walked through rooms filled with morning light, swept and garnished by one of the sprites that took care of the island, the one they called Housewraith. The kitchen was a large bright room at the back. She pulled open one of the drawers and took out a paring knife. She set the blade on her wrist. It was so sharp its weight was enough to push the edge a short way through her flesh; when she lifted the knife, she saw a fine red line drawn across the porcelain pallor of her skin. She put the knife down. It wasn't time yet. She wasn't tired enough of living to endure the pain of dying. Boredom . . . no, that wasn't enough, not yet.

She set the knife on the work table and drew her thumb along the shallow cut, wiping away the blood. The cut stung and oozed more blood. Rubbing her wrist absently against the side of her breast, she wandered outside, shivering as the frosty morning breeze hit her skin. For a moment she thought of going inside and putting on a robe, but she wasn't bothered enough to make the effort. She looked at her wrist; the cut was clotted over; the blood seepage had stopped.

Ignoring the bite of dew that felt like snowmelt on her bare feet, she walked down the long grassy slope to the water and stood at the edge of the small beach listening to the saltwater lap lazily at the sand and gazing across the narrow strait to a nearby island, a high rocky thing sculpted by wind and water into an abstract pillar, barren except for a few gray and orange lichens. All the islands around Jal Virri were like that; it was as if the lovely green isle had drawn the life out of them and spent it on itself. Arms huddled across her breasts, hands shaking though they were closed tight about her biceps, her feet blocks of ice with smears of black soil and scraps of grass pasted on them, she watched the dark water come and go until she couldn't stand the cold any longer. It's time we went to Kukurul again, Maks and me, or me alone, if he won't come. She stood quite still for a breath or two. I don't think I'm coming back. I don't know what it is I'm going to do, but I can't vegetate here any longer. She turned and walked back toward the house. I've been sleeping and now I'm awake. I never could stay in bed once I woke up.

2

"Hoist it, Maksi." She jerked the covers off him, slapped him on a meaty buttock. "Wake up, you bonelazy magicman, I need you."

He grunted and cracked an eye. "Go 'way."

"Uh-uh, baby. You've slept long enough for ten your size. Pop me to Kukurul, luv. I woke up wanting."

He closed the eye. "Take the boat."

She took his earlobe instead and pinched hard.

"Ow! Stop that." He grabbed for her arm, but she jumped out of reach. "Witch!"

"If I were, I wouldn't need you."

He groaned and sat up. "You don't need me."

"Come on, Maksi. Housewraith decided to make break-fast this morning. It's spelled to wait, but I'm hungry. I'll take the boat all right, but I want you with me."

He shoved tangled hair off his face and looked shrewdly at her. "What is it, Bramble? Something's eating at you."

"No soulsearching before breakfast, if you please. I've run your bath for you, I've had mine already. I'll wait twenty minutes no more, so it's your fault if your eggs are cold."

3

The fire crackled briskly behind the screen; the heavy silk drapes were pulled back to let in the morning sun. Brann paced back and forth, her body cutting through the beams, her shadow jerking erratically over the furniture. She swung round, scowled at Maksim. "Well?"

"Of course I'll go with you. Matter of fact, I've been thinking for several days now it's time for another visit." He rubbed his hand across his chin. "What's itching at you, Bramble-all-thorns?"

"The usual thing. What else could there be?" She turned her back on him and stared out the window.

"I don't think so."

"Oh you."

"Me."

She moved her right arm in a shapeless, meaningless gesture; she started to speak, stopped, tried again, had even less luck finding words for what she wanted to say; the trouble was, she didn't know what she wanted to say. "I'm useless. There's nothing to do here." She turned round, hitched a hip on the windowsill. "Nothing real." She lifted her hands, let them fall. "I don't know, Maksi. There's no point to anything. Nothing I try . . . works. I tried potting, you know that, you shaped my kiln for me. It was horrible. Everything I did . . . mediocre . . . bleah! At Shaynamoshu I was content a hundred years. Happy. Here. . . ? I paint a pretty flower, don't I. Dew on the petals, pollen on the stamens, you can see every grain. Lovely, right? Horrible. A dead slug has more soul. Useless, Maksi. Out to pasture like a broke-down mare. Even the damn gods don't need me anymore. Maybe I should go to Silili with you and give Old Tungjii a boot in the behind. Maybe something would come of that."

"It probably would. I doubt you'd be pleased with whatever it was."

"Pleased? That doesn't matter. It'd be something to do. Some reason to get out of bed in the morning. To keep on living. You know what I'm talking about; you're restless too, magicman."

"Brann, I. . . ."

"No. You don't need to say it. I know what's going to happen. You'll go to Silili to see your protége through her Passage Rite and you won't come back. Why should you?"

"Thornlet, come with me." He lay back in his chair and laughed at her and let his voice boom out, dark velvet rubbing her bones. "Come wandering with me and see the world. Sure somewhere there's a prince who needs his bottom whacked, a lord to be taught his manners, a bully who needs his pride punctured. Let us go out and do good, no matter how much chaos we leave behind us."

"Ah Maksi m'luv, you're such a fraud, you evil old sorceror, you bleed at a touch and put yourself to endless inconvenience. I don't know. Maybe we just need some hard living for a while so we can appreciate peace again.

Anyway, let's scratch our ordinary itches and see what comes of that."

4

Kukurul. The place where seapaths cross. The pivot of the four winds. If you sit long enough at one of the plaza tables of the café Sidday Lir, it's said you'll see the whole world file past you. Kukurul. Expensive, gaudy, secretive and corrupt. Its housefronts are full of windows with screens behind them like the eyes of Kukrulese. Along the Ihman Katt are brothels for every taste, ranks of houses where assassin guilds advertise men of the knife, women of the poison cup; halfway up the Katt there's a narrow black building where deathrites are practiced for the titillation of the connoisseurs, open to participation or solitary enjoyment. At the end of the Ihman Katt is the true heart of Kukurul, the Great Market, a paved square two miles on a side where everything is on sale but heat, sweat, and stench. Those last are free.

Brann patted at her face with a square of fine linen, removing some of the dust and sweat that clung to her skin. It was one of those fine hot airless days that early autumn sometimes threw up and the Market was a hellhole, though few of the shoppers or the shopkeepers seemed to notice it. She pushed the kerchief up her sleeve and lifted a graceful vase. Eggshell porcelain with an unusual glaze. She frowned and ran her fingertips repeatedly over the smooth sides. Unless she was losing her mind, she knew that glaze. Her father's secret mix and Slya's Breath, never one without the other. At Shaynamoshu she'd tried again and again to get that underglow, but it was impossible without the Breath. She examined the lines and the underpainting. It wasn't her father's work or that of any of his apprentices, but there was something there . . . the illusive similarity of cousins perhaps. Biting at her lower lip, she upended the vase and inspected the maker's mark. A triangle above an oval, Arth Slya's sigil. The glyph Tayn. The glyph Nor. These were the potter's seal. Tannor of Arth Slya. She carried the vase to the Counting Table. "Arth Slya is producing again?"

The old man blinked hooded eyes. "Again?"

"You claim this is oldware?"

"Claim?" He shrugged. "The mark is true, the provenance can be produced."

"I don't doubt the mark, the glaze alone is enough to guarantee it."

"You a collector?"

"No." She smiled as she saw the glitter in his eyes fade before that cool negative. "Earthenware is at once too heavy and too fragile to survive my sort of life. I will take this, though, for the pleasure it gives me. It's a cheerful thing when a dead loveliness comes to life again. Twenty silver."

He settled to his work and his pleasure. "New or old, that's Arth Slya ware. Silver is an insult. Five gold."

When the bargain was concluded, Brann had him send the vase to the Inn of the Pearly Dawn where she and Maksim were staying. She left the Market and strolled down the Katt to the café Sidday Lir, confused by the conflicting emotions awakened by the vase. She was pleased because her father had left workheirs; she was jealous because that place was hers by right and talent. She wanted to go home. Home? Arth Slya? What made her think that place was home more than any other patch of earth? Kin? She couldn't claim them, who would believe her. If they believed her, they'd back away from her, terrified. And could she blame them?

She chose a table with a view out over the harbor and sat watching the ships arrive and depart, wondering if one of them was a trader like Sammang's Panday Girl, like her working the islands north and east of the Tukery, like her calling in at Tavisteen on Croaldhu where Brann had started her wandering. She wallowed comfortably in nostalgia as she sipped at the tea and enjoyed the dance of the ships and the streaming of the ladesmen working the wharves below; she wondered what the Firemountain Tincreal looked like these days, whether the eruption and the weathering of two centuries since had changed her out of all recognition, wondered if she'd recognize the descendants of her kin if she saw them. Was there any more reason to go back to Arth Slya than there was to return to Jal Virri? I'd like to see it again, she thought. I'd like to see what the ones who went back made of it.

When the teapot was empty, she sat considering whether she wanted more tea or should call for her bill and return to the Inn for a bath and a nap until it was time to go looking for something to warm her bed. Before she reached a decision on that, she saw Jaril walking down the Katt and settled back to wait for him.

The changer wound toward her through scattered tables, drawing stares enough to make him uncomfortable; Brann watched him shy away from a clawed hand reaching for his arm, pretend he didn't hear a half-whispered suggestion from a Hina woman of indeterminate age, or drawled comments from a group of Phrasi highborns lounging at three tables pushed together. He looked a teener boy, fourteen, fifteen years old, a beautiful boy who'd somehow avoided the awkward throes of adolescence, hair like white-gold spun gossamer fine lifting to the caress of the wind, elegantly sculptured features, crystal eyes, a shapely body that moved with unstudied grace. He pulled out a chair and sat down, fidgeted for several moments without speaking to her.

"Add a few warts next time," Brann said, amused. She felt suddenly happy. Her son was come to visit her. She looked past him. Alone? "Where's Yaro? Saying hello to Maks?"

"No," he said. "Yaro's not with me."

She eyed him thoughtfully, caught the attention of a waiter and ordered a half bottle of wine. When he'd gone, she said, "Tell me."

Jaril touched a fingertip to a drop of spilled tea and drew patterns on the wood. "Remember the swamp before we got to Tavisteen? Remember what happened to me and Yaro there?"

Brann closed her eyes, thought. "That was a while ago," she murmured. She remembered gray. Even during daylight everything was gray. Gray skies, gray water, gray mud dried on sedges and trees, gray fungi, gray insects, gray everything. She remembered waking tangled in tough netting made from cords twisted out of reed fiber and impregnated with fish stink. She remembered little gray men swarming over the island, little gray men with coarse yellow cloth wound in pouty little shrouds about their groins, little gray men with rough dry skin, a dusty gray mottled with darker streaks and splotches. She could move her head a little. It was late, shadows were long across the water. A gray man sat beside a small fire, net woven about him and knotted in intricate patterns describing his power and importance; a fringe of knotted cords dangled from a thick rope looped loosely about a small hard potbelly. In a long-fingered reptilian hand he held a drum; it was a snakeskin stretched over the skull of a huge serpent, its eyeholes facing outward. He

drew from the taut skin a soft insistent rustle barely louder
than the whisper of the wind through the reeds; it crept
inside her until it commanded the beat of her heart, the
pulse of her breathing. She jerked her body loose from the
spell, shivering with fear. He looked at her and she shivered
again. He reached out and ran a hand over two large stones
sitting beside his bony knee, gray-webbed crystals each as
large as man's head, crystals gathering the light of the fire
into themselves, miniature broken fires repeated endlessly
again. Yaril and Jaril frozen into stone. She knew it and was
more frightened than before. He grinned at her, baring a
hard ridge of black gum, enjoying her helpless rage.

She blinked, brought herself back out of memory. "The
swampwizard," she said. "Ganumomo, that was his name.
Why him? Did you go back to Croaldhu and fall in that trap
again?"

"No." He sipped at his wine and gazed out across the
bay. He was uncomfortable and she couldn't make out why.
He was worried about Yaril, but that wasn't it. She watched
the level of the wine sink lower in his glass and remembered
something else; neither he nor Yaril would talk about their
people or their home. Had something happened to Yaril
that was connected to their homeplace? "Caves," he said;
he seemed to taste the word like hard candy on the tongue.
"Caves. We love them because they're terrifying, Bramble.
We could die if we were shut off from sun too long, we
would go stone and lie there in stone, fading slowly slowly
until there was nothing left not stone." He poured more
wine in his glass, tilted it and watched the rich red sliding
down the curve. "Yaro and me, we were poking about some
mountains, the Dhia Dautas, if you want the name, and we
found this set of caves. Splendid caves, Bramble. Shining
caves. We went a little crazy. Just a little. We soaked up all
the sun we could before we went down. We weren't going to
stay down more than a day or so, we'd have plenty of push
left to get us out of trouble should we run into any. Not that
we expected to." He gulped at the wine, went back to
staring at what was left.

Brann waited. His lack of urgency was reassuring. Yaril
wasn't dead. She was sure of that. Jay would be . . . different . . . if his sister was dead.

"She was flitting along ahead of me. Actually, I was
chasing her . . . it's an old game . . . from home . . . complicated rules . . . the thing he . . . whoever . . . didn't

count on." A crooked angry grin, a hunching of his shoulders. "I wasn't close enough to get caught with her. I was round a bend about twenty feet behind when the thing closed round her. The trap I mean."

"Trap?"

"It wasn't something natural."

"What was it?"

"I don't know. Yaro went stone before I got round the bend. I saw her sitting there . . . you remember how we looked . . . gone stone. . . ." He shuddered in his peculiar way, his outline melting and reforming, his hands growing transparent, then solid. "I tried to get to her. There was a barrier. I couldn't see it, I couldn't feel it either, not really, I just couldn't get to her. I tried going over it. Around it. Under it. I went into the mountain itself, I slid through the stone. That's dangerous, it's so easy to get confused so you don't know up from down, but I did it. No good. It was a sphere, Bramble, it was all around her. I couldn't get to her. I leaned against it and called to her; if I could wake her, maybe we could do something together. I couldn't reach her. I couldn't even feel her there, Bramble. Do you understand? My sister. The only being in this place who's LIKE me. If I lost her, I'd be alone. I couldn't TALK to her. Not even TALK to her, Bramble. I went wired for a while, I don't know how long." He shuddered again, the pulses of fleshmelt moving swiftly along his body, clothes as well as flesh because his clothing was part of his substance. "When I knew what I was doing again, I was miles south of the caves." He gulped at the wine, then with a visible effort steadied himself. Brann watched, more troubled than she'd been a short time before; Jaril was barely containing his panic and his control was getting worse, not better. "I was eagleshape, driving south as fast as I could fly. I couldn't think why for the longest, I wasn't capable of thinking, Brann, but I kept on flying. After a while, I decided I was coming for you. I knew you'd help us. And prod Maksim into doing what he can. He doesn't like us much, but he'd do a lot for you, Bramble."

Brann clinked her spoon against the teabowl and waited for the waiter to bring the check. "We'll go up to the Inn," she said. "And go over everything you can remember first, then you can hunt Maks up and bring him to me."

Jaril nodded. "Bramble. . . ."

She thrust out her hand, palm toward him, stopping him. "Later."

He shifted round and saw the waiter walking toward them.

##

A winding lane with flowering plums and other ornamentals growing at carefully irregular intervals along it led to the Outlook, a terrace halfway up the side of the dormant volcano which rose high above the lesser mountains that ringed the bay; the Inn of the Pearly Dawn sat on that Outlook, surrounded by its gardens with their well-groomed elegance, an expensive waystop but only moderately successful since the merchants, collectors, and more esoteric visitors preferred living in the heat and stench of the city where they could keep their fingers on its throb and profit thereby.

Brann and Jaril walked up the lane, feet stirring drifts of dead leaves; they talked quietly as they walked, with long intervals of silence between the phrases.

"How much time do we have?"

"Decades, if whoever's got her lets her have sun. If they keep her dark, a year."

Brann reached up, broke a small green and brown orchid from a dangling spray. "I see." A fragile sweet perfume eddied from the flower as she waved it slowly back and forth before her face as she walked. "We'd better expect the worst and plan for it."

Jaril's outline wavered. When he'd got himself in hand again, he nodded. "Maksim. . . ."

"No." Brann closed her hand hard on the orchid, crushing it, releasing a powerful burst of scent. She flung the mutilated thing away, wiped her hand on her skirt. "Don't count on him, Jay. He's got other commitments."

"If you ask. . . ."

"No."

"He owes you, Bramble. Weren't for you, he'd be dead."

"Weren't for me, he'd still have Cheonea to play with. It balances."

Jaril moved ahead of her, opened the Zertarta Gate for her, then followed her into the Inn's Stone Garden.

Brann touched his arm. "We can go up to my rooms, or would you rather take sun by the lily pond?"

"Sun." He shimmered again, produced a stiff smile. "I'm

pretty much drained, Bramble. I didn't stop for anything and it was a long way here."

She strolled beside him, following the path by the stream that chattered musically over aesthetically arranged stones and around boulders chosen for their lichen patterns and hauled here from every part of the island. The stream rambled in a lazy arc about the east wing of the Inn, then spread in a deep pool with a stone grating at each end to keep the halarani in, the black and gold fish that lived among the water lily roots. Three willows of different heights and inclinations drooped gracefully over the water. There were stone benches in their spiky shade, but Brann settled on the ancient oak planks of the one bench without any shadow over it. There was no breeze back here; stillness rested like gauze over the pond, underlaid with the small sounds of insects and the brush-brush-tinkle of the stream. She smiled as Jaril darkened his clothing and himself until he was sun-trap black, sooty as the dusky sides of the halarani. He dropped onto the bench and lay with his head in her lap; his eyes closed and he seemed to sleep.

"We were in the Dhia Dautas," he murmured after a while. "East and a half-degree south of Jorpashil. West on a direct line from Kapi Yuntipek. Dhia Dautas. Means daughters of the dawn in the Sarosj. The hill people call them the Taongashan Hegysh, they live there so you'd think travelers would use their name for the mountains, but they don't, the Silk Roaders always say the Dhia Dautas." His voice was dragging; she could feel him putting off the need to talk about the caves. She could feel the tension in him, he vibrated with it. "We were in Jorpashil five, six days, we heard about the caves there. Storyteller in the Market. A pair of drunks in a tavern. Seemed like we ran across at least one story every day while we were there. You want me to give you all of it?"

"Later, Jay. It's probably important."

"I think so. How could whoever it was lay the trap for us if he didn't know we'd be there to spring it. We weren't thinking about traps then, we took wing and went hunting for the caves. . . ." His voice droned on.

They talked for a long time that afternoon, until neither could think of another question to ask, another answer to give. Then they just sat quietly in the hazy sunlight watching the Inn's shadow creep toward them.

5

Brann stood at her bedroom window, a pot of tea beside her on the broad sill. Far below, the sails of the ships arriving and departing were hot gilt and crimson, then suddenly dark as the brief tropical twilight was over. Night, she thought. She looked at her hands. Idle hands. They'd lost strength over the past ten years. If I had to fire a kiln tomorrow, I'd be wrecked before I was half through splitting billets. She filled her bowl with the last of the tea, lukewarm and strong enough to float a rock, sipped at it as she watched the lamps and torches bloom along the Ihman Katt. Wisps of sound floated up through the still, dark air, laughter, even a word or two snatched whole by erratic thermals. Jaril was down there, looking for Maksim. She grimaced at the bite of the tannin, the feel of the leaves on her lips and tongue. Maksi, she thought, always underfoot when you didn't need him, down a hole somewhere when you did. I have to Hunt tonight.

When the Chained God weaned her nurslings from their dependence on her, at first she'd felt relief. Each time she went out to Hunt for them, she sickened at what she had to do, the killings night after night until Yaril and Jaril were fed and she could rest a month or so; later, when they were older, once a year did it, then once every two years. Drinker of Souls, sucking life out of men and women night after night—more than ten thousand nights—until she was finally free of the need. She quieted her souls by choosing thieves and slavers, usurers and slumlords, assassins and bullyboys, corrupt judges and secret police, anyone who used muscle or position to torment the helpless. All those years she yearned to be rid of that burden, all those years she thought she loathed the need. Then she stopped the Hunting and thought she was content. Now that the need was on her again, she wasn't sure how she felt . . . no, that wasn't true, she knew all too well.

She gazed at the lamps of Kukurul and was disconcerted by her growing impatience to get down there and prowl; her body trembled with anticipation as she imagined herself stalking men, drawing into her so much lifeforce she shone like the moon. Filling herself with the terrible fire that was like nothing else. Ever. She remembered being awash with LIFE, alive alive alive, afraid but ecstatic. In a way, though she didn't much care for the comparison, it was like a quieter time when she unpacked her kiln and held a minor miracle in her hands, like those few wonderful times all squeezed into that singular moment of fullness. . . . And for the past ten years she'd had neither sort of joy. Yes. Joy. Say it. Tell yourself the truth, if you tell no one else. Satisfaction, pleasure beyond pleasure, more than sex, more than the quieter goodness of fine food and vintage wines. She pressed a hand under her chin, flattened the loose skin, dropped her arms and pinched the soft pout of her belly; she was tired of aging with the aches and pains age brought. If she couldn't die, why endure life in a deteriorating body? She shivered. No, she thought, no, that's despicable.

She moved away from the window, started pacing the length of the room, back and forth, back and forth, across the braided rug; her bare feet made small scuffing sounds; her breathing was ragged and uncertain. She was frightened. Her sense of herself was disintegrating as she paced. The only thing she felt sure of was that her father would neither like nor approve of what she was turning into.

An owl dropped through the window, landed on the rug and shifted to Jaril; he crossed to the bed, threw himself on it. "I found Maksim. He was with someone, so he wasn't happy about me barging in. When I told him you needed to see him, he wanted to know if it was urgent or what, then he said he'd be back round midnight if there wasn't all that much hurry. I said all right."

She sat beside him, threaded her fingers through his fine hair; they tingled as threads of her own energy leaked from her to him. He made a soft sound filled with pleasure and nestled closer to her.

"Jay."

"Mm?"

"You need to go home, don't you."

He shifted uneasily. "We can talk about that after we get Yaro back."

"All right. We do have to talk. Never mind, luv, I won't push you." She slid her hand down his arm, closed her fingers around his. "I can't live on sunlight or grow wings."

"Flat purse?"

"Pancake."

Jaril laughed drowsily, tugged his hand loose. "So I go scavenging?"

"With extreme discretion, luv."

"More than you know, Bramble." He yawned, which was

playacting since he didn't breathe; that he could play at all pleased her, it meant he was not quite so afraid. He turned serious. "Not at night."

"Why?"

"Wards are weaker in daylight."

"Since when have you worried about wards?"

"Everything changes, Bramble. We've picked up too much from this reality. Things here can see us now. Sort of."

Brann scowled at him. "Forget it, then. I'll see what I can borrow from Maks. We'll pick up supplies on the road."

"Just as well, the Managers here are a nasty lot. I'll crash a while, tap me when Maks shows up." He moved away from her, curled up on the far side of the bed and stopped breathing, deep in his usual sleep-coma.

Brann looked at him a moment, shook her head. "I don't know," she said aloud. She went across to the window, hitched a hip on the sill and went back to watching the lights below.

6

"What's this Jay was hinting at?" Maksim was tired and cranky; she saw that he meant to be difficult.

"Come sit down." She stepped back from the door and gestured toward the large leather chair that stood close to the sitting room fire. "There's brandy if you want it, or tea."

He caught hold of her chin, lifted her face to the light. "Those nits have put you in an uproar. What is it?"

"We need your help, Maksi." Her jaw moved against the smooth hard flesh of his hand. She closed her eyes, wanting him intensely, roused by the power in him. The futility of that made her angry, but she suppressed the anger along with the desire and waited for him to take his hand away.

He crossed to the chair and poured a dollop of brandy into the bubbleglass waiting beside the bottle. When he'd settled himself, he said, "Tell me."

Keeping her description terse and unemotional, she reported what Jaril had told her. "So," she finished, "there's a time limit. If we're going to find her alive, we do it before the year's out. Will you long look for us?"

He held the glass in both hands and stared into the amber liquid as if he sought an answer there. "Where's Jay?"

"In the bed. Resting. He said to wake him when you came, but I decided not to."

Maksim's lips twitched, the beginnings of a smile. "Tact, Bramble?"

"Surprised? I think that's an insult."

"Never." The word was drawn out and ended in a chuckle. "Seriously, Thornlet, how quiet do you want to keep this? If I start operating around here, there'll be notice taken. Official notice. The Managers don't like outsiders mussing the pool."

"I haven't a clue what you're talking about."

"Security, Brann. Kukurul's boast. Do your business here and it stays your business."

"So?"

"Use your head. How do you think they enforce that?" He closed his eyes and looked wary. "If you want me to fiddle about under seal, we go back to Jal Virri."

"Will they know what you're doing or only that you're doing it?"

"Now I'm the one insulted."

She flipped a hand in an impatient gesture. "Can you work here? I mean, do you need tools you haven't got?"

"Words are my tools, all I need," he said. "Little Danny Blue explained that, remember? As long as my memory functions and my hands move, I'm in business." He smiled at her, his irritation smoothed away by hers. "I haven't noticed it falling off, have you? Don't answer that, mmh." He leaned forward, hands cupped over his knees. "I could get busy tonight, Bramble, but I'd rather wait until I can inform the Managers what I'm doing is no business of theirs."

"I have to Hunt, Maksi. For lots of reasons."

"Better wait."

"How long?"

"Two days, three at most."

"All right. Will you come with us?"

"No. I'll make up some *call-me*'s for you; if you run into trouble and I can help, break one under your heel and I'll be there." He lifted his hands, spread them wide in a flowing expressive gesture. "If it weren't for young Kori. . . ."

"It's my affair, not yours, Maksi; you needn't fuss yourself."

"Hmm." He got to his feet. "If you need money. . . ."

"I do. But I'll talk to you about that later. All right?"

"Fine. Third hour tomorrow morning?"

"All right. Here? Good."

She stood in the doorway to her suite and watched him stride off down the corridor. That's over, she thought. I was right. Neither of us is going back to Jal Virri. Healing time, resting time, it's done. She sighed and shut the door, went over to the fire and stood leaning against the mantle, letting the heat play across the front of her body. Tungjii, she thought. Say hisser name and step back. Maksi was right. I shouldn't have invoked the little god, look what happened. She brooded until her robe began to scorch, then she shifted to a chair. Slowly, with painful care and uncomfortable honesty, she confronted needs she hadn't expected to have and set these against the ethical code her father had taught her by example and aphorism.

Don't cheat yourself by scamping your work, whatever the pressures of time and need; you always lose more than you gain if you cut corners.

In your dealings with others, first do no harm.

If harm is inevitable, do all you can to minimize its effects.

Her eyes filled; she scrubbed her hand across them angrily. This cursed nostalgia was useless. All it did was undercut her efforts to deal with the things that she was discovering about herself, things that terrified her. Disgusted her.

"You didn't wake me." Jaril dropped beside her, knelt with his arms resting on the chair arm.

"Maksi was in a mood." She touched his hair. "Do you mind?"

"He going to help?"

"Yes. He'll start looking for Yaril tomorrow. He has to soothe the Managers first."

"Um. He coming with us?"

"No. It'll be just us."

"Good."

"Jay!"

"He'd be a drag and you know it."

"He's powerful. He can do things we wouldn't have a hope of doing."

"Who says we'll need those things? We haven't before."

"Imp." She tapped the tip of his nose, laughed. "What are we arguing about, eh? He's not coming, so there's no problem."

"When we leaving?"

"Maksi says he should have all he can get in two-three days, say three days. Then I've got to Hunt, he says wait until he finishes his sweep and I agree. Say two nights more. All right?"

"Has to be. You look tired."

"I am."

"Sleep."

"Can't turn my head off."

"Come to bed. I can fix that."

"I don't want to dream, Jay."

"I won't mess with dreams, Bramble. If you do, you need to. Come on."

"I come, o master Jay."

7

Maksim was embarrassed and worried when he came to her suite two days later. "I don't know who, I don't know why. I tried every means I know, Bramble, but I found out nothing." Hands clasped behind him, he went charging about the room, throwing words at her over his shoulder. "Do you hear? Nothing! Even the cave is closed off from me. All of it." He stopped in front of her, glared at her. "I don't think you should go there, Bramble. Not alone."

"I won't be alone. Jay will be with me."

He brushed that away. "You have a year. Give me two months. Come with me to meet Kori when she leaves the school. As soon as I finish there, I'll be free. I've never seen anything like this, Brann; god or man, no one has shut me out like this since I was a first year apprentice."

"No, Maksi. Now. It has to be now."

"If I don't snap you to the cave site, it will take you at least two months' travel to reach it. Give me those months."

"If that sled Danny Blue made hadn't gone to pieces, I wouldn't have to beg. I hate this, Maksi, but I've got no choice. Please. Do what you said you'd do. I'm not being stubborn or perverse. It isn't Jay working on me. This is . . . I don't know, a feeling, something. It says NOW. I don't know. Please, Maksi. Do you want me on my knees?" She started to drop, but he caught her arm in a hard grip that left bruises behind when he took his hand away.

"No!" He shouted the word at her. "No," he said more quietly. "Here." He stretched out a fist, held it over her cupped hands. "*Call-me*'s. If you need me, put one under your heel and crush it. I'll be there before your next breath. If I can find you." Grim and unhappy, he dropped half a dozen water-smoothed quartz pebbles in her hands. "If I can. If you aren't blocked off from me like the cave."

8

Drinker of Souls prowled the streets.

A band of prepubescent thieves came creeping through
the fog to find their Whip limp and lifeless on the filthy
cobbles.

A childstealer dropped from a window with a bundle
slung over one shoulder. A hand came from the darkness,
slapped against his neck. A mastiff howled until a houseguard
came out to throw a cobble at the beast. The guard heard
the baby crying, saw the bundle and the dead man, woke
the house with his yells.

An assassin prepared to scale the outside of a merchant's
house. When the streetsweepers came along, they found his
body rolled up against the wall.

Inside the BlackHouse a man was beating a boy, slowly,
carefully beating him to death. When he finished, he left the
place, strolling sated between his bodyguards. His gardener
found the three of them stretched out under a bush, dead.

And so it went.

In the cold wet dawns the streetsweepers of Kukurul
found the husks she left behind and put them on the rag and
bone cart for the charnel fires.

In the cold wet dawns the Kula priests went sweeping in
procession through the tangled streets, setting silence on the
newborn ghosts. Ghosts that were highly indignant and prepared to make life difficult for everyone around them. They
fought the grip of the priests but lost and went writhing off,
pulsing with blocked fury. The wind blew them off to join
the fog out over the bay and the debris from older cast-out
souls.

9

On the evening of the third night, with Jaril trotting
beside her, Brann climbed the mountain above the inn and
waited for Maksim.

The Wounded Moon was a vague patch of yellow in the
western sky, a chill fog eddied about the flat; the stones
were dark with the damp, slippery lightsinks and traps for
the unwary ankle. Brann pulled her cloak tighter about her
body, muttering under her breath at Maksim's insistence on
this particular spot for his operations. At the same time she
was perversely pleased with her surroundings, the gloom
around her resonated with the gloom inside her. Jaril was

even more unhappy with the place. He'd kept his mastiff form but replaced his fur with a thick leathery skin that shed the condensation from the fog like waxed parchment. In spite of that he was uncomfortable. The wet stole heat and energy from him. He was prowling about, rubbing his sides against any boulders tall enough to allow this, impatient to get away.

In the fog and the cold and the dark, Jaril whining behind her somewhere, Brann began to wonder if Maksim had changed his mind again. She eased the straps of her rucksack; though the leather was padded, they were cutting into her shoulders. Soft, she thought, but I'll harden with time and doing. She looked at her hands. They glowed palely in the dense dark, milkglass flesh with bone shadows running through it.

"You can still change your mind, Bramble." Maksim's voice came out of the dark, startling her; she hadn't heard or sensed his approach. That worried her.

"No," she said. "Jay, come here. Do it, Maksi."

10

Brann stepped from one storm into another. The slope outside the cave mouth was bare and stony; a knife-edged icewind swept across it, driving pellets of ice against Brann's face and body. Jaril whimpered, ducked under the snapping ends of her cloak and pressed up against her.

Brann dropped into a crouch, put her mouth close to his ear. "Where's the cave? We've got to get out of this."

Jaril shivered, grew a thick coat of fur. He edged from the shelter of the cloak, waited until she was standing again, then trotted up the slope to a clump of scrub jemras, low crooked conifers with a strong cedary smell that blew around her as she got closer, powerful, suffocating. She plunged through them and into a damp darkness with a howl in it.

Once he was out of the wind, Jaril changed to the glow globe that was his base form and lit up a dull, dark chamber like a narrowmouth bottle. He hung in midair, quivering with indignation and cursing Maksim in buzzing mindspeak for sending them into this cold hell.

Brann ignored the voice in her head as she would a mosquito buzzing; she slid out of the shoulder straps and lowered the rucksack to the cave floor. Her cloak was wet through, she was cold to the bone. "Jay, in a minute give me some light out there. I have to get a fire started before

I perish. . . ." She gasped and went skipping backward as a stack of wood clattered to the stone, followed by a whoosh and a flare of heat as a clutch of hot coals and burning sticks landed near the woodpile. She laughed. "Thanks, Maksi," she called. She laughed again, her voice echoing and re-echoing as Jaril darted to the fire and sank into it, quivering with pleasure as he bathed in the heat.

She bustled about, spreading mat and blankets, restacking the wood, organizing the coals and several sticks of wood into a larger fire. When she finished, she sighed with weariness and looked around. Jaril was gone. He couldn't wait, she thought. Well, she's his sister and night and day don't matter underground. She rubbed her back, frowned. What do I do if he's trapped like Yaro? Idiot boy! A few more hours and I could have gone with him. She dropped onto the mat and pulled a blanket around her to block off the drafts. Staring into the fire, she grew angrier with every minute lumbering past.

The glowsphere came speeding recklessly back. Jaril shifted to his bipedal form, flung himself at Brann, sobbing and trembling, cold for his kind and deep in shock. "She's gone, Bramble, she's not there any longer, she's gone, she's gone. . . ."

II. SETTSIMAKSIMIN

Kukurul, the World's navel
Settsimaksimin, alone and
restless
also: Jastouk, male courtesan
Vechakek, his minder
Todichi Yahzi, Maksim's
ex-secretary, now a
mistreated slave.
Davindolillah, a boy who
reminds Maksim of
himself, of no other
importance.
Assorted others.

1

Settsimaksimin yawned. He felt drained. It was brushing
against the trap in the cave that did it, he thought. The
block. Fool woman, lack-brained looby, ahhh, Thornlet,
that thing is dangerous. He stomped about the rubble-strewn
flat, uncertain what to do next; the fog was thickening to a
slow dull rain and the night was colder; it was time to get out
of this, but he was reluctant to leave. Fool man, me, he thought.
He wrung some of the water from his braid, shaped a will-o
and sent it bobbing along ahead of him to light the path so
he wouldn't break his neck as he went downhill to the Inn.

Jastouk would be at the *Ardent Argent* unless he'd got
tired of waiting and gone trawling for a new companion.
Gods, I'm tired. I don't want to sleep. Sleep, hah! Bramble,
you're damn inconvenient, you and those devilkids of yours
. . . fires die if you aren't there to fan them. . . .

He changed his clothes and took a chair up the Katt. He
found Jastouk sitting sulkily alone, watching some uninspired dancers posturing with the flaccid conjurings produced by an equally uninspired firewitch. He coaxed the
hetairo into better humor and carried him off to a semi-
private party at one of the casinos.

39

Company in his bed didn't chase the dreams this time. Maksim woke sweating, his insides churning. He swore, dragging himself out of bed and doused his head with cold water.

Heavy-eyed and languorous, Jastouk stretched, laced his hands behind his head. "Bad night?" he murmured.

Maksim snapped the clasp off the end of his braid, tossed one of his brushes on the bed. "Brush my hair for me," he said. He dropped into a chair, sighed with pleasure as the youth's slim fingers worked the braid loose and began drawing the brush over the coarse gray strands. "You have good hands, Jasti."

"Yours are more beautiful," Jastouk said. His voice was a soft, drowsy burr, caressing the ear. "They hold power with grace."

"Don't do that." The anger and worry lingering from the night made Maksi's voice harsher than he'd meant it to be. "I don't need flattery, Jasti. I don't like it."

Jastouk laughed, a husky musical sound, his only answer to Maksim's acerbities. He began humming one of the songs currently popular in Kurkurul as he drew the brush through and through the sheaf of hair. He was thin, with the peculiar beauty of the wasted; his bones had an elegance denied most flesh. He was neither learned nor especially clever, but had a sweetness of disposition that made such graces quite superfluous. Pliant and receptive, he responded to the needs and moods of his clients before they were even aware they were in a mood and he had a way of listening with eyes and body as well as ears that seduced them into thinking they meant more to him than they did. They were disturbed, even angry, when they chanced across him in company with a successor and found that he had trouble placing them. He was wildly expensive, though he never bothered about money, leaving that to his Minder, a Henerman named Vechakek, who set his fees and collected them with minimal courtesy. Jastouk had a very few favored lovers that he never forgot; despite Vechakek's scolding he'd cut short whatever relationship he was in at the time and go with them, whether they could afford his fees or not. Maksim was one of these. Jastouk adored the huge man, he was awed by the thought of being lover to a Sorceror Prime; there were only four of them in all the world. But even Maksim had to court him and give him the attention he craved; there were too many others clamoring for his favors and he had too strong a need

for continual reassuring to linger long where he was neglected and ignored. He was indolent but had almost no
patience with his lovers, even the most passionate; when
Brann's demands on Maksim's time and energies interfered
with his courting, Jastouk was exasperated to the point of
withdrawing, but when the interference was done, he was
content to let Maksim's ardor warm him into an ardor of his
own; this morning he was pleased with himself, settling
happily into the old relationship. He brushed Maksim's long
hair, every touch of his hands a caress; he sang his lazy
songs and used his own tranquillity to smooth away the
aches and itches in Maksim's souls.

When they left the Inn, the sun was high, shining with a
watery autumnal warmth. Content with each other's company, they moved along the winding lane, dead leaves dropping about them, blowing about their feet, lending a gently
melancholy air to the day. Maksim had the sense of something winding down, a time of transition between what was
and what will be. It was a pleasant feeling for the most part,
with scratchy places to remind him that nothing is perma-
nent, that contentment has to be cherished, but abandoned
before it got overripe. He plucked a lingering plum from a
cluster of browning leaves, tossed it to a jikjik nosing among
the roots. There were no real seasons this far south, but
fruit trees and flowering trees went into a partial dormancy
and shed part of their leaves in the fall, the beginning of the
dry season, and stretched bare limbs among the sparse hold-
outs left on whippy green twigs until the rains came again.

"When you were busy with your friend," brown eyes soft
as melted chocolate slid lazily toward Maksim, moved away
again, the chocolate cream voice was slow and uninflected,
making no overt comment on Maksim's neglect of him,
though that did lie quite visible beneath the calm, "I was
rather moped, missing you, Maksi, so I went to see the Pem
Kundae perform. Do you know them?"

"No." Maksim yawned. "Sorry, I'm not too bright today.
Who are they and what do they do?" He wasn't much
interested in Jastouk's chatter, but he was willing to listen.

The hetairo noted his mental absence; it made him unhappy. He stopped talking.

Maksim pulled himself together; he needed company; he
needed sex and more sex to drown out and drive away things
clamoring at him. Drugs were impossible; a sorceror of his
rank would have to be suicidal to strip away his defenses so

thoroughly. He needed Brann. He was furious at the changers for calling her away like that. He missed her already;
time and time again when he saw some absurdity, he turned
to share it with her, but she wasn't there. Instead of Brann,
he had Jastouk, pliant and loving, but oh so blank above the
neck. *I'm not going to have him, if I keep letting my mind
wander.* He set himself to listen with more attention. "Are
they some kind of players?"

Jastouk smiled, slid his fingers along Maksim's arm, took
his hand. "Oh yes. Quite marvelous, Maksi. They do a bit
of everything, dance, sing, mime, juggle, but that's only
gilding. What they mainly do is improvise little poems. You
shout out some topic or other and two or three of them will
make up rhyming couplets until there's a whole poem finished for you. And the most amazing thing is, they do it in
at least half a dozen languages. Delicious wordplay, I swear
it, Maksi. Multilingual puns. You'd like them, I'm sure; it's
the kind of thing you enjoy." He hesitated, not quite certain
how his next comment would be taken. "I've heard you and
your friend play the same kind of game.'

"Ah. I shall have to see them. Tonight, Jasti?"

"It would have to be, this is their last performance here. I
bespoke tickets, Maksi, do you mind? They're very popular,
you know. I had to pull all sorts of strings to get these seats.
They're a gold apiece, is that too much? They're really
worth it."

"No doubt they are." Maksim cleared his throat; he re-
gretted the sarcastic tone of the words; he knew Jastouk
wouldn't like it. "I'm looking forward to seeing them
perform."

They turned into the Ihman Katt and strolled toward the
harbor. The broad street was crowded with porters and
merchants coming up from the wharves, with other strollers,
visitors who meant to sample the pleasures of Kukurul before getting down to serious buying and selling; a few like
Maksim and Jastouk were heading for the café Sidday Lir
and noon tea or a light lunch and lighter gossip.

A line of slaves on a neck coffle came shuffling along the
Katt. Maksim's eyes grazed over them. He started to look
away as soon as he realized what they were, then he saw the
being at the tail of the line, separate from the others, tugged
along on a lease like some bad-tempered dog. It was Todichi
Yahzi, his once-amanuensis.

Maksim felt a jolt to his belly. Guilt flooded through him,

choked him. He'd dismissed the little creature from his
mind so completely he hadn't thought of him once during
the past ten years. Gods of time and fate, he thought, not
an instant's thought. Nothing! He'd snatched the kwitur
from his home reality, used him and discarded him with as
little consideration as any of the kings he so despised. He
couldn't even comfort himself with the notion that he'd
assumed Yahzi had got home; the trigger he'd left with the
kwitur only worked if he, Maksim, died. He hadn't assumed
anything because he hadn't bothered to remember the being
who'd spent almost every waking hour with him for nearly
twenty years. He saw the collar on Todichi Yahzi's neck,
the chain that tethered him to the whipmaster's belt. He saw
the lumps and weals that clubs and whips had laid on his
almost-friend's hide; he saw the hunched, cringing shuffle,
the sudden blaze of rage in the deep set dull eyes as they
met his. Todichi's body read like a book of shame, but
despite the abuse he'd suffered, he was as alert, intelligent
and intransigent as he'd been when he lived in the Citadel.

After that brief involuntary lurch, Maksim walked on. He
knew Jastouk had noted his reaction and would be wondering why such a commonplace sight as a string of slaves
would bother him so much. That couldn't be helped. He
looked around. They were passing a tiny temple dedicated
to Pindatung the god of thieves and pickpockets, a scruffy
gray-mouse sort of god with a closet-sized niche for a temple. He stopped. "Jasti, go ahead and get us a table. I'll
want tea, berries, and cream. I'll be along in a minute."

Jastouk touched Maksim's shoulder. For a moment he
seemed about to offer what help he could give, but in the
end opted for tact. "Don't be long, hmm?"

"I won't. It's something I'd forgotten that I've got to take
care of. Only be a few minutes. Don't fuss, luv."

Jastouk pressed his lips together; he didn't like it when
Maksim either deliberately or unconsciously echoed Brann's
manner of speech, but he said nothing.

Ruefully aware of offending, quite aware of where the
offense lay, Maksim watched the hetairo saunter off. Shaking his head, he slipped into the templet and settled onto
the tattered cushions scattered across a wallbench. He slid
his hand into his robe and took out his farseeing mirror.
He'd made it to keep watch on Brann so he could help her if
she needed him, but he had a more urgent use for it now. It
was an oval of polished obsidian in a plaited ring of Brann's

hair, white as a spider's web and as delicate. The cable it hung from he'd twisted from a strand of his own hair. He breathed on it, rubbed his cuff over it, sat holding it for several moments. What he was going to do was a very minor magic; there was even a good chance that the Guardians hired by the Managers wouldn't notice it. If they did, he might be booted out of Kukurul and forbidden to return. He scrubbed his hand across his face. He was sweating and angry at himself, angry at Todichi Yahzi for showing up and making him feel a lout, angry at Fate in all her presentations including Tungjii Luck.

Impatiently he pushed such considerations aside and bent over the mirror, his lips moving in a subvocal chant. He set the slave coffle into the image field, along with the agent and his whipmaster, followed the shuffling string to the Auction House on the edge of the Great Market and into the slavepens behind it. He pointed the mirror at the agent and followed him into the office of his employer, watched and listened as the agent made his report, the slaver made his arrangements for the sale of the string. Three days on. Maksim let the mirror drop, canceling the spell on it, and spent a moment longer wondering if he should bid for himself or employ an agent. Shaking his head, he stood and slipped the mirror back beneath his robes. He thrust two fingers into his belt purse, fished out a coin and tossed it in the bowl beneath the crude statue of the little gray god. "In thanks for the use of your premises," he murmured and went out.

He stood a moment looking down the Ihman Katt toward the café Sidday Lir where Jastouk waited for him. I am sadly diminished, he thought. From tyrant and demiurge I have descended to merely lover and bought-love at that. Poor old Todich. There's nothing grand in hating a little man. He started walking, chuckling to himself at the image the words evoked.

2

Maksim dressed with great care, choosing a good gray robe meant to present the image of a man moderately in coin and moderate in most other things, a third rank sorceror who could defend himself but wasn't much of a threat. He dressed his long hair in a high knot, had Jastouk paint it with holding gel until it gleamed like black-streaked pewter, then he thrust plain silver skewers through the knot. He loaded his fingers with rings. Quiet, moderate rings. He was a man it was safe to gull a little, but dangerous to irritate too much.

He finished buffing his nails, inspected them closely, dropped his hands into his lap. "Slave auction," he said. "Jasti, don't come. You don't want to see that place. Or smell it."

Jastouk smiled and took his buffer back, replaced it in his dressing kit. "The sun shines all the brighter for a cloud or two."

Snorting his irritation, Maksim got to his feet. He didn't want Jastouk along, but the hetairo had evaded him all morning, refusing to hear what he didn't mean to hear. He could order him to stay away, but he didn't dare go that far. Should he demand obedience, Jastouk would obey—and when Maksim got back to his rooms, he'd find Vechakek waiting with a graceful note of farewell and a bill for the hetairo's services. He wasn't ready for that, not yet. He knew he could easily find other company, but he wanted Jastouk. The hetairo excited him. Jastouk carried an aura of free-floating promise undefined but exquisitely seductive. Maksim didn't fool himself, it was part of a hetairo's portfolio, that promise never fulfilled, never denied so that hope lingered even after the sundering: *Someday someway I will find what I want, someday someway I will KNOW what I want.* It wasn't Jastouk and it was, it wasn't Brann and it was, he didn't know what it was.

The slavepens were a vast complex growing like mold over the hills south of the Great Market, apart from it, yet part of it, deplored by the genteel of Kukurul but patronized by them along with others who didn't bother about the moral issues involved. The shyer visitors rented thin lacquer halfmasks from the dispensary just inside the portal, beast mask, bird, fantasy or abstraction, a face to show instead of the faces they wore in more respectable circumstances; the bold put on masks for the whimsy of the act or played to their vanity by separating themselves from the nameless troglodytes who bought drudges for kitchens and stables or selected more delicate fruit for the pleasure Houses. Despite a compulsive overdecoration in all the more public areas, the pens were a meld of stench and ugliness. That didn't matter, those who came to buy didn't notice the ugliness and ignored the wisps of stink that cut through the incense drifting about the private views and the auction room.

Carved in Twara-Teng high relief, the massive portal was intricately chased, heavily ornate, monumentally ugly. On sale days the syndics had the twin leaves of the Gate swung outward and pinned to angular dragonposts, exposing the serpentine geometrics of their inner surfaces. Maksim walked past them, his nostrils twitching. He loathed this place, but was almost pleased because its aesthetic qualities were so wonderfully suited to the acts within, as if the building and its ornamentation were designed by some heavy handed and deeply offended satirist. He paused at the dispensary and rented a falcon's mask for Jastouk, taking a black bear's muzzle for himself.

Masked and silent, they strolled among the cages for a while, waiting for the first sale to be called.

Jastouk was restless, uneasy. Like most of the hetairos working with Minders or from one of the established Houses, he'd been meat in a cage like those around him when he was a child, a brown-eyed blond with skin soft and smooth as fresh cream, knowing just enough to be terrified because he had no say in who bought him or what use they made of him. But that was long ago, longer than he liked to think about. The years were pressing in on him, leaving their traces on his face and body. The day would come when clients would ignore him for younger, fresher fare; new lovers would be hard to find, his price would drop, his standards go. He'd seen it happen to others again and again, thinking not me, no, never. Anyway, that's a long time off, when I'm old, I won't be old for years and years. This place reminded him that those years were passing, each year faster than the last; it was time and more than time to begin planning, it was time and more than time to search for a lover he could stay with.

They passed a small blond boy, all eyes and elbows and numb terror.

Maksim felt the fingers on his arm tremble, caught the flicker of slitted eyes. He guessed at Jastouk's fears and felt pain at the loss of something he'd treasured, the golden gliding invulnerability of the hetairo. Jastouk had made several mistakes this morning, the biggest of them, underestimating the power of the buried anxieties this place would trigger, the effect they'd have on his judgment. Maksim looked at him with pity instead of lust and was saddened by

that. For a moment he thought of keeping the hetairo with
him now that Brann was gone and unlikely to return, but
only for a moment. He was fond of Jastouk but he didn't
like him much and he certainly wasn't in love with him; he
hadn't been in love for . . . how long? It seemed like centuries. It was at least decades. The last time, when was it?
Certainly before he went to Cheonea. Traxerxes from Phras.
The ancient ache of parting felt like pressed flowers, the
shape there but all the fragrance gone. Five stormy years
and more pain and fury than . . . faded and gone. No one
after Trax. He was too busy with his little Cheonenes, trying
to shape them into something . . . no time, no energy,
nobody. . . . Jastouk wasn't meant for longterm anything.
He was a diversion, delightful but ephemeral.

No, don't think about it, he told himself and made a
half-hearted pretense of inspecting the merchandise. Without his musings to distract him, outrage took hold, outrage
and helplessness. If he were given the rule of things, he'd
turn every slaver into pigmeat and lop the ears off parents
who sold their children no matter what the reason. He'd
outlawed slavery in Cheonea, skinned some slavers and
confiscated some ships—how long that would hold he had
no idea. He had to trust his farmers to keep the land clean;
they were tough old roots; they had their claws on power
and it'd take a lot to pry them loose. Ah well, it wasn't his
responsibility any longer.

He pulled the mask away from his face, mopped at his
brow and upper lip with the lace-edged linen wipe he twitched
from his sleeve. He settled the mask into place, tucked the
wipe away and strolled to the back of the room. Todichi
Yahzi was in none of the cages. That might mean the kwitur
was part of the first lot. If so, good, he thought, the sooner
I'm out of here. . . .

Maksim set his back against the wall, smoothed a hand
down the front of his robe, his stomach churning despite the
calm detachment he was trying to project. Or it might mean
Todich was already gone. Private sale. The dealer hadn't
planned to offer private views, but anything might have
happened since last night.

Jastouk leaned against him, responding to his tension,
offering warmth and support—and a voiceless warning that
he was broadcasting too much emotion.

Maksim sighed and did his best to relax. He was drilled in
self-control, but excess was an integral part of his power. He

drew strength from riding the ragged edge of disaster. Not
now, he told himself. This is not the time for power, this is
the time for finesse. Forty Mortal Hells, you great lumbering fool, finesse! He blinked sweat from his eyes and swept
the room with an impatient glance. It was rapidly filling up.
About a third of the newcomers wore masks, some of them
far too rich to be part of the Dispenser's stock; it was early
for such notables to be out, maybe that meant something,
maybe it was just chance. The rest were stolid types with
House Badges on dull tabards, some solitaire, some with a
clutch of clerks in attendance. Maksim bent toward the
smooth blond head resting against his ribs. "Tell me who's
here," he murmured.

"Some of the masks I don't know." Jastouk's whisper was
a thread of sound inaudible a step away. "They don't make
the night circles, I think. Goldmask Hawk, that's an Impe-
rial Hand from Andurya Durat; I don't know why he's here
now; this is a meat market. The skilled slaves go in the
evening sale. Black Lacquer Beetle with the sapphire bobs,
she's Muda Paramount from the Pitna Jong Island group,
that's out in the middle of the Big Nowhere, she usually
culls a girl or two from these sales, or a boychild if he's very
young and very beautiful. . . ." The creamy murmur went
on as the stage began to show signs of life. Two sweepers
emerged from behind tall black velvet curtains, swung brooms
in graceful arcs, almost a dance as they came together,
parted, then glided out, pushing before them small heaps of
dust and other debris.

"The Hina mix in gray with the Shamany Patch . . . um,
that patch is a lie, he hired it off the Shamany; everyone
knows that but goes along with it. The Shamany's a miserable poxHouse, makes its taxcoin from those patchrents. I've
seen him around in the dogends of morning, I think he runs
a stable of child thieves; he's probably looking for new
talent. . . ."

Three youths in black pajamas pushed a squat pillar out
to the center of the stage, fitted a curving ramp onto it. The
Block. Maksim shuddered, acid rising in his throat. It was
over a century since he'd been present at a slave auction; it
was two hundred and seventy-one years since he himself had
been sold in one. The sight of it still made him want to
vomit. As more sceneshifters brought in the Caller's Lectern
and a cage that glittered like silver in the harsh light, he
forced himself to listen to Jastouk.

"Rinta House, Gashturmteh, Aldohza, Yeshamm, all solitaire reps, they don't look like they're expecting much . . .
um, BlackHouse is here, that's why. Not a good idea to bid
too often against BlackHouse, bad things happen to you."
Jastouk shuddered, his body rubbing against Maksim's.

The Caller came onstage and stood behind his Lectern,
holding his hardwood rod a handspan above the sounder.
He looked out across the milling crowd, then he hammered
twice for attention, the harsh clacks breaking through the
buzz of conversation, pulling those still drifting among the
cages onto the auction floor. Maksim stepped away from
the wall and onto the floor though he stayed at the back of
the bidders. His size was an embarrassment sometimes, an
advantage here. He couldn't be overlooked. He folded his
arms across his broad chest and waited.

The first offerings were brought out to warm up the
crowd and get them bidding, two half-grown males and a
middle-aged woman; they went to clerks looking for muscle
and a reasonable degree of health.

"We have several items fresh in from the South; the first
is a healthy boy said to be Summerborn and in his sixth
year." The Caller tapped lightly with his sounding rod. A
Hina girl led a small M'darjin boy from behind the curtains,
walked him up the ramp and whispered commands to him
from behind the pillar, making him turn and posture, open
his mouth and show his teeth, go through the ritual of
offering himself for sale. He was frightened and awkward,
but already he'd learned to keep silence and obey his handlers.

Blind unreasoning rage shook Maksim, rattled in his throat.
Without warning he was that boy on the Block; all the
intervening years were wiped away, his control was wiped
away; another instant and he might have destroyed half of
Kukurul in his fury before he was himself destroyed by the
forces that guarded the city.

A short sharp pain stabbed through the haze, came again
and again; Jastouk had read him and reacted without thought
or hesitation. He had a come-along hold on Maksim's hand,
he was squeezing and pressing on it, generating such agony
that it brought Maksim out of his fit, sweating and cursing
under his breath.

"Bid," Jastouk whispered urgently. There was a faint film
of sweat on his skin, a frantic, half-mad glare in his eyes. "If
you want him, bid." He began massaging the hand he'd

mistreated, still disturbed, his eyes half-closed, his breathing
a rapid shallow pant.

"Could've been me," Maksim muttered.

"No. Stupid ordinary little git. Not you."

Maksim managed an unsteady chuckle. "I was a stupid
ordinary little git, Jasti."

Jastouk shook his head in stubborn disagreement, but he
said nothing.

The caller had already taken a few bids, starting low, six
coppers; he worked that up to thirty coppers, coaxing small
increments out of the motley group on the floor. All the boy
offered was his youth; he wasn't especially charming or
quick and the Caller continued noncommittal about his talents.

The BlackHouse Rep held up five fingers. Fifty coppers.

That jolted Maksim out of his brooding. He lifted both
hands, showed six fingers. Though he'd recovered from that
first shock of identification, he could not possibly let that
boy go to BlackHouse; there was only one use they had for
a child that age; it made him sick thinking about it.

The Rep looked around, scowling. Once they declared
interest in an item, they weren't used to being challenged.
He thought a moment, showed six fingers straight and a
seventh bent. Sixty-five coppers.

Maksim showed eight.

The Rep looked at him a long moment, looked at the
boy, shrugged and let the bid stand. Small coltish boys with
no special charm or talent were no rarity and he wouldn't be
reprimanded for letting this one go elsewhere.

There being no other bids, the Caller hammered the boy
to Maksim and the Hina girl led him off. He'd be held in the
back until Maksim brought the coin to pay the bid and the
tag-fee.

Another boy was brought out, older this time, a stocky
freckled youth with a long torso and short legs. "Journey-
man gardener," the Caller announced and the bidding started
again.

Maksim was annoyed at his loss of control, annoyed at
circumstances, Fate, whatever, forcing his hand. *What do I
do with him? Send him home? Chances are it was his own
family sold him to some traveling slaver. Complicating my
life. I certainly don't need complications, it's bad enough
now, what with Jastouk and his needs and Bramble with
those devilkids she dotes on and Kori coming out of school;
I've got to leave for Silili soon if I want to be in time to*

catch her before she starts home. And now there's old Todich, gods know how much he's going to cost me. Signs. All these signs. A closure coming. An era pinched off. Turn of the Wheel. I damn well better get myself in order or that Wheel will roll right over me. Offering to the Juggernaut, smashed meat.

As the bidding continued around him and Jastouk grew restless and unhappy at being ignored, Maksim brooded over the Signs. Sad, sad, sad. Melancholy like the dead leaves eddying around their feet when they came down from the Inn. The boy, what did he mean? Was he setting free his baby self so he could move to true maturity? What was maturity to someone like him who could extend his life as long as he was interested in living? Was it the willingness to let go, to die? He thought about death with a curious lack of emotion. To this point he'd fought death with everything he had in him, fought death and won—with Brann's help. Brann was gone. He thought about that. Odd feeling. Like an arm hacked off. Todich. A thread dangling from his past. Tie it off. Send him home. I owe Todich passage home or I'm no better than BlackHouse or old king Noshios I kicked out of Silagamatys. It was a debt he had to pay, a payment he'd put off far too long. It was going to cost. No more BinYAHtii to carry the load. Cost doesn't matter. Ah well. . . .

Todichi Yahzi was brought on at the tail of the lot.

"Here we have an exotic item, looks like a cross between a macaque and some sort of giant bug. It can talk a little and understand what you tell it. Our readers have checked it over and it's no demon, so you don't have to worry about waking up turned into a toad. . . ." The Caller chattered on, trying to stir up some interest as the handlers prodded the kwitur up the ramp and got him to crouch on the Block facing the audience. They poked at him, cursed him in angry hisses, but gave over their efforts at a sign from the Caller who didn't want his lack of spirit to become too apparent.

Maksim waited a moment. No other bids, bless Tungjii Luck. He thought it over, then he lifted a fist, opened up four fingers. Forty coppers. There was some stir in the others on the floor, but no more offers, no matter how cleverly the Caller wheedled them. Finally he gave up and hammered the kwitur to Maksim.

Maksim smoothed his fingers along the nape of Jastouk's neck. "Let's go," he said.

"That's it? It's that thing you came for?"

"Are you coming?"

"No. I think not."

"I'll see you tonight, then."

"Perhaps."

Maksim thought about coaxing him into a better humor. After a minute he decided better not. If it was ending, let it end.

3

Jastouk was gone when Maksim got back from provisioning the boat.

He couldn't send Todich home from Kukurul; if he had unfriends elsewhere, he had spitesons on his back in Kukurul who would sacrifice a firstborn to catch him when he was too whipped to defend himself. Spite and envy aside, the Managers who ran Kukurul would like nothing better than setting their claws into a sorceror of his rank; he couldn't call his breath his own if they got hold of him. Without BinYAHtii to give him support and control, he'd have to drain himself to a dishrag simply reaching the reality where he'd found the kwitur; sliding Todich there along the capillary he was holding open with will and bodyforce would drop him into coma for hours, maybe even a full day, it wasn't one of the easy reaches like the salamandri source or the tigermen's world. He'd be vulnerable to anyone who stumbled across him. A yearling bunny could make a meal of him. Better to sail deep into the Tukery and find himself a deserted rock where he could sleep off the throwjag and have a chance of waking with his souls still in his body.

He came back to the Inn weary and depressed, looking forward to a little cuddling and comforting, though Jastouk had turned cool and unforthcoming since the slave-auction. He walked into Jastouk's Minder.

Vechakek came from the SunParlor off the main lobby of the Inn; he stepped in front of Maksim, put his hand flat against Maksim's chest. "He's off," the Minder said. "He doesn't like being ignored, he won't put up with it. The association is terminated." he held up a sheet of paper folded once across the middle. "The account for services rendered. Pay now." He was a massive Henerman from Hraney, a half-mythical country supposed to be somewhere in the far west. His skin was pale mahogany, hard and hairless, polished to a high gleam; he wore his coarse black hair in twin plaits that hung beside his highnosed face; he had a taste for sarcasm and sudden violence that made folk walk tip-a-toe around him. Would-be clients tolerated his insolence; they had to if they wanted to arrange a liaison with Jastouk.

Maksim stared at him until he backed off a few steps. "Don't touch me again," he said quietly.

Vechakek's face went rigid and darkened across the cheekbones, but the Henerman couldn't quite work up the nerve to come at a man who was rumored to have few equals in power and none above him but the gods themselves. Then the anger washed out of his face and Vechakek was smiling, his pale blue eyes swimming with malice; he knew something. Something was going to happen, something which Maksim wouldn't like, no, not at all, which Vechakek planned to sit back and enjoy.

Maksim read that and wondered; the Henerman seemed very sure of what he knew; it was a thing to puzzle over but not just now. He held out his hand. "Give me the bill." He unfolded the paper, examined the list of charges; there were things he might have challenged, but in spite of the unhappy ending of this interlude, Jastouk was a dear and a delight; besides, he didn't feel like wasting energy on petty cheating. "Wait here," he said.

Todich and the boy were in the sitting room of his suite. The kwitur was curled up in one of the armchairs, either asleep or making an effective pretense of sleeping. The boy was standing by an open window, staring out into the foggy dank afternoon.

Maksim crossed to the fireplace and took down the battered leather box sitting on the mantle. As soon as he touched it, he knew the boy had been fooling with it, trying to get it open. A thief and incompetent at it. No doubt that was the reason his people sold him. Young idiot not to realize a sorceror would have wards on anything he wanted left alone. Maksim put the box on a table beside Todichi's chair. He grinned down at the little creature. "Ah! Todich, you should have told him it was futile fooling around with this." No answer. The boy's shoulders twitched, but he didn't turn around.

Maksim opened the box and counted out the coins he needed from his rapidly diminishing store of expense money.

He was going to have to tap one of his caches before he started to Silili; what with the auction and Brann's call on his purse, he had barely enough coin left to pay his bill at the Inn. Other years he'd have added a handsome tip when he paid Jastouk off; not this time, he couldn't afford it and the hetairo hadn't earned it. He divided the fifty Kukral aureats Vechakek demanded into four piles, wrapped them first in the bill, then in a clean sheet of writing paper. He sealed the ends with red wax from his private store, stamped his mark into the wax and spun a small bind about the packet, keying it to Jastouk's touch. If Vechakek intended to take his percentage before he handed over the coin, he was out of luck. It was a small favor, perhaps meaningless, all Maksim could do for his temporary lover—let the hetairo get full measure for once, not just what his Minder decided to hand over.

He tugged at the cord and gave the packet to the maidservant who came to answer the bell. "Take this to the man in the SunParlor," he said. He gave her a five cupra piece for her pains, watched, amused, as she pushed the broad coin into her sleeve, flirted her lashes at him, then bounced from the room.

He brushed his hands together, brushing away Jastouk and Vechakek with the nonexistent dust. For a moment he stood gazing at the door, then he sighed and crossed to the largest of the armchairs. When he was settled, his feet comfortable on the hassock, he laced his fingers together across the hard mound of his stomach and contemplated the narrow back of the M'darjin boy. Occupied with Jastouk's sulks and making the boat ready for a trip into the Tukery, he'd ignored his new acquisition, noticed the boy only as a minor irritation to be brushed aside when he got underfoot. With Jastouk gone and the trip imminent, it was time to find out what he'd got. "Come here, boy."

The boy came slowly away from the window. When he reached the hassock, he fell on his face, elbows out, hands clasped behind his head.

"Get off your belly, buuk." Maksim looked at the cringing figure with distaste; he understood why the boy was that way, but he didn't have to like it—and it woke painful memories he'd tried hard to erase. "What's your name?"

The boy scrambled to his feet. "Davindolillah." He looked sideways at Maksim, added, "Saör."

"So you're a thief."

Davindo opened his eyes wide. "No."

"And a liar." Some of his sourness washed away; the boy amused him. "A bad liar," he said, cutting off Davindo's parade of indignation before he could get it going. "By which I mean an incompetent liar. Unconvincing. Where did the slavers get you, Davindolillah? By which I mean: what is your homeland?"

"Majimtopayum," the boy said, pride thrumming in his voice. "The Country of the River Which is Wide as the Sea. My father is Falama Paramount, he has five hundred wives and his wives each have five hundred cows and five hundred boats and five hundred acres each of beans and maize and taties," he boasted, piling improbability on improbability, head back, eyes flashing, strutting where he stood. He shook himself and mimed a becoming humility. "I am not the eldest son. . . ."

Maksim suppressed a smile. The boy could prove amusing enough to earn the coppers he cost.

"And I am not the youngest son." Davindo slapped at his skinny chest. "Only the favorite. There was weeping and wailing and tearing of hair when the slavers stole me from my father's house. When I was born, the Wamanachi prophesied over me, the Great Wamanachi said of me, I shall be Puissant and Terrible to the Enemies of the Land, inside and out. I shall be Sung down the Ages, Father to many sons, Warchief to my people, Paramount among Paramounts. That is what he said."

"Most interesting. No. Be silent, Davindolillah." He inspected the boy more closely than he'd done before.

Davindo's small size and round face had fooled him as they had the slavers. The Caller had rated him about six. Maksim measured him against his memories of himself at six and rejected the number; he was at least double that though still on the child's side of puberty, a tough, clever little streetrat, defending pride and person with everything in him. Maksim saw the desperation behind the boasting, knew it intimately because it was his own when he was five, six, ten; it made him sick and turned him crueler than he'd meant to be.

"If I sent you back, would your people simply sell you again?"

The boy pressed his lips together. Anger flashed in his black eyes. His first impulse was to attack with the slashing invective he'd acquired in his home streets, but he'd learned

enough about being a slave to keep a tight rein on his
temper. "I was stole," he muttered.

"As you say. I am going to give you your papers. No. Be
quiet. I don't intend to discuss my reasons with you. If you
wish to go home, I will pay your passage and put you on a
ship with a master I trust to make sure you get there. If you
prefer to stay in Kukurul, I will arrange schooling for you or
an apprenticeship. Well?"

Davindo's eyes shifted from the door to the window. His
pale pink tongue flicked over his lips. "What do you want
me to say?"

"I know what you think you want, but I'm not going to
cut you loose; I've got enough guilt spotting my souls, I
don't need more. Do you have a talent or an inclination that
you'd like to pursue?"

Davindo looked sly. "You teach me."

"Do you know what I am?"

"The beast told me. Sorceror."

"Yes. You have no Talent."

"How do you know? You haven't even looked at me."

"Talent shouts. You don't have to look for it. I can hear
it across a city, young Davindo. There's nothing I can teach
you. Don't take that as an insult; you wouldn't blame a
singing coach for not training you if you couldn't hold a
tune. Do I send you home?"

"No." Davindo swallowed, kicking at the rug. After a
minute he squared his narrow shoulders, stared defiantly at
Maksim. "As long as I'm here, I might as well take a look
round the place."

"Wise of you. Who would neglect the opportunities that
come his way is a clothhead not worth the name of man.
Can you read?"

"Of course I can, I had teachers since I could walk. Um,
but not this jabber they speak up here.'

"Right." Maksim swallowed a smile, his need to deflate
the boy's air castles dissipated by his appreciation of Davo's
deft footwork. "The more languages you can read and write,
the more control you have over your circumstances." He
moved his feet, freeing a part of the hassock. "Sit down.
School or tutor?"

Davindo hesitated, then dropped warily beside Maksi's
ankles. "Tutor."

"I hear. You didn't answer me. Do you have a talent or
an inclination you'd like to pursue?"

"I will be Warleader in my time."

"So you said. I take it that means you have no scholarly interests?"

Davindo twisted his face into a scornful grimace, but said nothing.

"So. Apprenticeship not scholarship. I'd best find you a place in one of the guilds. Merchant, military, seaman, priest, artisan, player, singer, musician, thief, beggar, which? There are others, but those are the chief."

"Thieves have a guild?"

"They don't put it about, but they do take apprentices and they have teaching masters who'll work your tail off. That amuses you. Hmm. I suppose it is funny to see the darkside aping the bright, but it's useful. If you go that route, you'll learn something and they'll house and feed you, which is more than you can expect outside. And there's this, if you don't have Family here to back you, you'd better have a Guild or you're fair game for the Pressgangs supplying meat to the pleasure Houses and the Whips who run the childgangs and anyone else with a taste for boys and the power to gratify his whims. And there's BlackHouse. Let me warn you, keep clear of BlackHouse.

Davindo shivered. "They told me at the Pens."

"Yes." Maksim closed his eyes. He was tired, but taking care of the boy—finding a tutor, arranging the apprenticeship, setting up a trust account to support Davo while he was being taught, all that meant it would be hours before he could rest. He knew why he was doing it; he was using Davindo to cancel a portion of his guilt for abandoning Todich, using the boy as a parlor wipe to polish up his amour-propre. "Choose," he said, impatience sharpening his voice.

"Thief." Davindo looked defiant, as if he expected Maksim to try talking him into something more respectable.

"You're sure?"

"Yes."

"So be it." Maksim got wearily to his feet, crossed to the door. "You should be set by tomorrow evening. I'll pass over your papers and after that you're on your own."

Davindo bit at his lip. "Why?" he burst out. "Why are you doing this?"

Maksim pulled the door open, looked over his shoulder at Davindo. There was no way he could answer that question, the boy was too young, too limited to understand the things that drove a man. "Call it a whim," he said and left.

4

Late that night Maksim went up the path behind the Inn to the flat where he'd sent Brann and Jaril on their way. Using a broom he'd borrowed from a tweeny at the Inn, he swept the stone as clean as he could, then he drew a circle with a length of soft chalk. Working quickly, he finished the sketchy pentacle; precision wasn't important for what he planned, there was little danger in casting mantaliths. What he wanted, what he needed was privacy.

The chalk had a tar base so the damp from the fog didn't wash it away; he stripped off the cotton gloves he'd used to keep it from clinging to his hands and knelt at the heart of the pentacle. He drew out a soft leather pouch and twitched the knot loose that held the drawstrings tight. Muttering the manta chanta under his breath, he poured the rhombstones into the palm of his left hand. He closed his eyes, visualized the reality he needed to reach, then spoke the word: WHEN? And spoke other words: WHAT DAY? With a snap of thumb against finger on his free hand, he shouted the Trigger, his deep voice booming through the fog, echoing back at him, the overtones lovely in their murmurs and their silences. When the echoes died, he threw the mantaliths and read their answer.

Two days hence. Third hour past noon.

At that time Todichi Yahzi's home reality would in some inexplicable way be closer to this one, easier to reach, the membranes between the two softer, thinner, the number of realities between them lessened somehow. He passed his hands over the stones, murmured the releasing manta chanta, the blessing on the mantaliths, the delivery of his gratitude for the answer he'd received.

He gathered up the stones and the broom and went away, leaving the rain to wash away his traces.

5

Maksim raised sail an hour before dawn on the chosen day; Todichi Yahzi sat in the bow of the boat, looking out across the black water, his back to his one time master. He hadn't said a word to anyone since he left the Pens, his anger was too deep. As Maksim sent the small boat scooting south into the Tukery, he glared at the kwitur and choked on his guilt and smoldered with an anger of his own—and sometimes was sad at losing an almost-friend.

By the time the sun rose they were deep into the narrow crooked waterways. Already he had crept through the patches of dense fog that swung in complex orbits around and about the Tukery, fog inhabited by howling souls cast out from Kukurul, souls spilling over with fury and despair, doing their futile best to drive him onto razor-edged rocks or into quicksands that could swallow a boat between one breath and the next. Twice he'd driven off ambushing bands, throwing fire and dissolution at them, pulling their sailing canoes apart under them and dropping them into schools of hungry needlefish. He didn't know exactly what he was looking for, he just sailed on and on, waiting for his Talent to seize onto a place.

Through all this Todichi Yahzi sat silent and brooding in the bow, ignoring Maksim, staring at things only he could see.

When the sun was directly overhead, Maksim saw a rocky islet with vents in its precipitous sides voiding steam into the cold dank air; it was a truncated cone rising about a hundred yards above the water. Here and there swatches of orange and faded-olive lichens interrupted the drab dun stone; near the vents ferns were lush lacy patches of a green so vibrant it hurt the eyes. There was a small halfmoon of sandy beach on the north side, the side he came on first; he circled the islet and came back to the beach, drove the nose of the boat up onto the sand and tossed the anchor overside. He slipped his arms through the straps of his rucksack and got cautiously to his feet. "Todich, you think you can make it to the top?"

The kwitur dragged himself up, moving with painful slowness. Maksim watched, frowning, angry at first, then amused. "Ooohhh, tragedy, the very image of it." He laughed for the first time in days, the sound booming back at him from the hollows of the cliff. He held to the mast, his weight keeping the boat steady as Todich clambered out.

The kwitur sank ankle-deep into the damp sand. He hummed his distaste for the clinging stuff and continued cursing in his insect voice as he trudged to the rock and began picking his way carefully upward, climbing with the steady sureness of his kind.

Maksim contemplated the slope and considered snapping himself to the top; his mass and relatively high center of gravity made him less than sure-footed on rock faces and he was beginning to feel the weight of his years despite his skill at using earthfire to boil off the poisons of aging. He dropped overside into the shallow water, pulled the boat higher on the sand and moored her to a handy rock; he wasn't about to thrust an anchor here in the Tukery.

He got to the top, weary, shaking, scraped about like a stew carrot. Todich was crouching in a pitiful knot, looking more miserable and mistreated than ever. Maksim snorted. Todich was overdoing the victim to the point of absurdity. He began building a small fire with the coal and tinder he'd hauled up in his backpack. In the middle of this business, he looked up to see Todich watching him. He'd never been sure he read the kwitur's minimal expressions with anything like accuracy, but he thought he saw a flash of amusement, even affection there. That startled him so much he forgot about fanning the tiny fire and it went out on him. Exaggeration? Resentment caricatured beyond absurdity? Beyond? Absurdity? THAT LITTLE GIT WAS PAYING HIM BACK FOR THOSE TEN YEARS AND HAVING SOME FUN AT THE SAME TIME!!! "You! YOU! You perfidious inglorious diabolic old fraud."

"Slow," Todichi hoomed. "Got old, han't you."

"Yeh, you right. Looks like any brains I had 've turned to suet." He dug into the backpack, tossed a blanket to the kwitur. "You're shivering. You'd better wrap this round you till I can get this damn fire lit."

The reluctant coals finally caught. Maksim set a pan of water on a tripod, watched it a moment to see that the tripod was stable and the fire was going to keep burning, then he sat on his heels and contemplated Todichi Yahzi. "Tell me about it," he said and settled himself to listen.

6

They talked and sat in a shared silence and talked some more, drank tea when the water boiled, made peace with memory while they waited for the appointed hour.

When the time came, Maksim sent Todichi Yahzi home as gently as he could, then collapsed beside the remnants of the fire.

7

When he struggled back to awareness, at first he couldn't

remember where he was or what had happened to deplete him so thoroughly.

Memory crept back slowly, so slowly he was disturbed; his mind was not working right.

He tried to sit up.

He was tied.

His arms were tight against his body, his hands were pressed against his thighs; ropes passed round and round him; he couldn't wiggle a finger; he could barely breathe.

He tried to speak.

His tongue was bound, not by ropes but by a force he couldn't recognize.

He tried to mindcall a firesprite to work on the ropes, something he was able to do before he could read his name.

His mind was bound.

He sweated in claustrophobic terror until he managed to override that bloodfear, then he gathered will in shoulder and neck and got his head up off the stone.

Fog.

Like white soup, ghosts bumping about in it, swirling about him and whoever had caught him.

He ignored the ghosts.

Jastouk, he thought. I talked in my sleep and he betrayed me. He wept and was furious at himself for weeping.

Time passed.

He couldn't feel his body or count the beats of his heart.

There was nothing he could use to tick off the minutes, nothing to tell him if a day had passed, a week, or only an hour.

He eased his head down.

He fought the helplessness that was worse than the claustrophobia. He called on two centuries of discipline, then waited with the patience of a cat at a mousehole. His captors had given him time to collect himself. Stupid of them. Or maybe they didn't care. Overconfidence? He produced a wry smile. I hope it is overconfidence.

Time passed.

The ghosts backed off.

New shapes solidified in the fog.

He heard a foot scrape against stone and decided he was still on the islet.

Someone spoke.

He heard the voice but couldn't make out the words.

Answers came from several points.

He strained to make out what was being said, but it was as if his ears were stuffed with something that deafened him just enough to make sure he learned nothing from what he heard.

The exchanges continued.

It began to feel like ritual rather than speech.

He couldn't tell if that was a trick of his fettered mind or something real. This irritated him, his incapacity was like nettles rubbed against his skin.

By the Gods of Fate and Time, I will make you suffer for this, he thought at them; he struggled to shout it; his jaw ached with the need to shout at them.

The binding held.

Not a sound came out, not a sound!

With such a cork shoved in his mouth, need was building up in him.

He was going to explode.

He visualized himself blowing apart, hot burning pieces of him rushing outward, colliding with the things out there prattling like fools, colliding with them and ashing them.

I'm getting giddy.

Gods of Fate and Time! Keep hold of yourself.

Think of Vechakek and Jastouk.

I owe them.

I'll pay them.

I pay my debts. Always.

Feeling trickled back into him.

The chill of the damp stone struck up through his body, sucking away what warmth he had left.

He pressed his fingers into the meat of his thigh and won a little space.

He worked his fingers, trying to gain enough movement for a simple gesture.

The stone softened under him, flowed up around him.

Lumpy, faceless elementals like animate gray clay lifted him and carried him down a spiral ramp that created itself before them.

Complaining about the abrasions of the sand in subsonic groans like rock rubbing against rock, they lumbered across the beach and rolled him into his boat as if he were a dead fish.

He managed to keep his head from crashing into the deck but collected bruises over every part of his body.

Fog billowed about him.

Ghosts hoomed in the distance, frightened off by those other entities, whatever they were, who stood on air about the boat, thickenings in the fog, featureless, serpentine, bipedal.

He didn't recognize them.

Smell, aura, everything about them was unfamiliar.

He wasn't surprised.

The layered realities were infinite in number and each sorceror had his own set of them in addition to those that they all shared.

His head wasn't working right, but he settled grimly to learning what he could about them.

Two figures dropped onto the deck.

They dragged him into the hutch and laid him out on the sleeping pad.

They wore black leather top-to-toe like the Harpish and black leather cowls with only the eyes cut out.

They weren't Harpish.

Forty Mortal Hells, who are you and who is running you? Amortis?

Gods of Fate and Time, I hope not.

She'd watch me burn and throw oil on the fire.

They tossed a blanket over him and went out.

He felt the boat float free.

She shuddered, yawed, rolled.

Those two didn't know codswallop about sailing.

They got the sails up finally and the boat underway.

Maksim settled to working trying to free his hands a little.

There were gestures so minimal they required almost no space but could focus sufficient energy to cut him free.

The way those numb-butts were handling the boat, there was a good chance he'd end up on the bottom of some Tukery strait, food for prowling needlefish.

The rope was spelled to cling.

Every millimeter of freedom he won from them was gone as soon as the spell reacted.

He fought the ropes as long as he had strength, then he slept.

He nudged at the spells that bound him.

He tried to work out their structure.

He couldn't counter them without word or gesture, but knowing that structure would let him act the first chance he got.

He probed and pried, sucked in his gut, drove his thumbs into his thigh muscles and got nowhere.

The bonds holding him responded automatically and effectively to every effort.

The boat went unhindered through the Tukery despite the clumsiness of the crew.

Not long after sundown he felt the lengthening swells as the boat broke into the Notoea Tha.

He heard the basso wail of a powerful following wind that drove them northwest, away from Kukurul.

He stopped being afraid of drowning or dying, but his determination to get out of this trap only grew stronger.

Late at night, the boat hove to, the sails came crashing down.

The two pseudo Harpish dragged Maksim up on the deck and left him there.

Their companions swung in slow circles overhead, maintaining the same distance between them always, no matter how they moved.

The boat was bobbing beside a dark, rakish ship, a Phrasi Coaster, ocean-going and river-capable, a favorite of smugglers, pirates and those merchants who needed speed and a shallow draft from their ships.

He could hear men talking; they spoke Phrasi.

A davit swung over the rail and a cargo net was winched down.

The net settled over him, dragging back and forth as the boat rocked with the heave of the sea.

The pseudo Harpish loaded him into the net.

He was hauled up, jerk by jerk, the winch squealing with every turn of the spindle.

As the sailors caught hold of the net to pull him inboard, a wisp of smoke floated by him.

Woodsmoke?

He muscled his head around and looked down.

His boat was burning.

He fumed.

Phrasi sailors hauled him over the rail and dumped him on the deck.

Wisps of smoke rose past the rail.

There were flickers of red on the white sails that rose as the ship prepared to go away from there.

He cursed and struggled to break loose.

He was fond of that boat. There were good memories laid

down in it, memories of Brann and the Tukery, Jal Virri and Kukurul, days full of brightness scudding before the wind with the sails bellied out, the sheets humming.

Seven pseudo Harpish came for him.

They rolled him out of the net and carried him to a crate near the foremast.

They dumped him in the crate and nailed it shut around him.

They chanted in their buzzing incomprehensible langue and tightened another layer of bonds about him.

He was smothered into unconsciousness.

III. KORIMENEI PIYOLSS

Silili on the double island Utar-Selt

Korimenei at the end of her schooling, goes through a passing-out ordeal and starts on her journey to free her brother. also:

The Eidolon of her
Sleeping Brother
The Old Man of the
Mountain
The Gods Geidranay
Groomer of Mountains
Isayana Birthmistress
Tungjii Luck
and Assorted Others
Spirit Guides.
Shahntien Shere,
headmistress
Firtina Somak, Kori's best
friend at school

1

"No! You can't come back. Not yet."

The eidolon of the sleeping boy was the size of a mouse; he lay curled in a crystal egg that floated in the darkness over Korimenei Piyolss. She saw him whether her eyes were open or shut, so she kept them open. She moved impatiently on her narrow bed. "Why?" She kept her voice low. The walls between this sleeping cell and the next were paper and lath; after ten years at the school she knew well enough how sound carried. "I thought you wanted out of there soonest possible."

"And then what?" Her brother looked like the six-year-old boy the Sorceror Settsimaksimin had spelled to sleep; his body hadn't changed a hair. His mind certainly had.

66

Those three words aren't a boy's complaint, she thought, he's so bitter. "Dance to the Chained God's contriving?" he spat at her. "No!"

"I don't see how you can change that."

"Why do you think I had you do all that work on the Great Talismans?"

"I didn't want to ask. I didn't know what might be listening."

"So?" there was an acid bite in the single word, a touch of impatience.

"And what does that mean?"

"Use your head, Kori. If HE listened, the asking itself would tell HIM all HE wanted to know."

"Then how can we do anything?"

"If, Kori. Did you hear me? IF. Listen. HE has BinYAHtii now, HE got it off Settsimaksimin after Brann and the Blues took him, but I don't know how much good that's doing HIM, that stone is hard to handle even if you keep it fed." He stopped talking. His body never moved, nonetheless, Kori thought she felt a shudder pass through him. "HE has been keeping it fed. I don't want to talk about that. HE's a god. I don't know all that means but for sure HE has limitations, otherwise HE could've squashed Settsimaksimin without bending an eyelash. Listen, listen, isn't it true when old Maksim had BinYAHtii round his neck, didn't he keep Amortis on the hop? I could feel how nervous Amortis made HIM. What I've been thinking: if I could get hold of the right Talisman, I could block HIM, keep HIM off me. Off you too."

Korimenei closed her eyes, pressed her lips together. She couldn't blame him, not really, and it was her fault he was stuck in that cave, but including her was so obviously an afterthought that it hurt. It hurt a lot. A belated tact disastrously untactful. Oh gods and gunk, I'm as bad a phrasemaker as Maks is, even if I can't roar like him.

Her enforced sojourn at the school was almost over. Just that morning the runner Paji came to the exercise court to say Kori should come to the Shahntien's office at the end of second watch tomorrow. He didn't say what it was about. She didn't need telling. It was her graduation exercise. She'd been strung out for days now, waiting for Shahntien Shere to decide what it would be and when it would happen. Tomorrow, the next day, maybe the next, then she'd be free to leave. She wanted to go to Trago as soon as the Shahntien cut her loose, she wanted to go as fast as she could for the cave where her brother slept in crystal waiting for her to touch him free, she wanted to go NOW, not after some indefinite period devoted to some sort of nonsense Trago had dreamed up. How sane could he be, after all, confined to that stupid crystal for so many years? Three, nearly four years blocked off from everything outside. Then he finally managed to free his mind enough to reach her. Six years since and all he could do was look over her shoulder. Does he visit other places too? Does he look through other eyes? She was appalled at herself when she felt a twinge of jealousy. "What do you want, Tré? Do you really want me to hunt up a talisman and fetch it to you?"

"Yes, Kori. Yes yes yes. Please. The one called Frunzacoache."

"All right, if you say so. Why that one?"

He ignored the question and went on, "Frunzacoache disappeared years ago, but I found it. It's in the torbaoz of a Rushgaramuv shaman. He doesn't know what he's got. There's barely enough magic in him to light a match. He has a vague idea it's a thing of power, so he hides it away down at the bottom of his essence pouch. If you pattern up a good copy and sink some energy into it, he'll never know the real thing's gone. Bring it to me, Kori. Pleeease?"

The eidolon winked out before Korimenei could say anything. She lay staring into the darkness where it'd hung. It was a long time before she went back to sleep.

2

Korimenei pulled the half-hitch tight, glanced across the bay at the paired islands Utar-Selt, then left the stubby pier and started up the mountainside.

She was lanky and tall, thin for her height with long narrow hands and feet that looked too big for her. She had fine curly flyaway hair the color of dead leaves, a pale gray-brown with shines of an equally pale gold when the sun touched it at the proper angle. Her eyes were a light gray-green like shadowed water; her skin was thin and pale with a spray of small freckles across a longish nose and high broad cheekbones; every ebb and flow of blood showed through, to her frequent embarrassment.

She wore old canvas trousers frayed and soft as velvet from many washings, trousers inherited from a student long gone, and a sleeveless pullover with a high neck, several badly botched patches, assorted pulls and snags. Over this she'd pulled on a knee-length canvas coat with huge pockets and wide cuffs; it was slightly newer than the trousers, but even a ragman would turn up his nose at it. On her feet she wore a pair of heavy-soled sandals, fairly new but as scuffed and scarred as her ankles. She was carrying an old leather rucksack, not heavily loaded, with a thick blanket rolled into a tight cylinder and tied below it.

She climbed the Old Man's Mountain, walking along an unobtrusive but well maintained path. Much of the time she was moving through lowslope woods, maple, beech, aspen, oak, the morning light glowing through leaves like translucent slices of jade, dark and light, gold and green, the leaf shadows moving mottles on the red earth of the path. A hundred kinds of songbirds flittered and swooped over her, hidden by the leaves, singing extravagant solos, or blending in pleasant cacophonies. Now and then the path moved out of the trees across an area of open slope or along a cliff edge where she had a clear view out over the bay.

Halfway to the Old Man's Meadow, she stopped walking and turned to gaze at Silili; she could see the gilded roofs of the school buildings peeping through the dark yews, oaks and willows planted along the walkways and in the watergardens. She was startled by how much of the south slope of Utar's Temple Mountain the school took in. There were no vistas inside the walls, just gardens like green gems for teaching and meditation, so it was impossible to judge the size of the place when one was in it. She'd known the school was important from the way that merchants treated her when they saw the patch sewn on her shirt, but this was the first time she'd had any real idea how important it had to be. Only the Temple grounds were larger. You did me well, Maks my friend. I suppose I'll have to thank you for it. She sighed again and trudged on. Hmm. I expected to see you before this. Well, busy busy, I suppose, setting the world right. She'd gotten very fond of the man and was a little hurt because he hadn't come.

Watersong filtered through the trees; she went over a hump on the mountain's flank and looked down into an ancient cut at a stream leaping along a series of steps, swirling about black and mossy boulders. The path continued along the rim of the ravine, crossed over it on an elegant wooden bridge, each timber handhewn and handpolished and fitted together with wooden pegs and lashings

of thin tough rope. On the far side the path curved through
a stand of ancient oaks that almost immediately opened
onto the Old Man's Meadow.

His small neat hut was across the meadow, half-hidden by
the droopy limbs of a monster oak; like the bridge the hut
was built of ax-smoothed planks with a roof of cedar shakes.
Korimenei pulled off the rucksack, rummaged inside and
took out the gift she'd brought for the Old Man, a half
pound of the most expensive tea found in Silili Market; it
was wrapped in a swatch of raw silk and tucked into a
carved ebony box.

The Old Man was kneeling between rows of onion sets,
pulling gently at grass and tiny weeds growing around them.
Ghost children ran in silent games among the dying vines on
the beanpoles, ghost grandmothers so ragged they were
little more than sketches watched over them, ghost grandfa-
thers squatted beside the Old Man, chatting with him, pointing out weeds for him. A strangled man ghost hovered close
to the trees, watching Korimenei with frightening intensity.
A headless woman, her battered head clutched under one
arm, came rushing at Korimenei, veered off, trailing behind
her an anguished wail more felt than heard. Korimenei
ignored all of them, stopped at the end of a row and waited
politely for the Old Man to reach her. Her first sight of the
ghosts of Silili had startled her, Owlyn ghosts stayed de-
cently among the treetops until they dissipated, but habit
and time had made her accustomed to the sometimes vocal
and always present dead.

The Old Man settled onto his haunches, his dirt-crusted
hands dropping onto his thighs. Morning light cool as water
and filled with dancing motes picked up every wrinkle, wart,
and hair on his still face. He blinked, mild ancient eyes
opening and closing with slow deliberation; with his shaggy
brown robe, the tufts of white hair over his ears, his round
face, he looked like a large horned owl. He also looked
harmless and not too bright, but there were many stories
about him and certain brash intruders who thought they
could force his secrets from him. "Saöri?" His voice was the
dry rustle of dead leaves.

Korimenei bowed and held out the chest. "This unworthy
student will be much honored if the Saör considers accepting this handful of miserable tea."

He took the chest, tucked it into a pocket of his robe.
"Leave the mountain as you found it," he said.

"This one hears and swears it will be so, Saör."

He grunted, swung round still squatting and began pulling grass from around a set.

Korimenei flared her narrow nostrils, but swallowed the laughter bubbling in her throat; the Old Man could be touchy about his dignity at the most unexpected times. She resettled the rucksack and began walking again, following the path.

3

The tiny meadow was stony and dry in its upper reaches. An ancient conifer had fallen to a storm a decade or so past and now lay denuded of bark, slowly rotting into the earth it had grown from. Thinner now and noisier, the Old Man's Stream curved around the stubby root-shield and squeezed past boulders at the bottom of the roughly circular meadow and disappeared into shadows under the shivering gold leaves of a grove of aspen saplings. Korimenei shrugged out of the rucksack, set it on the dead trunk. She wriggled her body, reached high, stretching all over as she did so, stayed on her toes for a long long moment, then exploded out a sigh and dropped on her heels.

She pulled loose the thongs binding her dream-blanket to the rucksack, shook it out and spread it on the grass. Toward the end of her first year at the school, she'd bought wool in Silili Market. She dyed it and wove it into a dreampattern blanket which she kept wrapped in silk for the day she'd need it, for now. She sat on the trunk and smiled at the sharp-angled patterns and the brilliant colors. I did good, she thought, pleased with herself. She unbuckled her sandals, closed her eyes and flexed her toes; the earth was cool and silky against her soles and she had a curious sense that she was momentarily cut off from the flow of time, that she was a part of the Mountain. Her mind drifted into phrasemaking, ephemerally eternal, eternally ephemeral. The Mountain and the life parasited on it changed, died, was continually reborn. She sighed and yanked herself back to her own purposes. Settling herself on the blanket, she folded her legs and dropped her hands onto her knees. Her mind drifted to yesterday. . . .

##

Shahntien Shere sat behind her desk and frowned at Korimenei. She was a tall woman, thin, her abundant gray hair dressed in a soft knot at the nape of a long neck. She wore a simple white dress with close fitting sleeves and a high soft collar, over that an unadorned sleeveless robe of heavy black silk. It was her customary dress, effectively elegant, underlining her authority without making too oppressive a point of it. Abruptly, unexpectedly, she smiled, her dark eyes narrowing into inverted echoes of her mouth. "The ten years are up," she said. "Of course you know that. You've done well, better than I expected. Maksim is most pleased with you, though he seems rather shy about telling you himself." She paused, rubbed the tips of her fingers together. "I don't know what his plans are, Kori; I expect he'll show up when he's ready. I've taught you all I can," the ends of her thin mouth tucked deeper into their brackets, turned into a mirror image of her earlier smile, "All anyone can, I think. The rest is up to you."

Korimenei laced her fingers together and stared down at them. She couldn't think of anything to say, so she said nothing.

"Yes," the Shahntien said, "and that is essentially what this is about." She sighed. "To it, then. I have consulted yarrow and water and tortoiseshell and considered your family lines. Your people are . . . um . . . remarkably untouched by Talent, always excepting that imposed by the Chained God on his priests; however, that has nothing to do with you since the priests are always male and as far as I can determine chosen by the God himself without much concern about any inborn Gifts. Your Talent has come to you from your Ancestress Harra Hazhani, the Rukka Nagh; there were, no doubt, other women before you with much the same abilities, but things being the way they are among your people, the Gifts were denied and they withered without being used." She tapped her nails on the desk top, a tiny clatter like a flurry of wheatsized hail against a window. "An obscenity. . . ." She spread her hands flat on the desk, frowned at them. "Which is a digression . . . I'm explaining too much. It's not needed. More than that, it's probably counterproductive. You are to go to the Old Man's Mountain across the bay. You are to find a sufficiently quiet and secluded place. You are to fast and meditate for three days. Do nothing. Accept what comes to you. Forget nothing. You won't understand most of it now, you don't know enough about the world or yourself. Accept for the moment what I tell you, it comes from my own experience, Kori Heart-in-Waiting; you will return again and

again to this time, finding new richness, new meaning in it."
She straightened her back, looking past Korimenei. "Again I
explain too much. You seem to have that effect on me, young
Kori. Go and do."

##

Korimenei settled into her fast-vigil. She sought to re-find
that sense of connectedness with air and earth, with plant
and beast that she'd gotten as a gift for those few moments
when she sat on the trunk and dabbled her feet in the dust.

The sun rose higher, dust motes danced in the rays that
slid through openings in the needle canopy above and behind her. She was all sensory data, perception without self-
awareness. Then lost it. Then had it again. Then lost it. And
lost it. And sank into self-doubt and sourness. Shadow
shrank about her, hot yellow sunlight crept toward the blanket, came over it, touched her knees, her fingers. She rubbed
at her eyes, looked up. The sun was almost directly overhead. "Three days," she said aloud. "Three days."

She rocked on her buttocks, straightened her legs, flexed
and loosened the muscles in them until the stiffness was
gone. She stood, stretched, shivered all over. Two hours
only and already the exercise seemed futile, a fanatic's flag-
ellation of body and spirit. She let her arms drop. There you
go again, you silly maid, aping Settsimaksimin, roaring phrases
in your alleged mind. Her fast had begun this morning with
a breakfast of juice and a hardroll. She was hungry, her
stomach was grumbling and she had that all-over sense of
debilitation she got when she went too long without eating.
Three days, she thought again and just managed to stifle an
obscenity, one of the many she'd picked up when she was a
rebel child wandering Silagamatys' waterfront when she was
supposed to be in bed.

She fished a tin cup from the rucksack, filled it at the
stream and sat on a flat rock with her feet in the water. The
stream went down a long shallow slide here, with a steady
brushing hum punctuated occasionally by the pop of bubbles
or a troutling breaking surface. She sipped from her cup and
watched the clear cold stream smooth as glass slip over her
bare toes. The sun was hot on her head and shoulders;
behind her she could hear the buzz and mumble of insects.
Her stomach cramped. She closed her eyes and willed the
nausea to go away. It was mostly imagination, she knew that

well enough, but knowing didn't seem to help. Three days. I'll be a rag. Why am I doing this?

She rinsed the cup, filled it again and took it back to the blanket. She lowered herself onto the dreampattern, set the cup beside her and folded her long legs into the proper configuration. Ten years she'd spent learning control of her Talent. That's all it is, this school, Maksim told her once, control. And maybe expanded possibility. Maybe. She could testify to the truth of that now. Control and the limits of control. She told herself she knew her limits, she told herself she had earned a degree of confidence in her skill and in her strength. She'd survived each trial so far, but every new step was a new threat. She didn't believe there could be more for her to learn; the last two years she'd spent consolidating what she'd dredged up out of herself during the first eight years of her schooling. She didn't want to believe there was more power out there waiting for her to tap into it; she was afraid of touching any hotter, wilder sources. There were times during the past ten years when she was working hot that the power she was shaping threatened to consume her. She managed to hang on, but each time was worse than the last, each time she came closer to losing it, a lesson she took to heart. She had an edgy uncertainty working in her now, a fear that the next time she touched heat, she wouldn't be strong enough, that she'd die, or worse than death, find herself controlled.

"Trago," she said aloud. "Come talk to me." She waited, hands on her thighs, opening, closing, short ragged nails scratching erratically at the canvas of her trousers. He didn't come. She never knew if he heard her when she called him; sometimes he showed up, sometimes he didn't. This looked like one of the latter. "Damn." If it weren't for Trago locked dreaming in crystal, she'd run and trust her reflexes to keep her loose. But he was the hook that bound her to the Shahntien's whim and she had to play out this farce.

#

I put him, Maksim said, where his god can't reach him. If I kill him, child, there'll only be another taking his place, another and another, no end to it. He'll sleep and sleep and sleep . . . Maksim turned his head and smiled at her . . . until you and only you, young Kori, until you come and touch him awake. He is in the Cave of Chains. If you can get

*yourself there, Kori, all you have to do is touch the crystal
enclosing him. It will melt and the boy will wake. No one else
can do this. No one, god or man. Only you.*

She scratched at her nose. All over the place, she thought.
I did better concentration my first year. "Tré," she said,
"give us a look, will you?"

Nothing. Obviously he was busy with other things, things
more important than a long gone sister. She moved her
body impatiently. He'd been looking over her shoulder for
years, studying what she studied, maybe even nudging her
when he wanted something she wasn't dealing with at the
moment. She'd been driven, those first years. She'd thought
it was because she wanted to get away as soon as she could
and free her brother. She had to learn, to grow accustomed
to working hot and fast, she had to find a way to outwit the
Shahntien so she could escape her claws. To outwit Maksim
who made a habit of sending his eidolon to chat with her.
Maybe it was more than that, maybe it was Trago pushing
her. One thing she did know, he was watching and studying
a long time before he started talking to her. She worked her
mouth. It hurt, thinking that way, but the most important
thing she'd learned (besides control, of course) was never lie
to yourself. No matter what extravagances you practice on
other people, it's fatal to lie to yourself. She had the Shahntien
to show her the truth of that, she had Maksim. Odd, the
way he treated her. She could swear he never lied to her,
never even shaded the truth. It was hard to take at times,
but in the end she was grateful to his habit, in the end she
saw this as the starkest compliment he ever paid her. In the
end it was why Shahntien Shere stopped hating her. And
life at the school got to be a lot easier.

The sun slid down its western arc; shadow crossed the
stream and crept around her, cold and silent. Depressing.
She was tired and hungry and she hadn't managed more
than a moment or two of real meditation the whole futile
day. Her stomach cramped repeatedly through that interminable afternoon, at times she could think of nothing but
food. She dreamed of roast chicken with brown-gold gravy
pooling round it. She thought of shrimp fried in a batter so
light it might have floated off at a breath of wind, succulent
pink shrimp. Peaches, peeled and golden, dripping with a

rich fragrant nectar. Strawberries, plump tartsweet, floating in whipped cream. She wrenched her mind away and contemplated a blade of grass she pulled from a clump beside the blanket. She considered the greenness of it, greenness as an abstract idea, greenness as it was expressed in this particular physical object, mottled with lines of darker color, with pinpoints and patches of black and tan; she considered the edge where the blade left off and the air began, the finely toothed edge that was not so much green as an extraction from the colors combined into green, a pale anemic yellow fading to white, to no-color.

The sky put out its sunset flags and the wind rose, chill enough to knife through Korimenei's coat and pullover, stir the hairs on her arms and along her spine. Gentle Geidranay came walking along the mountain peaks. He squatted among them with his head against the sun, his fingers grubbing among the pines, absurdly like the shadow of the Old Man in his garden, grotesquely enlarged and cast against the drop of the darkening sky. The Groomer of Mountains came closer, his fingers swept across the small meadow, brushed against Korimenei and passed out without noticing her. The fingers were like semisolid light, translucent, melting through the air without agitating it, dreamlike and disturbing, a beautiful nightmare, if such could exist. Korimenei shivered and shut her eyes.

A dozen heartbeats later she cracked a lid; the god was gone. She sighed and broke posture. Her head was swimming, but the dizziness faded when she had moved about some more. She went to the stream, refilled her cup and stood watching the water darken to black glass as the last color faded from the sky. She carried the cup to the dead trunk, sat down beside her rucksack and took sip after slow sip until the cup was empty. The largest bulge in the sack was a heavy, knitted laprobe. She thought a moment, then with some reluctance took the laprobe out and dropped it on the blanket; dying of pneumonia was not a desirable outcome of this minor ordeal. She plucked a handful of dry grass and went deeper into the trees to void her bladder; when she was finished she washed her hands at the stream, using sand for soap.

She settled onto the blanket, folded her legs properly and pulled the laprobe about her shoulders.

In the distance an owl hooted. She thought about the Old Man, wondered vaguely who and what he was. Some odd manifestation of the Earthsoul, thrust from the soil as stones are ejected by a combination of earth and thaw? Or a creature as ancient as old Tungjii, perhaps even a kind of kin to himmer? Older than the gods themselves, older than the earth she sat on? Or was he the face of the Mountain itself? Was her blanket spread across his flesh? She moved uneasily, that was an uncomfortable thought. She considered the Old Man and the Mountain and Geidranay, Tungjii and her brother, Maksim and his assorted peculiarities, whether he'd managed to rise above his prejudices, sexual and social, and take her as an apprentice. She wanted that rather desperately; she knew by study and experience now what she'd guessed the first time she saw him: there was no one like him. If he taught her . . . if he taught her, maybe she wouldn't be so afraid of what she sometimes saw in herself, what she scurried from like a scared mouse whenever she caught a glimpse of it.

The laprobe trapped warmth around her; sleep tugged at her as she grew more comfortable, threatened to overwhelm her as the night turned darker. A fat, mutilated crescent, the Wounded Moon was already high when the sun went down; its diminished light fell gently on the quiet meadow, cool and pale, drawing color out of grass and trees, turning Korimenei and her blankets into a delicately sketched black and white drawing. Moon moths flew arabesques above the stream, singing their high thin songs. Fireflies zipped here and there, lines of pale gold light, the only color in the scene. A white doe came from under the trees on the far side of the stream. For a long moment the beast gazed at Korimenei, her eyes deep as earthheart and dangerous, Korimenei felt herself begin to drown in them. The doe turned her head, broke contact; as silently as she came, she vanished into the inky shadow under the pines.

A fragment of old song drifted into Korimenei's mind, one of Harra Hazani's songs which had been passed with another gift from daughter to daughter down the long years since she came to Owlyn Vale. Korimenei was born with that gift, Harra's ear for pitch and tone and her sense of rhythm; she'd long suspected it was a major part of her Talent, when she thought of Maksim's extraordinary voice she was sure of it. "I am the white hind," she breathed into the night; the darkness seemed to accept and encourage her, so she sang the song aloud. Not all of it, it had hundreds of lines and three voices, the white hind, the gold hart and the fawn; the hind spoke, the hart answered, the fawn questioned both. Korimenei lifted her voice and sang:

> *I am the White Hind*
> *Blind and fleet*
> *My feet read the night*
> *My flight is silence*
> *My silence summons to me*
> *Free and bold*
> *The Gold Hart.*

> *I am the Gold Hart*
> *Artful and fierce*
> *I pierce the night*
> *My flight is wildfire*
> *Desire consumes me*
> *She looms beside me*
> *Fleet and unconfined*
> *The White Hind.*

Korimenei let the song fade as the doe had faded into the darkness. Why? she thought. What does it mean? Does it mean anything? She closed her eyes and banished memory and idea, accepting only the sounds of the stream. Fragmented images prodded at her but she pushed them away. Hear the stream sing, she told herself, separate the sounds. First the coarse chords. She heard these, named them: the shhhh of the sliding water, the steady pop of bubbles, the brush-brush tinkle against intruding stones and boulder, the clack-tunk of bits of wood floating downstream, bumping into those boulders, swinging into each other. She listened for the single notes of the song, teased them from the liquid languorous melliflow, concentrated on one, then another and another, recognized them, greeted them. Concentrate, she told herself. It's gone, it's gone. Narrow your focus, woman. You know how, you've done it a thousand times before. It's gone. Get it back. Concentrate, separate, appreciate, she chanted. Symmetry, limitry, backbone, marrow, she chanted, the phrasemaker in her head plundering her wordstore. Separation, isolation, disseverance, disruption, rent, split and rift, cleavage and abruption, she chanted, the words drowning the water wounds.

The Wounded Moon slipped down his western arc, crossing the spray of stars with a ponderous dignity that dragged

at Korimenei's nerves, setting her to wonder if this interminable night would ever end, if she could possibly get through
two more nights like it.

Sometime after moonset, she felt a presence come into
the meadow. It was a small meadow with young pines clus-
tering tightly around it. She sat in the center like a rat in a
pit. Owl eyes looked at her, immense golden eyes. Owl flew
round and round the pinepit meadow, his wings stretched
wider than the grass did, but somehow Owl flew there
round and round Korimenei. Feathers touched her, wings
brushed her head, her shoulder, she smelled him. She trembled, her bones turned to ice. She heard Owl cry something,
voices spoke inside her head, there was something they
were saying to her, she could not quite understand them.

She was suddenly on Owl's back, spiraling up and up until
she was high above the meadow. She looked down and saw
her body sprawled across the dreampattern blanket, the
laprobe bunched beside her hip. She was at once frightened
and exhilarated. Owl circled higher yet until she saw points
of light sprayed out beneath his belly; stars, she thought, we
fly above the stars.

Owl tilted suddenly. She slid off his back. She fell. Down
and down and down she fell. She was terrified. She was
screaming. Her throat was raw from screaming.

Then she was inside her body looking up into the face of
Geidranay, a Geidranay made small, his golden flesh like
sunlight given form.

The Groomer of Mountains touched her pullover and it
fell open, baring her breasts. He plunged his left hand into
the earth and brought it up again; he held an amethyst, a
single crystal glowing violet and blue. He set it on her chest
above her heart and watched it slip inside her, melting
through her flesh. He thrust his right hand into the earth
and brought it up again; this time he held a moonstone the
size of her fist. He touched the closure of her trousers and
they fell open, baring her navel. He set the moonstone on
her navel and watched it slip inside her. He touched her
forehead. His fingers were cool as the stones. He said nothing, but she knew she must not move. He took up the tin
cup she used for drinking and drew a golden forefinger
about its rim and it turned transparent, gleaming in the
starlight like polished crystal. He reached into the air, closed
his hand into a fist; when he opened his fingers, diamonds
cascaded into the cup. He knelt, dipped the cup into the

stream and brought it back to her, the diamonds like ice
floating in the water. He cupped his hand behind her head
and lifted her gently, tenderly; he put the cup to her lips and
she drank. The water was delicately sweet and smelled of
spring orchids. The diamonds melted into the water. She
drank them also.

When she looked up, Geidranay was gone. The cup was
tin again, ancient, battered, as familiar as her hand.

Feathers brushed across her and her clothing vanished
utterly, the laprobe was gone, the dreampattern blanket was
gone. She lay on earth and grass. Great wings brushed
across her and were gone. Owl walked toward her. It was
the Old Man. He stood at her feet and looked down at her.
She was ashamed at first because she was naked before him,
but she was not afraid. He sank into the earth, slowly
slowly. She wanted to laugh when she saw his round stupid
face resting on her great toes, then the face slid down and
vanished into the earth.

He was reborn from the earth, rising from it as slowly,
silently, easily as he went into it. He was covered with red
dust, otherwise he was naked and young and beautiful. He
put his left foot on her right foot; gently, delicately he
moved her leg aside. He put his right foot on her left foot;
gently, delicately he moved this leg aside. He knelt between
her legs and put his hands on her thighs. She shivered as she
felt fire slide into her flesh. He looked at her, smiled. She
cried out with pleasure, as if that smile were hands touching
her. He bent over her, his hands moving along her body;
they left streams of red dust on her skin.

His hands moved over her, stroking, rubbing, even pinch-
ing where the small sharp pains intensified her pleasure.
When he finally pushed into her, the pain was briefly terrible, he burned her, wrenched her open, then she was on fire
with a pleasure almost too intense to endure. It went on and
on until she was exhausted, too weary to feel anything
more.

He rose from her. She cried out, desolate. He stood
beside her, his broad tender smile warmed her once more.
As Geidranay had reached into the air for diamonds, the
Old Man Reborn Young reached up and plucked a square
of fine linen from the shadowy air. He came back to her and
pressed the cloth between her legs, catching the blood that
came from the breaking of her hymen. He sat on his heels
and folded the cloth into a small packet, the bloodstains

hidden inside. He leaned over her, touched her left hand, laid the packet on her palm. Again he said nothing, but she knew it was very very important that she keep the cloth safe and hidden, that she should never speak of it, not to Shahntien Shere or to Maksim, not even to her brother.

He set his right hand flat on the ground beside her thigh. The dreampattern blanket was under her again. He stepped over her leg and squatted beside her, drew the fingers of his left hand from her ankles to her waist, drew the fingers of his right hand from her waist to her shoulders and she was dressed again. He snapped the fingers of his left hand, spread his hands; the laprobe hung between them. He laid it over her and smiled a last time, touched her cheek in a tender valediction. And was gone.

She slept. When she woke it was midmorning. The first day and the first night was done.

4

At first she thought the events of the night were a dream, but when she moved her legs, she found she was still sore. The linen packet fell away when she sat up; she looked at the bloodstains for a long moment, then folded it up again and put it in her rucksack. Feeling more than a little light-headed, she took the tin cup to the stream and filled it. She drank. The liquid was merely cold water with the acrid green taste common to most mountain streams. She remembered water flavored and scented with diamonds, but that might have been something she did dream. She sipped at the water and thought about sleeping. She wasn't supposed to sleep, she was supposed to keep vigil. She didn't feel like worrying about her lapse. After filling the cup once more, she carried it up the gentle slope to her blanket and set it on the grass by her foot. She looked around.

The meadow space was filled with stippled sun rays, the misty light slanting through the dark needle-bunches on the upslope pines and cedars; there was no wind, the quiet was so thick she could feel it like the laprobe pulled heavy and close against her skin. Her mind was weary; it was hard to tie one word to another and make a phrase of them. She walked about a little, her legs shaky. Her inner thighs felt sticky, the cloth of her trousers clung briefly, broke away, clung again. She grimaced, disgust a mustiness in her mouth. She stripped, dropped her clothing on the blanket and took a twist of grass to the stream. She waded in. The water was knee-high, the cold was shocking. She shivered a moment, then gathered the will and went to her knees. She gasped, then examined her thighs. She'd bled copiously which surprised her, but she didn't waste time worrying about that either. She splashed water over the stains, began scrubbing at them with the grass. Each move bounced her a little on the gravel lining the streambed, she felt the bumps against her knees and shins, the rubbing, but the cold was so numbing she felt no pain until she climbed out of the water, put her clothes back on and warmed up a little.

She grunted as she tried to fold her legs; the bruises and abrasions she'd acquired in the stream made themselves apparent, so she crossed her ankles and straightened her back and began feeling her way into further meditation.

Flies came from everywhere and swarmed around her; they settled on her and walked on her hands and on her arms and on her legs, everywhere but her face; they were a mobile armor of jet and mica flakes, buzzing through a slow surging dance up and around and down, black twig feet stomping over every inch of her. She sat and let this happen. When the sun was directly overhead, the armor unwove itself and flew away.

She sat. Something was happening inside her. She didn't understand anything, but she had fears she didn't want to think about.

A one-legged woman stood under the trees across the stream. Vines grew out of her shoulders and fell around her. There was emptiness on her left side; the vines swayed parted, unveiling nothing; the vines on her right side grew round and round her single leg. She hopped. Stood still. Hopped again. The vines bounced. Arms outspread, she began jumping up and down on the same spot, turning faster and faster as she hopped. Korimenei heard a whining sound like all the flies singing in unison. The woman went misty and the mist went spinning away into the dim green twilight under the trees.

Korimenei considered this. She slid her hand up under her pullover and touched the place where the amethyst had seeped into her. Her skin was cool and dry; there was nothing to show it had really happened. She pulled her hand out, let it rest on the slight bulge of her belly; it seemed to her she could feel a thing growing in her, growing with a speed that vaguely terrified her. She took her hand away, closed her eyes and began humming to herself. After a while she plucked a song from Harra's Hoard, an Owlsong, and focused all of herself on it.

Around midafternoon another woman came slithering from the trees across the stream. She was writhing on her stomach like a great white worm; her legs were all soft from hip to toe; she had no toes, her legs ended in rattles like those on a snake's tail. She reared up the forward half of her body and danced with her arms and shoulders, shook her rattlefeet to make music for her dance. She had the polished ivory horns of a black buffalo, horns that spread wider than the reach of her arms. Her face was broad, her nose and mouth stuck out like the muzzle of a flat-faced dog. Her ears were pointed and shifted independently, a part of her body-dance. The hair on her head was like black broomstraw and hung stiffly on either side of her face. The hair under her arms was rough and shaggy like seafern; it hung down her sides, lower than the flat breasts that slapped against her ribs. There was a terribleness about her that rolled like smoke away from her, invisible emanations that filled the round meadow and squeezed Korimenei smaller and smaller.

Before Korimenei shriveled quite away, the horned woman sank into the earth and was gone.

The sun went down. Korimenei watched for Geidranay, but he didn't come this dusk; she felt sad, lonely. "Tré," she said aloud. "Trago, brother, talk to me." He didn't come. She was alone in the growing darkness with a thing growing in her.

She curled her hands and stared at her palms. "I don't understand any of this," she said aloud. That wasn't quite true. The crystals were for eyes to see and ears to hear the things beneath/behind the things one saw in ordinary light. She'd read about them in the books that Shahntien Shere had drawn to her library from the four corners of the world, she'd heard about them from the wandering scholars the Shahntien collected on the temple Plaza and invited to lecture to certain students, those she thought would profit from contact with other symbologies, other systems of visualization. Sometimes the crystals weren't crystals but roots or flowers, insects or beast organs; the effect was much the same. Her initiation had its parallels also, the event though not the details. The flies . . . she could call from memory a score of similar happenings and each of these had at least a score of interpretations, meaning one thing to the newly initiate, something else to the same person when he or she

was a mature practitioner, something else again to that
person when he or she was in the twilight of his or her life.
The two women had no referents, but both frightened her,
both reeked of danger, of power on the verge of erupting
from control. She remembered what the Shahntien said and
smiled, then went back to being frightened; she pressed her
hand against her swelling body. This . . . she laced down
her fear, tying it tight inside her . . . had no parallel she
knew of, only the familiar terror before dangers she hadn't
the knowledge or strength to fight against, the terror that
swept through her when Trago came into her bedroom and
showed her the Godmark that meant he was doomed to
burn at the stake unless she could manage something, the
terror that swept through her when the drunk caught her on
the street and she thought he was going to hurt her, kill her
before she could reach the Drinker of Souls, the terror that
swept through her when Settsimaksimin snatched her from
her bedroom and so arbitrarily threw her to the Shahntien
like a beast thrown to a tamer. Terror. . . .

Sometime after moonset the white doe came from the
woods; she stood gazing at Korimenei for several moments,
then she lifted herself onto her hind legs, shrinking as she
did so until she had the doe's head still, but a woman's body
with white milky breasts; the breasts were bare but the rest
of her wore the doe's pelt; it glinted like silver wire in the
starlight. Music came from somewhere, a flute played, a
drum, a lute, something with a high sweet woman's voice,
singing. The doe spoke: "There is music. You are not
dancing."

Korimenei stood. Her clothing fell away from her. She
began to dance. She didn't know what she was doing, her
feet were moving, she felt awkward, she was awkward.

The doewoman waded across the stream. She took
Korimenei's arm. "Be still," she said. "I will teach you the
proper dance. Come with me." She led Korimenei toward
the stream, choosing the place where there were two stones
in the middle of it. She stepped on the first stone and pulled
Korimenei onto it with her. There was very little room,
Korimenei pressed against her guide, smelled her strong
deer smell, gland and fur. The doewoman stepped across to
the second stone; it was smaller than the first, there was no
room for Korimenei but the woman tugged her after her
anyway. Somehow there was room. They stood without
moving. Korimenei looked around her. The stream was a

river now, split into two strands; it was the widest deepest
river she'd ever seen. The water was deep and silent as it
flowed, it looked like green-blue grass. There was power
and terror in it. And great beauty.

The doewoman made the waters rise. Korimenei lay down
in them, her body pointed in the direction of the flow. The
water took her. Her body began to undulate like the serpent
woman, back and forth in sweeping s-curves. She went that
way for a long time. She didn't know how long.

The singing began again, louder. The drum was louder
also, the flute more piercing. A man lifted her, carried her.
His head was the head of the Gold Hart. His antlers spread
like a great tree of heavy rough-beaten gold. His eyes were
hot and piercing, they were gold, molten gold. Force came
out of him like heat from a fire. It went into her. He laid
her on the water; he stood at her feet, holding onto them.
He made her sit up. She discovered that she was under
water and she gasped for breath. She started struggling. "Be
still," he said to her. " I am making you drink this water.
Drink it. Drink."

After she drank, he carried her out of the river and set
her on her feet. Water ran out of her, pouring from her
eyes, her mouth, from every orifice in her body. The
doewoman was there, waiting, a small male fawn pressed up
against her. The Hart strode over the grass to the Hind; he
put out his hand. She rested her hand on it. They danced, a
slow stately pavanne, circling each other, parting and coming together, face to face, then back to back. The dance
went on and on. Korimenei should have been cold, but she
was not. A Whole Moon larger than the moon she knew
swam high overhead, full and white with traces of blue like
a great round of pale cheese. The trees around them were
bone white and still as stone, though they were not dead;
Korimenei felt a powerful life in them. The grass was thick
and short and black as the fur on a silver fox.

The dance changed, grew wilder. The Hart came to her,
took her hand, pulled her into the dance. The three of them
circled, parted, came together, face to face, then back to
back.

Korimenei had no idea how long the dance lasted, she
suffered no fatigue, she flowed with the pattern and felt
only a cool pleasure.

The Hart and the Hind and the Fawn drew back before
her. They sank onto four legs and trotted away, waded

across the stream and vanished under the trees on the far side. The river was gone, or perhaps it had merely shrunk to what it had been before the white doe came. She was standing on the red dirt of the meadow; she was dressed again in trousers, pullover and coat. She went back to the blanket, settled herself on it, pulled the laprobe about her shoulders. She touched her swelling body, but the fear was gone. Something was going to come out of this, but she knew the dance now and nothing could hurt her unless she let it. Behind her the eastern sky flushed palely pink.

The second day and the second night were done.

5

Korimenei was no longer hungry. She was exhausted, her head swam whenever she moved it. She wanted no more visions, no more harrowing of her flesh and spirit. She refused every flicker of thought, pushed out of her mind's eye everything but what her body's eyes saw and she restricted that to the blanket pattern centered between her knees. Her body continued to swell. She ignored that. Her bladder ached. She ignored that as long as she could, went to her latrine bush when she had to. She snatched a handful of needles as she went back to the blanket, rolling them between her palms, crushing them to release the clean acrid pine scent. She threw the wad away as she reached the rim of the meadow, wiped her hands on her sides. She sank onto the blanket and went back to contemplating the patterns on it.

The day lumbered along. Nothing happened.

She refused to think about anything, especially about events and images of the past two nights, but she could feel, down deep inside her, those experiences sorting themselves out, dropping into their proper pattern. The thing growing in her settled into a similar consolidation of its forces; it lay still and serene within her. It was alive, she had no doubt of that; it glowed like an iron stove in midwinter, not with heat, but with a cool power beyond any the doewoman or the deerman could show. It was like the great Owl come to nest inside her.

Nothing happened. She waited in a state somewhere between sleep and waking for the day to be over.

The sun crept down the western sky. She saw gold firedragons undulating around it, they were so beautiful she wept awhile; quietly, effortlessly she wept and smiled.

Geidranay came strolling along the mountaintops; he stopped when he was between her and the vanishing sun, lifted a hand in greeting and gave her a great glowing smile. He wandered on, vanishing into the clouds blowing up from the west.

Korimenei sighed and rubbed the back of her hand across her eyes. After the sun was completely down and the sky darkened to a velvet blue-black, she walked shakily to the stream and splashed water onto her face. She scooped up more water and drank from her hand. She straightened and stood rubbing her back. One last night, then this thing was over. What good it was, she had no idea. She smoothed her hands over her swollen front, grimaced, then walked upslope to her blanket.

The Wounded Moon went down, the clouds thickened overhead; the night grew darker and darker. Korimenei wasn't trusting her senses much, but sometime late, she thought it was around midnight, she had her first contraction.

Cool hands closed on her shoulders, eased her flat. Isayana Birthmistress bent over her, humming a song that flowed over her like water, calming her; she floated on a bed of air that the god rocked like a cradle. She retreated to a distant place, looking down on the body she'd left behind. The contractions came closer together. Isayana touched the body and left it bare where her fingers wandered. Korimenei snickered soundlessly, gods were great valets, no bother with buttons or ties.

After an hour, Isayana lifted Korimenei's laboring body onto its feet and held it in a squat. A thing emerged, slick with blood and mucus. It dropped to the blanket, crouched a moment between Korimenei's knees, then it tried to scuttle away. Isayana laughed and let Korimenei care for herself as she scooped it up, cradled it in gentle hands. "Oh, oh, oh," she crooned. She held the small creature against her generous bosom with one hand, stroked it with the other, cleaning it. It was a tiny gray-furred beast with huge eyes, black hands and feet, like a combination of ferret and marmoset.

Korimenei lay back on the blanket, watching, not knowing how to feel about what had happened to her. Her insides churned. She had birthed the creature, what did that mean? What was it? What had she done? NO! what had been done to her?

This is a mahsar. Isayana's voice was deep and caressing, she spoke in sounds like a warm wind makes when it threads through a blowhole, sounds that turned into meaning inside Korimenei's head. *Your womb received and nurtured her, child, but she is no flesh of yours. Quiet your fears, child, untrouble your souls. Your body was prepared to receive her . . .* Isayana raised a delicate brow; her large brown-gold eyes glimmered with amusement, *and a pleasant preparing it was it, not so? Don't speak, child, your blush answers me. Your body was made ready to receive her and she was drawn into you from the place where she and her kind dwell. She was drawn little by little into you until she was wholly here. She is tied to you, Kori Heart-in-Waiting; were you a witch, she would be your familiar; as you are more, so she is more. She has many talents and more uses, they are yours to discover. She will stay with you until your first true-daughter is born, then go to your child to protect and serve her.* Still cuddling the creature against her breasts, Isayana bent over Korimenei and stroked her clothing into existence as the Old Man Made Young had done, as the doewoman and the deerman had done. She tucked the mahsar into the curve of Korimenei's left arm, touched Kori's temple with gentle approving fingers and was gone, melting like mist into the night air.

Slowly, dreamily Korimenei sat up, bringing the mahsar around into her lap. She sat drawing her hand over her not-daughter's small round head, down her springy spine and along her whippy tail. Over and over she drew her hand down, taking pleasure in the exquisite softness and silkiness of the mahsar's short gray fur and in the warmth of the tiny body where it cuddled against her. "Mahsar, mahsar, mahsar . . ." She chanted the species name in a mute monotone, making a kind of mantra of the word. "Mahsar, mahsar, mahsar . . ."

She stilled her hands and sat lost in a deep oneness with air and earth. Time passed. The clouds thickened. Rain came, no more than a fine mist that drifted on the intermittent wind and condensed in bead-sized droplets on every surface.

When she was damp and cold enough, she surfaced and pulled the laprobe around her head and shoulders. She tucked it around the mahsar too, smiled dreamily as she felt the little creature nestle cosily in its folds and vibrate with a sawtooth purr. "Ailiki," she said suddenly. "That's your name, daughter-not. Yes, Ai . . . li . . . ki . . . Ailiki. Yes. She knew most surely, with a shock that broke her free from her drift that she'd found the first NAME in all the NAMES

she'd know the rest of her life, the first great WORD in all
the WORDS she'd know. She drew her forefinger over the
curve on Ailiki's head, along her shoulder and down her
foreleg to her three-fingered black hand. Ailiki edged her
hand around and closed it on Korimenei's finger. Kori
laughed. "Words," she said aloud. "Do you know, I think
I'm going to be a sorceror. Maybe even a prime." She laughed
again, cut off the sound when it turned strange on her.

She pushed the damp hair off her face. Her hand felt hot.
"You're a little furnace, Aili my Liki. Sheeh!"

Later she threw off the laprobe and lifted her face to the
unseen clouds. The mist droplets landed on it and puffed
into steam. Heat was a river pouring irresistibly into her,
coming from the heartroots of the earth and flowing into
her. She sat unperturbed and bled it out again, until the air
around her was white as daylight with the power of it and
she the suncenter, a glass maid filled with fire.

The heat came harder, the river widened into a flood. She
bled it off still, but the air burned her now, the radiance
reached for the trees and she was suddenly afraid they
would catch fire and burn like she was burning. She tried to
control the flow, to pinch it down into a thread she could
handle, but the attempt to control was enough in itself to
send the river flaring hotter. She whimpered, allowing herself that small outlet for the uneasiness building in her,
while she concentrated on channeling and, more important,
understanding. She saw realization of her potential as a key.
What she allowed now would determine the extent of her
access to that potential. At worst she would burn to ash . . .
no no, at worst she'd end a mediocrity, death was better
than that. At best she had that chance of rivaling Settsimaksimin. Of wresting from him all he was and all he knew.
She wanted that. She needed it.

She threw her strength against the flood. She could smell
singed hair, the blanket under her was burning. Not that
way, no no . . . all she'd been taught was control, all the
Shahntien knew was control. But Shahntien Shere was limited, magistra not sorceror, immensely learned and knotted
into that learning. Korimenei drew back as much as she
could without giving her body to fire and ashing; she cooled,
the heat flowed around her as the river had flowed when the
White Hind took her to the island. She'd gone into the river
then, she'd given herself to the current, let it take her where
it must. Was that the answer? No, not the whole answer.

The Gold Hart held her underwater, forced her to drink, to make the water most intimately a part of her. She gasped and pulled a shield like glass about her. She could endure this, she saw that as soon as the glass closed around her. She could endure and be what Shahntien Shere was, not so bad an outcome. Not really mediocrity. But not majesty either. She stared at the white-gold flames coursing about her, rising in shimmering stabbing tongues to touch the clouds overhead. She felt rather than heard Ailiki hissing with a terror answering her own. "Ahhh. . . ." she said aloud. "Tushzi," she cried in a voice to match her desires, using an ancient word from the Rukka Nagh ancestors buried deep in her cells, a word that meant fire. "TUSHZI VAGYA. I AM FIRE," she cried. It was her second WORD. She cast away the shield, she threw Ailiki into a spiraling loop above her head and stretched her arms wide, surrendering body and souls to the fire.

For a moment she was without thought, without perception, she was light itself, heat itself. She flowed with the stream wherever it would take her and it took her on a circle of the layered realities, bursting into one and out between one blink and the next. She was traveling with such speed she took with her only a blurred fragment of each, putting it into memory for the time when she would return though she was not thinking of returning now, she was not thinking at all, she simply WAS. Galaxies turned beneath her, she crossed a universe in the blink of an eye, dived into another and crossed that. . . .

The stream slowed, cooled; she began to draw back into herself, to seek home. A thing called her without words, a fireheart pulsed, drew her to it. She fell like the mist-rain, as slowly and insubstantially and blown about by the sullen wind. She fell into the meadowpit again and landed as she had before so lightly not a blade of grass stirred. Ailiki leaped into her arms and murmured a wordless welcome. She laughed. Her hands were translucent, filled with a light as cool and pale as moonglow. She felt immensely powerful, as if she could walk the mountaintops beside Geidranay and never miss a step. Yet there was more gentleness and love in her than she'd felt before, an outreach to all there was around her, a welcoming in her for all that was, name it good, name it evil, she welcomed all and gave it respect and dignity. She ran her hands over her hair and laughed again. The ends were singed into ashy kinks, as if someone had passed a torch too close to her. She looked around. The ground was charred where her dreampattern blanket had burned. Leave it as you found it, the Old Man said. Yes. Let me think.

Before she was ready, fire leaped to her hand, startling her. She wasn't afraid now. Without knowing how she knew what she had to do, she shaped the fire and threw it from hand to hand, played with it like a juggler with his props; she squeezed it into a ball, spun it on a finger until it spread like flatcake dough into a wide disc. She dropped the disc on the burnt grass. It soaked into the earth and left behind it crisp new grass, green and springing, smelling like spring. She laughed again and stretched out beside the new patch, weary but immensely content. After a while she slept.

The third day and the third night were done.

6

She woke in cool green morning light.

The Old Man was standing beside her. When she sat up, he held out a battered pewter bowl filled with potato and onion soup. The smell was at first nauseating, then with a shocking jolt, was everything good; she took the bowl and forced herself to eat slowly though she was ravenous. A sip at a time, a chunk of potato or onion, slow and slow, the soup went down. The warmth of it filled her, the earthsoul in it wiped away the haze that blurred her mind. The Old Man sat on the new grass at her left side, watching her, smiling. She snatched quick glances at him, embarrassed at first, but there was nothing of the red-gold lover visible in him so her uneasiness faded. When the bowl was empty, she sat holding it and smiling at him.

Tungjii came strolling from under the trees. Heesh snapped hisser fingers and Ailiki lolloped over to himmer, her odd high-rumped gait comical but efficient. She climbed himmer like a tree and sat on hisser shoulder, preening herself and murmuring in hisser ear. Male and female, clown and seer, bestower and requirer, the old god stood at Korimenei's right side and smiled down at her. Heesh pointed at the bowl, snapped hisser fingers again.

Korimenei scrambled to her feet. Bowing, she offered the bowl.

Heesh cupped it in hands of surprising beauty, long-fingered shapely hands that looked as if they belonged with another body. Eyes twinkling, heesh whistled a snatch of song currently popular in Silili. A warm yellow glowsphere formed momentarily about hisser hands, dissolved into the pewter. The bowl was changed. It was a deep-bellied bubbleglass filled with a thick golden fluid.

Korimenei took the glass and obeyed the flapping of heesh's hand; she sank down, sat cross-legged and sipped at the liquid. It was a mixture of fruit juices, sweet and tart, rich and cold; even the Old Man's soup was not so wonderful. Tungjii plumped down beside her, nodded across her at the Old Man, then sat beaming at her while she continued her sipping. There was no urgency in their waiting, so she took her time finishing the juice. They were enjoying her enjoyment and she was content to share it with them.

Tungjii took the glass when she held it out to himmer, touched it back to pewter, tossed it into her lap.

Amused by the absurd routine, she fished up the bowl, bowed deeply over it and passed it to the Old Man.

His dead-leaf eyes shone at her. He bowed in answer, then took the bowl in both hands, blew into it and held it out. When she took it, he folded both his hands over hers, his touch was warm and releasing. He got to his feet and wandered off, vanishing under the trees.

Korimenei watched him leave, a touch annoyed because he hadn't bothered to speak to her, to say something cryptic and satisfying as rumor said he did at other times for other questers. Potato soup, she said to herself, suffering gods, potato soup? She frowned at the bowl and wondered what that meant. She turned to Tungjii to ask himmer to explain, but the plump little god had taken hisser self off somewhere. Nothing from himmer either. Potato soup and fruit juice. The school cook could do as much. She laughed aloud. Well, maybe not quite as much, gods and demiurges and tutelary sprites seemed to be better cooks than retired witches. She stretched, yawned. Three days and three nights. I'd say I've done my time. She was changed, she knew that, but she didn't want to think about it now. She wanted the security of the person she'd known for twenty-four years, not this new thing, this battered creature tampered with by crazy gods and whatever took a notion to have a go at her.

Groaning as sore muscles complained, she got to her feet. She put the bowl away in her rucksack, then stretched and twisted, ran her hands through her hair and grimaced at the burnt straw feel. She was tired, but not so tired as she had been. The potato soup and the fruit juices were in there working. Swinging the rucksack onto her back, she pushed her arms through the straps; it pressed wrinkles into her coat and the pullover underneath so she tugged them flat and smoothed the coat around her lips. "Ailiki?"

The mahsar came running across the meadow; she took a flying leap and landed on Korimenei's shoulder where she crouched, singing into Kori's ear.

Korimenei laughed. "So you'll be riding, eh?" She walked to the stream, found the path that brought her here and started down it.

The Old Man was working in his garden again. She called a greeting but got no reply. She hadn't really expected one, so she kept on walking. The clouds were blowing out to sea and the sun broke through more and more as she went down the mountainside. The boat was where she left it. She slipped the knots, settled herself on a thwart and began rowing across to Utar-Selt.

7

Korimenei held a shirt up and inspected critically but rather absently its collection of patches and the numerous threadbare places. Behind her the door opened.

"That might do for a dustrag." Firtina Somak lounged against the door jamb, her arms crossed over the plump breasts she found more an irritation than an asset. "Unless you plan an involuntary strip some windy day."

Kori threw the shirt on the bed. "It's not all that much worse than the rest of my stuff."

"Tell me, hunh, me who's had to look at them all this time." Firtina laughed. "You only have to wear them." She came into the sleeping cell and plopped herself on the hard narrow bed, twitched a shirt from the pile and snapped it open. "T'k t'k, you can't wear this in public, Kri, people will throw coppers at you thinking you're a beggargirl." She folded the garment into a neat rectangle, sat scratching absently at a forearm. "The Shahntien passed you then."

"Mmh." Korimenei pushed the mound of clothing aside and sat on the bed next to her friend. Firtina was intensely curious about everyone; she never talked about what she learned and she wasn't pushy about it or malicious, but you could feel her feeling at you. "She said anything to you yet? About your test, I mean."

"She said sometime in the spring. If I work on voice control I'll be a Witch of Witches which is nice to know, but there's that damn IF. She says I go so flat sometimes it's a misery and she'd be shamed to claim me as one of hers." She narrowed her eyes, glanced slyly at Ailiki who was sleeping on the window sill, body coiled into a pool of sunlight, gray fur shimmering like tarnished silver. "I never thought you'd go for a witch."

"Haven't." Korimenei could feel Firtina wanting to ask about that and the mahsar, but her friend managed to swallow her curiosity, for the moment, anyway. Relenting a little, Kori said, "She's not a Familiar, she's Something Else."

Firtina waited a moment to see if Korimenei was going to add to that, then grinned at her, shook her head. "Clam. You for home?"

"Not for a while, I think." Korimenei spoke slowly; she hadn't told anyone about her brother, not even Frit,who was her best friend; she didn't want to lie to Frit, but she couldn't tell her the whole truth, so she pinched off a little of it and produced that. "My um sponsor sent some money, I'm going to spend it poking around here and there before I settle to something. You going home?"

"Have to, I think. The Salash Gazagt. . . ."

"Huh?"

Firtina scratched at her thigh. "I thought you knew the Nye Gsany."

"To read, not to speak." Korimenei left the bed and crossed to the window where she stood smoothing her fingers along Ailiki's spine. Over her shoulder she said, "And only the Nye of the Vanner Rukks. I don't know the hissery-clunk you talk, village girl."

"Hunh! talk about tin ears. Nye is Nye. I think you're digging at me, li'l Kri. Should I apologize for calling your clothes rags?"

"Idiot."

"All right, all right, here it is, the Salash Gazagt, he's the oldest male, the head of my family. When you come to visit me, I'll introduce you. If I know the two of you, it'll be dislike at first sight, but I'll do it."

"Am I going to visit you?"

"Aren't you?"

"All right. So what's your Salash Gazagt on about?"

"He's getting impatient, old bull; he wants me home before I wither into uselessness."

"Haah?" Kori swung round, hitched a hip on the window-sill and began chewing at a hangnail. "Wat th' hay, Frit?

Tink and Keiso and RayRay and I'm not going to waste breath naming the rest of your tongue-hanging court, the way they pant after you, you're not exactly declining into decrepitude."

"Them." Firtina wrinkled her nose. "They don't count. Thing is, if I'd stayed home like my sisters, I'd be wedded and bedded and by now hauling around a suckling and a weanling or two." She slapped at her breasts. "My doom," she said. "My folk have a thing about virginity, they tend to marry off a girl as soon as her shape starts showing. Just to make sure."

"Hunh! Just like my lot."

"Hmm. Sounds to me like you're not going home. Or maybe just a visit to show 'em what they'll be missing?"

"You got it." Korimenei plucked at the ancient white blouse she was wearing. "I never paid much attention to clothes."

"You finally noticed?" Firtina giggled, flicked another sly glance at Kori. "If three nights fasting will do that for you, it gives me hope. Maybe my Ordeal fixes my ear."

"Nothing wrong with your ear, you just don't keep your mind on what you're doing." Korimenei was briefly amused at this delicate hint for confidences, but the Passage Test wasn't something you talked about, it was too intimate a thing, more intimate than sex or family secrets. "I'm no good at line and cut and yelling at shopkeepers. Come help me spend my money."

"Why not." Firtina slid off the bed, held up a hand. "Let me get this straight. You really are going to spend REAL coin on NEW clothes?"

"Mmh-hmm." Korimenei took an ancient vest off its peg, shoved her arms through the armholes and smoothed the leather over her hips. She scooped up Ailiki and tucked her into one of the sagging thigh pockets. "Something easy but dignified."

"Oh oh oh." Firtina giggled. "Dignified. Dignified. . . ." She repeated the word twice more; each time she put a different spin on it, snuffling little laughs up her too-short nose as she walked from the cell. She stopped a few steps down the hall and waited for Korimenei. "Seriously," she said, "you have any idea what you want?"

Korimenei pulled the door shut, put her personal seal on it and followed Firtina out of the Senior Cott onto the maze-walk around the Dorms. "More or less the same thing I always wear," she said. "Better material, newer, that's all."

The autumn afternoon was warm and sunny; all evidence

of the brief storm three nights ago was cleared away, the stones underfoot were dry and powdery, as were the bright-colored leaves scattered on the granite paving by first year students who spent most of their days cleaning and sweeping, cutting grass and pulling weeds. Somewhere among the clipped yew hedges two girls giggled and chatted while they worked in a flowerbed, having lost much of their first awe of the place and at the moment at least some of their grim determination to succeed here. Two teachers came walking past, M'darjin drummers exchanging grave gutturals and spacious gestures. A squad of second-years paced along a nearby path, breathing in time with their coach, a student, like Korimenei and Firtina, nearing the end of his studytime. Kori stretched and sighed, lifting her head to look beyond the walls. The school was near the top of Selt's single mountain; at her left hand the gilded Temple roofs rose above the treetops, but everywhere else what she saw over the wall was the deep bright blue of the sky.

"You'll need some skirts too," Firtina said thoughtfully. "Boots, riding gear, a cloak, hmmm. . . ."

"Skirts, gah. No."

"Don't be stupid, Kri. You know well enough there are places where a woman gets stoned if she's not in skirts. It's better to be tactful than dead. Besides, a skirt can feel nice fluttering about your ankles, make you feel elegant and graceful."

"Gah."

"Don't bother then, go home and wear your trousers chasing after cows."

"Double gah."

"It's a cold cruel world out there that the Shahntien's going to boot you into. By the by, when's the parturition due?"

"Two, three days, depends on when I can get passage out."

They passed through a narrow arch in a thin, inner wall, walked into the rectangular formal garden at the front of the school and strolled toward the main gate. Short-stemmed asters were masses of pink and purple, yellow and vermilion; white tuokeries foamed around them. Manicured to an exquisite polish, oaks and cedars and plum trees grew alone or in carefully balanced groups of three. Patches of lawn like rough velvet changed color as a chancy wind blew blades of grass about. The paving stones in the curved walks were cut and placed so the veining in the marble flowed in a subtle endless dance of line and stipple. There was a fountain at the golden section; it was a sundragon carved from clear crystal spitting a stream of water from a snout raised to the sky. Korimenei and Firtina fell silent as they passed into this garden, respecting its ancient peace.

The porter came from his hutch, read their senior status from the badges, and opened the wicket to let them through into the city.

The street outside the school was a cobbled lane rambling between graceful lacy mimosas growing in front of walls that closed in the villas of the richest and most important Hina merchants. Ghosts were caught like cobwebs in the bending branches; they stirred, twitched, flapped loose for the moment to flutter about the heads of every passerby; they struggled to scream their complaints, but produced only a high irritating whine like a cloud of mosquitoes on a hot summer night. Though they refused to banish the haunts, considering exorcism a kind of murder, Kula priests working out of the Temple wove a semiannual mute spell over these remnants. The merchants had to suffer the embarrassment of the haunting (everyone knew that earthsouls only hung around those who injured them or their kin), but escaped more acute indictments by paying for the Kula muterites. Ignoring the eroding souls, Korimenei and Firtina walked north toward the Temple Plaza.

"So." Firtina clasped her hands behind her and looked up at Korimenei who was the taller by more than a head. "Are you looking for a Master, or is that already fixed up, or shouldn't I ask?"

"I don't know. It's like going home, I've got to do it sooner or later, but there's no hurry about it." Her mouth tilted into a crooked smile. "After all, I've got to visit you first and you won't be home for half a year or more."

"Ooh ooh ooh," Firtina chanted. She pinched Korimenei's arm and danced away as Kori slapped at her, swung round and danced backward along the lane. "While I'm waiting for that treat, where'll you be? North or south?"

"I thought I'd go south a bit, Kukurul maybe."

"Then you want light stuff." Firtina waited for Korimenei to come up with her, walked beside her. "Cottons and silks, nothing to make you sweat."

"Well. . . ." Korimenei fidgeted uncomfortably; she loathed having to hedge every statement, but what could she do? "I'd better have some winter things too. There'll be mountains, I'm pining for mountains, it can get cold in mountain vales, even southern ones, come the winter."

"Mmh-hmm. Fur?"

"Extravagance. Good wool and silk will do me." For a few steps she brooded over the idea of fur, then shook her head, her fine curls bouncing. "Definitely not fur." She bent a shoulder and touched the lump that was Ailiki asleep in the pocket.

They went on without talking through a shadow-mottled silence; no city noise came this high. The crunch of their feet, the soft flutter of the mimosa fronds and the whine from the ghosts only underlined the peace in the lane. It was one of those golden autumn days when the air was like silk and smelled like potpourri, something in it that bubbled the blood and made the feet dance.

Korimenei and Firtina came out of the quiet of the lane into the bustle and noise of the Temple Plaza like bathers inching into the sea. It wasn't one of the major feastdays, but the Plaza was filled with celebrants and questers, with merchants looking for a blessing on their cargoes or a farsearch to locate late ships, with mothers of unwed daughters dancing bridal pavannes for Tungjii and Jah'takash, with pickpockets, cutpurses, swindlers, sellers of magic books, treasure maps and assorted other counterfeit esoterica, with promisers and procurers, with lay beggars and holy beggars, with preachers and yogin and vowmen in exaggerated poses, with dancers and jugglers and players of all sorts, with families up for an afternoon's half-holiday, come to watch the evershifting show, with students sneaking an hour's release from discipline, or earnestly questioning Temple visitors, with folk from every part of the known world, Hina and Temueng locals, westerners (Phrasi, Suadi, Gallinasi, Eirsan, Henermen), southerners from the Downbelow continent (Harpish, Vioshyn, Fellhiddin, M'darjin, Matamulli), Islanders from the east (Croaldhese, Djelaan, Panday, Pitnajoggrese), others from lands so far off even the Temple didn't know them, all come to seek the Grand Temple of Silili, Navel of the World, the One Place Where All Gods Speak.

Korimenei and Firtina edged into the swirling chaos on the Plaza and went winding through it toward the Temple. A pickpocket attracted by the bulge in Kori's thighpocket bumped against her; he suppressed a scream of pain as Ailiki bit him, let the press of the crowd whirl him away from them. Frit grinned, twitched plump hips in a sketch of a dance, jerked her thumb up. Kori shook her head at her, amused by her friend's exuberance and the pickpocket's optimism; she knew better than to carry coin in any pocket she could get into without unbuttoning something. They eeled through the mob on the wide shallow stairs going up to the Temple, passed in through the vast arches.

They dropped coppers through a slot and accepted incense sticks from the acolyte. Firtina lit hers and divided them between Isayana and Erdoj'vak, the land spirit of her homeplace. She bobbed a bow or two, then followed Kori from Geidranay to Isayana to the little alcove where Tungjii's image was. Kori thrust the last of her incense sticks into the urn between hisser turned-up toes, then rubbed hisser belly for luck; for a moment she let herself remember her Ordeal, then she pushed away the troubling images, laughed, and followed Frit into the light.

They plunged into the market, bought wool and silk, linen and cotton, Frit taking the lead and Kori backing her, bargaining energetically and vociferously with the vendors. A sewing woman next, a quick measure and a more protracted back-and-forth over styles and cost. Bootmaker. Glover. Perfumer for soaps, creams and scents. Saddlemaker for pouches to hold all the above.

When they were finished, they sat over tea in the Rannawai Harral and watched the sun go down. Geidranay was a golden shadow against the sun, squatting among the mountaintops, his fingers busy among the pines; a translucent sundragon undulated above the horizon for a while, then vanished behind a low flat layer of clouds; the Godalau surfaced out beyond the boats of the Woda-an, and played among the waves, her long white fingers catching the last of the sunlight, her saucy tail glinting as if its scales were plates of jade.

"The gods are busy tonight." Firtina spoke idly, turning her teabowl around and around in her short clever fingers. "I haven't seen so many of them about since the New Year feast."

Korimenei sipped at her tea and said nothing. Her Ordeal was taking on the haze of myth. Not quite dream. Not quite memory. If I let myself slide into megalomania, I could think all that's put on for me, she thought. She smiled. Not likely, I'm afraid. She glanced at Firtina, smiled again. She almost believes it. I can see that. I wonder why? She's got a special touch for divining. "You think something is stirring?"

Frit chewed on her lower lip. She reached for the teapot

and filled her bowl again. "You've got the right word," she said finally. "Stirring."

"What?"

"Ah. That's the question. I don't know." She frowned, pushed back the dark brown hair that fell in a veil past her eye and curved round to tickle at her mouth. "It's, it's well, like standing over a grating and hearing things, you know, *things,* slithering about under you. You don't know what they are and you're quite sure you don't want to know. That sort of stirring." She gulped at the tea, shivered, refilled the bowl and sat holding the warm porcelain between her palms. "Yuk."

"Well, it can get on with it without me, I'm off as soon as my things are finished."

"Well. . . ." Frit set the bowl on the table and frowned across the bay at the mountains, dark and quiet since Geidranay had vanished with the sun and her attendant dragons. "I get the feeling . . . I just started noticing . . . it smells stronger every breath I take . . . I think you're some kind of . . . of magnet for it. When you move, it moves. I'll do some looking when we get back, see what I can find."

"Thanks. I think." Korimenei made a face. "Portents. Gah! I don't believe a word of it, you know. Come on, you're still under Rule, we don't want to get you chucked out before your time is up."

8

Six days later Korimenei Piyolss, sorceror in posse and possessor of portents too nebulous to grasp despite Frit's efforts and her own, Korimenei followed a porter and her pouches onto the merchanter Jiva Marish and sailed south for Jade Halimm.

IV: DANNY BLUE

a. The pocket reality of the
Chained God
b. The village at Haven Bay
c. The city Dirge Arsuid
Danny Blue
After ten years, he emerges from
the sleep pod and is propelled
on his way to his meeting with
the Talisman Klukesharna
    also: Lio Laux, owner of the
        ship *Skia Hetaira*
    Braspa Pawbool, fifth-
        rate sorceror in the
        employ of the Prenn
        Ysran of Dirge
        Arsuid
    Felsrawg Lawdrawn,
        thief and assassin
    Simms Nadaw, thief
    Trithil Esmoon, secret
        geniod, Phrasi
        courtesan

1

The Daniel Akamarino part of him woke first because Daniel had been through this before.

He opened his eyes and saw the translucent white petalform
of the pod cap slanting up away from him. Sleep pod? He
swallowed. The taste of burning insulation that filled his
mouth warned him he'd been down for more than a few
hours. He stared at the cracks clouding the cap and trembled with terror/rage. The starship was older than time and
rotting to dust. He could have died in that pod. If the
coldsleep system had broken in the smallest part, he would
be dead now and rotting with the ship.

Dead and rotten. For a god's whim, Chained God playing
Spin the Boogie with Fate. Live? Die? Who cares.

Mutely cursing the god and h/its reckless interference in his life, hands shaking with anger and inanition, Daniel Akamarino stripped leech-feeders off the emaciated body he inhabited and tried to sit up.

Your life? Our life! The words exploded in a head already blind with pain. Ahzurdan was coming awake. Sharing the body with Daniel, he shared the terror, the rush of adrenalin, though he couldn't know what caused it since he was entirely ignorant of starships and their mechanisms. *My life also.* Daniel saw the words as black against red with liquid white halos flowing around the outside of the letters. He cursed again, shoved angrily at the intruding Other. "Go away," he shouted, asserting control of the voice they shared. "Leave me alone."

Ahzurdan seemed to acquiesce, then slammed into Daniel with a sudden flare of power, trying to expel him from the body.

Their joint flesh humped, twitched, threatened to boil off the bone, their shared bones creaked and shuddered. Ahzurdan screamed, the SOUND tearing at their throat. Daniel howled and tried to shape the howl into words, to grasp at words and use them to kill the Other or, if killing were impossible, to force him from the body. This was a mistake. Words were Ahzurdan's technology, he could unmake with them as well as make and he strove desperately to unmake Daniel Akamarino and control the body that was born from the forced melding of their flesh.

Danny Blue, their rueful and unappreciative sort-of-son, woke and hovered like a ghost above his battling half-sires.

Not so long ago in conscious time, impossible to know how long in world time, Daniel Akamarino was walking down a road in another reality, was a starman/trader looking for a bargain, was a man who had a deep contempt for self-styled magicians, considering them deluded idiots with a yen for power but too inept or lazy to acquire the real thing, or charlatans, milking the deluded idiots that swarmed about them. On that day when he was walking along that road, Daniel Akamarino was past his first youth, with blue eyes bright in a face tanned dark, was bald except for a fringe of hair over his ears like a halfcrown of black thorns, was a tall man, lanky, loosely put together, but fast and hard when he had to be. Amiable, competent, unambitious, and generally somewhere else when you needed him.

Not so long ago in conscious time, in this reality where

magicians are the technocrats, Ahzurdan was a sorceror of high rank with a dreamdust habit that was killing him. Back then he was a tall man with a handsome ruined face and eyes bluer than the sea on a sunny day, with fine black hair, a beard combed into corkscrew curls and a bold blade of a nose. Among ordinary folk for his vanity's sake he spread a glamour about himself, wearing pride along with wool and leather, wearing power like a cloak, pride and power put on to cover the blind weak worm within. An ineffectual driven man, despite the power he commanded. Bitter, angry, dominated for too long by a neurotic mother, then a charismatic master.

Danny Blue's half-sires, fighting insanely over a body neither had the strength to control.

He snorted with disgust when he discovered what was happening. If one part of him destroyed the other, it would be an act of suicide. Ahzurdan and Daniel Akamarino were ghosts, incapable of independent existence; apparently neither of them could or would recognize this. Since he had no soft yearnings for easeful death, he gathered himself, slapped his warring parts into order and rolled his fragile body up until he was sitting with his legs hanging over the edge of the pod, his head cradled in dry bony hands.

He sat that way for several minutes, trying to dredge up sufficient strength to hunt out his quarters and see how much time had passed while he was stashed away in coldsleep. He scrubbed a hand across his mouth; his lips were cracked and dry. Painful. Whole body's in bad shape, he thought. He shivered; the clammy chill of the pod chamber was seeping into him. He reached up, caught hold of the cap and levered his wasted body off the cot.

He swayed, pressed his free hand hard against his eyes as his head threatened to explode. He lowered his hand and frowned at it. I look like the tag-end of a seven-year famine, he thought. He trembled again and his knees went soft on him. That miserable conglomeration of rot, I could have died in there. He clutched at the cap, steadied himself, then took a tentative step toward the open arch between the squat, cylindrical pod-chamber and whatever was outside it; he didn't lift his feet but shuffled along like an aged, aged man, body bent and swaying. When he reached the arch, he closed his hand around a broken bit of the wall and stood panting and shaking as he looked about.

The chamber was only slightly larger than the one behind

him. Halfway across it, shoved up against the right-hand
wall, there were two wide flat couches raised waist-high off
the floor and surrounded by skeletal instruments he managed to identify through a painful stretch of his imagination
and Daniel's memories. Sick bay, he thought. Thick scummy
webs hung in veils from the vines that crossed and recrossed
the ceiling and grew out of shattered screens ranked along
the walls. Unseen vermin scuttled about. He heard the
click-clack of their feet, the tentative whisper of the limp
pallid leaves as they brushed past. He scowled at the mess
of weed and web. This decay reminded him how lucky he
was to be alive. He worked his mouth, spat on the first two
fingers of his left hand, reached across his body and rubbed
his fingers on the wall beside him, an offering to Tungjii
Luck. He did this automatically, a habit pattern from
Ahzurdan's past life, as he struggled to think around pain
that struck in from his eyes whenever he moved his head
and between times was a dull, grinding ache.

Sick bay. Small. Must be officers only. Hmm. Colony
ship, converted battleship, given what that misbegotten patch-
work told me. That means I'm not too far off from my
quarters. Shee-it, how long was I out of it? God, I wish I
knew what happened while I was down. My legs feel like
spaghetti, I'll be crawling before I get there. Come on,
Danny, anyplace is better than this, it's enough to make a
goat sick. Start shuffling, man. He set his teeth and began
creeping toward the exit. It was half open and he could see
a pale light beyond. A corridor, probably. And it was lit. A
good sign. Could be it was still passable. There was air
wherever you went in this ancient ship, he knew that now;
metal and forcefields could exist in vacuum, but too much of
the Chained God's life or essence or whatever had spilled
out of the natal computer into that cobbled together mess,
bits of brain matter, bone and sinew, vegetable growths and
swarms of necessary symbiotes for h/it to shut off the flow of
air.

He started across the chamber, clawing awkwardly at the
ancient webs, his skin crawling as he visualized spiders dropping into his eyes. The dust he knocked off the webs and the
leaves drifted slowly onto him with the silky ponderance of
the half-g gravity decreed by the Chained God throughout this pocket reality; he breathed shallowly, his lips pressed
together, but that exuviae, that ancient scurf filled his mouth
with the taste of death. He caught hold of the rail at the foot

of the first cot and stood bent over it, feeling it give slowly slowly under the pressure of his diminished weight. The dust fell harder, the leaves above him shook with the agitated trotting of the creatures that lived up there. He moved on.

For the next half hour he moved along corridors as overgrown and dusty as the sickbay. The transition into a clean well-lighted section was abrupt, as if he passed through a membrane that blocked contamination from the unregulated life outside. He leaned against a sterile white wall, closed his eyes, sick with weariness, knowing he was near the living quarters which the Chained God had cleaned up for outsiders, the apartments he'd occupied for a month and a half before the god caught him plotting and dumped him into coldsleep. Because he was so near, the will that kept his body moving drained out of him . . . so near and so far. He sank onto his knees, hugged his arms across his chest and tried to dredge a last effort out of a mind and body on the verge of collapse. Just a few turns more, only a few turns more and he could rest and eat. The thought of food nauseated him, but he had to replace the flesh melted off him while he vegetated in the pod. He had to begin rebuilding wasted muscle. He rocked onto hands and knees and crawled, head hanging, eyes blind with sweat and the hair that must have kept growing while he slept; it fell in a coarse gray-streaked black curtain long enough to sweep the rubbery floorcovering. He hadn't thought about hair before, it'd just been there on his head. He crouched where he was and scowled at the hair falling past his eyes. The Daniel memories told him that in a properly working coldsleep pod even hair growth stopped, but there was enough play in the stasis field to let small changes occur if the adjustment wasn't precisely tailored to the metabolism of the sleeper; the wasting of his body was one of those changes, a serious one if he'd stayed much longer in the pod, the hair growth was another. And it was a crude way to measure time. He started crawling again, moving blindly along the corridor as he considered available data. The hair he'd inherited from Ahzurdan was eight to ten cm long when the god put him down. Now it was . . . he stopped crawling, pushed up into a squat and jerked a hair from the back of his head. It was close to thirty cm now which meant . . . two cm a year was a good average, take off ten already there, that left twenty which meant he was in that pod for roughly ten years. He threw the hair away and went back to crawling. Ten years?

He snarled at the friable mat that crumbled each time he set a hand down. Ten years cold storage. I'm supposed to be a good boy now, eh? Or you put me down again and maybe this time I'm snuffed? No joy, stewmeat. His mind blanked as rage took hold of him; his arms quivered and he collapsed to the floor, his body shaking with dry sobs.

His half-sires whispered sarcasms into his ears, mocking his suffering as extravagance and nonsense, a whimpering of a hypochondriacal organism, puppy looking to be petted. He slapped his hands against the mat, lifted himself on trembling arms and crawled on, fuming; his anger at the Chained God for risking him so casually was shunted aside by this annoying persistence of his sires; he was beginning to wonder if Daniel and Ahzurdan would ever fully merge with him and leave him without those irritating chains that kept jerking him back into his double past. Hair swaying in front of his nose, limbs trembling, he inched along the corridor, staying close to the left-hand wall.

A door sighed open. He stopped, blinked, then fumbled around and passed through the doorway into the chamber beyond where he collapsed in the middle of a painfully clean, faded blue carpet. He lay there and thought about pulling himself up and putting himself properly to bed, but the will to move died with his consciousness and he sank into a sleep that was close to coma.

2

For the next two weeks Danny Blue ate, slept, quelled his sires when they threatened to come apart, built back his weight and strength. And he grew more puzzled as each day passed.

He remembered the Chained God being powerfully present everywhere, sending a fantastical web of sound throughout the starship—cascades of beeps, oscillating hums, bings, bongs, twangs, murmurs, sibilant sussurations, squeals and twitters, subsonic groans that raised the hair on his arms and grumbled in his belly—the god communing with h/its various parts. That continuous, pervasive noise was barriered from the living quarters, but back then, when he was living there alone, the unheard vibrations filled the rooms despite the filters, buzzing in his bone. The vibrations were gone, replaced by a silence as intangible and impenetrable as the god's alleged mind. Silence filled the quarters, except for the sough of air through the ducts, the minor ticking of the support systems, and the noises Danny himself made. The god had withdrawn from his realm.

At first Danny was too intent on his own needs to notice that absence, except for a vague unease that wasn't intrusive enough to break his concentration on himself. When he was no longer an animated skeleton, though, he heard the silence and wondered. And started worrying. The Chained God in h/its ordinary aspect was spooky enough. This was worse.

He worked out in the gym, his mind seething—what's happening? what's that obscenity getting up to? He fiddled with recalcitrant controls on the food machines—god, I've got to get out of here, this ship is collapsing under its own weight, it's a wonder I lived through ten years of coldsleep, what do I do when the food and water quit? when the air goes? What is that abomination planning for me now? It has to be something or h/it wouldn't 've waked me. What? what? what? He coaxed the autotailor into fabricating new underwear and some multi-zippered shipsuits for him—how do I bust loose? is there anywhere in that backroad reality h/it can't reach? H/it's got h/its hooks set deep in me.

By the end of a month-standard, Danny Blue's body was repaired sufficiently to let him settle into a workout routine; he'd trimmed his hair, leaving it long enough to brush his shoulders (the mane he'd inherited from Ahzurdan was one of his not-so-secret vanities); he'd found his Heverdee vest and his sandals, their leather dry and cracking but intact because the god had put them away where the vermin couldn't get to them; he oiled the sandals and rubbed them until they were reasonably supple, then began a much more careful refurbishing of the vest.

3

He stood in the middle of a room like the inside of an egg, walls painted eggshell white, a fragile ivory carpet on the floor; there were a number of lumps about, chairs and couches folded in on themselves, put away for the moment, there were ovals of milky white glass at intervals around the walls, long axes parallel to the floor. The room was filled with soft sourceless light, as if someone had bottled sunlight and decanted it there.

"Hey," he bellowed. "Kephalos! God! Ratmeat! Talk to me. What the hell's going on?"

Silence.

"What do you want? I can't read your alleged mind,
Garbage Heap."

Silence.

"Look, Rotbelly, I don't intend to spend the rest of my
life hanging round this dump."

Silence.

Danny Blue wiped his hand across his mouth. He waited
one minute, two, five. . . .

Silence hung thick and sour about him. He brought his
hands a slight distance from his body, fingers curled, palms
up. He frowned at the palms as if he were trying to read the
god's answer in the lines. He dropped his hands and walked
from the room.

4

The Bridge.

The visible portion of the Chained God was a queasy
amalgam of metal, glass, vegetable and animal matter, shimmering shifting energy webs, the plasma of the magic that
was the source of the lifestrength of the god. Instrumenta-
tion stacked blind face on blind dead face, dials, sensor
plates, keyboards, station on station grouped in a squared-
off horseshoe about the massive Captain's Chair. Dusty
sweep of milkglass forescreen, fifty meters by thirty like a
blind white eye dominating the chamber.

Danny Blue stepped warily through the half-open valve
and stopped just inside. Powerdown, he thought. The energy webs were ghostwriting across the heavy decaying metal
and plastic of the stations, the readouts were dead, most
lights were shut off. Even so he could see sketchy attempts
the god had made to refurbish h/its mainplace, attempts that
some time ago had trickled into nothing. There were carpets
spread across the crumbled remnants of the floormat; even
in the gloom he could see the rich colors and intricate designs, he could also see the film of dust and grit laid over
the pile. There were plants in ceramic tubs, dead, all of them.
Rustling at long intervals when the airflow stirred their dry
leaves.

Beside the Chair the floor was bared to metal, deckmetal
plated with silver in a paper-thin disc twenty meters wide,
polished until it gleamed like ice in the half-light. A design
was scribed on the disc, fine black lines set into the silver, a
circle within a six-pointed star which itself lay within a
second circle; lines inside the star crossed from point to

point and intersected at the center of the design. *Hexa, get away from it.* The thought came from Ahzurdan; he didn't want anything to do with that figure. BinYAHtii lay in a sprawl of heavy gold chain where the lines crossed. Ignoring his half-sire's urgings, Danny stood scowling at the talisman. Why? he thought. Though his memory was uncomfortably vague, it seemed to him that the chain and its pendant lay much as they had when he dropped the thing ten years ago. But that couldn't be true, he'd been back to the Bridge several times since and BinYAHtii was nowhere in sight. Why was it here now, why arranged like that? why? He took a step toward the silver. The Ahzurdan phasma mindshouted a warning: AVOID AVOID.

"All right," Danny Blue said aloud. "Hey! God! What's going on?"

Silence.

Hands clasped behind him, arms tucked cautiously against his sides, he moved along the instrument array, examining everything minutely, touching nothing.

Dark. Blank. Dead.

Here and there a few lights wavered, monitors hooked into energy flow and life-support. The god had powered down so far h/it was in a kind of coma.

Fear stirred in Danny Blue, colder than a wind off Isspyrivo's glaciers. The god had waited too long, whatever h/its plan was. H/it underestimated the ravages of age on h/its material fabric. Even hullsteel was mortal, given sufficient time and stress. The Chained God was dying, h/its slow time-death accelerating toward total dissolution even as Danny watched.

Danny Blue moved back to the central bank of instruments. An impulse to try taking control of the computer stirred in him—that was Daniel Akamarino fighting to surface, the Akamarino phasma retreating to memories of a reality so different that his reactions had no connection to what Danny Blue had to cope with; even with all he'd seen since he'd been pulled into this reality, down deep Daniel then and his phasma now simply didn't believe in magic and wouldn't, perhaps couldn't, incorporate it into his worldview. Danny clamped down hard on his half-sire's urge, knowing it for the stupidity it was. He moved away to stand at the edge of the silver, staring down at BinYAHtii.

The Ahzurdan phasma stirred uneasily; he was uncomfortable this close to the Hexa; his anxiety sent cold chills

down Danny Blue's spine. Daniel Akamarino was trying to
be heard, saying: Pattern a drain, set it on delay and let's
get out of here. If you won't try breaking the Kephalos free
of the god, at least destroy it. I know we tried that before. I
know the god caught us at it and put us down. It's different
now. That thing is dormant. Can't you feel it?

Like eels in a sack, Danny's half-sires were fighting against
his control, flexing and writhing, punching at him; he was
getting more and more impatient with this nonsense, it was
distracting him when he needed all his intellect focused on
the problem before him. The Chained God was dying and if
he couldn't get out of here, he was going to die with h/it.

Danny Blue frowned at the talisman; he could feel his
half-sire Ahzurdan coveting the stone despite the phasma's
fear of the Hexa. If Danny could get at it somehow, he
knew from a sweep of Ahzurdan's memories that he could
use its power to protect them all from the god. From that
sweep he learned also that the Hexa he saw was a dangerous
variation on the more usual pentagram. Ahzurdan had never
used one and knew very little about them, but he was afraid
of this one; he didn't know why the god had laid it there, he
didn't want anything to do with it. He fought to keep Danny
from touching it.

BinYAHtii lay dull and red, sucking such light as there
was into its rough heart. It was close enough to be tempting,
two long strides would take him to the center of the pattern.
Rubbing at his chin, Danny looked about, hunting for a
pole or something he could use to rake the talisman from
the silver.

His half-sires began wrestling with him and each other
again, leaving his brain a muck of half-thoughts, half-desires,
half-terrors.

Impatient and angry, he swore aloud, backed off a few
steps, then took a running leap into the center of the Hexa.
With a smooth continuation of the motion, he bent and
grabbed for the chain, planning to straighten and leap again
as soon as he had it.

His hand passed over a surface like glass. He couldn't
touch the talisman. He thought suddenly, No dust, there's
no dust on. . . .

5

He dropped a few inches, stumbled and fell to his hands
and knees on black sand.

He got to his feet, brushed sand off his knees and hands.
To his left, diminishing black hills curved around a placid
bay. The sun was low enough in the west to glare into his
eyes and dazzle off wrinkle-waves. He knew this place.
"Haven Bay," he said aloud.

There was a ship anchored out near the narrow mouth of
the bay, a sleek black hull with a green and black port flag
snapping in the wind. I know that ship, he told himself. He
scowled at it, disconcerted. Unless she has a twin, that's the
Skia Hetaira. What's going on here. . . ?

He shook his head and starting trudging along the beach,
heading for Haven Village, out of sight around a bulge in
the foothills.

6

The corral was empty. The erratic wind lifted then dropped
clouds of ancient dry manure and sent the gate creaking on
its cracking leather hinges. The stable doors gaped wide;
several of the windows were cracked or broken; all of them
were smeared with gray dust and veiled with dusty cobwebs.
The cottage beyond had lost part of its thatching. Like the
stable, its door was open and a litter of leaves, twigs and
dirt had been blown through the gap into the kitchen beyond.

Danny Blue walked along the rutted street, frowning and
nervous. The village was deserted; it looked like it'd been
empty for years. He had a chilly feeling he knew what had
happened to the people living here; that freaking Ratbait
had fed them to the Stone. BinYAHtii. Haven was as dead
as the god was going to be. Danny smiled at the thought,
then shivered, thinking about the hook the god had set in
him; he was afraid his fate was linked somehow with that
abomination.

He came round a curve and saw a pale skim of yellow
lantern light laid out across the ruts; it came through the
open door of a tavern. He hesitated, glanced toward the
bay. He couldn't see it now, but nodded anyway. Someone
off the ship. He stepped through the door.

Lio Laux was perched on a stool at the bar, a lantern
beside him, the only light in that stale dessicated room.
There was an open bottle and a tankard at his side. He was
sitting with his elbows on the bar, his bare feet hanging
loose beside the legs of the stool. He wasn't drunk, but
elevated enough to watch the mirror with philosophic melancholy as Danny Blue walked toward him.

Danny dusted off another stool, wiped his hand on his pants and sat down. "No one about."

There was a flicker as Laux moved his head slightly; his silver and moss agate ear dangle shivered in the lantern light. The light touched his ancient dark eyes, snuffed out as horny eyelids closed to slits. "No." After a moment, he added. "You live round here?"

"Just passing through. There another of those tankards left?"

"Ahind the bar."

"Ah." Danny slid off the stool, sauntered around the end of the bar and squatted so he could inspect the cluttered, dusty shelves. It looked very much like the proprietor stepped out for a breath of air and never came back. He found a tankard; it was thick with dust so he hunted some more until he discovered some clean rags in a tilt-out bin.

When he was back on his stool, he filled the tankard from Laux's bottle, took an exploratory sip, then a larger gulp. "That your ship?"

Danny saw ivory glints as the old man's eyes darted toward him and away; Laux was puzzled by a vague sense that the two of them had met before, but he couldn't pin down time or place. He had plenty of reason to remember Ahzurdan and Daniel Akamarino and Danny had something of each in his face and form. The resemblance to either wasn't all that strong, but it was there, a family likeness as it were.

"Yah. Looking for passage?"

"Might be, say we can do a deal."

"What you got to offer?"

"I could whistle a wind should you be wanting one. And I can do another thing or two if the need arises."

"Wizard, mage?"

"Nothing so grand. A bit of Talent, that's all."

"You set wards?"

"Yah."

"How far you want to go?"

"Next port bigger'n this."

" 'S a deal. You ward if we need it, give us a wind if we draw a calm, take a hand if we run into sharks round the Ottvenutt shoals. And I'll carry you on crew as far as Dirge Arsuid, that's ten days west of here. It's a chancy port, but you won't have to sit around long, there's a lot of trade in and out this time o year, take you just about anywhere you want."

"Good enough."

Laux drained his tankard, his ear dangle clattering musically as he tilted his head. He squinted at the bottle; there was half an inch of wine left in it, wine thick with wax and wing. "Reach me another of those bottles . . . ah . . . what do we call you, man?"

"Lazul, Laz for short."

"And while you're ahind the bar, hunt out the biggest of those rags, Laz. I wave that out the end of the pier, my second'll come fetch us."

Danny took one of the dusty bottles lined up below the mirror, set it on the bar. "Need something to open that?

"Got something." Laux drew the cork, sniffed at the neck, poured a dollop into his tankard and tasted it. He grunted with satisfaction and filled the tankard. "Found that rag?"

Danny shook out a gray-white rectangle that might once have been a flour sack. "This do?"

"Should. Toss it over. You been here before?"

"First time."

Laux sucked at his teeth, tilted his tankard and contemplated the dark red wine. "Haven't been here for some years now," he murmured, talking more to himself than to Danny Blue. "It was quiet, the glory days were gone, long gone . . . time was there was near a thousand here, a dozen taverns, a casino, the place wide open day and night . . . yah, it was quiet when I was here last, but not so quiet as this. Two/three hundred people hereabouts, more down along the inlet. Don't know about them, maybe they're still around. You see anyone?"

"No."

"Mmh. Funny. The notion come to me one night, I ought to go see Haven again. Don't know why. Just something I ought to do. Wish I hadn't."

"Know what you mean." Danny put his elbows on the bar beside the rag, scowled into the tankard Laux shoved across to him. The wine was past its peak, but it wasn't that put the sour taste in his mouth. It didn't take a lot of thinking to see why Laux and his ship were here right now. Jerking my string, he thought. Whatever it takes, I swear I'm pulling that hook out. He gulped at the wine, wiped his hand across his mouth. "Any reason you're hanging about? Tides or something?"

"Ah the vastness of your ignorance, young Laz." Old

Laux grinned at him, shook his head. He sobered, looked depressed. "Crew took a look round an hour ago. Got spooked and left. I told them to fetch me come sundown, I wanted to poke about some more. Haaankh." Having cleared his throat, Laux spat the result into the dust on the floor. "Being you're over there, shove a couple bottles in the pockets of that thing you're wearing and push another couple across to me. I saw a vest like that once, some years back. Never seen another."

"Gotcha. Never saw another myself. Could be it's the same one. I picked it up in Kukurul Market a little over a year ago."

"Ah." Lio Laux collected his bottles, slid off his stool and ambled toward the door. Over his shoulder he said, "Bring the lantern, Laz."

Danny grinned. Getting his money's worth, old thief. Well, I'm riding for free. So what's a dime's worth of flunkying.

7

Danny Blue, Laz to his companions, emerged into the abrasive cold, shivered as he wandered over to stand beside Lio Laux who was leaning on the port rail, watching the play of light across the walls and towers of the city on the horizon. The pointed roofs of Dirge Arsuid glittered blackly in the dawnlight; it rose in white and crimson and raven black over the dark drooda trees and the broad reedfields of the mouth-marshes of the Peroraglassi.

Danny/Laz folded his arms across his chest. "What's the problem? Why aren't we moving?" The *Skia Hetaira* was hove-to a half mile out to sea, riding the heave of the incoming tide, lines and spars humming, clattering in the brisk wind.

"No problem, Laz. We just waiting till it's full light before we go closer."

Danny inspected the water and what he could see of the city. "No rocks."

"Nah. Arsuid's built on mud."

"How come it don't sink?"

"It's Arfon's toy. You didn't know that?"

"Never been out this way. Arfon?" In the back of his head, the shade of Ahzurdan sneered. *You know,* the phasma said in a thin scratchy mindvoice, *if you condescend to remember. Fool. All right, go ahead, show your*

ignorance. Who cares if he despises you for it.* Danny Blue
ignored his fratchetty half-sire and waited for Laux to answer him.

"River god. Dwolluparfon, which is too much of a mouthful so Arsuiders just say Arfon. Never, huh?"

"No. I come from way out where the sun pops up. I'm a
rambling man, Laux; can't stand sitting around watching the
same scenery all the time. If it's not silt or rocks, why are
we sitting out here? We waiting for high tide?"

"Nah. Lemme tell you something, Laz. Darktime in Arsuid
is a thing a smart man keeps shut of. Unless he's an Arsuider
and even then, hmm. We're not going to move for another
couple hours, so I might as well spend it telling the tale of
Dirge Arsuid." The plaques of his ear dangle clattered
softly as he tilted his head to look up at Danny/Laz; the
silver shimmered, the moss agate insets seemed to alter as if
spiders crawled about under glass; there was a quizzical
amusement in his old dark eyes. "You may have noticed I
like to talk." He twisted his head around further, beckoned
to the ship's boy who happened to be passing. "Pweez, tell
Kupish to burn some duff for us, eh?" To Danny, he said,
"You turning blue. Han't you got a coat or something? It's
getting on for winter, jink."

"I didn't expect it to get this cold this south."

"Winter's winter. Let's go below. I'll spin you the tale
over hot grog an' one o Kupish's fancier fries. Taksoh
caught a gravid kuvur last night, we'll have roe an' cheese to
start."

8

"In the time before time when the Wounded Moon was
whole. . . ." Lio Laux sucked up a mouthful of thick hot
grog, let it trickle down his throat. "And the gods were
sorting themselves out and sharing up the world, Dwalluparfon
found he'd got hisself a river, a swamp and a handful of
vipers. The story goes like this; he took a while to root
round and get to know his mud, then he stuck his head up
and looked round at his neighbors. And lo, they had lots of
things he didn't. They had cities and farms, most of all they
had people. He had fish and snakes. He didn't like that no
way, wahn't fair. So he caught him a mess o snakes and
made hisself some people." Laux's eyes slid round to Danny,
the wrinkles round them crinkling with his sly-fox grin. "Not
a tale Arsuider mams tell their lovin' infants. Lessee. He

watched the snake people slither round in the mud and that
was amusing for a while. But it was kind of drab, so he
decided they were going to build him a city. He thought
about it a long while, being slow that way; like his river he
takes a long while to get anywhere, lots of detours, but he
finally reached a conclusion. He wanted a shining city like
the other gods had. He built up a mound of mud at the river
mouth and cooked it until it was hard, then he drove a grid
of canals through it and fixed the canals so the water was
always moving in and out of them in good strong currents to
keep them scoured clean. He went snooping around to the
cities people built in other godplaces and picked out the
things he liked about them and made hisself a city pattern.
When he got back home, he scooped up a clutch of his
snake people, rinsed them off and set them to work with
ovens he made for them, turning out tiles, red, white and
black. He spread his plan out for them so they'd know what
he wanted, then he drove them generation after generation
till he had his city built. Then he said, go live there and
follow my rules and do me honor. And there you have it,
Dirge Arsuid."

"Snake people, hmm?"

"To know 'em is . . ." Laux sucked up more grog, twin-
kled at Danny ". . . to know 'em."

"So, tell me more. If I'm going to be knocking about
there, I better know what to look out for." In the back of
his head, the Ahzurdan phasma snorted but said nothing.
Danny ignored him. For a lot of reasons, he wasn't willing
to trust the information in the memories his half-sire made
available to him.

Laux ran his tongue over his teeth, stared past Danny at
the cold white light coming through the porthole. "Been
thinking 'bout that. I'll tell you a thing or two first, then . . .
well, that can wait. Arfon say you get a trial if you accused
of something. He say you got to be guilty 'fore they can
send you to the strangler. Guilty o something, if not the
thing they say you did. That's the law an' Arsuiders, they
hold very strict to it. Arsuid honor. Hmh!" He shook the
grog jar, emptied the last drops into his mug. "Trouble is,
most folks have a thing or three staining their souls, an' if
they don't, well a smart ysran, what they call their judges,
he can f'nagle it someway to shift someone else's guilt onto
that poor jink's head. Arfon don't care, long as the look o
the thing's right. Mostly he don't notice what's happening;

like I said, he's not too swift. Keeping all that in mind, it's a
pretty loose guarantee 'less old Arfon, he sticks his head up
and takes your side. It do happen. Can't count on it, but it
do happen. I know. I run into something first time I showed
up wanting to trade. Nearly got my neck in the strangler's
noose too. But Arfon took a notion, don't ask me why, he
stick his weedy head through the floor an' tell the ysran let
me go. Ysran don't like it, but he do it. I don't have a smell
o trouble the rest of the time I was there, I got some mighty
profit out of it too. Why I bother to come back an' why I
don't go in while there's dark on the canals. Trading here's
worth walking the edge awhile. That f' sure. Long's you do
it in daylight and watch the 'ifs' and 'buts' in your bargaining, they good folk to do business with. Arrogant bastards,
make you want to skin 'em the way they act, but they keep
their word. An' if they tell you something 'bout what they're
selling, it's true. An' they got a lot to sell. Hennkensikee
silks, for one thing. Better price than you can get just 'bout
anywhere. Lessee, what else . . . ah! Stay inside once the
sun's down. All bets 're off after dark. Strangers on the
walkways or riding the canals, they dead. Don't think you
could argue your way loose or fight 'em off, you won't. You
dead. Floating out to sea. Sacrifice to Arfon. Arsuiders,
they know what their god likes." He wrinkled his nose, sat
back in the chair, dark fingers laced over his small hard pot.
"Lots o pretty red blood and fancy screaming. Long's it's
foreigners making the noise and doin' the bleedin'. Way I
see it, old Arfon, he never did get over other gods gettin'
the jump on him with their cities an' their temples an' their
busy-busy little folk, and he kinda likes seeing outsiders
wiggle for it."

Danny lifted his mug. "Here's to the Arsuiders. To know
'em . . ." he gulped down the last of the lukewarm grog,
". . . is to know 'em."

"Yeh." Laux ran his tongue over his teeth, making his
lips bulge. "Look here, Laz, you whistle up a good wind."
He grunted with impatience and stopped talking as Pweez
came in to clear away the dishes; when the boy was gone, he
went on. "Taught some manners to those top'sh off Ottvenutt
shoals. First time I've got past without taking some damage.
You say you're a rambling man, no place you have to be, no
one expecting you here or there. What I'm saying, if you
don't fancy taking a chance on that," he flicked a hand

toward the porthole, "why not stay on board? Say we can
settle on what you get out of it."

Danny Blue picked at a hangnail and thought about it. He
was tempted. He didn't know where he was going—except
away. Away from the Chained God and his manipulations.
Which did the god want him to do? Stay? Go? Enough to
send a man biting his tail. His half-sire Daniel Akamarino
had spent his life drifting from one place to another with no
goals, no ambitions, his work the only center his life had.
That kind of work wasn't available here, that reality was a
place Danny found himself wanting to visit, but it was out of
reach and he wasn't about to waste time yearning for what he
couldn't have. His other half-sire Ahzurdan never took
one step without plotting out a hundred steps beyond, though
for him too, work was justification, a reason for being. And
that was gone too, not available. With the war going on in
his head, Danny Blue couldn't reach the degree of focus a
sorceror needed for all but the most ordinary activities.

Stay, fool, Ahzurdan's phasma said, *you won't find a
better place. Things will only get worse.*

Don't listen to that mushbrain, Daniel's phasma said,
*you and me, we're going out of our skull shuttling around
on this crackerbox. We can get along just fine on the ground.*

Danny Blue liked old Lio Laux, the M'darjin was close to
being a friend. He liked the crew. But he agreed with his
half-sire Daniel, he most definitely did not like living on the
ship. He was cramped, uncomfortable, and bored most of
the time.

"Thanks," he said. "It's a good offer, but Dirge Arsuid
sounds interesting, it's a place I've never been, I think I'll
take a look at it. How long you going to be in port?"

"In by noon, out by dark. I don't overnight here ever."

"That's that then. See you round, I suppose. Maybe on
my way back."

9

Danny Blue followed the guide Laux had summoned for
him, a boy, twelve or thirteen, sallow skin with a greenish
tint, stiff spiky hair dyed in green and yellow squares, green
paint on his eyelids, yellow triangles painted under each
eye, lips carefully tinted green. Heavy round ceramic plugs
swung in rhythm with the swing of his meager hips, hanging
from flesh loops stretching down from his earlobes, green in
the right, yellow in the left. He had ceramic armlets clamped

above and below the elbow on his left arm; they were
striped in green and yellow. He wore a glove on his right
hand, snakeskin dyed a rich dark green. His left hand was
bare, the nails painted blood red. On his feet he wore
snakeskin slippers dyed to match the glove. Instead of trousers he wore knitted hose, right leg green, left leg yellow,
with a bright red codpiece and belt. To cover his torso he
had a tight sleeveless green shirt with pointed yellow darts
slashing downward diagonally, starting from his right shoulder, aiming toward his left hip. He strolled along as if he
were going that way from choice and had no connection
with the scruffy drab creature following him. His was a
conservative dress for his kind, a simple walking-out costume. Warned on the ship to mind his manners, warned
again before Laux turned him loose, Danny Blue managed
not to stare at the show around him, but sometimes it was
not so easy to keep his eyes straight ahead. As when a
creation in feathers and gauze fluttered past, its species as
uncertain as its outline. The boys he saw all had painted
faces but no masks; every adult, male and female alike,
wore halfmasks, stylized serpent snouts as if they adopted
the insult in the old tale and made it something to flaunt.
Laux said they carried viper poison in the rings they wore
and could shoot it into someone with a special pressure of
the hand. They usually refrained in the daylight, it was bad
for business, but you didn't want to push them much, their
restraint was delicate as a spider's thread.

It was a city of silences and shadows, of walls and towers;
it smelled like clove carnations; they grew in the walls, red
and white carnations, they floated in the water, bobbing
past him as he walked along the roughened tiles, red and
white carnations with white orchids and a rose or two,
swirling around the narrow black boats poling along the
canals. Red and white. The whole city was red and white.
Every wall was faced with glossy red and white tiles. Panels
of red tiles, columns of white tiles. Patterns of cut tile, red
and white swirling together, sweeping along in dizzying flows.
Red and white, white and red. Except for the pointed roofs.
Those were black tile, shiny black. It rained most days from
two till four, thunderstorms that dumped an inch or more
into the grooves that ran in spirals from the peaks and
dropped into channels that fed the glossy black gargoyles;
the rain water spewed from their mouths, arching out over
the walkways to spatter into the canals.

The boy led Danny Blue past a water plaza.

There was a black tile fountain in the middle and lacy
white footbridges arching to it from the corners of the
square. There were seats round the fountain. Several
Arsuiders sat there, in groups like flocks of extravagant
birds, heads close, talking in whispers. They stopped talking
when they saw Danny, watched him until he went round a
corner. He didn't look back, but he could feel the pressure
of their whispers following him.

The Stranger's Quarter, local name Estron Coor, was laid
out near the heart of the City, not even the Ahzurdan
phasma knew why. The Stranger's Wall was a swath of
murky red with black diamonds in a head-high line march-
ing around the enclosure. The single door in that wall was
iron thickly coated with a shiny black paint, nicked and
bruised and smeared, the first dirt Danny Blue had seen in
the city; the opening was narrow, a man only marginally
bigger than average would have trouble squeezing through
it.

The boy stopped before the door, his costume swearing at
the wall; next to its heavy brooding solidity, he seemed
more a concept than a living person, a player in some
fantastical drama. He whistled a snatch of something, a
complex tonerow sort of thing, stepped aside when he got a
matching answer from the gatehouse perched over the entrance, no windows in it, only arrowslits with oiltraps in the
base of the overhang. Danny Blue kept his face noncommittal but wasn't liking this much at all. Laux said they barely
tolerated outsiders in their midst; this tower underlined that
and went beyond. Strangers were treated like disease germs,
encysted, kept away from the rest of the organism.

The door creaked open, a sound that felt like a rusty
knife twisting in the bone. No sneaking out of here, Danny
thought. He went through the narrow opening into the
Estron Coor. The boy was still watching when the door was
maneuvered shut by a complicated arrangement of ropes
and pulleys. Making sure I stay where I'm put. What a
bunch. Danny Blue looked around.

There was an Inn, three stories high and tight against the
Wall; from the look of the second story windows and other
signs it was eight rooms long and barely one room thick.
The third story was tucked in under toothy eaves with
shuttered unglazed holes too small to qualify as windows.
Next to the Inn were several miniature stores with living

quarters above them, a cook shop, a grocery, a butchery, a miscellany. Across the canal from the Inn there was a ponderous godon with offices or something similar in part of the ground floor and a line of portals with chains and bars enough to suggest that behind them were rare and costly things. Next to the godon there was a sort of multi-purpose temple with seven flights of steps leading to seven archways, no two alike; ghosts in various stages of preservation drifted in and out of openings that made a sieve of the cylindrical tower emerging from the squat ground floor; they undulated past women with painted breasts who sat in those openings, they mingled with the drifts of smoke from the incense which kept the air inside the walls smelling rich enough to eat. The Ahzurdan phasma sneered at the women. *Temple whores. Tempted, Danny?* The Daniel phasma muttered something Danny couldn't hear, didn't particularly want to hear.

All those buildings were fairly new and constructed of wood by someone with a fixation on sharp points; the eaves looked like the bottom jaws of sharks, there were spearheads or something similar jutting from the corner beams, edges sharp enough to split a thought. The window bars were no meek retiring rods; on the outside they had ranks of needles like the erectile spines of a hedgehog snake, and the needles had discolored points. Poison, Danny thought, sheeit.

There were people looking at him from the corners of their eyes, shoulders turned to him. A motley collection, scarce two alike though they were mostly men. They were standing around as if they had nothing more important on their minds than sneaking peeks at a new arrival; the whole place had a feeling of stagnation, constipation, though the water in the broad canal ran clear and clean with scattered flowers riding the wind ruffles, slipping in through one grating and out the other. One of the men sauntered away from a group, crossed the humpy bridge to the temple and went inside. A few women swathed in drab veils that covered them head to toe hurried from one store to another, trotted back to the Inn or climbed the stairs to the cramped quarters over one of the businesses.

Unhurried, giving those side-eyes a bland mask to look at, Danny Blue strolled for the Inn, wondering rather seriously how much it was going to cost him. He had an assemblage of coins, a very mixed lot, some left over from Daniel's first days in Cheonea, some from Ahzurdan's hoard, some he'd found scattered about the starship. Though it wasn't much when he piled it up, it was enough to cushion him until he decided how to make some more—as long as he was quick about it. He pushed through the door.

The room inside was small and smoky, lit by a brace of sooty lamps. There was a staircase vanishing around a sharp corner, swallowed by shadows as sooty as the lamps and in the corner opposite it was an L-shaped counter with barely enough room for the youth dozing behind it. Danny woke him up, talked him out of a room and went to it to think about things.

In the middle of thinking, he fell asleep.

10

He woke, startled out of sleep so suddenly he sat up confused, slammed his head into something hard and cold. He swore, moved more cautiously. He was in a stone cage, granite by the look of it, squat, heavy, ugly. It sat inside a pentacle in a domed room without windows or any apparent doorways. No one about. He ran his hands over the stone, there wasn't a crack in it, not even where stone joined stone. "No doors in this thing, how'd they get us in here?"

C'vee mir, Ahzurdan phasma said, detached appraisal in his insect voice.

Danny was briefly amused, as he suspected he was meant to be. "What's that?" he said aloud.

Cage. Meant to hold magic wielders. Us.

"Not good, you mean?"

Not good.

"What's going on?"

I suspect we'll find out soon enough.

"You don't know?"

Like Lio Laux, I've avoided this place. There was no reason to seek it out. They don't welcome stray sorcerors here, no matter how high the rank.

"They don't welcome stray anybody. Any law against unregistered sorcerors?"

None that I know of.

"Gods, I haven't been here long enough to bruise a rule, let alone break one. What do they think I did? Spit in their canal?"

There'll be something. Unless Arfon intervenes.

"I think we can forget about that. This cage carved out or patterned?"

You mean, can I unmake it.

"Yeh."

I can't. You can.

"What a hope." Both his sires had learned whatever they needed to learn as easily as breathing; Danny Blue had assumed he could relearn Ahzurdan's sorcery in much the same way. After all, he didn't have to do the original work, only shift the WORDS and gestures to match his new psyche. Two problems with that. First, he wasn't given the time he needed; he'd spent the past ten years in an artificial coma. Second, he kept slamming into Daniel Akamarino's bone-deep disbelief in magic. In short, he discovered the truth in the aphorism: Sorcery requires will and the proper application of will requires belief. In those first months after the battle with Settsimaksimin when Danny was confined within the starship body of the Chained God, before the god caught him plotting, he'd worked harder than he could remember in either of his lives to rebuild a full range of WORD, IMAGE and gesture, though it was like fighting a tiderace to overcome the Daniel phasma's resistance, his unconscious rejection—and the Ahzurdan phasma's jealousy. Danny recovered some small confidence in his skills, though he was frustratingly unable to move among the realities, his half-sire clutched that ability to his insubstantial chest and wouldn't let Danny near it. Danny got far enough along to contrive a way of shorting out of the shipbrain, but the god woke up and time ran out on him. The Ahzurdan phasma might harbor illusions of competence; Danny Blue knew better. His hold on fire and wind was deft enough; he could play what games he wanted with the unTalented, but until he could make free with his realities again, put him against a fumble-fingered apprentice and he'd go down smoking. The phasma was right, he could dissolve that cage, he knew that after some tentative exploration, but he couldn't do it without making such a noise that the cage-maker would come running. Annoyed at the waste of his work, no doubt he'd impose a nastier sort of coercion. Best leave things as they were and see what happened.

Be ready, the Ahzurdan phasma said, tension sharpening his gnat's voice. *If there is a challenge, you need to be prepared. Search my memories. Now!*

Danny Blue paid no attention to his half-sire's agitation; there simply wasn't time to acquire skills he didn't already have. He floated his fingertips across the stone, seeking to read the status of the sorceror who made it, and tasted the air around him to pick up ghost images of past events in this unlovely chamber, a psychometric survey that even the Daniel phasma believed in since it mimicked the activity of electronic sniffers.

From the air he got: Images of dark-robed men, of menacing faces looming over him. A fog of fear and cringing, rage, outrage and helplessness swirling about him. Voices booming words that never quite took specific shape. A sense of death and desolation and dissolution. Trials without defense where the verdict was given before the questions were asked.

From the cage, the c'vee mir, he got: Arrogance and malevolence, prissiness and paranoia. And a name. Braspa Pawbool.

There was a burst of insect laughter from the Ahzurdan phasma. *Poo Boo,* he squealed. *Poo the Boob, he couldn't scratch his way out of a spiderweb.* A moment's silence; Danny waited. *But he can talk, Danny, oh can he talk, I remember once he talked me into . . . mmh, never mind that. I can see how he tickled the Brin Ystaffel into hiring him. He's a water man, Danny. Fire makes him piss his pants. If it comes to a crunch, throw some salamandri at him and see if we can snap out of here before Arfon interferes.*

"I can't touch the realities, you forgot? Even if I could, we're inside this pentacle; I throw a salamander, it bounces back on me and whoosh, we're all gone."

The Ahzurdan phasma refused to hear what he didn't want to know. He ignored the first part of the statement. *A pentacle of Poo's making. Cobwebs. Breathe on it and it breaks.*

Danny Blue worked his body around until he was lying on his stomach. He reached through the cage, edged his fingertips to the nearest of the glimmering lines.

A nip, pain in his hand, like putting his finger in a live socket—the image slipped in from the Daniel phasma who was watching with cool skepticism. It wasn't as bad as his memories forecasted. He touched it again, let the pain flow round him and slip away without bite or afterbite. He tasted it, savored the flavors, got to know it, learned the WORD to dismiss it, translated that WORD into his own framework. He drew his hand back. "Yes," he said aloud. "One-two and it's through."

Yessss.

The satisfied vibrato tickled through Danny, made him smile. He crossed his arms, dropped his head onto his forearm and settled himself to wait for events to unfold. After half an hour when nothing happened, nothing changed, he slept.

11

There was a portentous knocking, the butt of a staff pounding on the wood of the dais with the five throne-chairs. The chairs were filled now with black hooded figures, velvet halfmasks reinforcing the shadows from the hoods; the men wore heavy jeweled chains with jeweled pendants that caught what light there was and broke it into particolored glitters, they wore silks and velvets subtly draping about their hidden forms, richly tactile, magnificently sweet to the eye. A sixth man stood with staff in hand, robed and hooded too, but more simply, with plainer stuffs and a plainer chain. The six of them had slipped in while Danny Blue dozed and arranged themselves in dignified poses; now they waited for the drama to begin, waited in a silence as portentous, as theatrical, as essentially hollow as that knocking—a reaction Danny shared with the Daniel phasma who saw it was the sort of idiocy that disgusted him in the by-the-book, spit-and-polish conformity he had to put up with whenever he shipped on carriers like the Golden Lines. Danny Blue sat up warily, folded his legs and waited. What he saw was far tawdrier than the images he'd evoked; the phantom impressions of past trials were realer than the reality. The Ahzurdan phasma was annoyed with Danny and Daniel both and irritated by the figures in the chairs. In the days before he got tangled in the plots swirling about the Drinker of Souls, he cultivated such men and found a validation in their acceptance; they acknowledged his power as he paid homage to theirs, tacitly, placidly, both sides blessed by the certainty of their superiority. But the recognition, the certainty were missing now and he resented that. They should have known. If they were the real powers of Dirge Arsuid, they should have seen the power he had, or rather, the power possessed by the body he dwelt in. They should have given Danny the honor he deserved even if he was too stupid to demand it.

"I am the Prenn Ysran of Dirge Arsuid." The voice echoed hollowly; it took a moment for Danny to identify who spoke; it was the man in the center seat. If Prenn Ysran

meant what he thought, this was the high judge of all
Arsuid. He wasn't happy with the identification; it told him
he was in more trouble than he liked to think about. The
man spoke again, "State your name, felon."

Danny thought that over before he answered; Daniel
prodded him to demand an explanation; Ahzurdan wanted
him to be meekly courteous. "My name is Lazul," he said.
"Why am I here?"

"You lie. Your name is Ahzurdan."

"No. Ahzurdan is dead."

"You are a sorceror. You are addicted to dreamdust and
come seeking it here. The sale of dreamdust is illegal here.
To attempt to buy it is to break the laws of Dirge Arsuid."

"I am who I say I am. If I'm a sorceror, that's my
business, unless you passed a law against them. Have you?
Not only am I not addicted to the dust, I'd put a knife
through anyone who tried to force it on me. Who says I
court such idiocy? Who says I importuned him to sell me
anything? Bring him. Show him to me so I can call him the
liar he is."

"The deed is not required, only the intent."

"Intent? You reading people's hearts now?"

"It is not necessary. You are here. Your habits are known.
You are guilty. Do you repent?"

"How can I repent what I've neither done nor thought?
How can I repent another man's sins?"

"He is contumaceous, brothers; he is intent on his illegal
purposes. I say there is no point to further deliberation.
How say you?"

"Guilty," intoned the figure to the far left. "Guilty."
"Guilty." "Guilty." The lesser judges condemned him in
whispers, squeaks and muted bellows.

"So say I. D'wab-ser, dissolve the cage and bring the man
before us."

Danny Blue prepared himself, ready to move when he felt
the eventflow shift. He watched the cowled sorceror change
his grip on his staff, saw the silver lines inlaid in the wood
come to life, running like moonwater from tip to butt. He
saw a shifting of shadow under the hood as the man's lips
moved, though he couldn't hear words. The cage melted
away around him. He stood up.

Free hand twisting through complex, awkward gestures,
D'wab-ser Braspa Pawbool came down the stairs.

Danny waited, ready to counter if he could figure out

how, waited for the moment when the man broke through the pentacle, expecting the attack then. Ready to attack the stone beneath Pawbool, the air around him, ready. . . .

No attack.

Braspa Pawbool simply reached across the lines, cancelling them. "Come," he said. "Don't be foolish. Come." He took hold of Danny's arm near the wrist, tugged at him. "Face your sentencing like a man not a child."

Startled, Danny took a step toward him. Pawbool's grip shifted. The Ahzurdan phasma screamed, *Pull away, pull . . .*

He was too late. Danny Blue felt the pricks from the twin fangs of the ring on Pawbool's center finger. His wrist burned. He started to jerk his arm away, Pawbool tapped the point of his shoulder with the staff; his arm went limp. "What . . . what are you . . ."

"Nothing to worry you. It's just to keep you quiet. Come with me."

Pawbool took his hand away. The fangs withdrew, the burning cooled until Danny couldn't feel it. Slowly, slowly the strength began returning to his arm. He followed Pawbool. The Sorceror stopped him with a touch of the staff when he was in front of the Prenn Ysran. Danny stood there rubbing at his wrist; he could feel the drug beginning to work in him. A pleasant euphoria spread through his body; he felt lethargic, didn't want to move or think.

The Prenn Ysran waited until Braspa Pawbool climbed the stairs and resumed his place beside the last chair on the right, then he leaned forward until his nose and chin were visible as the light from one of the three lamps edged under his cowl. "The D'wab-ser lied," he said. "You have your death inside you, but you need not die." He spoke quickly, nervously; his heavily gloved hands tightened on the arms of his chair. "There is a way of atoning for your guilt, felon. There is an antidote. You can earn it. It will save you if you get it within the next four months. After that you die." He cleared his throat, his hood swayed as he turned his head slightly side to side as if he watched for something he feared to see. "What say you?"

"What do I have to do?"

"Say the words, felon. Say you accept the task." Again that twitch of his head, the shimmy of the hood.

Danny thought it over; he didn't like anything about this business, he also didn't have much choice. "If I can do it, I accept the task."

There was an odd creaking sound, a plopping like bubbles breaking in hot mush. Startled, Danny looked around.

A large head had pushed up through the stone, dark and shifty, quivering as if it were sculpted from gelatinous mud; on hair like seagrass it wore dripping, leathery leaves in a limp off-center wreath. Large dull eyes stared at them all, passing along the line of judges, dropping, stopping at Danny Blue. They fixed on him, gray and filmy fisheyes.

Danny Blue began to understand more of this. The god was behind what was happening. Arfon. Dwalluparfon. Mixed up somehow with the Chained God and his convoluted plots. The Daniel phasma sniggered. *Traded to a bush league, that's you, old Dan. Traded like a broke-down offwing.*

Be quiet, Danny snarled at his half-sire, *I need to pay attention here.*

The Prenn Ysran settled back in his chair, his relief palpable. "There is in the city Hennkensikee one of the Great talismans, Klukesharna. You are a sorceror, you must know of Klukesharna."

"Sorceror or not, I know of Klukesharna."

"Do you know what it looks like?"

"It's star-iron, shaped like a key about the length of my palm."

"Good. Bring us Klukesharna and we will give you the antidote."

"In four months? Impossible."

"We will underwrite your expenses and provide useful companions."

"Why me? The Peroraglassi passes through Lake Patinkaya; if his Riverine Sanctity over there wants the talisman, why doesn't he reach out and take it?"

"It is not for us to question the tasks the Great One sets us, felon; even more is it unseemly for you to intrude yourself."

"Hmh! Fancy language for blackmailers."

"Watch your tongue, felon, or your back will suffer for your insolence."

"Oh really?"

"We can find another easily enough."

"That I believe. However. . . ." He yawned, patted the yawn, hooked thumbs into loops on his vest. "Dead is not what I want out of life, so let's talk about this underwriting business. I need a reason to visit Hennkensikee. What do you suggest?"

The Prenn Ysran stood. "This is nothing to do with the Ystaffel. Make your arrangements with the D'wab-ser; he has our authority to proceed." He walked along the dais, skimming past the knees of the sitting judges and vanished behind an ancient dark arras that shifted slowly in the many drafts wandering about the chamber; after he was gone, Danny Blue deciphered the image embroidered there, it was a repeat of the Head silently watching the business, the river god protruding from the floor. Silently the other four judges rose and marched out, leaving Braspa Pawbool alone with the prisoner and the god.

Pawbool settled himself into the end chair. "Well, Ahzurdan, you've changed the furnishings somewhat, but you smell the same."

"Ahzurdan's dead," Danny murmured; in his head the Ahzurdan phasma gibbered a denial, but he ignored that. "Call me Lazul."

Pawbool laid his staff across his knees. "The dreamdust must have rotted your brain, you were easier than a first year apprentice, not a ward in sight. Makes me wonder if we were right involving you in this business. Well, what's done is done. Your question. It's the end of the trading season; the Silk Road is shut down though there's no snow in the passes yet, which is odd, there should be some by now, the last caravans left for the east a couple weeks ago. What that's got to do with this is this: every year when the season closes, the Lewinkob Spinners get rid of the ends and bolts that didn't sell. They cut the selvage off so the Hennkensikee sigil is gone and reduce the price to something like a third of what it would have been. What happens is small-time traders come in from everywhere to hunt through the leavings and get what they can. Even without the name, Lewinkob silks bring big money. You play things right, the Wokolinka's Amazons will think you're just another trader."

"I know as much about silks as you do about fire, Poo Boo."

"There you come, sneaking out, Firenose. Say your greets to the real world." Pawbool ran his fingertips delicately along his staff. "We know how ignorant you are, Little Zhuri. We have provided. Of your three companions, two know as much about silks as any specialist would. One steals them, the other wears them."

"A thief and a. . . ."

"Courtesan."

"And the other?"

"Thief and assassin, you get two for one with her. Oh, you needn't be worried about their commitment to the enterprise; the basis of their loyalty is much the same as yours."

"I see."

"I'm sure you do."

"Right. If you want this thing to work, I'll need a few items. An up-to-date map of the city. I presume you know where the talisman is housed, so lay out for me whatever information you have about that, a floor plan of the structure, if you can come up with one that's reasonably accurate, a description of how the thing is guarded—and warded. I assume it's powerfully warded and our silent friend back there would have got his fingers singed if he tried this on his own. I need what you know about the local god and what's his or her attributes." He paused a moment, thought a question at the Ahzurdan phasma, got back the equivalent of a shrug. "I've never been there and I haven't bothered to learn the basics. Too busy with more immediate concerns. I need to know them now."

Pawbool glanced at the god, then nodded. "Everything we have will be ready for you before the day's out."

"Good. I need to meet with and assess these aides you've roped in for me; any plan I make has to include their weak points and strengths. I'll go there by river, but I want strong, fast horses waiting for me and the others when we leave Hennkensikee. If things go well, we'll get out without raising a stir, but it's stupid to count on that. You know as well as I do, if anything can go wrong, it will. Set up relays along the river so we can change mounts and come straight through to Arsuid without stopping to rest."

"Travel both ways by river. We can guarantee protection as long as you're on water."

"Lovely. It's my skin, Poo. I know what I can do, I'm not all that sure of your um protection. It'd be so very easy to take that talisman off me and leave me to the tender mercies of the Wokolinka. If you want me to do this, set up the relays."

"You don't do it, you die. Painfully."

"Without the relays, I'm even more apt to die. Painfully."

There was a bubbling grunt from the god. Danny stiffened, then relaxed as he recognized the sound. Arfon was laughing. "Do it," the god said; his voice was like mud flowing, liquid and thick. "I like this one's wits; he doesn't cringe like you worms and he uses his head. I like him."

Pawbool's hands tightened on the staff; he waited until he was sure the god had finished, then his hood jerked as he nodded. "Agreed," he said to Danny, carefully not speaking to the god. "I will arrange for the relays come morning. What else?"

"If the three you've planted on me look like everyone else in this city, they'll need less conspicuous clothing. I won't travel with things out of some dye-master's nightmare. I'll need more gear myself; set me up as a Phrasi on the tawdry side, a small trader just barely making it. And I'll need enough coin to be convincing. Over and above what you found on me, which I'll want back. I'm supposed to be going there to buy, not shoplift. Everyone's heard that much about Hennkensikee; they don't let deadbeats through the gates."

"That has already been arranged. We will send you properly equipped."

"Nice of you. I'd better not go back to the Estron Coor, I don't want rumors to get out connecting me to anything Arsuider, especially your lot. I presume you've thought of that and set up quarters for me here, wherever this is."

"Yes."

"You left my gear in my room?"

"Yes."

"Transfer it. I'm tired and hungry and filthy. I want food and a bath, then I want to see the three I'm supposed to be working with."

"Snipsnap, Firenose, is that all? Shall I send along some dreamdust too?"

"Stuff it up your own nose."

"Hostile, aren't you."

Danny Blue looked over his shoulder. The god was gone. He snorted, it took that to give Poo Boo some stiffening in his spine. He stretched, rubbed at the back of his neck. "How much more time we going to waste playing one-up games?"

Braspa Pawbool stood. The light flared in the silver inlay of his staff as he fashioned a small amber will-o which drifted over to Danny and hung before his face. "Follow the light, Firenose. I'll follow you."

12

"Felsrawg Lawdrawn." The small wiry woman in boy's

tights and tunic glanced at him, went with quick nervous
steps about the room, whipping back draperies, opening
doors to see what lay behind them, stopping to touch the
bars on the window. She was a narrow sword of a woman,
tensile and darting, filled with energy, with anger at the
world; she looked like she'd give off sparks if you touched
her. When she finished her inspection, she perched on a
small backless chair, hands resting lightly on her thighs,
her sleeves loose about her wrists, the knives she wore on her
forearms not visible but ready if she needed them. Her tights
were black and white, the stripes spiraling about her legs
down to soft boots of dark crimson. There was a matching
glove on her left hand; the nails of her right hand were
painted green. Her tunic was divided into squares, black,
red and white in a dizzying spiral; she wore a loinskirt of
leather strips dyed a bright green, studded with black iron
and silver. Her hair was black with silver stripes; it was
pulled tightly up and bound at the crown with a green
thong, the fall coiled into black and silver corkscrews that
trembled past her shoulders. She had small ears that sat
tight against her head pierced along the rim; she wore six
black studs on the left side, six silver studs on the right. She
had a lean and angular face, a wide mouth whose corners
turned down. She was young, not more than twenty, and
she could have been pretty if she'd wanted that, but she
refused it with every breath she took. "Who're you?" she
said; her voice was hoarse like an old singer's might be after
fifty years in cabarets.

"Lazul."

'That doesn't tell me a whole helluva lot."

"I doubt you need telling much, being the one that Poo
the Boob brought in to put a knife in me and take the
talisman soon as we get clear of the city."

"At least you're not a fathead like him."

"There's only one of him, gods be blessed for that. He
said you're a thief. How good are you?"

"You mean if I got caught, I couldn't be worth much."
Her face was taut with an anger only just under control.
"Him. He set his thumb on me. Arfon." She shrugged. "I
was a whore when I was eight, killed my pimp when I was
ten and got rid of his ghost before it squealed." She laughed
when he raised his brows, mildly surprised that she would
tell him something like that. "I'd just say you lie and they'd
believe me, I'm Arsuider, you're outsider. Think about it,

toop." Another shrug. "Since then my life's been mine, I
have not been cheated or caught. I trust myself and no one
else. I am good, Lazul. It took a god to get me. And I don't
know shit about this business, except that blinbaw Pawbool
told me I was to do what you said and when you got what
they wanted, to get it off you and bring it to him."

"Wait till the others get here, I don't want to go through
this more than once."

"Others? What others?"

"Two."

She got to her feet, began pacing about the room; there
was too much fury in her to let her rest a moment.

13

"Simms Nadaw." The second thief had a spiky thatch of
coppery hair and the translucent too-pallid skin some red-
heads were cursed with; the pink/purple flush of his face
clashed awkwardly with that orange/red hair. His tunic and
tights were a mix of reds and pinkish oranges in assorted
plaids and stripes, his glove and boots were a bright brown
of surpassing awfulness. He was such a disaster, so wrong,
you looked away from him in embarrassment, remembering
the ensemble while you forgot his face.

Amber eyes sleepy under fat eyelids, he produced an
amiable grin, nodded without grace in answer to Danny's
greeting and ambled over to sit in the single armchair.

Felsrawg stopped in front of him. "You, huh?"

Simms blinked at her. "Me, yeh."

She examined his outfit, shuddered. "I've seen you in
bad, but that's the worst."

He grinned again, his eyes almost disappearing into the
crease between upper and lower lids; he seemed barely
intelligent enough to know which end of a shovel to dig
with. "I try. Arfon?"

She shuddered again. "Yeh. You?"

"You think the 'staffel got me?" He had a light tenor
voice that made sleepy laughter of the words.

"No."

"Sh'd hope not."

She swung round to face Danny Blue who was watching
this, bland-faced but amused, planted her fists on her hips.
"Well?"

"There's one to come yet."

"Who?"

"I don't know. She's supposed to be a courtesan of some kind. Knows silk. Poo the Boob said one of you knows silk. Which?"

She jerked a thumb at Simms. "You wouldn't think it to look at him, would you."

Danny folded his arms, leaned against the wall. "Oh, I think so; he's a very clever man, isn't he."

"So are you, if you see that." She stood stone-still for a moment, her eyes narrowed, her head thrusting forward; she looked like a poison lizard poised to strike. Then she relaxed and perched on the edge of the backless chair where she'd been sitting before. "Maybe we'll get out of this alive."

14

"Trithil Esmoon." She came through the door with a sussurous of whisper silks. Despite the play she made at concealment, a narrow serpent mask across her eyes, she was immediately and astonishingly beautiful. Despite that mask, she was not Arsuider. No Arsuider had eyes of that deep smoky blue or hair fine and white as spidersilk; it was combed back and to one side, flowing in long shimmering waves to her waist. Her skin was cream velvet, delicately pink about the cheekbones. Her wrists were pencil thin, her hands small and tapering. She wore a simple robe that slanted from her shoulders to a fullness about her feet; it was made of layer on layer of transparent blue silks that shifted across each other with every movement, every breath she took; her body was a hint of darker blue beneath them, slender with round full breasts and a tiny waist; the sleeves were tubes, the upper edge open and falling away in swags from silver tacks, gathered at the wrists into silver bracelets. She wore silver and sapphire earrings as long and heavy as a Panday shipmaster's ear dangle and on her ungloved hand had silver and sapphire rings on every finger plus her thumb; most of the sapphires were faceted and glittered bluely when she moved her hand, but the thumb ring was cabuchon cut, a mounded oval, a star in its heart. Her slippers and glove were silver, her perfume subtle as the shift of blues in her robe. She smiled at Danny Blue, held out her gloved hand, the glove being a guarantee the hand was safe to take.

Since she seemed to expect it, Danny took the hand, bowed over it. She was a piece all right, artificial as a wax flower, advertising her pliancy to his needs with every move, every twitch of an eyelash. He thought he disliked her pretentions and was put off by her profession. Half-sire Daniel disapproved of prostitution; besides, he'd never needed to buy women. They liked him. He drifted in and out of their lives as easily as he drifted in and out of his jobs. Half-sire Ahzurdan was ambivalent about women at the best of times, which these most decidedly weren't; his sex life was mostly imaginary, taking place in the heroic fantasies he experienced during his dust orgies.

Then Trithil's perfume hit Danny and he wasn't so sure what he thought of her.

He straightened, led her to the bed and lent his arm as she sank gracefully onto the quilts and sat there with her little hands laced together, half-hidden in the folds of her draperies. When he turned, Felsrawg was looking as if she'd been carved out of hot ice into a personification of indignation and disgust. Simms screwed up his face and panted like a dog, tongue lolling, then relapsed to idiot.

Danny Blue went back to leaning against the wall; he crossed his arms and scowled at two-thirds of his strike force. "You're a pair, you are. Insolent, impudent and smarter than any three like me, right?" He spoke with weary impatience and a deep-down anger he wasn't about to surface, not now anyway. "Insubordinate because you earned it, right? Individualists who aren't about to take orders from me or anyone else, right?" He yawned. "I know you, see? I've been you. Nothing you can show me I haven't done already and done better. I don't give a handful of hot shit for any of your games. It comes down to this, my friends, we've got four months to do a job. We bring it off or we die. I'm not going to waste time tickling your vanities. Either you help or you hinder. If you hinder, you're out. Now or later." He moved his eyes from Felsrawg to Simms to Trithil, then fixed on Simms. "What I say now, you better believe. I don't need any of you. You're in this because the ones working this scam figure you can be useful. And you're here because they don't trust me farther than they can spit, they figure poison isn't enough of a hold on me. Well, I intend to survive. I'm good at surviving. Just remember that."

Felsrawg simmered; Simms looks stupider; Trithil smiled slowly and fixed her blue blue eyes on him as if she couldn't bear to look away.

"Right, I can see how impressed you are. Did they tell you what we're going after?"

Simms rubbed a long spatulate thumb over his wrist, a gesture Danny recognized; he'd been doing the same thing since Pawbool injected the poison into him. "They say come here." He sounded as if he were speaking through a yawn, letting the words fall out of his mouth. "They say back up him I found here any way I c'd. They say when he gets sa thing, steal it an' bring it back. Nobody bother sayin' what IT is."

Felsrawg stirred. She glanced at Simms, very unhappy at his singsong discourse. Which told Danny more than words would about the man and his talents. "Same with me," she said finally. "I told you that, remember? And you said something about a talisman."

Danny turned to Trithil, raised his brows. She didn't have anything to contribute but the graceful lift and fall of her breasts. He looked hastily away, ignored Felsrawg's muttered insults. "We're going to Hennkensikee," he said. "We're going to steal Klukesharna."

"Broont! We're dead." A flicker of Felsrawg's hands and she was holding twin stilettos, the blades needle-fine, hardly longer than her middle finger and coated with a dark gummy substance. "I swear, before I'm dead, they are."

Simms sat placid as a milk pudding with cinnamon trim. "Sorceror?"

"Not the one they think I am, but yes, a sorceror."

"Not a prime."

"Too true. Poo the Boob caught me hopping, it's not something I'm proud of, but there it is." He glanced down at the scabbed pinpricks on his wrist, grimaced. "I'm not asleep now. For what that's worth. Make up your minds, the three of you. In or out?"

Simms' eyes dropped completely shut. "In," he said. "Long as you stay awake."

"In." It was a liquid murmur, promise of delight, all that in one tiny syllable. Trithil reached up, smoothed the hair back from her face, her rings glittering.

"In," Felsrawg said, biting off the tail of the word as if she'd like to bite something else. She looked down at the knives, slipped them back into their sheaths. "What choice have we got?"

"You got a choice, Felsrawg. Enthusiasm or out."

"In. In! IN!"

"Now that that's done, I need to know what you all do best. I'm a whiz with wards, I can tease the densest knot open without a whisper and throw a knot of my own that only two people I know can undo. But there's bound to be more involved than wards. Poo tells me the Wokolinka uses witches and the local god to run her security. Which is not good news, witches tap into earth forces I can't touch; that means traps. And a god even a local one is always trouble. Which you know as well as me." He tapped a forefinger on the wrist where Pawbool had sunk his ringfangs. "Any of you been to Hennkensikee?"

"Not me." Felsrawg leaned forward, her interest caught at last. "I do locks. All kinds of locks. Walls. I'm good at walls. Blowpipes and sleep powders, nobody's ever sneezed when I puff the powder in. That happens, you know, if you're sloppy. It can embarrass the hell out of you because they wake up." She was sparkling, almost laughing; apparently she'd decided to lay her resentment aside and treat the problem as a challenge. "I know metals, if that helps. And I'd be a lot more useful if I had my keys and files and picks and the rest of my kit. The 'staffel took it away and haven't give it back which seems rather stupid, considering."

"Agreed. I'll have a talk with Poo and see if we can fix that."

Simms yawned, blinked slowly. "Get 'm to gi' me mine too," he murmured. He ruffled his spiky hair, smiled sleepily at Danny. "Like li'l Felsa there, 'm a born and bred Arsuider. N'er stuck my nose outside the place. No point in it. I know silks, yeh, like to know why y' wan' to know that, don' seem connect t' Kluk'shar'. Want me t' brag a bit, 'm the only thief 'round better'n Felsa at ticklin' locks." Another sleepy smile, this time directed toward Felsrawg. "She w'd argue that, but tis true. Got 'nother talent. Talk t' rocks."

"What?"

"Not so dumb as it sounds. I'm a Reader. Rocks chatter like ol' Grannas if you know how to tickle 'em. An' I'm good with ghosts. Be s'prised what they tell you 'bout their folks. Just 'bout all ghosts hangin' round thick 'nough to talk got a grudge. Ol' grandfa once take me right to a abdit full of pretties. Bein' lazy, I'm a patient man, I like to know all I can find out 'bout a place 'fore I go in. I'm good at piecin' too. Bit here, bit there, you know. Drawin' plans. That sorta thing." He stopped talking, having said all he meant to say.

"I know Hennkensikee," Trithil said quietly.

Danny Blue turned to her, startled. She'd shut off the hithery and lost her gloss. She was still beautiful, that was in the bone, but she'd added at least ten years and subtracted most of the life from face and eyes.

"I know grades and prices," she said. "Pawbool said you wanted in as a trader, I can handle that for you. And I can get information for you." There was an unreadable look in her eyes, animal eyes with nothing back of them, now that he paid more notice to them. "Man or woman, both find me pleasing. And if that fails, I have certain potions that loosen tongues or do other things you might find useful." She didn't so much stop speaking as let words drift away from her.

Danny Blue frowned, wondering about her. His half-sires stirred in him, equally uneasy.

Maybe she's on something and it just let her down, the Daniel phasma muttered. *How much can you trust what she's telling you?*

I don't like her, the Ahzurdan phasma said. *I don't trust her. I don't think she's what she seems. Maybe she's a demon of some kind. I don't smell demon on her, but there's something. . . .*

Can you watch her?

Sense of shrugging. The Ahzurdan phasma brooded a moment. *If you watch her, we see her. Otherwise not.*

Well, do what you can. I have to get on with this. Aloud, he said, "Just a few things for now. We can talk more on the way there. Are there many Arsuiders in Hennkensikee?"

After waiting a moment for the others to answer, Trithil said, "No."

"Why? There has to be trade moving along the river."

"Not as much as you might think. The Lewinkob are suspicious of the South. They prefer to deal with the caravans that come in from the east." She spoke in a marshmallow monotone that he had to strain to hear; she was passive, almost inert, giving out information like a robot. "Most of the Hennkensikee silk leaves that way, that's why it's called the Silk Road." She glanced briefly at him, looked down again, eyes fixed on the toes of her silver slippers. "They are more than suspicious really, they hate the South; they call the disputed land between the two domains the Bloody Fields. There have been raids across the Bloody Fields since before the cities were. And wars. Seven bloody wars,

Dirgeland against the Tribes. No. Arsuiders are not welcome in Hennkensikee."

"Would the local noses be able to sniff them out?" He waved a hand at Felsrawg and Simms. "If we stuffed them into normal clothes."

"Probably not, as long as they use the kevrynyel tradespeech even in private and forget they know the Dirgefoth." She looked distantly at the others. "Trade is blood in Hennkensikee. Blood can blind."

Danny pulled his hand across his mouth. "I can't hear an accent in your kevrynyel, I can in theirs." He nodded at Felsrawg and Simms. "Heavy. What about that?"

"Traders come from everywhere to buy the silks, especially this time of year. They all speak the kevrynyel. They all have accents. One accent merges with the others."

"How much of a background will we need? What I mean is, how many questions are we going to have to answer?"

"None or too many."

"I see. The personas have to be fleshed before we come near the city."

"Yes."

"Hmm. Simms, ever heard of a place called Croaldhu?"

"Neh."

"Island off the east coast, about twelve days sail from Silili. You know Silili?"

"Who don'?"

"Let's do this. Your family left Croaldhu for reasons of their own and your grandfa or gre'grandfa, something like that, set up as merchant in Silili, hmm . . . how old are you?"

"Chwart."

"I take it that means old enough."

Simms grinned sleepily at him.

"All right. We'll say you're a third son, rambling about looking up new possibilities for the family business. You signed on with me because I said I'd get you into Hennkensikee. That's the heart of it; we can set the details later. Any questions? objections? whatever?"

"Why Croaldhu?"

"You have the look. Or would in what the rest of the world calls clothes. I'm half-Phrasi by birth, shouldn't be any problem with that. Trithil?"

"No."

"Felsrawg?"

"Tell me, o master, what's you got for li'l me?"

"Got any preferences?"

She shrugged, slipped a throwing knife from her boot and began flipping it and catching it.

He watched it loop lazily through the air, nodded. "Know anything about the Matamulli?"

She caught the knife, held it, looked at him from narrowed eyes. "That a joke?"

"Neh, assassin. They're Southrons; they claim the Mulimawey Mountains beyond M'darj." He rubbed at his nose, inspected her. "You could pass with some rearrangement here and there." She didn't want any part of that, he could feel her resisting. "The men are the homebodies; they farm, care for the herds. The women hunt and trap and do most of the trading. Very independent lot they are, too." Felsrawg flipped the knife again, caught it, flipped it. There was time left and Danny was willing to spend it persuading her; if time ran out and she was still fighting him, he'd cut her loose; it didn't matter how loud Poo yelled. "What's useful for us is this, before they settle down with a husband or two, younger daughters generally go outland to make a dowry for themselves since they don't have land." He pointed at the knife. "They carry half a dozen of those and can split a mosquito at thirty paces."

"That all?"

"All for now. Make up your mind."

"Enthusiasm or out?"

"Yep. Ground rules."

"I hear you. Just call me Matti. When do we go?"

"If Poo doesn't drag his feet, by the end of the week." He ran his hand through his hair. "Wait here, the three of you, if you don't mind; Poo sent over some charts, I'd like to get your ideas on them."

THE REBIRTHING: PHASE TWO
The stonebearers are pointed toward the stones

I: BRANN/JARIL

> The Cavern was empty so they
> went searching
> for Yaril in the only place they
> knew to look:
> Dil Jorpashil

1

"All right," Brann said calmly, using voice and body to quiet her changer son. "So Yaro is gone. She didn't just walk out?"

"No." Jaril stopped shuddering as Brann stroked his hair and fed him snippets of energy. "No, if she was free enough to walk, she'd be here, waiting for me."

"That being so?"

He lay still, his eyes closed. After a minute, he said, "That being so, whoever set the trap came and got her."

"Yes. When you feel up to it, Jay, go back and see if he left some traces, anything to tell us who to look for. If we're lucky, he isn't finished with this, he's after you too. And me."

"You?" Jaril pulled away from her, stared at her, startled.

"Think about it. Yaro's either food or part of a bigger trap. Which would you prefer?"

Jaril started convulsing; in minutes the shudders were waves of dissolution passing along his body, threatening to tear him into gobbets of mindless energy.

Brann snatched a burning billet from the fire and slammed it into and through him, feeding fire to him to strengthen and distract him; she caught up another and repeated what she'd done. Then she seized hold of him and began flooding him with energy, draining herself to help him stabilize.

He broke away, appalled at what he was doing. When he

141

was steady enough, he crawled into the fire and crouched there. "Brann?"

"No no, luv, I'm all right. For awhile anyway. You?"

"Sorry, Bramble. I didn't mean to. . . ."

"I know, Jay. Don't fuss, my fault, I shouldn't have been so abrupt."

"Bramble. . . ."

"Yes?"

"If anything happens to Yaro, I will DIE. I can't BE the only Surraht here."

Brann nodded. "I know." She got heavily to her feet, collected several scattered billets and piled them on the fire around Jaril. She gathered her blankets, folded one into a square and sat cross-legged on it, wrapped the other around her shoulders. "You and Yaro have always avoided talking about your people. I need to know more about you, Jay, so I can read this trap. Maybe send you home. You and Yaro." She grimaced. "I'll miss you, both of you."

Jaril fluttered a hand at her, looked away. "Bramble. . . ."

"I know. We've been together a long time. It's hard, mff." She managed a fragment of a laugh. "Talking Slya into sending you home isn't going to be the easiest thing I've ever done. You think you could crawl out of that fire long enough to set some water to boil? A little tea would be a help."

Jaril nodded. His limbs glowing red-gold like the flames, he cooled one hand enough to pour water from the skin into a pot, then went back to the fire and sat holding the pot on his thighs until the water boiled. He scolded Brann back to her blankets when she started to get up, made the tea and took a mugful to her. He retreated to the fire and watched as she sipped. "If we talked, it meant we had to remember. It's not easy, Bramble. Not even with you."

Brann sipped at the tea and waited; she said nothing, it was up to Jaril now, he had to decide what he was going to tell her.

"It wasn't so bad when we were aetas, that's uh children who aren't babies any more. Aetas are supposed to wander around, usually two or three or maybe four together. When they're twins like Yaro and me, they generally go in twos. That's how Slya caught us, we were off by ourselves, poking into a stuvtiggor nest. Stuvtiggors eat Surrahts, they pick on afas, that's babies, and agaxes, that's adults. Aetas are too fast and too tough for them. It's one of the things we do

when we're aetas. Eat stuvtiggors. They're uh like ants, sort
of, their uh essence is like ours, not yours, Bramble; they
taste good, like um those fried oysters you pig on sometimes. Not really, I don't know, it's the same idea. Close
enough. They can do what we did when we made that horse
for you, remember? They can merge to make one curst big
stuv clot. If they catch one alone, it's good-bye Surraht.
That's why, when you said Yaro might end up food. . . ."
He started to shudder again, stopped himself. "We lost a
. . . I suppose you'd call her a sire-side cousin . . . we got to
her late, we saw the stuv clot eating her . . . agh! We
scragged it, ate. . . ."

He stopped talking, flowed briefly into his globe form,
sucking in great gulps of heat energy, almost killing the fire
before he changed back. "We were aetas when Slya snatched
us. She changed us back to afas, sort of, so we had to have
you feed us, Bramble, so we had to change you, so she
could use you and us. You know all that. Anyway, the thing
is, we're not aetas any more, Yaril and me. We're aulis. All
that godfire, it kicked us all the way past . . . uh . . . it's a
kind of part-puberty. We aren't fertile yet, that happens
later, but we uh make out like minks. Or we would if there
were other aulis around. Not a sister . . . or a brother . . .
we can't . . . uh . . . it doesn't work. . . . Ahh! gods, Bramble, sometimes in the past year or so, Yaro and me both, we
felt like we were going to go nova if we didn't get somewhere there were more aulis than just us. We were working
up to ask you if you'd please please figure a way to . . . it's
more than uh sex, Bramble. Aulis make bonds. Communi-
ties. Like families here. Sort of. It's more complicated. We
NEED to do that or we go uh rogue. Round the bend.
Insane. We get worse than stuvtiggors. We eat . . . uh . . .
it's bad. Well, you get the idea." He cupped his hand about
a wisp of flame, let his flesh go translucent, showing shadows of bones that weren't really there. "This might be more
important, Bramble. When we were aetas, we were uh
simpler and uh tougher. You know how fast we came back
after that webfoot shaman stoned us. We can't do that now,
it takes time for us to uh unfold, it takes more uh force to
bring us back and the longer we're down, the harder it is
to come back. You don't want to count on Yaro being able to
help us, well, fight or run, even if we can bring her all the
way back from stone."

"And I was complaining about being bored." Brann rubbed

her fingers across the hollow at her temple. "I do want you
to look around more carefully down there, Jay; keep in
mind what we decided about Jorpashil, see if you can find
anything to support or cancel that."

Jaril deformed, his version of a yawn. He blinked sleepily
at her over the tongues of fire curling about his legs. "You
brought some wine, didn't you, Bramble?"

"I brought some wine. I'll have some hot for you when
you get back."

"Holding my nose to it, huh?" He smiled, that sudden
flash-grin that could twist her heart and remind her that he
and Yaril were the only children she'd ever have. Then he
shifted to the firesphere and went darting off.

She looked after him until even the faint glow on the
walls went dark. First Maksim splits, now the children. No,
that's the trouble, they aren't children any more. She thought
about the Arth Slya that existed when she was a child and
mourned for what had been, a long flow through the centuries since the first artisans moved there, teacher/parent passing skills to student/child who taught in his turn, her turn.
My children will be gone beyond my reach after this is over.
If they were dead, at least I'd have their ghosts to comfort
me a while. If they stay here, they're dead or mad. Dead or
mad. I never have a choice, do I? She grimaced. "Tchah!
Brann, oh Brann, you know it's not so bad a world. Stop
glooming. A month ago you were bored out of your skull.
Hmp, Maksim was right, watch out what you ask for, you
might get it."

"Talking to yourself, Bramble?" Jaril dropped into the
fire, wriggled around until he was comfortable. He tossed
her a copper coin. "Tell me what you think."

She rubbed her thumb across the obverse. "I don't know
this writing."

"Sarosj. It says Blessings to Sarimbara the Holy Serpent."

"Ah. A coin from Dil Jorpashil?"

"What they call a dugna. Fifty to a silver takk."

"You're feeling better."

"It was not knowing, Bramble."

"I know. How far is Jorpashil from here?"

"Yaro and me, we flew it, took us five days and part of
the sixth. 'Less we can get you mounted, you'll be walking.
Probably triple that and then some, say twenty days for
you."

She pulled the blankets tighter about her, shivering a little as stray currents of icy air sneaked through crevices in her clothing. "I could use one of Maksi's *call-me*'s. If he was here, he could pop us over in a wink."

"How many he give you?"

"Six."

"I have a feeling you ought to save them for something more important."

"More important than my poor little feet?"

"Brammmmble!"

"Mmh. You've been there, I haven't. What face should I put on?"

"Old and ugly. The base culture is nomad Temueng; an offshoot of one of the grassclans gone to seed. Settled by Lake Pikma a couple thousand years ago. Since then they've mixed with Phrasi, Rukka Nagh, Lewinkob, Gallinasi, and whatever else trickled up the river, but that didn't change how they look at women. You know Temuengs."

"That I do. You going to spend the night in that fire?"

"Oh yes. Any reason why I shouldn't?"

"No, just pop a billet on now and then, hmm?"

"That's me, is it? Automatic fire feeder."

"Where could I find a better?" She grinned and got to her feet, taking the blanket she'd been sitting on with her. She snapped it open, folded it in half and spread it close to the fire. "Wake me sometime round dawn. Might as well get an early start." She wrapped the second blanket around her and stretched out. "Slya bless, this rock is hard." She yawned, rolled onto her side so she was facing the fire and in minutes was deep asleep.

2

Twenty days later a tall gaunt holywoman came striding along the Silk Road, a gnarled staff in one hand, the other swinging loosely at her side. She wore an ancient tattered overrobe and gathered trousers of coarse homespun; her sandals were worn, mended with cord. Her lank gray hair was loosely braided into a single plait that hung down her back, its ragged end bobbing against her buttocks in time with each step. Straggles of gray hair fluttered about a weatherbeaten face. Her mouth was a flat line bracketed by deep furrows curving down from the nostrils of a long bony nose. A big black dog with a blanket-wrapped bundle strapped to his back paced beside her.

She stopped at the edge of the rivermoat, sniffed at the

thick green mat of jeppu plants and the hoard of leaf hoppers that started a frantic piping when she climbed up the levee and stood looking down at them. "So how do we get in?"

The dog looked up at her, then he turned south and trotted away along the levee path. The woman stumped after him.

There was a ferrylanding near the place where the moat branched away from the river, a gong on a gallows at one side. A rag-padded stave hung beside it; the leather loop tied through a hole in one end was hooked over a corroded nail on the gallowpost. A narrow lane was cut through the mat of jeppu, baring a strip of water wide enough to let the flatboat pass. The ferry was across the river, the ferryman nowhere in sight. Brann shaded her eyes with one hand, peered along the river. She could see other landings opposite other gates. At every crossing the ferries were snugged up on the city side. She shrugged, lifted the stave off its nail and beat a tattoo on the gong.

Nothing happened.

She looked at the stave, shrugged again and hung it where she'd found it. "I suppose he'll come when he feels like it."

The black dog yawned, sank onto his stomach. Tongue lolling, head on his forelegs he was a picture of patience.

Brann laughed and dropped beside him. She arranged her legs in the lotus cross and prepared to wait.

Across the river a stumpy figure came from a shed and stood on the bank, hands on hips, staring at her. He wiped the back of his hand across his mouth, spat into the mat of jeppu; his lack of enthusiasm was louder than a shout. He glanced up at the barbican behind him when a guard leaned from an arrowslit and bawled a garbled comment in the sarosj that Brann was only beginning to understand. He spat again, slapped his right hand on his left forearm, then turned his back on the guard. Impatiently he thrust his hands through his thick curly hair, shouted something incomprehensible at the hut and stalked onto the ferry; he stood at he shoreside end, his hands back on his blocky hips, watching as two boys ran from the hut, cast off the mooring lines of a longboat and rowed across the moat.

The boy at the forward oars inspected her with a lively curiosity in his black eyes, but he asked no questions. "To cross, a takk," he said.

"Don't be absurd. Three dugnas is more than enough for that leaky tub."

He smiled, a smile sweet as honey and as guileless. "Our father will beat us, baiar. Forty dugnas."

"He should beat you for your impudence, pisra. Five dugnas and only because you have the smile of an angel, though doubtless the soul of an imp."

"See my sweat, baiar. Consider how far it is. And you have that no doubt dangerous beast with you. Thirty dugnas for the two of you."

"There's not enough sweat on you and your brother both to tempt a gnat. Seven."

"Twenty for you, five for the dog."

"Ten for me, two for the dog."

"Done. Pay me now, baiar." He held up his hand, the palm horny with long labor at the oars.

"Why not. Make room for the dog, hmm?" After Jaril-hound jumped into the boat and was standing with legs braced, Brann got to her feet, thrust two fingers in her belt pouch and fetched out twelve dugnas, counted them coin by coin into the boy's hand. When the count was done, she eased herself stiffly into the longboat and settled on a thwart with Jaril-hound sitting up between her knees. The boys started rowing.

On the other side, she followed Jaril onto the landing and stalked off, paying no attention to the ferryman or his sons, ignoring the guard who yelled at her but was too late to catch her as she passed through the gate and into Dil Jorpashil.

3

The first week Brann spent her nights in doorways with Jaril standing guard over her; she spent her days looking for someplace to go to ground.

She found an empty hovel on the edge of the Kuna Coru, the quarter where the sublegals lived when they weren't in prison or on the street due to a stretch of Tungjii's Buttocks in the Face. The hovel had three small rooms, one of them a kitchen of sorts; the roof leaked and the front door wouldn't close because the leather hinges were cracked, the scraped sheepskin on the windows was cracked or mostly missing, but the walls were thick and solid, the floor was intact and there was a jakes around the corner that she shared with five other households and a branch of the aqueduct brought city water close by; the tap on it was illicit, but no one paid much attention to that. All the discomforts of home and a bouquet of wonderfully varied and powerful stinks besides.

She paid the latch bribe to the local caudhar, hustled some furniture and had the roof and the floor fixed, then moved in. Her neighbors weren't the sort to ask questions and she wasn't talking anyway. Not then.

Once she was settled, she went to one of Sarimbara's shrines and sat there all day, neither eating nor drinking, her legs in a lotus knot, her gaze blank as the stone eyes in Sarimbara's icon. It was the most boring thing she'd done in all her long life, but she kept it up for a week, her presence there as a certified holywoman was cover for Jaril as he flew over the city in his hawkform, probing for any whiff of Yaril or her captor.

On the fifth day of this boredom, when Jaril came in from another sweep, this one as fruitless as the others, Brann was staring gloomily at a pot, waiting for the water to boil so she could drop in a handful of rice and some chopped vegetables. She was almost as bored with her own cooking as she was with the shrine-sitting; it'd been years since she'd bothered about meals, the ten years on Jal Virri, thanks to the cosseting by Housewraith. She looked up as Jaril flung himself into a tottery old chair by an equally dilapidated kitchen table. "You look like I feel."

He drew hardened nails across the table top, scoring grooves in the soft gray wood, making an ugly rasping sound. "This isn't working."

"Nothing?"

"Tell me what I should be looking for. Besides Yaro." He slapped his hand on the table. "Bramble, we have to DO something."

"What?"

"I don't know!" He kicked at the table leg, watched the table shudder. "I don't know. . . ."

"So what have you done, Jay? I see you about three minutes every third day."

Ignoring its creaking protests, he leaned back in the chair, crossed his arms and scowled at the fire in the stovehole. "I figured anyone who could build a trap like that would likely be up around the top, so I started with the hills and the Isun sars. I found a couple sorcerors living in the sars, neither of them anywhere near Maks' class. And a couple dozen mages, but mages don't deal with other realities so it isn't likely they'd know how to make that trap. I marked them anyway; if it comes to that, I can go into them and read as many of them as I can before they start yelling for help." He leaned back farther and put his feet on the table. "I spent a while sniffing about the Dhaniks since they're the ones that really run the city, I snooped on judges, tax farmers, priests in their shrines, caudhars of the districts. Nothing there either. Some Dhaniks hire Talents, but they sure take care not to associate with them. These Talents live in the Kuna Kirar with the lesser merchants. I checked out their hirelists, some witches for farseeing and truthreading, some shamans, mainly as healers, and low-grade mages to set wards about their offices and their sars. I looked at the lot of them; if you added their talents together, they wouldn't have enough gnom to light a fire in a jug of oil. I checked out the doulahars of the High Merchants. Pretty much like the Dhaniks, they hire Talents but don't want them around day to day. Yesterday and today, I did the Great Market. The same mix, mostly. Some street magicians whose hands are quicker than their Talents, especially when they're in your purse, fortunetellers, card and palm readers, dealers in potions and amulets, curse setters and layers, and none of them worth the spit to drown them. I looked at every Slya-cursed one of them. I thought maybe the trapper might be hiding behind a charlatan's mask. Be a good front, if you think of it much. If he is, he's too good for me. I'm whipped, Bramble, down to a frazzle. I don't know what to do now. Maybe I ought to dangle myself for bait."

"Hmm." Brann glanced at the pot, snorted as she saw the water busily boiling; she scooped up the vegetables and the rice, dumped them in, stirred them briskly and put the lid on. "Let's save that for desperation time. I don't think we've got that desperate, not yet. What about around us? The Kuna Cora."

"In this collection of losers?"

"It marches with your idea about the streetsers. If there's ever a place where people don't ask questions. . . ." She lifted the lid, stirred the mix inside some more, then moved the pan off the fire to the sandbed where it would continue cooking at a much lower heat.

"I'm tired, Bramble."

"I know. You ought to try spending your days looking that damn snake in the face. I think I'm going to set up as a wisewoman, Jay; this holy bit is getting us nowhere. Why don't you stay home a day or so, rest."

"You mean be your familiar and friendly sneak and read those women on the sly. That's a rest?"

"They say a change is as good as a rest." She lifted the lid on her supper, replaced it, and walked briskly to the box where she kept her bowls and flatware. She laid a place for herself, hunted out a napkin and dropped it beside the spoon. "Get your feet off the table, huh?"

"They say. Who they? I doubt that they ever did a day's labor."

"Quibble. Feet, Jay. I don't care to stare at your dirty boots while I'm trying to eat. You going to stay?"

"Oh yes."

4

On the first day, one woman came timidly into the warm steamy kitchen and sat at the table. She had a badly infected hand that was turning gangrenous. Brann poured up a cup of bitter herb tea, made her drink it and sat holding her hand, eyes closed; Jaril came padding around the table and sank to his stomach beside the woman, his body pressing against her leg. A few minutes later the woman was looking at a hand with all the swelling gone, the redness gone. The splinter that had caused the trouble was out, the wound was closed over, not fully healed but well on its way. Ignoring the woman's excited incoherent thanks, Brann took a dugna for her efforts and sent her off. Come the next morning, she had scarcely a minute to herself. Established healers made some trouble for her, but she was formidable in herself and handy with that hardwood staff and when a pushy Minder or one of the caudhar's bullyboys got a good look at Jaril-hound's teeth, they turned polite very quickly. The caudhar tried to up his bribe, but she persuaded him that would be uncourteous and unwise.

Sambar Day came round again.

Brann closed down her clinic and went to sit in the shrine; she had a hard time staying awake, she was exhausted and depressed, but she did have a lot to think over. The hunger to Hunt was growing in her; the more she drained herself to help those miserable women, the more urgent that Hunger became. As if there were some sort of measure-stick inside her that tripped a valve when her energy dropped below a certain point. It was a frightening idea. She had to decide if

she believed it and if she did believe it, what she was going
to do about it. I'm tired of this nonsense, she thought, it's
too complicated to think about now. Jaril was restless; nothing he gleaned from the women gave him any new leads, so
he wanted to go wandering the Market as he had when he
was here before with Yaril, hanging himself out for bait,
trusting Brann to make sure he wasn't eaten. Slya Bless, I
don't want him to do that. Let's hope he finds something
today. Sarimbara, if you're bothering to listen, give him a
nudge. Sleepy Sarimbara, you're a good match to my sleepy
god. Slya Fireheart, what a sight she was, stomping through
the Temueng Emperor's Audience Hall like a big red house-
wife chasing down vermin. Sleep, Slya, sleep, we sang,
because when you woke. . . .

> Slya wakes
> mountain quakes
> air thickens
> stone quickens
> ash breath
> bringing death
>
> Slya sleep   sleep Slya
> Yongala dances dreams for you
>
> Slya turns
> stone burns
> red rivers riot around us
> day drops dark upon us
> beasts fly
> men fear
> forests fry
>
> Slya sleep   sleep Slya
> Yongala dances dreams for you

Look at me, idiot woman, singing Slya's lullaby at
Sarimbara's shrine. Impolite, to say the least, impolitic for
sure. Going home . . . got to go home for more than one
reason now. I have to talk Slya into sending the changers
home. Forty Mortal Hells, like Maksim says, what a bit of
work that'll be. Why forty I wonder? Maksi, oh Maks m' luv,
I'm missing you like hell.
Rocking on her buttocks, muttering to herself, her mind
wheeling here and there and finding no ease anywhere,

Brann passed the daylight hours in the shrine. When the sun went down and the lamplighters were out, she went home to her hovel.

5

When Jaril came in from his search, the Wounded Moon was up and swimming through dry clouds; Brann had supper on the table and was just emptying the tea leaves out the back door. He shifted almost before his talons touched the grass mat, stumbled, caught himself and went running to the chest where she kept the wine jars.

She raised her brows, pulled the door shut. "Last is best, eh?" She poured herself a bowl of tea and stood sipping at it as he brought the jar and two glasses to the table. "Mind if I eat first? I've been stuck at the shrine all day. Which is enough in itself to make one dizzy without adding wine on an empty stomach."

"Mind?" His grin split his face in half and he waved the jar perilously close to a lamp. "I'd even kiss old Maksi's toes should he stand here now. Eat, Bramble. Eat the table if you want. . . ." He splashed wine in one of the glasses, gulped it down, then filled both and handed one to her. "First, lift a glass to Tungjii Luck."

"I take it you found her. Or him."

"I found something. Drink, Bramble, drink!"

She laughed, raised her glass high. "Tungjii, love!" she cried and spilled a goodly dollop of wine, laughed again as the libation vanished before it hit the table. The little god wasn't one known for wasting wine. She watched Jaril do the same, then she drank and slammed the glass to the table at the same time he did.

"Tell me." She pulled up the box she was using as a chair, began spooning up the mutton stew she'd left simmering on the stove while she was gone, taking sips of tea between bites, as excited as he was, but a lot hungrier since she didn't feed on sunlight.

"I told you about the stuvtiggor, remember?"

She nodded.

"Well, I started on the west, the side closest to the Market. You know how much I expected to find anything interesting. Well, I didn't, but it was all I had left and I wasn't really panting to lay myself out as bait. All morning there was nothing. About like I expected, there were some thieves and some others with hot talents I couldn't pin, but nothing for

me. A bit past noon, I moved into the highrent section, such
as it is, fences, you know, slave dealers, courtesans, a couple
assassins and so on. I started getting nervous. I didn't know
why, it was a weird shivery feeling. Thing was, it's a long
time since I *sphined* a stuv nest and I'm not aeta any more so
my *sphine* has got the reach of a drunk's breath. And it
wasn't really stuvtiggors, just something that has the same
. . . uh . . . the same I suppose you could say smell. Anyway, I went on searching, trying to ignore the feeling. It got
worse. After a while I knew where it was coming from.
Right at the edge of the Kuna Coru there's this doulahar;
it's sitting on a bit of a hill, tall enough so folk on the top
floor or the roof can look out over the Lake; it's got gardens
and stables and a pond deep enough to swim in. Fancier
even than some of the Isun sars. I don't know who owns it,
some courtesan lives there, I saw her; she might even own
it, though that's hard to believe, given the laws here. She
was out visiting the first time I flew over. I stayed long
enough to see her come back with a string of carriages
bouncing after her. The Grand Isu himself was in the first
one. She's got some client list, that whore. I wonder what
they'd say if they knew she was a demon."

"What!"

"Well, I'm one, aren't I, by the way folks here think."

"Don't be silly." She frowned. "That kind of demon?"

"Is there any other kind?"

"I'm not the one to ask. Go on."

"Well, by the time she showed up, I was pretty sure what
was happening to me. I was putting a shape to things. Them
down in the doulahar, they weren't stuvtiggors, but they
were at least first cousins. Hivesouls. Shoved together to
look like people. And hungry. And dangerous. Stuvtiggors
don't have magic, they just jump you and eat you. This
bunch was something else. Spooky, sheeh! I think even old
Maks when he had BinYAHtii would've taken a look at
them and backed off. I backed off fast. I didn't try to get
close. They didn't know I was there, I'm fairly sure of that.
But they would've if I'd got closer. What I think is, we've
got stuvtiggors in our reality, they've got something like
Surrahts in theirs, so that's how they knew what we were
when we were here. Five of them. Stuv clots, I mean. Six
when the woman got back." He wriggled in his chair. "Feels
funny calling that thing a woman. Gods, she's powerful. If

she came after me, I'd go stone so fast . . . I'm scared, Bramble."

"Hmp." She took the glass he pushed across to her, sipped at the wine and frowned at the curtain stirring over the mended sheepskin in the window where the tape was peeling off. "What about Yaro? You think they've got her in that doulahar?"

"If she's there, they've blocked me off. She IS alive, Bramble. The tie's too tight between us for her to be dead and me not know. Anyway, where else would they put her?"

"Then we have to get inside somehow." She dragged her hand across her mouth, sat scowling at the amber wine running down the sides of the bell as she tilted the glass back and forth. "Without them knowing."

"Yeh. Otherwise they could eat her before we get close."

"Predators."

"I think."

"I think . . . I think we'd better add Maks to this plot." She set the glass down, pushed the box back and got to her feet. "Wait here, I'll get the *call-me*'s." A moment later she was back with a soft, leather pouch. She fished out one of the pebbles and set it on the table. It shimmered in the lamplight, a milky quartz stone water-polished smooth. "Crush it under the heel he said. You want to do the deed or shall I?"

"You're the one with the mass, Bramble."

"Never say that to a woman, urtch. Mmp. Better put this over there by the door. Maks does need considerable space." She looked up, chewed her lip. "And he's like to crash his head into the ceiling. Maybe I should take it outside."

"And maybe you shouldn't. We don't want to tell the neighbors all our business."

"Especially Jahira. I swear that woman knows every belch. Well, he'll just have to duck." She picked up the *call-me* and almost dropped it again. "Yukh, the thing feels alive." Squatting, she set it on the floor near the threshold; when she was satisfied, she stood, brought her heel down on the pebble, crushing it to powder. As soon as she felt it go, she jumped back.

Nothing happened.

"Maks? SETTSIMAKSIMIN!"

Nothing.

She stirred the powder with the toe of her sandal. "I am

going to have your black hide for this, Maksi." She flung the door open, snatched up a broom and swept the glass bits into the yard muck. When every sliver was gone, she yanked the door shut, slamming it loudly enough to wake half the quarter, so hard that the latch didn't catch. It bounced open again. She ignored that. "All right, Jay. We do this ourselves."

Shudders passed along Jaril's body, escalating to a sudden convulsion. He spewed out most of the wine he'd drunk and went suddenly stone.

Brann swore, snatched up a dishtowel; she mopped at her arms and face, flung the towel into the mess sprayed across the table. She straightened Jaril's chair, picked up the warm pulsing crystal and opened her blouse. With Jaril stone cradled against her breasts, she felt with her foot for the chair, sat and waited.

Time passed. She understood then just how afraid Jaril was. And she saw what he meant when he said aulis take longer to recover than aetas. She began to be afraid; if he couldn't come out of this by himself, she hadn't a clue how to wake him up.

The crystal softened. It stirred against her; it felt like a baby wanting to suck. She bit her lip. There was no point in futile dreaming; she'd been effectively sterile since her eleventh birthday. Slowly, so slowly, the boy's form unfolded until, finally, Jaril filled her lap, his head resting between her breasts. He opened his eyes, looked blankly up at her, then remembered.

Stiffly, he pushed away from her, slid off her lap and went to stand in the doorway, staring into the stinking darkness outside.

Brann frowned at him. After a minute, she said, "If you go stone every time I mention that place or you-know-who, we're not going to get very far."

He pressed his body against the doorjamb, stretched his arm up it as high as he could reach. He said nothing.

"Hmm. Tell me this, is everybody at the house a demon?"

He twisted his head around. "I saw some gardeners that weren't. Some women went out to the Market, I suppose they were after supplies for the party the courtesan was throwing that night. They weren't. I didn't actually see more, but she'd need a lot of servants or slaves to run a house that size. I only counted five smiglar plus the courtesan."

"Smiglar, Jay?"

Rubbing at his neck, he swung around, strolled to her box and sat down on it. "Have to call them something. I'm uncomfortable when I hear talk about demons. The way you folk define these things, I'm a demon. I don't like the fringes that word has, you know what I mean. Stuvtiggor clots are smiglar, these hive types are like them, why not call them smiglar? Better than demon, isn't it?"

"Smiglar's fine. All right." She pushed fluttering strands of hair out of her eyes, began rebuttoning her blouse. "First thing. We need to know how the inside of that house is laid out, who lives there. You're sure they'd spot you?"

"Yeh."

"That's out then. Too bad. Trap . . . trap . . . um, you think the courtesan is the whiphandler of that clutch?"

"Yeh." He dipped a finger in a pool of wine, drew glyphs on the wood. Set. Tsi. Ma. Ksi. Min. "The uh fetor she gives off is ten times what I got from the others." He drew a line through the glyphs, canceling them. "Like I said, even Maks would back off that bunch. Her most of all." He frowned. "Maybe that's it. Why he didn't come."

Brann brushed aside his dig at Maksim, it was nothing but an upsurge of Jaril's old resentment. "And she's flying among the Isu?"

"If her guest list for tonight's party means anything."

"Courtesan, hmm. Big house. Lots of dependents. Living high. All that in spite of the Temueng base for the culture and what that means about woman's place, especially a woman without a family to back her. She has to be clever, Jay; power in itself wouldn't get her those things. You said there were sorcerors in some of those Isu sars?"

"Yeh." He drew two circles on the table, pulled a line from the left circle to the right. "One of them might have matched Ahzurdan when he wasn't drugged to the eyebrows. While he was still himself, that is."

"And they haven't smelled out what she is. Interesting, isn't it. And this. They're predators, but Yaro's still alive. They didn't take her to eat her. She's bait, Jay. For you, sure. For me, probably. Which means I've got to keep away from there too. Ahh! What a mess."

"Mess." He crumpled the stained towel between his hands, then began wiping up the wine. "You expected it to come out like that, didn't you."

"Why?"

"You asked about the servants. Only thing left is getting

at one of them." He tossed the towel at the tub where the stew pot was soaking. "So?"

"So we go looking for a servant or slave or someone from that house that we can get next to without letting the boss . . . um, what's the singular form of smiglar, Jay?"

"Same. One smiglar, twenty smiglar. Hive things."

"Right. Without letting the boss smiglar know what we're doing. Get some rest, luv. We start tomorrow early."

6

One week later.

Midmorning, just before the busiest time in the Market.

A huge brindle mastiff stopped suddenly, howled, shook his head. Foam from his mouth spattered the serving girl who stood beside an older woman so busy arguing over the price of tubers she didn't notice what was happening around her. The girl screamed and backed away.

A gaunt old woman appeared between two kiosks. She swung a heavy staff at the beast and bounced dust off his hide. He howled, then yelped as the staff connected again; he swung his muscular front end from side to side, trying to get at her. Foam dripped copiously from his mouth.

People around them scrambled to get away. The girl had dived behind the old woman, trapping herself in a short blind alley between two rows of shops. Her companion looked around, yelped and went running off. The place emptied rapidly except for the three of them, the woman, the girl and the dog.

The mastiff whimpered, backed away from the whirling staff. He stood for a moment shivering convulsively, then he went ki-yi-yipping off, vanishing into the crazyquilt of alleys about the market, the noises he made sinking into the noises and silences of the dank cloudy afternoon.

The old woman knocked the butt of her staff against the flagging underfoot, grunted with satisfaction. She tugged her worn homespun shirt down and shook her narrow hips until the folds in her trousers hung the way she wanted them. Finally she tucked a straggle of gray hair behind her ear as she turned and inspected the deserted chaos around her. She saw the maid, raised her scraggly brows. "You all right, child?"

The maid was rubbing and rubbing at the back of her hand where some the dog's spit had landed. Tears welled up in her eyes and spilled out; she wasn't crying so much as overflowing. She was young and neatly dressed, her brown hair was smooth as glass despite her agitation, pinned into a three-tiered knot atop her head; she might have been pretty, but that was impossible to say. Puffy and purplish red, a disfiguring birthmark slid down one side of her face, hugged her neck like a noose and vanished beneath her clothing. Her arms were covered from shoulder to wrist, but the backs of both hands were spattered with more of that ugly birthstain.

She lowered her eyes. "I think . . . I think so," she murmured, speaking so softly Brann had trouble hearing her.

"You're shivering, child." Brann touched her fingertips to the marred cheek. "Your face is like ice. Come, we'll have some tea. That will make the world look brighter."

The maid shrank back. "I . . . I'd better find Elissy."

"Surely you can take five minutes for yourself." Brann rested her hand on the girl's shoulder, using the lightest of pressures to start her moving. "Don't be afraid of me, I am the Jantria Bar Ana. Ah, I see you've heard my name. Why don't you tell me yours."

Reassured, the girl began walking along beside her. "My name is Carup Kalan, Jantria." She looked uneasily at her hand. "It didn't bite me, but I got its spit on me. Will that do bad to me?"

They turned a corner and plunged into the noisy, dusty throngs of the Market, walked around a group of highservants arguing over some bolts of silk and velvet. "No. If your skin is not broken, there's no harm in that foam. If you're worried, there's a fountain two ranks over; you can stop and wash your hands." She smiled at Carup. "I expect you were with—Elissy, was it—just to carry things, so it will be my pleasure to pay for the tea."

They stopped at the fountain and Carup Kalan scrubbed her hands with an enthusiasm that made Brann smile as she watched. Carup might have heard of her healings and find her presence reassuring, but she wasn't about to take any chances she could avoid.

There were a number of teashops scattered about the Market, each with a little dark kitchen, a counter and tables under a battered canvas awning. Brann took her unknowing catch to the nearest of these and sat her at a table while she went for tea and cakes.

Circling the crowded tables, lifting the tray and dancing

precariously around clots of customers coming and going. Brann carried her cakes and tea back, shushed Carup as the girl jumped up and tried to take the tray from her. The tea was hot and strong, the cakes were deep-fried honey wafers, crisp and sweet. "From your name, you come from Lake Tabaga." She slipped some cakes on a round of brown paper and slid them across to Carup, poured tea for both of them.

"Ay-yah." Carup looked briefly surprised. "The Ash-Kalap have a farmhold close to a village called Pattan Haria on the west shore of Tabaga." She gulped at the tea. It was too hot; she shuddered as her mouth burned, but seemed to welcome the pain. When the bowl was empty, she set it down and stared into it; her face twisted with . . . something. There was tragedy in what birth had done to her. The mark distorted and denied all her expressions. Nothing came out right. Suffering was grotesque, a laugh was uglier than a snarl. "My father sold me when I was eight," she whispered. Trembling fingers stroked the mark on her face, then she jerked them down and began crumbling a cake into sticky fragments. "He said no one would want to marry me or even take me in to warm his bed. I was too ugly. He said he'd never make back the cost of my food and clothes, so he might as well get what he could out of me. He said they had perverts in the city that might find me. . . ." She took the bowl Brann had refilled and gulped at the steaming tea. "Might find me. . . ." She sobbed. Her hand shook, but she took care to set the bowl down gently. It didn't break. No tea spilled. "I'm sorry."

"No, child, don't. Say what you want to say." Brann took one of Carup's hands and held it between hers. As she'd spoken to many of the women visiting her, keeping up the role of holywoman, Jantria, she spoke to Carup: "Hearing what comes to me is the task the Gods have set me. Say what you must and know that I will hear it." She waited, feeling the tension in Carup, the need to talk and the fear of casting herself into deeper trouble. It was hard for Brann to understand the girl. Her own life was complicated and often dangerous; for the most part, though, she'd managed to control events rather than endure them. Time after time, one god or another had meddled with her, driving her this way and that; even so she was able to finesse a degree of freedom. She could see that Carup was different, that the options she had were much more limited; she could even see reasons why this was so, but that was the mind's eyes, not the heart's.

A bad taste in her mouth because she was going to use this unfortunate girl as unconscionably as the girl's beast of a father had, she leaned closer and smiled at Carup and prepared to entice from her everything she knew about the courtesan and her doulahar. "Were you brought right away to Dil Jorpashil?"

Carup sighed and freed her hand so she could sip at the cooling tea. "Ay-yah, the Agent brought us straight here."

"What happened then?"

"I was afraid . . . what my father said . . . but it didn't happen. The Chuttar Palami Kumindri's agent bought me for a maid." Carup sighed with weariness and managed at the same time to project a touch of pride. "You must have heard of her. The Chuttar Palami Kumindri is the premiere courtesan in all Dil Jorpashil." Her mouth turned down. "The Housemaster treats me like a dog. I work hard, I'm up before the sun every day, he never says word one to me, he pretends he doesn't even see me."

"Then you're still a part of the Chuttar's household?"

"Ay-yah." Carup sighed again; her eyelids drooped. The emotional storm had passed and she wanted nothing more than to lie down and sleep. A group of merchants came bustling past their table, kicking into her. She cringed automatically, tugged her chair farther under the table, made herself as small as she could.

Brann pressed her lips together, angry at the merchants because they were arrogant and thoughtless, angry at the girl because she hadn't spirit enough to resent them, at herself because she couldn't do anything about either. Her voice deliberately mild, she said. "How long has it been?"

"Ten . . . years. . . ." Carup blinked, straightened. The color drained from her face, leaving the red-purple stain more glaring than ever. Her eyes were fixed past Brann's shoulder.

Brann twisted around. The stocky woman, Elissy, Carup called her, was standing under the scalloped edge of the canvas, looking angrily about. Brann saw her and she saw Carup at the same moment. She came charging across to the table. Brann stood, held up a hand, palm out. "Gods' peace be on you, Elissy friend."

"I'm no friend of yours, beggar. Carup, get over here. By Sarimbara's Horns, what do you think you're doing, lazing about like this?" She turned her scowl on Brann. "Who you? What you think you doing with this girl?"

"I am the Jantria Bar Ana." Brann suppressed a smile as she saw the consternation on the woman's face, the sudden shift of expression. The past two weeks had apparently given her a formidable reputation.

She nodded gravely at Elissy, shifted her gaze to Carup. I need more, she thought, a lot more than I've got. Ten years that girl has been in that house. She's not stupid, poor thing, might be better for her if she was. Get to it, woman. . . . She set her hand on Carup's shoulder, turned the girl to face her. "Carup Kalan," she said, lowering her voice to its deepest register, speaking with a deliberate formality. "Would you care to serve me? My household is small, but you will not go hungry. You will clean my rooms and yours, you will do the laundry, you will buy food for our meals and do such cooking as you are trained for. In return, I will buy you out of your present place and register you at the Addala as a freewoman. I will provide a room and a bed, food and clothing and I will pay you five dugna a week."

Carup's face twisted into a gargoyle grimace as she struggled to decide; she had security, she knew where she would sleep, where her meals would come from, that she would be safe on the streets from pressgangs, pimps, muggers and assaults and she had a shadow share in the prestige of the Chuttar Prime, but she also knew that she'd be thrown out like refuse if she got sick or hurt too badly to work any more. Or when she was too old to work, though too-old was a long time off, at eighteen you're immortal. She hated her life, that was obvious, but she was afraid of venturing from its comfortable certainties, that too was obvious. Brann as holywoman/healer had prestige also, was presumably trustworthy, Carup being gullible enough to accept communal judgment about what was holy and what wasn't, but the Jantria was a stranger. From another land, another people. That was suspect, frightening. Brann was poor; Carup had a slave's ingrained contempt for the poor. Brann had treated her with kindness and acceptance, had stood between her and the rabid dog and had beaten it off, a powerful omen for the superstitious, and like most slaves Carup was deeply superstitious. Brann offered her manumission and a degree of control over her life. That was attractive in theory but terrifying in actuality.

With a suddenly acquired dignity that made Brann as suddenly ashamed of how she was using the girl, Carup said, "Sarimbara's Blessing, Jantria Bar Ana, I will serve you."

"So be it, child. Go with your companion now. Wait and trust me. I'll send for you when the thing is done."

7

Two days later.

The Housemaster tugged at heroic mustaches that hung from the corner of his tight mouth down past his chin to tickle his collar. He scowled at the Basith, a go-between Brann hired to handle the exchange because she didn't want to go anywhere near the doulahar. "Why this object?" He jerked a thumb at Carup who was kneeling at his feet, but didn't look at her. She offended his eyes and he'd let her know that every day of her life since she'd walked through the service portal.

The Basith was a typical Jana Mix. He had black hair like the coarse baka wool the nomad tribes wove into tent cloth, a tangle of watchspring curls about a widening bald spot; he had a nub of a beard on the point of a long chin; he wore a Phrasi merchant's ring in his left ear and a Gallinasi coupstud in his right ear, one of the prized ruby studs. His eyes were dark amber, long and narrow, set at a tilt above prominent cheekbones, clever eyes for a clever man. He was the son of a courtesan and an unusually rebellious Dhanik who took the boy into his sar despite the screeches of his proper wives and saw that he got a lawyer's education. A week ago the Basith's wife had ventured timidly into the Kuna Coru to see the holywoman about an ulcer on her leg; she came back with the ulcer closed over, with the cancer that caused it cleaned out of her and with a proper appreciation of Brann's worth. Which was why he was here now. He masked his distaste for the man in front of him, for that unfortunate creature crouching at the Housemaster's feet, and prepared to do what he was hired for. "The holywoman is but following the instruction of her god. This is the slave she wants. This is the slave she shall have. Place a price on her, if you please, Callam. Then we will see."

Half an hour later the Basith handed over one takk and five dugnas and received a bill of sale. He left the doulahar with the bill and Carup Kalan, took both to the Addala, did the paperwork and paid the manumission fee while the Tikkasermer stapled the bronze firman into the girl's left

ear, signifying she was a freewoman. He delivered Carup
and the documents to Brann, smiled with genuine pleasure
as she thanked him and paid his fee. Then he went home to
collect the gratitude of his wife.

8

Brann went back to being the Jantria, listening to women
from the quarter and beyond, farther and farther beyond
these days as her reputation spread, there were even a few
wives from the lesser Isun, healing their bodies and doing
her best to prop up their souls. It was draining, but she
accepted it as the appropriate payment for the use she was
making of the girl and for her bi-nightly prowls. Drinker of
Souls was walking the streets of Dil Jorpashil. She came
back sated and destroyed, swearing to herself she'd never go
out again. But when the hunger was on her, she went.

Carup bloomed. She cooked, cleaned, sewed, she used a
part of her meager pay to buy a chair for Brann, recaned
the back and the seat, burnished the ancient wood until it
glowed. She moved about the tiny house singing cheerful
dirges, polishing the place until it gleamed. And she talked.
Night after night, she consumed pots of tea and talked. And
Brann listened. She nudged the girl now and then in a
direction that would give her the data she needed about the
workings of the doulahar; she didn't have to nudge hard or
often. No one had listened to Carup Kalan since she was
weaned or showed her in any way that they valued her. Not
even her mother.

Jaril was restless and irritable during this time, as fidgety
as a dog with fleas. He went back again and again to the
doulahar like a tongue to a sore tooth. He couldn't keep
away from it.

##

"The Chuttar left during the afternoon," he told Brann,
"in her fanciest litter, the ebony one with the silver mount-
ings. She went up the hill to the Isullata sar. She's still
there, very entertaining she must be."

##

"She stayed home tonight," he told Brann another morning, "two Adals and a sorceror came by. They were there

about two hours, then the Adals left. The sorceror was still there when I came away."

##

"She went to the Market; she bought two slaves, a live bullock, some bolts of cloth. I don't know why she went herself, maybe she was bored or something."

##

And so it went. He watched the Chuttar Palami Kumindri day and night; overflying the doulahar far enough up to escape notice, staying over it twenty minutes at most with two to three hours between visits. He was cautious, but he could not keep away.

Days passed.

Brann acquired charts and lists and schematics of each floor, timetables, locations of all forbidden areas, everything she needed for a fair notion where the Chuttar might be hiding Yaril, everything she needed to get into the doulahar with a chance of getting out again, but she still had no plan for handling the smiglar. And no plan for Carup's future. She had to have both before she could act.

Sambar Day.

She went as usual to the shrine and sat among the penitents and petitioners, surrounded by the slip-slap, click-clack of prayer beads rotating through work-worn fingers, the insect hum of the old women who came there because they had nowhere else to go, the rattle of drums and the chants of the celebrants as they did their best to sing Sarimbara deeper asleep.

Wreathed in incense drifting copiously from swinging censers as the celebrants made their hourly procession about the praiseroom, she cursed Maksim a while, but halfheartedly. Then she began to worry about him. Something must have gone wrong for him. That Jastouk? Little creep, he'd sell his mother for the gold in her teeth. That girl in Silili? What was her name? Kori something. Speculation was futile. And she had neither time nor attention to waste on him right now. Carup. She called up an image of Carup. If you ignored that mark and looked at her bone structure, her nose, mouth, eyes, she was almost beautiful. She was slim with wide hips and full breasts, the sort of body men in this culture valued above all others. She kept herself covered, but Brann was certain the red-purple flesh was spattered the length of her body, neck to heel. Strip that away, though, and maybe her family would take her back. I wonder if I could do that? Well, Jaril and I. I can't leave her here on her own, free or not. I might as well strangle her myself, it'd come to the same thing. I can't do like Maks did with his Kori and put her in school somewhere. No Talent. No interest either. She's bred to be some man's wife. Dowry? That I can do. The skin, the skin, can I do ANYTHING about that mark? Jaril and I, we've done harder things. Yes. take the curse off her face. Can't take it off her heart, can I. Takes more than magic to erase eighteen years of cringing.

A lanky boy with a shaved head came in, awkward and diffident, all bone and gristle, carrying a dakadaka under his arm, gray dust ground into the skin of his feet and knees, smeared over the rear folds of his bunchy white dhoti. He went shuffling to the raised area where Sarimbara's icon was and dropped clumsily to the planks. He wriggled around, adding more stonedust to his person and his clothing, got his legs wrapped around the dakadaka and began tapping at its twin heads, drawing a whispery rattle from the taut snakeskins. Several older celebrants straggled in, men with shaved heads and orange dhotis; they sat in a ragged arc behind the boy and began a droning chant, a weary winding sleepsong for the god whose attention they feared more than his neglect. The visitors to the shrine, mostly women, added their wordless hums to the chant, filling the praiseroom with a sound like dry leaves blowing.

Brann hummed with the others, taking a break from the dilemmas that plagued her. She passed her prayer beads through her fingers, slip, slap, rattle-tattle, dark brown seeds fingerpolished to a mottled sheen, round and round, a soft, syncopated underplay to the drum, the song, the hum.

The day passed slowly, but it did pass, taking with it her hesitations and uncertainties. She went home to her hovel determined to peel off her problems one by one, Carup Kalan scheduled first to go.

9

Three days later.

Morning, about two hours before dawn.

Raining outside, little wind, water coming down in near vertical lines, the sort of rain that seems like it will never end, as if the rest of life will be gray and chill and damp, the sort of rain that makes a pleasure palace of the most wretched of shelters as long as there's a bit of fire to chase away the damp.

Brann pushed aside the curtain that closed off her bedroom doorway, edged around it into the cramped livingroom where Carup was sleeping. Her hair hung loose, a waving mass of white, fine as spidersilk; she wore her own face, young, unlined, her eyes green as new leaves, her mouth a delicate curve, soft and vulnerable. She wore a black velvet robe embroidered with gold and silver and rubies. Jaril stole it for her from the wardrobe of an Isu whose taste in decoration was so bad it was almost a Talent. He grinned as he held it up for Brann to inspect; when she said finally, I suppose bad taste is better than no taste, he had a fit of giggles that she shushed quickly, afraid he'd wake Carup. In her left hand she held a heavy wooden candlepole taller than she was and covered with tarnished silver-gilt that she'd been afraid to clean because the gilding was so thin it came off if you looked at it hard. There was a fat white candle impaled on the spike, but she hadn't lit it yet. The only light in the livingroom came from the fireplace where faint red glows from last night's fire seeped through the smother of gray ash.

Jaril brushed past her, black panther with crystal eyes, moving with an eerie silence. He padded across to Carup, sniffed at her, came padding back. *She's ripe, Bramble. Her eyes are moving, she's starting to dream.*

She nodded, brought the candle pole down until the wick was beside his head. "Light me, Jay," she whispered.

He spat a spark at the wick, smirked as she swung the pole hastily upright when the twist began burning. *Handy to have round, am't I, huh?*

"Sometimes, but don't let it go to your head." She inspected him. "Maybe you should turn yourself white. You disappear into the murk like that."

His mouth dropping into a feral cat grin, he purred at her. His eyes began to glow silver-white, the tips of his coathairs went translucent and shone with a clear white light. He was still a black cat, but one outlined in moonfire.

"Impressive," she murmured and grinned back at him. "All right, let's do it."

##

The candle made an aura round her shining hair, dropped dramatic shadows into the hollows of her face and touched with fire the rings on the hand that held the pole. "Carup," she called. "Carup Kalan. Wake up. Carup. Carup Kalan."

The girl woke, startled, then afraid, scrambling back under the covers until she was pressed against the wall; she pulled her knees up, threw her arms across her face and whimpered.

"Have no fear," Brann said. Her voice was deep and caressing, the words had a smile in them. "I am she who was the Jantria, Carup Kalan. Look at me, child. I mean you no harm."

Still trembling, Carup pulled her arms down, lay peeping at Brann over the delicate halo of hair on her forearm.

Brann lifted a hand in blessing. At first Carup cringed away, that was what her life had trained her to do, that was the only way she'd found to turn aside or lessen the pain about to be inflicted on her. Then she saw Brann's smile, only a little smile, a quirking upward of the ends of her mouth, but it was approval, fondness even, and Carup began to unfold like a flower opening in the sun.

"You have served me faithfully and well." The words were solemn but the tone was gentle, friendly, and Carup relaxed yet more. "You have given more than service, child. You have shown generosity of spirit, expecting only a little kindness, a trifle of shelter from the world and those who would do you ill. Carup Kalan, I am a servant of One I may not name. I am at times given word to do this, or do that, to go here, to go there. Word has come to me that I am required elsewhere soon." Brann kept her face a smiling mask as she spun her web of lies, but again she wasn't liking herself much, especially when she saw the look on Carup's face.

The girl's lips trembled, but she didn't dare protest. Fear was flooding back into her, more than fear, a flat despair. Once again Fate was tearing her from her happiness, casting her aside like garbage.

"I would take you with me, if that were permitted. It is not. But there is a thing I can do for you, a gift I can give you, Carup Kalan. I can send you home to your own people with the dowry of a queen."

Carup's right thumb moved over and over the marks on the back of her left hand. She didn't say anything for several

breaths, then she bowed her head. "I thank you, Jantria."
Her voice was dull, lifeless.

"Stand before me, Carup Kalan."

Carup glanced at the shining panther, then shrugged;
there were far more terrible things waiting for her than that
eldrich beast. She hitched herself to the edge of the cot and
stood. She slept in a sleeveless shift of unbleached muslin. It
had a meagerly embroidered neck with a faded ribbon
threaded through the eyelets and tied in a limp bow at the
front.

"Remove your shift."

Moving like an automaton, Carup pulled the bow loose,
spread the neck of the shift and let it fall about her feet. She
didn't try to cover herself, she was too deep in despair for
shame to touch her. The spongy red-purple flesh ran the
length of her body, more of it than Brann had expected to
see. There were spatters on her right side, drops like spilled
blood on her breast. A wide river of the wine flesh ran
down her left side, slashed across her navel and flowed
down her right thigh.

"Straighten the blankets on the bed, then lie down on
them."

Obedient as always, refusing to acknowledge anger or
pain, Carup worked with the skilled neatness with which she
did everything, even turning square corners as she made the
bed.

"Lie on your back," Brann said when Carup was finished.

All this while Jaril panther had been pacing around Brann,
his crystal eyes reflecting the candle flame. Now he melted
into a mist and the mist settled over Carup, seeping into
her.

Carup lay rigid, eyes squeezed shut.

Brann leaned the candlepole against the chimney, went to
kneel beside the bed. With Jaril guiding her, she began
restructuring the blemishes, wiping away all trace of them.
All that the night prowls of the Drinker of Souls had brought
her, she poured into the girl. And more. When she was
finished, Carup Kalan was a lamb without blemish, an
unpierced pearl whose price was the price of queens.

Shaky with exhaustion, perspiration dripping down her
face and body, Brann got to her feet and went to the
candlepole, removed the candle and set it on the box that
served as a bedtable; the candle was thick enough to stand
by itself. She looked down at the rigid, unhappy girl, shook

her head and crossed to the bedroom. Jaril emerged as mist, solidified to black nonluminous panther and padded into the kitchen; a moment later he was a mistcrane powering into the rain, heading for the doulahar and his obsession, cursing the damp, the cold and his unruly needs.

Brann came back with the hand mirror she'd bought as a gift for Carup once the metamorphosis was complete. "Open your eyes, Carup Kalan, and behold my second gift."

For an instant the girl resisted, then she sighed and did as she was told. Brann bit at her lip. Where is your spirit, girl? You aren't grass for everyone to step on. She said nothing. It wouldn't help. Carup was what her culture made her.

"Sit up," Brann said. "Look at your hands, child."

Carup pushed up until she was sitting with her legs over the edge of the bed. She looked at her hands, gasped. She felt at her thigh, at her breasts, she touched her face.

"Take your last gift, this mirror, and behold yourself, Carup Kalan."

Brann left the girl staring into the mirror and feeling at her face as if she were unable to believe what her eyes saw and needed the confirmation of her fingers. In her bedroom, Brann stripped off the robe and with some difficulty took on once more the aspect of the Jantria Bar Ana. She put on her ordinary clothes and sat on the bed for a while, gathering her strength.

"Jantria?" The voice that came from the other room was hesitant, shaky from excitement and a lingering fear.

"One moment, Carup." Brann got to her feet, felt at her braid to make sure it was properly clasped so it wouldn't unravel at the first movement of her head. I feel like I'm going to unravel, she thought. Hoo! If I can get that girl to sleep, there's some dark left, maybe I can go find me a juicy murderer or two. No. A slave dealer. More appropriate, I'd say. Almost a pun. Spend on a slave, recoup on a slaver. Hah!

She moved to the crate she used as a linen chest and dressing table, grunted as she lifted a small iron-bound box. Shoulders bent, she elbowed past the curtain.

Carup was sitting on the bed. She'd put the shift on again, and pulled a quilt around her shoulders, but she blushed when Brann came in, then looked uncertain as she saw the old woman who'd bought her free. She stole a look in the mirror—it was on the box beside the candle; she'd put her sandal behind it to tilt it up so she could see herself when she glanced that way. She blushed again, stared down at her hands as they rested in her lap, fingers twined tightly together.

Brann nodded at the candle and the mirror. "Push those aside, will you, Carup? So I can set this down. It's heavy."

Hastily the girl tossed the mirror onto the bed, brushed the sandal off the box and pushed the candle back. "Is that enough?"

"It should be." The flimsy box creaked under the weight of the small chest. "This isn't locked now, though you should keep it so later. Open it."

"Me?"

"It's your dowry, young Carup. Now, do what I tell you. Open the chest."

"Oh." Carup turned back the lid. Inside, there were two doeskin bags and a small belt-purse. She loosened the drawstring on the larger bag, reached in and took out a handful of coins. Gold coins, thick, heavy, with a cold greasy feel to them. "Jorpashil jaraufs," she whispered. "Sahanai the Siradar's daughter wore hers at her wedding, threaded round her neck."

"One hundred," Brann said. "I promised you a queen's price, child."

"She only had ten." Carup turned the broad coins over and over, rubbing her fingers across them, then she put them back in the bag and pulled the drawstrings until the opening was gone; neat-fingered as always, she wrapped the thongs into a smooth coil and tucked it between the side of the box and the bag. She opened the second bag. Silver this time. Takks.

"Fifty," Brann said. "Those are for you alone. A woman should always have her own money, Carup. It means she has a way out if she needs it. Pass what you don't use to your daughters; tell them what I've just told you. It is a trust, Carup Kalan."

"I hear and I obey, Jantria Bar Ana." She put the takks away and opened the purse. There was a pile of worn dugnas inside it.

"One hundred dugnas, Carup, to buy clothing, hire a bodyguard and transport to get you home."

"I don't want to go home." The words came out in a rush. "My father will just take the dowry and give it to my brothers. He did that all the time with the money my mother brought in."

"Gods! Does nothing go right? I can't leave you here.

The vultures would be down on you before I was gone an hour."

"Take me with you, Jantria. I'll serve you. You said I was good at serving you. The One Without a Name, I'll serve that One too."

Brann sank onto the hearth, her back against the rough bricks of the fireplace; their heat seeped through her shirt and into her bones. Sleep flooded through her, waves and waves of sleep. Thinking was like shoveling mud. "Carup, I can't." The lies were catching up with her, twisting around her like a fowler's net. That last bit was true enough, though. She couldn't keep the girl with her. A deeper truth was, she didn't want to. Carup was reading that, though she wasn't fully aware of it, and trying to fight against it, flailing out helplessly, futilely. Brann drew her fist across her mouth, let her eyes droop closed for a minute. Fine time for the girl to dredge up some independence. "Where I go, no one can come." Make it convincing, Brann; she's going to be stubborn. "Even if you tell him the dowry is the gift of a god?"

"He wouldn't listen to me. Even if he listened, he wouldn't believe me." Carup wrapped the quilt tighter about her body, pulled her legs up and tucked them under her. She was fighting now, at last she was fighting for what she wanted. "If I go home and he takes me back as his daughter, I belong to him. Listen," she said. Her voice broke in the middle of the word. "This is how it went in my home, Jantria. My mother made shirts and sold them in the Pattan Haria Market; she had made herself a name for her broideries. Sometimes she got more from her shirts than he did off the land." She cleared her throat; her hand crept from beneath the quilt and stroked the side of her face where the mark had been. When she spoke again, it was in a hoarse whisper; she was talking about family things, breaking one of the most rigid taboos of her culture. "He took her money whenever the tribes came to Lake Tabaga and my brothers wanted to go into Pattan Haria and get drunk with them. My mother spent her eyes and her fingers on those shirts, she took from sleep time to make them and he took her money for my brothers to waste. Didn't matter what she said, what she wanted to do with the money; he owned her so he owned what she earned. If I go back, he'll do the same to me."

Brann rubbed at her eyes as her plans fell in rubble about her. She'd been so sure she could send the girl home and let her family have the care of her. Double damn, Tungjii help! What do I do now? She sneezed. What I do now is sleep. She sighed and got to her feet. "I'm too tired to think, Carup. It's late. Get some sleep. If you're up before I am and you find people waiting for me, send them away, will you? Tell them I'm meditating; it will be the truth, child. Get some sleep yourself, you should be tired too." She didn't wait for a response but pushed past the curtain and fell on the bed, asleep as soon as her body was horizontal.

10

Brann rubbed her eyes and sipped at the near boiling tea that Carup had brought to her as soon as she heard her moving around. She yawned and tried to clear the clots out of her head.

Hands clapped outside the curtain. Brann's hand jerked and she nearly spilled tea down her front. She swore under her breath, brushed some drops off her trousers. "Yes, Carup, what is it?"

"Subbau Kamin brought fresh bread this morning, she says her grandson is full of devils and laughter and her son is over the moon about the change, she blesses you and hopes you will accept this small gift. Piara Sansa came with her and brought sausages. Would you like me to bring you some of this? The bread smells wonderful."

"Yes, yes, but take some for yourself, hmm?"

"I will, thank you, Jantria."

Brann finished her breakfast and stretched out on the bed, her fingers laced behind her head. She stared up at the ceiling, traced the cracks and played games with the stains, but found no answer anywhere. She was still tired, her energy badly depleted. And her head seemed to have shut down completely. She closed her eyes.

The sounds of the Kuna trickled in, women gossiping as they did the wash at the aqueduct overflow across the alley, slap-slapping the clothing against the washboards, laughing, scolding their children, the children running in slap-and-kick games, screaming, laughing, bawling, creating a cacophony thick enough to slice like sausage. Dogs barking, howling, whining and growling in sudden fights that broke off as suddenly when someone threw a brick at them or tossed water over them. Several streets off, some men were fighting, she couldn't tell how many, others were gathered around them yelling encouragement or curses, making wagers on the outcome. Voices everywhere, the Kuna was stiff with noise, wall to wall, every day, all day, late into the night. There were always people in the alleys, going and coming from the lodgings, thieves coming back from their nightwork, pimps with their strings of whores, gamblers inside and out, running their endless games. To say nothing of the people who couldn't afford even the meager rents and were living on the street. And the caudhar's baddicks sniffing out those pimps who didn't pay their bribes, running down thieves suspected of dipping their fingers into high purses, pride having outmatched sense, or just looking out for healthy youths who'd make good quarry in the Isun chases. Though she despised these hunters of men, they smelled like rotten fish to her, she left them alone when they were working the alleys; if one was found dead, the whole quarter would pay.

She pulled her mind back from that morass and tried to concentrate on her current problem. *I can't spend all this time on her. Yaril means a lot more than she does; I don't even like her all that much. What in Forty Mortal Hells am I going to do with her?* She sighed. *Hmm. It's been ten years since she left home, that's a long time . . . I wonder how old her father was then . . . maybe he's dead. Would that make a difference? Sounds to me like those brothers were spoiled rotten and might be worse than the old man. What did she say the family name was? Ah! Ash-Kalap. I need mother's name, father's name, eldest brother's name. All right. Let's get at it.* She sat up, swung her legs over the edge of the bed and scowled at nothing. She moved her shoulders, opened and closed her hands, clenched and un-clenched her toes, working the muscles of her arms and legs. "Carup," she called. "Come in here. I need to talk to you."

11

Two days later.

Night. Late.

The rain had stopped for a while, but the alleys were noisome sewers still.

Brann was picking her way across the mud, thankful her days in the Kuna Coru had deadened her nose so she couldn't smell the fumes rising from that muck. A large nighthawk swooped low and went climbing into the darkness.

Hunting. Jaril's mindvoice was filled with accusation and

annoyance. *You know you shouldn't go out when I'm not there for backup.*

Go home, Jay, and wait for me. I don't intend to argue this up to my ankles in mud in the middle of a street.

Trailing disapproval like a tailplume, the hawk shot ahead.

Brann shook her head. Like I'm his child. She frowned as she reached the hovel and sloshed around to the kitchen door. Jaril was sitting at the kitchen table, the wine jar at his elbow, along with two glasses. He'd lit the lamp.

She kicked off her sandals, stepped out of her trousers and took the kettle from the sandbed. She touched it; there was still a little heat left. She poured the lukewarm water into a pan, put her feet in it and sighed with pleasure. "You can give me a glass, if you feel like it, Jay."

He was still temperish and glared at her. "You don't deserve I should, going out like that, you could have been killed." He splashed some wine in the glass and pushed it across to her. "You could have been KILLED. I can't get Yaro without you." Radiating misery, anger, fear, he gulped at his own wine. "I might as well go knock on the smiglar's door and say here I am, eat me."

Brann swished her feet in the water, mud swirling off them. "I was careful, Jay. But I needed to go."

"You needed to go." Despair and disgust sharpened his voice. "You didn't need anything, you got filled up the night before I left."

"All right, have it your way. I went because I wanted to. Does that satisfy you?"

"Satisfy! Bramble, what's got into you? It's like you're twelve, not two hundred plus."

"I don't want to talk about it. What'd you find out?"

He shook his head at her. "Bramble. . . . All right, all right, here it is. You had the right hunch. The father is dead. Stroke. Five years ago." He relaxed as the wine was absorbed into his substance, his eyes dropped and his face softened. "The oldest brother took over the farm, he's married, two wives, I counted five children. It's a big house for that size farm, it's got packed dirt walls, two stories, flat-tile roof. It's built inside a ten-foot wall, packed earth with a canted tile top. There's a garden of sorts, the mother keeps it in order. She's still alive, looks a hundred and two, but probably isn't more than sixty, sixty-five. Tough old femme, like one of those ancient olive trees that just gets stronger as it gets older. One of her daughters is living with her in a two room . . . I suppose you'd call it an apartment, built into a corner of the wall. The other daughters are married to farmers in the area, mostly second wives. The younger brothers seem to 've moved out; no sign of them at the farm or in town. After the father died, I expect the heir cut off supplies. It's a small farm, it can't really afford to support five grown men with a taste for beerbusts. I did some nosing about. Your Carup was exaggerating a trifle. Even if her father were still alive, she would have her mother's protection, should her mother care to give it. Once a woman who's had children makes it past fifty, all bets are off. She's got whatever freedom she wants; the rules don't apply to her any more. She can tell her old man to take a flying leap and get away with it. I expect that's how she kept the daughter home. If she wanted to shelter Carup, no one could stop her. Your Carup knows all that and she knows how old her mother is. Do you think she just forgot to tell you? I don't. You can shove her in a coach and send her home with a clear conscience."

Brann took a towel from the table, set her foot on her knee and began wiping it dry. "That is . . . marvelous, Jay. One incubus off my shoulders." She yawned. "Ahh, I'm tired."

"Get rid of her, we can't waste more time on her. Bramble, Yaril keeps . . . trying to wake, I can feel it. She's wearing herself out. I can't really touch her, it's like seeing her in a dream. A nightmare. I can't talk to her, let her know we're here. She won't rest. She's wasting herself. I'm afraid she thinks I was caught too. I said a year. I think we've got less than half that."

"Slya Bless." She traded feet, rubbed hard at her sole, scouring off dead skin and the last of the mud stains. "I used to think Carup was so passive she wouldn't try to get away if there was an open door in front of her, I used to think she'd stand there crying and let herself get eaten." She laughed, an unhappy sound. "I wouldn't mind having a little of that passivity now; I get the feeling she's set her teeth and she's not going to be pried off. Never mind, I'll manage somehow." She looked at the filthy towel. "I don't know how I'm going to explain this. Hmp, I won't try. There's something I thought about last night, nearly forgot it when you came ramping at me. This is a trap, right?"

"Right. So?"

"The Chuttar's been going about her business as if she

doesn't give a counterfeit kaut whether we show up or not. Why? What does it mean? Maybe she knows all about us and is just waiting for us to make the first move. Why she'd do that, I don't know, I haven't the least notion why any of this is happening. What about it, Jay? Am I right? Are they just sitting there? Have you seen any sign of agitation? Well?"

"I hear you, Bramble. I think . . . a memory search . . . let me . . ." He looked at the inch of wine left in the glass, pushed it away, pushed his chair back and stood. Abruptly he shifted form and was a sphere of glimmering gold light that rose and floated over the table.

Brann watched as he drifted with the wandering drafts. She emptied her own glass, looked at the jar and decided she'd had enough for the moment. She glanced at Jaril-sphere again, then picked up her trousers and inspected the mud drying on the folds and the ends of the drawstrings that tied about the ankles. She reached for the towel and started to scrub at the scummy cloth.

The lightsphere quivered, came drifting back. Jaril changed again and dropped into his chair. "Memory says the smiglar aren't concerned about anything. They haven't upgraded security, I mean there are no new guards human or other-wise. And they don't leave the place except for the Chuttar and all she does is visit her clients. No one's out looking us, at least no one connected with that doulahar."

Brann brushed mud off a fold of cloth. "I haven't seen any unusual interest in us. A couple baddicks hang around, but that's just the caudhar making sure we don't short him on his rakeoff." She held up the trousers, scowled at the stench from the muck that impregnated the cloth. "Tchah!" She threw the trousers to the floor, dropped the towel on them. "Jay. . . ."

"Yaro is in there."

"You said it was like a dream."

"Yaro is in there."

"All right, you're the one that knows. How do we neuter them? Can we?"

Jaril frowned, shook his head. "Back home, we didn't fight them, we just ate them. Stuvtiggors, I mean. The stuv weren't as . . . well, smart as this bunch and they didn't play round with um magic; these smiglar stink of it. So I don't know. Except, maybe you should try Maksi again."

Brann nodded. She left, came back with a *call-me* cupped

in her palm. She dropped it on the floor, knelt beside it and hammered it to dust with the heel of her mucky sandal.

The glassy fragments vibrated wildly; miniature, hair-fine lightnings jagged over them, died away. Nothing else happened.

Brann dropped the sandal, got to her feet and wiped her hands on her shirt. "That does it, Jay. He's in trouble. Slya bless, everything's twisting into, I don't know." She bent and brushed her knees off, straightened and gazed at the fluttering curtains. "You didn't fight them," she said slowly, "You ate them. You could still do that, I mean even if you've passed from aeta to auli?"

"Yeh. So?"

"The *Skia Hetaira*, remember? We did have Ahzurdan to shield us, but. . . ."

Jaril blinked at her, puzzled. Then he grinned, beat his hand on the table. "Don't fight 'em, eat 'em. You and me and Yaro, we ATE Amortis. We whittled her down and sent her scatting off, scared to her toes."

She sat. "Quiet, Jay. We don't want to wake Carup. Pour me some wine." She lifted the glass, took a sip and sat watching the red change as the lamplight wavered. After a while, she shook her head, as if she were shaking out uncertainty. "We'll keep it simple. If we're lucky . . . though the way things are going, I doubt we get any breaks . . . maybe the Chuttar will be gone for the night, give us less to cope with. Whatever, we go in tomorrow, after midnight, when the servants and so on will be asleep. You circle overhead until I'm inside, then come down fast. That could reduce the time they have for reacting. Unless they can locate me as easily as they can you. We'll just have to hope they can't. Argument?"

"None. Go on."

"Everything we've learned says the Chuttar's personal suite is the heart of that place, so that's where she'd most likely keep Yaro. No one goes in there but smiglar, not her clients, not the maids, no one. It's on the third floor, the main house. There's a smiglar guarding the roof, another at the top of the stair and a third guard stays in the suite whenever the Chuttar's not there. Not counting the Chuttar, that leaves two other smiglar. One of them acts as relief, the other is the Chuttar's Housemaster. Camam Callam, Carup called him. Got his nose in everything, day and night. You say he's second to the Chuttar in power and if the two of them get together, that's trouble for us. I think you're right. Without Maksi to back us, all we can do is try whittling them down. Eat 'em." She gulped some wine, drew her hand across her mouth. "I'll get over the wall and into the house, shouldn't be too hard, break a pane on the glass doors that open on the terrace, turn the latch. You overfly first, let me know where the Housemaster is and the spare guards. I'll avoid them, if possible, drain them if I have to. That'll warn the others, won't it?"

"Yeh. When a bunch of aetas hit a stuv nest, they suck them up and get the hell out, fast, because the place is going to be swarming in minutes."

"You'll feel it too?"

"Yeh."

"Good. You stay high and keep track of me. If I make contact before I reach the stairs, you come in, take out the roof guard and if need be, the stair guard. Eat 'em fast, Jay, I don't want them landing on my back. If there's no contact, if I get up those stairs with no trouble, I'll mindyell as soon as I'm ready to take the guard there, that's when you come in. We'll try hitting the stair and roof at the same time. Then it's a dash for the bedroom. If the Chuttar's out for the night, we hit the guard there, grab Yaro and get out before the others converge on us. If the Chuttar's there, I'll keep her busy while you see if you can get Yaro out of stone and mobile. Yes, yes, you told me, it's likely to be a slow unfolding. If you can't get her out, can you fly and carry her?"

"I suppose. You mean leave you there?"

"If you have to. I'll be doing what I did with Amortis. Draw and vent. Draw down the Chuttar and use her energy to fry the other smiglar if they come at me." She smiled at him, lifted a hand. "Once you get Yaro someplace fairly safe, if you feel like coming back, I wouldn't mind a bit."

"This sounds more like a stampede than a plan. Bramble, there are at least a hundred ways we could screw up."

"I'd say more like a thousand." She shrugged. "Nothing ever goes like you plan it, you should know that, Jay. If we keep moving fast enough, maybe the momentum will carry us through. It's got to be fast. For Yaro's sake." She pushed the straggling gray hair off her face. "If you can think of a better way, tell me."

He shook his head. "I'm not even going to try."

12

Veiled and cloaked, dressed with a subdued richness, she'd absorbed taste from the Chuttar if nothing else, Carup took the bodyguard's hand and climbed into the traveling gada; she ignored his blatant appreciation of her body, but she was pleased by it. Her dark eyes flicked to his face for a moment, then she settled back and he closed the door. He climbed to the seat beside the driver, slapped the man's arm; the driver snapped his whip over the ears of the lead pair and the gada started north along the dusty, rutted road, heading for Pattan Haria.

Brann watched for a while, wondering if Carup would relent and wave. She didn't. From the moment they stepped onto the landing, Carup had refused to see her. She hadn't said good-bye and she didn't look back now. Her resentment had gone deep; she would have rebelled if she'd dared, but she knew too well the futility of fighting powers greater than her own. Bitter, resentful, and rich. A bad combination. She was going to make someone's life a hell.

Brann sighed and stepped into the longboat. "Go," she said, and settled back as the man pushed off and began rowing her across the moat. I've done the best I can, she told herself, I can't change the world by myself. Maksi tried changing a piece of it and look what happened to him.

13

Raining again.

Strong winds, sleet, heavy cold.

The next storm would probably bring snow.

Brann huddled in the entranceway of a kotha, a house built directly on the street without the size, the grounds or the enclosing wall of a doulahar. The kotha belonged to an ancient fence who'd survived purges, investigations and other worries thought up by the Isun, not only survived those but managed to hang onto the greater part of his profits. The door at the back of the short passage was small and massive and there was a trap in the ceiling in front of it; persistent and annoying visitors got a most uncivil welcome; more than once his guards had poured burning oil on a man who wouldn't take *go away* for an answer. He was even nastier to street folk who tried to sleep there, but she was safe enough if she didn't linger too long or make a fuss.

Jaril came trotting in; he was using the horny, water-shedding form he'd dreamed up that night above Kukurul. He shifted and stood shivering before her. "She's staying home tonight. I'm not surprised. With weather like this I'd rather be inside myself. Callam smiglar is in his room, the one on the third floor; he's busy about something, I couldn't see what, I was too far off to do anything but place him. Be better if he was downstairs, soon's we make a noise he'll be over with the Chuttar. Can't help that, though. The relief is at the back of the house in another wing doing something with the other smiglar, the one who stays in the suite when the Chuttar's not there. That's all right, they're nowhere near the terrace, you can go in there without worrying about them. The stair guard and the roof guard are in their usual places."

"Anything I should worry about?"

"Callam. He and the Chuttar are wide awake and up to something. Most nights they're resting by now if the Chuttar doesn't have a client. Dormant. Like Yaril and me, you know. Otherwise nothing different."

"What do you think, should we call this off?"

"There'll always be something."

"You're right. How's your energy level?"

"The cold and the wet are pulling me down. I could use a shot."

"And I'm more dangerous when I'm hungry. Take my hand, yell if it gets too strong."

Brann fed him till he started to glow and she felt a hollow pulse inside her. A Need. When he pulled free, she touched his shoulder. "If you see anything I should know about, give me a tweak, hmm?"

"Bramble!"

"I know, I don't need to say it. Go on, get!"

After he left she stripped to undershirt and loincloth, stuffed her clothing and sandals into a waterproof bag and plunged out of the passage into the rain. She ran along the street, settling to a long easy lope, her feet splatting steadily on the muddy cobbles; she was in her original body again, the old woman banished for the moment. The rain beat into her face, half-blinding her, but she wasn't bothered by that, there wasn't much to see. Most of the street lamps were out, either water or wind had got at them. Splat and splat. On and on, feeling good because the waiting was over, feeling good because her body was fire and iron, working like a fine timepiece, alive, alive, so alive.

She loped past the doulahar's gatehouse, a glassed-in lamp putting out enough light to show her where she was. She slowed, moved closer to the wall and followed it until it turned and she could no longer see the lamp. She unwound the rope from her waist, swung the end with the climbing claw several times, then threw it up. The claw caught. She tugged. It held. She walked up the wall, switched the claw over and slid down, landing up to her ankles in the sloppy mud of a flowerbed. Leaving the rope dangling, she ran for the house, jumping low hedges, plowing through more flowerbeds, swerving to avoid ornamental trees she could barely see, laughing idiotically as she ran, riding the kind of high she hadn't felt for a century or more.

She slapped her hands on the stone railing at the edge of the terrace, vaulted over and ran across the slick streaming tiles; her feet slapped down noisily, she was panting like a swayback mare at the end of a race, but she didn't care, the wind was howling, the rain came swooshing down, the storm was loud enough to cover a stampede, let alone the small sounds she was making.

When she reached the array of glass doors, she looked up into the murk and waited for any comment Jaril wanted to make. Nothing. Good enough. She swung her pack down, reached into an outside pocket and took out a glove; the back was plated with iron and the tips were curving claws. With that on her left hand, she smashed a pane, reached through, and unlatched the door.

As soon as she was inside, she closed it again, threw the latch, and stuffed a wad of drape into the hole. It was black as a coal cellar in there, cold and silent, the sounds of the storm muffled by the thickness of the walls and the heavy draperies drawn across the doors. Working by touch, she took off the claw and dropped it on the rug, then stripped off her sopping clothes and dressed in dry things from the pack. She rubbed her feet, then her hands and head on the draperies, removing much of the wet, enough so she wouldn't drip on the stairs and betray her position by the noise she was making. She hesitated a moment, then pushed the pack behind one of the drapes. Her hands were her best weapons, her empty hands. No point in cluttering them or weighing down her body with unnecessary paraphernalia. Move fast, move clean, momentum's the word, she told herself.

There was a splotch of gray on the far wall, a night-light filtering through a tightly netted doorweb. She moved cautiously across the room, stopped before the web and ran her fingers lightly over it. It was beaded, with beaded fringes, a misery to get past without enough clatter to break through the storm noise. She swore under her breath, gathered a handful of webbing and eased it aside enough so she could edge through. Keeping the fringe still, she spread the web out again until she could take her hand away without shaking the beads.

She listened. The storm sounds were a muted background; there were the usual night noises from a large old house. Nothing more. She ghosted away from the door and plunged into a nest of interconnecting rooms; there were small nightlights scattered haphazardly about, wicks floating on aromatic oil in glass bowls shaped like half-closed tulips. Annoyed and disoriented, she slowed. Jay, you've got it easy, luv. Sheeh! if I just had wings I could cut all this nonsense.

She emerged finally into an immense atrium three stories high with a graceful staircase curling around the rim like a climbing vine, its steps and rails made of white-painted wrought iron with more of the tulip bowls set on the outside edge of the steps, a shimmering loveliness in the tall dark. She listened again. Nothing. All right, she thought. Let's get at it. She glided across the black and white tiles and started up the stairs.

She was wary at first, but by the time she reached the first turn she was running, her bare feet making no sound on the lacework iron steps. Up and around, up and around, first floor, second. She stopped, stared into the murk; she couldn't see anything, but there was no point taking chances she didn't have to. She swung over the rail, hung for a moment until she found footing on the end of the step. Hand over hand, feet feeling for holds, she moved up the outside of the stair, ignoring the abyss below her.

The guard was restless; she could hear him kicking at the floor mat. She hung where she was and peered through a lacy panel. The staircase ended in a dark hole, made all the darker by the faint light from one of the tiny lamps. She couldn't see the guard, not even as a blotch in that blackness, but from what she could hear, he had to be a few steps down the hallway. She shifted her grip and went on.

When she reached the top, she rested a moment, mind-shouted intent at Yaril, then gathered herself and pushed off, using the strength of her legs to counter the relative weakness of her arms and shoulders. She went flying over the rail, landed running. Before the guard had a chance to react, she was on him, her hands slapped against him, drawing the life from him.

At first he went limp, then he began to dissolve; it felt like she had her hands on a sack full of hot-tailed scorpions. She increased the drain until she was taking in at her limit. The dissolution went faster, he was losing his shape, parts of him struggling to escape. He wasn't fast enough. She took everything he had and left him as dust on the mat.

Jaril met her at the door to the Chuttar's suite. He was glowing and grinning, wild and strange, more alien than she'd ever seen him. He nodded at her, shaped his hands into a parabola and shot a stream of fire at the lock, melting it and a good portion of the door around it.

Brann kicked the door open and plunged inside, running at the women who sat near a bank of windows, her hands folded over a black velvet cushion on her lap. The Chuttar Palami Kumindri, smiling and unconcerned. The other smiglar in the room, a big man with black mustaches hanging from the ends of his mouth, stood beside her. Cammam Callam, the Housemaster. He smoothed his mustaches, stepped in front of the chair and raised his hands, palm out. Brann slammed into something as resilient as a sponge, strong as oiled silk. Jaril changed and a blazing lightsphere hit the resilience beside her, rebounded, came at it again and yet again; each time he was flung back, each time he punched a deeper hollow in it. Brann flattened her hands against the shield and drew; somewhat to her surprise, she began pulling in a trickle of power. She laughed and pulled harder; she'd never managed to tap into a magic shield before; apparently this one was so much a part of that smiglar, was maintained so intimately out of his inner strength, she could attack it as if it were his flesh. Callam staggered, paled. He shrunk, grew denser, braced himself and shoved out the sags in the shield.

The Chuttar Palami Kumindri watched calmly for several minutes, then she began unfolding the black velvet. It wasn't a cushion. The milky, flawed moonstone that was Yaril sat on the velvet, pulling in light from all around her. Palami Kumindri lifted an elegant pale hand and splayed it out an inch or so above the Yaril stone. "Be still," she said. Her voice was low and lovely and full of the consciousness of her power. "Stop what you're doing or watch me eat her."

Jaril settled to the floor. He changed and stood radiating fear and rage, his eyes fixed on the Yaril stone.

Brann dropped her hands. "If that viper beside you attacks, I will defend myself," she said, "I will not stand still and allow myself to be destroyed, even for her."

"I have no intention of destroying you, Drinker of Souls. You are going to be much too useful."

"Not if I can help it."

"That's the question, isn't it." Palami Kumindri cupped her hands about the gleaming stone, still not quite touching it. "There's something I want. You can use that to ransom your friend." She took her hands away, rested them on the chairarms. "I will see that she is bathed in sunlight so she will keep as well as possible in this state. I will not harm her in any way, but I cannot prevent her from harming herself. I see you understand."

"What do you want?"

"In the Temple of Amortis, in the holy city Havi Kudush, there sits one of the Great Talismans. Churrikyoo. A small glass frog rather battered and chipped and filled with thready cracks. Bring it to me and I will give you your friend."

"There's a problem. Amortis. She doesn't love me and she knows me far too well. If I go near her, she'll eat me alive."

"You are a clever woman, Drinker of Souls, you will find a way."

"There are other talismans, send me after one of those."

"Churrikyoo is the only ransom I will accept, Drinker of Souls. Bring it here and claim your friend."

"Why should I trust you to keep your word?"

"I repeat, you are a clever woman, work that out. In any case, you have no choice."

Brann clasped her hands behind her, let her shoulders go round. She took time for a leisurely examination of the Chuttar, then the Housemaster. *Jay.*

What? His mindvoice was sullen, unfriendly.

Can they hear this?

No.

You sound very positive.

I am.

You know any way out of this?

No.

Terse.

What's to say?

We snapped up the bait, didn't we.

Yeh. Trolled us right in.

Trust me?

You know it.

Stay quiet, then, I'm going to do some pushing. She finished her look round the room, faced the Chuttar. "I have no choice if I let you dictate terms, if I value my friend's life above everything else. Listen and weep, whore. I do value her, but not beyond a certain point. Beyond that I WILL NOT BE PUSHED! Believe it. I will go after Churrikyoo. I will trade it for my friend. But not here. The exchange will be on my terms, not yours. I won't come back to this house. I won't come near this city."

"Where?"

"Let me consult with my friend." She turned to face Jaril. *Any ideas, Jay?*

Yeh. A Waystop in the Fringelands. Yaro and me, we've been past there more than once. It's just north of the Locks. The place is called Waragapur.

Tell me more about it. Why there?

It's a truceground, which should mean something, but probably won't and there's an old fossil of a sorceror there, one of the Primes. Tak WakKerrcarr. If that bitch smiglar starts playing games with us, she'll have him on her neck. He's the one laid down the guarantee and it's one of the few things he gets stirred up about.

Good. Maybe we can use him to kick something loose.

Anything's better than here.

Agreed. She faced the Chuttar, straightened her shoulders and put her hands on her hips. "These are my terms, I will get Churrikyoo and bring it to Waragapur on the edge of the Fringelands. As soon as I get there, I'll send a message north by one of the riverboats. Come there. Bring her with you and we will make the exchange."

"Why should I?"

"You get nothing if you don't. If you refuse, we fight. You can destroy our friend, but we'll get you. One way or another you die. If not now, later. I have friends I can call on and I will, if you force it, and if you think you can stop me getting out of here, dream on."

"Calmly, calmly, Drinker of Souls. I too must consult. Step outside, please. I will call you when I am ready to answer you."

Brann bowed her head, strolled out.

Jaril hesitated, then followed her. *Bramble. . . .*

What could I do?

Nothing, I suppose.

Be patient, Jay. Our time is coming, has to.

Yaro's in there.

I know. Does she have any idea we're here?

It's that shield, Bramble. The same as the one in the cave. I can't feel anything through it, so Yaro can't feel me.

Damn, I was hoping we'd get at least that much out of this.

We could still try breaking through. I think I was close.

So do I. But we'd have to start over again and we couldn't break it fast enough to save Yaro. Well, we might have to try it. I meant what I said, Jay. If she gets us back here, none of us will get out.

I know.

One thing, we'll have the talisman.

You can't use it.

No, but WakKercarr can and from what Maksi said, he might not be a friend, but he's no enemy.

I didn't think of that. After all these years you can still surprise me, Bramble-all-Thorns.

Let's hope I can surprise them.

Yeh.

"Drinker of Souls." It was a surly growl. Cammam Callam held the door open for them, then went back to stand beside Palami Kumindri, glowering like a chastised boy, obviously hammered into an agreement he wasn't strong enough to refuse.

Brann went back into the room. She waited, saying nothing.

The Chuttar sat with her hands cupped about the Yaril stone as if she were warming them at the changer's glow. "We have considered your terms, Drinker of Souls. We find them acceptable. We will meet you at Waragapur and make the exchange there."

Brann nodded, swung round and stalked from the room. Jaril backed up after her, not taking his eyes off the pair.

They went down the stairs in silence and left the doulahar without breaking that silence.

14

For the next several nights Drinker of Souls hunted through the streets of Dil Jorpashil, soaking up energy so she could assume a new shape. During the days she was the Jantria

Bar Ana and kept up her healing, Jaril taking the form of a small M'darjin boy and acting as her attendant. A few of the local women asked about Carup; they were pleased, angry, happy for her and jealous, when Brann said she'd sent the girl home with a dowry.

Those same nights Jaril flew in and out of Isu sars and the Merchant doulahars, collecting clothing, jewelry and gold for the trip south. He was profoundly disturbed at the thought of leaving Yaril, churned to the point of instability because the days were passing and there was nothing he could do to shorten the time ahead and each day Yaril died a little.

15

One week after the abortive attack of the doulahar, an hour after dawn, when the new-risen sun was a muted blur in the clouds, providing little light and less heat, and the incessant east wind was whipping whitecaps off leaden water, a wealthy Jana Sariser widow attended by a M'darjin page dismounted from a hired palanquin and went aboard the riverboat Dhah Dhibanh.

About mid-afternoon the Dhah Dhibanh cast off her lines and started south, widow and page standing at the rail watching the city recede behind them.

II: SETTSIMAKSIMIN

Sending Todichi Yahzi home
drained Maksim so completely
he was easy prey to a party of
demons (geniod) sent to capture him. He woke unable to
speak or move; it was hard to
think, impossible to act. The
demons put him into his boat
and took him out of the Myk'-
tat Tukery into the sea called
the Notoea Tha where they
transferred him into a small
sleek Coaster and nailed him
into a large crate.

1

When Settsimaksimin surfaced enough for self-awareness,
he was still in the crate and from the dip and sway of it, still
aboard the Coaster. His thoughts oozed across a heavy, dull
mind with the ponderous loiter of a sleep-drugged snail.

How long?

No thirst, no hunger.

Not much of anything.

I see.

Preservation spell.

He tongued at it sluggishly, smelled at it.

The stripes of light that came through the cracks between
the boards of the crate crept across him, marking the passage of a day. Dark came before he finished the plodding
exploration. He drifted into sleep, more from habit than
need, almost despite the spell.

In the morning he thought:

No water.

No food.

How long?

Why do I think? Feel? See? Hear?

It was an extraordinarily subtle spell in that it left him aware of what was happening around him while keeping him in stasis until he was handed over to whoever or whatever had orchestrated all this.

Why?

Yes. I see.

They want something.

They want me to do something.

They want me to do something I probably won't want to do.

They're softening me up.

The stripes climbed over him, moving across his motionless body while he produced these long slow thoughts. Slowly so slowly like a sloworm crawling from one hole to the next, he considered the spell. Night came and his sluggard metabolism reacted again, dropping him into sleep.

Yellow light running across his eyes woke him.

He considered the spell.

It was a strange one, he couldn't place the personality of the sorcerer or other who cast it, but he had nothing to distract him and the effort it took to think acted as a focusing lens. When the swift twilight of the tropical seas dropped over him once more, he almost had it. There was a sense of something distantly familiar, the cousin of a cousin of a cousin of a memory from the part of the past he'd suppressed as soon as he escaped from it, his apprenticeship. He slept.

He woke with the same taste on his tongue.

He burrowed through memory to the time when he was sold into a pleasure House in Silagamatys, six years old, a street rat, father unknown, mother rotting to death from diseases she'd picked up when she worked the wharves as a stand-up whore. He remembered Musteba Xa.

He was bought out of the House by that anciently evil man, a dried-up old bag of perversions who had forgotten how to feel so long ago that even the loss was a dim memory, the most powerful sorceror in the world. He kept that claim real by sucking up life and Talent from his apprentices. Coveting Maksim's Talent, he began to train the boy . . . no, he didn't even see the boy, all he saw was the Talent. He cultivated that Talent like a gardener cultivating a rare plant; he put his hands on it and shaped it the way he wanted it to go. He made only one mistake—he taught Maksim too well, a mistake born out of his inattention to

the whole boy and too much confidence in his ability to jerk
him about like a puppet. With his icy precision and un-
matched learning, his cutting tongue and hypertrophied intelligence, his ability to read muscle twitches and fleeting
shifts of expression so that he knew every thought or intent
that crossed Maksim's mind even before Maksim knew it
was there, he'd forced the angry passionate boy to learn an
equally icy control. When he decided to harvest what he'd
nourished, he summoned entities that were. . . .

Were like these.

Yes.

Like these pseudo Harpish who controlled him.

Maksim's mind shut down on him, the sudden burst of
excitement drowning the delicate control he'd achieved over
his spelled and dreaming body.

Later. Sun stripes hot on him.

He recovered enough to lay phrase against phrase and
began teasing at that memory, pulling out strands of it and
setting them beside his impressions of his captors.

The demons Musteba Xa summoned were similar to the
ones who were holding him now.

But not identical.

The web those earlier demons threw about him was similar to the cocoon that prisoned him now, but weaker.

Back then, he'd reacted from instinct and training; he broke
the bonds and provided Musteba Xa with the first surprise
he'd had in centuries. He killed his master and flung his
body into an empty reality as far off as he could reach.

Similar, yes.

Now that he had some idea what to taste for, he used his
fingertips like a tongue to taste the bonds that held him.

Time passed.

Sometimes he was aware of the thin lines of light running
round him.

When he looked again, more often than not the lines were
gone, the day gone with them.

Sometimes he overworked himself and his mind shut down
again.

Sometimes he was focusing so intently, so narrowly, he
wouldn't have noticed if the ship were on fire.

Interminable and immeasurable, the hours crawled past,
turned into days, the days into weeks and so on.

He reached a point where he needed to know more about
where he was going.

He rested from his labors and watched the sunlines move.

From the way the sunlight shifted about the crate, he decided the ship was heading west.

West of Kukurul the first port of any size was Bandrabahr.

On an average, in the autumn of the year, it was thirty days from Kukurul to Bandrabahr.

He tried to count the days he'd been in the crate, but he could not.

There was a brisk following wind.

A wizard's wind.

He could smell the power in it.

Great galloping gobs of power.

Whoever wanted him was spending it like water.

Bandrabahr. Phras.

He considered the implications of that and wanted to scream his outrage at this, using the sound of his voice to hide his fear.

Amortis.

Phras was her ground, the source of her godpower.

Her Temple was there.

Her priests were trained there.

Gods of Fate and Time, not Amortis!

The surge of emotion shut him off again.

When he came out of the dark, he felt a change in the ship's motion.

He heard port sounds, shouted orders, men calling to each other or to boat whores, the women answering, bargaining, exchanging insults, laughing. Water taxis scooting about, their sweeps shrieking like the ghosts of murdered children.

The language was Phrasi.

The smells were as familiar as his own armpits.

Bandrabahr.

He waited for the shipmaster to heave to and drop anchor.

The ship kept moving.

Slowly, carefully, it wound through the heavy traffic of the busy port.

He listened.

He heard the sounds of cranes and winches, but not the ones on this ship.

He heard the grunts of the rowers on the towships, the drums that set time for them.

He felt the ship yaw slightly.

For a minute he didn't understand this, then he knew the

ship had entered the outflow from the river that ran through Bandrabahr, the Sharroud.

Forty Mortal Hells, am I being hauled off to Havi Kudush? He struggled to control his body's reactions.

He couldn't afford to go black now, he had to get loose. HAD TO GET LOOSE.

He almost lost it at that moment, but suppressed his sense of helplessness and went back to his investigations.

The preservation spell was wearing thin.

His body was speeding up.

His senses were freer.

He could almost shake his mindreach loose.

He was distantly aware of the smells and sounds of the water quarter as the ship clawed upriver through the city.

He was aware of time passing, the minutes ticking faster and faster, moving from loooong looong pulses to the heart count of real time.

The sounds and smells of the city faded and finally disappeared.

He smelled gardens and plowed fields.

He heard birdsong, sheep bleating, the squeal of an angry horse.

They were in the Barabar Burmin, the Land of Hidden Delights, the rich, fertile hinterland of Phras.

He knew this county, he'd spent a century here, a lusty wasteful wonderful century.

Three days upriver was the junction of the Kaddaroud and the Sharroud.

He'd have his answer then.

If the ship turned up the Kaddaroud, Amortis was waiting for him in the Temple at Havi Kudush where she'd fry him alive and eat him for breakfast.

Crossgrained, intemperate bitch god.

She had reason to be annoyed, she'd lost a hefty portion of her substance running his errands, going after Brann for him when he was still trying to kill the Drinker of Souls before she got him.

Hunger began to nag at him.

By the second day on the Sharroud, thirst grew into a torment.

He ignored hunger and thirst and continued to tease ravels out of his bonds, dissolving them as soon as he had them loose so they couldn't wriggle away from him and rejoin the parent weave.

He was beginning to burrow his way out. Soon, soon. . . .

By the beginning of the third day, thirst had him hallucinating.

He saw lightlines turn to serpents of gold that writhed and knotted and coupled in a frenzy of lust and rage, he cringed away from them, thinking that Amortis was coming for him.

Amortis was the patron of lust and frenzy.

He saw polymorphous gold beetles shimmer into uncertain being and drop onto him.

They crawled all over him.

The tickling of their feet grew worse and worse until it was unendurable.

There were other torments, all the worse for being self-inflicted.

He rode out the first waves of that disorientation, husbanding what strength he had left until he saw a chance to seize control. . . .

He shaped a mind-drill and drove it through the decks into the river.

He turned the drill to a drinking straw and sucked up water through it. It was unfiltered river water with all that meant, the suspended soil, the sublife swarming in each drop, but it flooded with grateful coolth into his arid mouth and slid down his aching throat more welcome than the finest wine.

His stomach clenched, cramped and he almost vomited up what he'd swallowed, but he kept the water down and drew in more.

The hallucinations went away.

He returned to his raveling of the spellbonds.

Time passed in its uncertain way.

He looked around.

His vision was no longer confined to what his eyes could see.

He inspected the river banks, felt a flood of relief and pleasure.

They were deep into the great arid plain called the Tark that made up most of Northern Phras.

They were past the junction of the Kaddaroud and the Sharroud.

It isn't Amortis who has me.

Tak WakKerrcarr in the Fringelands, we'll be reaching him soon. If I can *call* him, if he's in a mood to listen. . . .

If I can't, it looks like Jorpashil's the endpoint of this voyage.

Interesting.

Thinking about Dil Jorpashil reminded him of Brann; he smiled.

Bramble, whoever's got that devilkid of yours has put his hands on me, I'd bet my stash on that.

He drank some more river and slept a while.

The hot wind that blew incessantly across the Tark crept through the cracks in the crate, turning it into an oven.

He had to reroute some of his meager resources into cooling himself.

He had to find a way of ridding his bladder of urine without voiding it into the crate; the stench would bring attention he didn't want.

When the ship came to the first of the Locks, he had almost reached the key strand.

One last sustained effort and he would make these bastards wish they'd never been whelped.

Outside the crate, there was frantic activity as the sailors prepared for the entrance into the lock.

The noise and shuddering of the ship faded from his senses as he narrowed and narrowed his focus.

He drew power from the heat in the planks he lay on and prepared himself for the strike that would free him.

He heard an immense rumbling roar and force smothered him.

The Others were awake finally.

He fought them, but he was still more than half bound by the old spinning so his reach was lamentably short, the power he could call on so small it was whiffed out immediately.

He screamed hate and rage at them, but could not get his curses past his tongue, the ties on it were iron-heavy, iron-hard.

He struggled to unlock his hands, but failed.

They were knowing and swift with their binding, but this time he was awake when they handled him and he learned more than they realized. Or so he hoped.

It was godFire they called on, no mage or sorceror, witch or warlock could wield that Fire without a god behind him. Or her.

Not

Amortis

His mind slowed and stiffened.

Not

Amortis

I know
I am sure
Who?
Don't
Know
Don't . . . kno . . . o . . . ow. . . .

2

When he slid out of the darkness, his mind and body were slooow annnnd stiifff.

More than they were when his captors first nailed him in the crate.

He remembered.

That was the first thing he managed.

While he was remembering, the sunlines appeared and disappeared in one blink of his eye.

Appeared and disappeared, appeared and disappeared.

Sound came to him, slowed down and stretched until they were no more than hollow groans without meaning.

He listened and looked.

A concept at a time, a word or a phrase, he explained to himself where he was and what was happening to him.

The ship shivered continually.

That bothered him until he understood it.

The ship was moving with her usual grace at her usual speed; it was the difference between his timerate and hers that made her seem so jerky.

She kept moving, no halts, no major changes in her motion.

They were through the locks.

He was angry.

They'd slid him past WakKerrcarr before he had a chance to *call* the Prime.

He wondered about WakKerrcarr.

Tak must have known something peculiar was happening, he must have ignored it. That was typical of the man and his whims.

He thought about Brann.

It was a better world she lived in.

She wouldn't have dozed as someone was carried past her trapped in a web of demonspin. She'd have been down there finding out what was happening.

He thought about Cheonea and wondered how his experiment was progressing.

He hoped he'd laid a strong enough foundation to carry it on without him.

Brann wouldn't let him go look. You go back, she said, you won't keep your hands off, you'll adjust this thing and lop off that and before you know it, you'll be the old kings reincarnated. Do you realize, he told her, how irritating it is when someone's always right? She laughed at him and patted his cheek and went away to work on a pot or a drawing or something like that.

He missed her.

She was dear. Mother and sister and child in one.

He thought of her walking into a trap like the one that had closed on him and he lost control.

His mind shut down before he could gather its ravels, the world turned black, a mix of fear and rage like pine tar painted on him waiting to be fired.

He woke thinking of her.

How odd it is, he thought. In Kukurul I knew that she wouldn't come back to Jal Virri, that I wouldn't see her again, perhaps for years. I could contemplate that absence with equanimity because I knew . . . he thought about that . . . yes, because I knew we'd come together again. How odd it is. I hadn't the least idea how painful the separation would be. We argue and she runs her hands through her hair, certain we'll never ever resolve our differences. Or I go stomping off, sure of the same thing. A few hours later she laughs, or I laugh, it's all so stupid, not worth remembering. She is dear.

He started working at his bonds again.

Much to his satisfaction, the erosion went faster this time.

He knew them now, he knew the twists they put on their spells.

He knew their arrogance; he'd felt their surprise as he'd come so close to escaping them.

He knew how much an accident it was that they discovered his work before it fruited.

He didn't waste time cursing that accident; what happens, happens.

They watched him closer for a while. He felt their probes sweeping through the crate whenever they decided to check on him.

They'd left him alone for days now, he wasn't sure how many days.

Slipping into their old ways. Careless and rather stupid. Bang not brain. Use it or lose it.

He grinned into the darkness, imagining Brann's acerbic, probably nonverbal response to that list of clichés.

He rested a while and considered his captors.

His mind was moving more fluidly these days and he was again feeling the first touch of thirst.

They should have suspected that might happen.

They should have watched him more closely.

They weren't bothering to watch him.

He smiled, a feral baring of his teeth that might have warned them if they'd been watching him, but they weren't.

Bang bang. Power. They trusted their power.

They didn't seem to understand how tricky a man could get even though he couldn't match their power. Maybe they thought it would take him another thirty days to do what he'd done before. Maybe they expected to reach their homebase before he could get loose again.

Dil Jorpashil.

Sarimbara the Horned Serpent was god in Jorpashil.

He thought about trying to wake the god.

Sarimbara wouldn't be happy knowing other gods and their demons were meddling in his territory.

Sarimbara was a lazy god and spent decades dozing, merged with the earth below Jorpashil, his serpentine length coiled in complex knots; the Jana Sarise had hundreds of lullaby rituals because he was also a god with an infantile sense of humor or it might be a sublimely satiric sensibility; one's idea about which concept applied depended on who he was doing what to. He was touchy about his prerogatives. Those who got too arrogant or proud found their noses rubbed in the mud. The Grand Isu, first among the Isun, could wake and find he was a rag-and-bone dealer, while a beggar sat in his place, eating his food off his fine porcelain, wearing his embroidered robes, enjoying his concubines. It had happened more than once. ANYTHING could happen when Sarimbara woke.

The ship began slowing, weaving from one side of the river to the other as the channel permitted.

There was traffic on the water now, going and coming.

At times the master had to shift his ship as far out of the main channel as he could without grounding her and wait for barge strings to trundle past.

In those quiet times Maksim heard the blatting of the

long-legged sheep that the grassclan Temuengs raised, the
whooping of the drovers as they moved a portion of their
herds to market in Jorpashil.

Sometimes he heard the shouted boasts of young clansmen
heading for one of the river villages to celebrate this or that,
get drunk, spend what coin they had, get themselves in
trouble with the sedentaries and more often than not end up
imprisoned or dead.

The noises from the Grass got louder and more confused,
the traffic in the river denser and slower.

They were closing on Lake Pikma ka Vyamm.

His hands shook.

He fought down the urgency that screamed through him
and continued with his slow, steady attack on the ties that
held him helpless.

A ring of ghost fragments hung like a neck-high mist
outside the walls of Dil Jorpashil. The ship slid through the
part of the ring that drifted over the river, warning him he
had almost no time left.

The soul mist flowed silently through the cracks in the
crate, eddied about him and slowly drained away; the dead
were silenced here as they were in most large cities, so all he
got from them was a vague sadness and scattered pricks of
rage.

He clenched his teeth and continued picking at the spells
that held him.

The river didn't enter Jorpashil, it flowed around the city
in two broad streams, a moat thick with carp and flowering
floating jeppu plants that together almost managed to clean
up the sewage that emptied every day into the sluggish
flows. The island thus created was five miles wide and six
miles long. It rose from the lakeshore to green and lovely
hills like multiple breasts; the high lords, the Isun, and the
lesser lords, the Dhaniks, planted their gardens and built
their elaborate sars up there, above the dust and noise of
the busy, hectic city. Just below them were the whitewashed
doulahars of the richest merchants. For the rest, the poor
lived where they could, the artisans and small merchants
had their quarters, the sublegal professions had theirs, traders and other visitors had their small enclave. Inns and
taverns, theaters and arenas, local markets and businesses
were dotted about wherever there was space and the pros-
pect of customers.

With acres of intricately intersecting alleys, clusters of

cubby stores, daggerflags fluttering before them announcing their wares, ragged lines of open face kiosks piled with meats and fruit and every sort of foodstuff, the Great Market was laid out across the Lakequarter. Stuffed with bales, barrels, jugs, and sacks filled with the rich flow of goods that came up the river from Bandrabahr and by land along the Silk Road and lesser trade routes, low thick walled godons were built between the citywall and the lakeshore. The moorings for the river traffic were on the Lakeshore also, long heavy piers jutting half a mile into the water. Sarimbara's piers. They were built on piles made from the trunks of giant drakhabars brought up the river on huge barges, three trunks to a barge, barge after barge during the summer cutting-season, year after year for fifteen years. A dozen piers splayed out like the fingers on two six-digited hands.

They were there because Sarimbara woke from a doze one day and was annoyed with the clutter of ships scraping their keels against his mud, churning his waters into stinking soup. He decided the Grand Isu was going to do something to stop that nonsense. He demanded coin or service as worshipduty from everyone who ate from the Lake or the river, directly or indirectly, everyone who lived from the fruit of the land, directly or indirectly; in other words, he demanded something from everyone who lived in and around the city. He did some fancy manipulations on the wealthy and powerful to convince reluctant merchants, furious Dhaniks and supercilious Isun to contribute their proper share of the effort. After several haughty matrons and their puissant lords had visions of themselves scrubbing floors, gutting fish or mucking out stables, their enthusiasm for the project was exemplary.

Fighting the powerful sweep of wind that came ramming across the Grass and then across the Lake, sending whitefoam flowing across knifeblue glitter, blowing east to west, eternally blowing, fighting that wind, tacking and tacking again, the ship crossed to the north shore and dropped anchor by cliffs of crystalline white marble, screened from the east wind by a tall vertical fold of that marble.

3

Maksim kept working.

He was so close to breaking the ties. So close.

The ship jerked erratically at its mooring cables.

The minutes stretched and stretched.

He was close. So close.

The crate fell apart around him.

He screamed with rage.

The iron locked his tongue down, no sound came out of him.

The demons hovered about him, spherical glows like Yaril and Jaril but considerably larger.

They began to move, flowing round and round him, faster and faster until they were a ring of light.

He threw off the clinging remnants of his bonds.

With a shiver of triumph, he bounded to his feet and flung himself at the rail.

He passed through the shimmering ring, screamed aloud, finally finally aloud, vaulted the rail and plunged toward the water.

And landed on his feet in an immense cavern, a great shimmering gem of a cavern like the inside of a monstrous geode.

The demons hovered about him, seven nodes of golden light, adding a rich amber cast to the glitter of the crystals embedded in the stone arching over him, dipping under him.

He screamed again, a basso bellow that echoed and re-echoed, reinforcing and canceling the original sound.

The figure on the massive throne raised a hand and compelled a sudden silence.

Maksim lifted his hands to fight, opened his mouth to pour forth the syllables he'd stored against this moment.

Nothing happened.

Nothing came to him.

He was mute.

He was erased.

His hands shook.

His arms went limp, falling to his sides.

"Maks, Maksi, Maksim, is that the way to greet your Master?"

He stared, swallowed. He didn't believe what he saw.

Musteba Xa. Line for line, gesture for gesture, it was Musteba Xa.

It couldn't be.

"You're dead," he said, was momentarily pleased to hear his own voice, then was afraid and angry.

"I killed you," he said. "I flung you into a place where nothing was."

Did they get him from my mind? he thought.

No, he thought.

I would know.

I would know if they plundered me like that.

Trembling with an ancient rage, an even older fear, he glared at the ancient evil old man.

"I will not believe it," he said.

"You are dead, you are ash and nothing," he said.

He gazed into the eyes of what had to be a simulacrum and saw himself.

Whoever or whatever sat there, it knew him to the marrow of his bones.

"You always were a stubborn git, li'l Maks." Musteba Xa (no, it wasn't him, no, it couldn't be him) lifted a crudely polished gemstone, a star sapphire the size of a man's fist.

Maksim tried to snap elsewhere, but the stone anchored him and he could not move.

He fought to break free, but could not.

The stone was one of the Great Talismans, Massulit the Sink, Massulit the Harvester, Massulit awkward and impossible, taking more skill to wield than any of the other talismans. Massulit in the hands of Musteba Xa. No. In the hands of that THING who chose to take his Master's form.

The Thing on the Throne began to chant, drawing threads of soulstuff from Maksim's helpless body, gathering the threads in the heart of the Stone.

He tried to fight.

He slammed into a wall.

For an instant he lost control and beat helplessly, futilely at that wall.

Then he gathered himself and waited for what would happen next.

They want something.

They need me to get it.

They need me alive.

Their mistake.

He managed a slight smile.

I hope.

The Thing watched the souls spin into the Stone, watched the stone glow brighter until its clear blue light filled the cavern.

The Thing laughed, a tottery wheezy giggle that should have made him sound senile and silly. It didn't.

Maksim knew that sound, it was like remembered pain.

He watched his souls spin out of him into the hands that

seemed to belong to Musteba Xa and it was as if none of the intervening years had happened.

"You should thank the geniod for our reunion, Maks." Having settled Massulit into the crack between his withered thighs so his hands would be free to gesture, he waved at the seven glowspheres ranged in an arc behind Maksim, then at the hundreds of smaller lights that oozed from the walls of the cavern and floated free. "They have a little quest for you, dear boy. I told them you'd be stubborn, but you weren't stupid. So here we are. No questions? You haven't changed, have you, Sweetness." Another shrill giggle, then he straightened his bony shoulders and fixed his eyes on Maksim's face. "The Magus of Tok Kinsa has a talisman at the heart of his Keep. One of the Great Ones. Shaddalakh." He clicked his horny yellow nails on the curve of Massulit. "The geniod want it. Matched set, eh? You are going to get it for them. Do it and you get your souls back. Still no questions?"

"Swear on Massulit for your souls' sake that I will get mine back if I bring Shaddalakh out and hand it over."

"You don't want to qualify that, dear boy?"

Maksim shrugged. "Tell me what more I could get if the lie pleases you."

"For old time's sake? For the love that was once between us? Ask, my sweet boy, and you shall receive."

Maksim shuddered, but refused to let his sickness show. "Swear on Massulit for your souls' sake that I will get mine back if I bring Shaddalakh out and hand it over."

The bones in Musteba Xa's face were suddenly more visible; there was spite in him and anger, but he did as Maksim asked. He swore and Maksim was satisfied the oath was complete.

"Let him who is first among the geniod swear the same," he said. "I have lived long enough to know how to die if I must. Let him swear."

The glowspheres grew agitated, went darting about in complex orbits, maintaining a set distance between them no matter how recklessly they careered about. After some minutes of this confusion, the largest of the geniod came rushing toward the throne; it hovered before Musteba Xa, changed form, was a beautiful woman, naked and powerful in her nakedness. She reached out, took Massulit from Musteba Xa's trembling hands. Her contralto filling the cavern with echoes, she declaimed the oath that Xa had sworn, then she dropped the talisman into Xa's lap and stalked over to Maksim.

She caught hold of his arm. Her fingers were strong, but they felt like flesh. He could feel no strangeness in her, see no sign she was other than woman. She stared at him a moment, measuring him, then she snapped them both from the cavern.

4

He slammed down on the backward-facing seat of a closed carriage, a traveling gada, he thought. The woman settled herself opposite him, knocked on the window shutter beside her and braced herself as the gada started moving over a rutted track about as bad as any road he'd ever tried out. The gada swayed wildly enough to nauseate him, lurched and jolted even though the team that drew it was moving at a walk.

He was stiff, cold, filthy, half-starved, and half-crazy with thirst.

On top of that, he was a brittle shell of himself and his body was already beginning the slow agonizing death of the unsouled.

He sat staring at the veiled woman without really seeing her, trying to work out his next move.

Somehow he had to get hold of Massulit and take his souls back with his own hands.

Oath or no oath, he couldn't trust any of them to leave him alive once they had Shaddalakh.

Massulit and Shaddalakh. What talisman did they send Brann after? That at least was clear to him. Someone, something, was gathering the Great Stones.

Who? And did it matter?

All knowledge mattered. How could he plan without a basic piece of information like that?

He scowled at the woman. Geniod?

Who or what were geniod?

Kin to the demons his Master had controlled. Yes. That he'd believe.

He passed his hand across his face, his dehydrated palm rasping across the dry leathery skin. No stubble, thank his unknown father for that and the M'darj absence of face hair.

The geniod woman wore the gauzy voluminous trousers, the tight bodice and silken head veil of a Jorpashil courtesan, having acquired all of these in mid-passage between the cavern and the carriage. She swept the veil aside, let him see her astonishingly beautiful face, skin like cream velvet, brilliant blue-green eyes, hair the color of dark honey falling about her face in dozens of fine braids threaded with amber beads that matched the amber lights the lamps on the carriage wall woke in that honey hair. There was nothing to tell Maksim's ordinary senses or his sorceror's nose that she was demon, not mortal. He found that astonishing also. She smiled and lowered her eyes; one lovely tapering hand played with the amber beads that fell onto the swell of her breasts. She was a superb artifact, a perfect example of what she pretended to be. He suppressed a smile. If she was supposed to be an added inducement, that was one mistake they'd made. Perhaps because I've been living with Brann, he thought. Something else I owe my Thornlet.

He thought about that Thing on the Throne and decided he'd been too precipitous in accepting appearances. He settled himself to endure his physical hardships. I'll beat the bastards yet.

The geniod stopped smiling when he didn't respond. She took a fur rug from the seat beside her and tossed it to him. "Wrap this around you and stop shivering," she said. "You look like a simm kit in a wetfall."

He eased the rug around him and sighed with pleasure as warmth began to spread through his battered body. A moment later the carriage swung about and climbed at a steep angle; it turned again and seemed to glide along. Road, he thought, some kind of highroad with a metalled surface. It was like being in a cradle; the sway was steady and soothing. He began to feel sleepy; his eyelids were so heavy he could barely keep them lifted.

"Stay awake," she said; she kicked his shin hard enough to draw a grunt from him. "Listen. My name is Palami Kumindri. I am Chuttar of the first rank."

"Courtesan," he murmured.

"Yes. I'm taking you into Jorpashil. You will not speak to anyone while you're there, not to people in the street, not even to my servants. I have my choice of lovers, Settsimaksimin, and I choose the most powerful and they do whatever I ask of them; they will not believe anything you say about me, they will have your head off before you get two words out. Remember that. Yes?"

"Yes." Maksim wondered drowsily why she was saying

any of this; she was powerful enough to lay down her own rules for what was, after all, her game. He was too sleepy to ask.

"My doulahar is on the edge of the Kuna Coru. Yes, I have a doulahar and it is larger and richer than any other in all of Jorpashil. I have gardens and slaves enough to keep them groomed. I am rich, Settsimaksimin. And I am going to be richer. I am powerful, Settsimaksimin, and I am going to be more so. We are going to my doulahar, Settsimaksimin, slave." She played with her hairbeads and watched him like a cat with aquamarine eyes. "Take note of my doulahar, slave; that's where you will bring the talisman."

"I hear." Maksim struggled to make his mind work through the waves of sleep. Not to the cavern? Are they going to bring Massulit into that house so they can resoul me? Maybe they're not even going to make a pretense of keeping their oath. Can't think. My brain is like stale mush.

She left him alone after that and he slept until her servants were hauling him out of the carriage, taking no pains to be gentle about it. He stumbled into the room she assigned him and fell on the bed. In minutes he was drowned in sleep.

5

She came herself to rouse him before dawn.

He tried to pull sleep back around him and not-hear her.

She wouldn't let him escape that way; she muscled him out of bed, held him upright while she slapped and pinched him awake. She looked delicate as a rose petal, but she had the strength of a wrestler and a stubbornness greater than his own. After harrying him out of the room and through a series of corridors, she threw him into a bathtub the size of a small pond. It was filled with ice water. She laughed at his indignant roars and left him to his ablutions. At the door she turned. "Breakfast is waiting in the terrace room; ring the bell when you're ready and a servant will bring you there." She left.

Maksim shivered and gritted his teeth. He examined the taps and managed to pump up a stream of water warm enough to take the curse off that already in the tub. Shivering and running through a thousand ringing curses, mostly to hear his voice again, to hear words come pouring from his throat, he scrubbed the accumulated grime off his body. When he climbed from the tub and found clean robes laid out for him, robes tailored for his size and even for his taste in such things, he laughed aloud. Despite the loss of his souls and his miserable predicament, he felt alive and eager to get on with his work. He yanked on the bellpull and followed the servant to his breakfast.

He was surrounded by empty plates and sticky beakers and draining his last bowl of tea when the Chuttar Palami Kumindri came strolling in. She wasn't wearing her veil and her honey hair hung loose about her face; it was long, down to her waist, finer than spidersilk; the drafts from the door and windows teased it away from her head, making it ripple and wave like grass in a stream. She wore beads about her neck, rows and rows of them, ivory, turquoise, jasper, carnelian, beads carved from scented woods, from crystallized incense. She halted just inside the door, smiled at him and stroked her beads, waiting for him to acknowledge he was finished with his meal.

He set the bowl down, got to his feet and bowed. A little courtesy wouldn't hurt. He didn't have to mean it.

A graceful wave of her hand acknowledged and dismissed the bow. "I have purchased a travel dulic for you and two mules to pull it." She smoothed at her hair, tucked strands of it behind a delicate ear. "I doubt if there's a horse in the whole North Country up to carrying a man your size."

"My profound thanks, Chuttar Kumindri. The thought of riding that far put a shiver up my spine." He damped a napkin in a fingerbowl, began working over his hands. When he was finished, he tossed the napkin aside, looked up. "One thing. . . ."

She raised a brow, fluttered a hand.

"It seems to me we'd all be better off if you just snapped me there. Why don't you? You have power and to spare for that minor bit of magic."

"Forget that, Settsimaksimin; you will go the mortal road and keep your head down. The Magus is. . . ." She shrugged; the beads clattered with the shift of her shoulders. "He has discovered somehow there's a magicman pointed at his talisman. Read the omens, I suppose. His reputation says he keeps his fingers on the strings of will-be, old spider. Now that he's alerted, he seems to be delighted with the challenge. He is a very subtle man." She said the last indifferently, the words came out flat and cold as if they meant nothing to her.

He was furious but kept it to himself. "I'll need financing," he said. "Or do you want to pile that on me also?"

"My Housemaster has a map of Tok Kinsa which you might find useful and a plan of the Zivtorony where Shaddalakh is kept. These things are waiting for you when you decide you're ready to leave. He also has a purse with fifty gold jaraufs, five hundred takks and a double handful of dugnas. Make it last, Settsimaksimin, you'll get no more from us." She looked him over, head to toe, a scornful sweep of sea-colored eyes, then she swung round and stalked out.

He chuckled, pleased with himself, hauled on the bellpull and asked the maid who came in to take him to the Housemaster.

6

The HourGong in the drumtower boomed twice as Maksim drove the dulic onto a ferry landing. He was the only one there, the to-ing and fro-ing of the morning was long finished. The ferryman was annoyed at being called from his afternoon nap and took his time winching the cable off the riverbottom where he had to leave it between trips so he wouldn't tear the keels off the riverboats. He demanded a takk for his efforts, but accepted ten dugnas after several minutes of shouts and groans and beatings of his breast. It was too much, but Maksim didn't feel like arguing any longer, he didn't have the energy for it. He drove the dulic onto the flatboat and chocked the wheels while the ferryman whistled up his sons. A small boy who couldn't have been more than five started beating on a gong to warn off ships and barges; the ferryman and the two older boys got busy at the windlass. With the clumsy craft groaning and complaining, the water boiling around it, shreds from the jeppu mats bumping about its side, the man and his sons wound the ferry across the south branch of the river, sweat turning their arms and shoulders to shining brass.

When they reached the other side, there were several riders with a small herd of sheep wanting passage into the city, so the ferryman's sweat on the return trip wouldn't be wasted. As the bargaining got noisy, then noisier, Maksim unchocked his wheels and drove onto the landing. He clucked the mules into a quicker walk and headed toward the Dhia Asatas which were lines of pale blue ink written on the paler blue of the sky.

III: KORIMENEI

Under the prodding of her brother-in-eidolon Korimenei sailed south along the coast to the Jade King's city, Jade Halimm. She was on her way to steal Frunzacoache from the spiritpouch of a Rushgaramuv shaman and take it to the Cave of the Chained God where her brother waited for her to touch him awake.

1

"No, no, no," her brother screamed at her. The eidolon of the sleeping boy floated beside Korimenei as she leaned on the sill of her bedroom window and looked out across the busy harbor at Jade Halimm.

"Why?" She watched a Coaster from the north glide in and drop sails. "What's wrong with taking a Merchanter to Bandrabahr, then a riverboat up to Dil Jorpashil? The Rushgaramuv pass the Lake on their way to wintering in the Dhia Asatas; it'll be easy to pick them up there and follow them until I know enough to take the talisman. I'll have to go more miles that way, but a well-found Merchanter can outpace a caravan in anything but a calm. I don't get seasick, so it's more comfortable than land travel. The most important thing is, it's safer, Tré. I'm a woman traveling alone. I'm young and not hideous. Let me tell you what that means. I'm fair game, Tré. Anything on two legs that fancies his chances will have a grab at me."

"Kori, listen to yourself. You sound like AuntNurse lecturing naughty girls on chastity and virginity. That's not you."

"You think I'm just being female? You haven't been watching the past few days. Aaah! I was spoiled by Silili. I had the school back of me there. I'm not in school now and no one's backing me but me. It makes a difference, Tré. A big difference. I went to the Market this morning. It was like I was running a gauntlet. Ailiki bit one man. I singed another who wouldn't back off. I got pinched and fondled and squeezed and rubbed against. I spent an hour in the baths when I got back here and I still feel dirty. I want to go by ship, Tré, I want civilized surroundings, I want folk around me who know I'm not safe to mess with and who'll leave me alone."

"You're not doing it right, that's all. Don't go out by yourself. Hire a guide, that's what they're for."

"Dream on. Tré, all I have is the money Maksim gave me. It has to last until I can get to the cave and wake you. I can't waste it on extras like guides." She tried to see him more clearly, gave up after a minute. Foolish. It was just an image he was projecting, not him. She felt like crying. They'd been so close, once. He didn't even sound like him any more. I've changed too, she thought. For a moment she rebelled against his demands; let him lay there, he was safe enough; let me get on with my life. She sighed and pushed the temptation away. He was her brother, her dearest. Well, he had been, and she owed something to that memory. "Another reason for going by ship. When you count in everything you need for land travel, the sea is cheaper."

"Not when you count in Amortis."

"Who said anything about Amortis? You won't let me near Cheonea."

"Who said anything about Cheonea? I'm talking about Havi Kudush. That's where her Temple is, that's her ground, the well of her power, where she went when Settsimaksimin fell. By now she's replaced what the Drinker of Souls stripped from her, but she hasn't forgot it."

"The well of her power, hmm. You sound like one of my teachers."

"Kushundallian discoursing on the fundamentals of godhood?"

"Right. You were watching?"

"You know I was. Stop dithering. If you go upriver from Bandrabahr, you pass through the heart of her ground. Do you think she's forgot you, Kori? Do you think she doesn't know who brought the Drinker of Souls to Cheonea? Do you think you can slip by her? Well?"

"No, I don't think any of those things. You've made your point. What I don't understand is why you let me come this

far south. I could have gone north to Andurya Durat and
been on my way by now."

"Durat? Don't be an idiot, Kori. It'd take you a year and
a small fortune to get a pass to the Silk Road. No. Jade
Halimm is the place to start if you need to travel the Road.
You take a riverboat up the Wansheeri to Kapi Yuntipek;
you get what you need there and take the Road to Jorpashil.
It's too late for caravans; you'll have to travel by yourself.
You can handle that, Kori; you know you can."

"What if the passes are closed?"

"They aren't. Not yet."

"How do you know?"

"Trust me. I know. There's been one storm in the mountains, it laid down three, four inches, but they've had rain
since, so most of that snow is gone. You've got around a
month before you'll have trouble getting through."

"So now you're Kiykoyl tosNiak, weather wizard?"

"I see what I see."

"That's the fact, huh?"

"That's the fact, yeh."

"You weren't around on the Mountain. I needed to talk
to you, Tré."

He didn't answer. As he hadn't answered then. She straightened. "It's suppertime. I'll catch Our Host, see what riverboats are in and when they're leaving. With a little luck, I'll
be out of here tomorrow."

2

The Miyachungay cast off and started upriver an hour
after dawn, her slatted sails clacking and booming in the
wind that came sweeping onshore most mornings as if it had
dragons on its tail. After counting and recounting her coins,
Korimenei had paid the premium that bought her a tiny
cabin for herself; it wasn't much larger than a footlocker,
but it had a bar on the narrow door so she'd sleep in peace
and comparative comfort. As a cabin passenger she took her
meals at the Captain's table, which meant she'd eat well and
since the cost was included in the price of her cabin, she felt
she'd made herself a satisfactory deal.

She stayed in the cabin as long as she could that first
morning. She was uneasy; she didn't know how to behave as
a traveler; she didn't know what the rules were. Settsimaksimin
had translated her directly from Cheonea to the school in
Silili. And she hadn't traveled after she'd got to school,

Shahntien Shere kept a thumb firmly planted on her students. She'd gone from one tight supportive society to another. She didn't want to make mistakes. The short trip downcoast on the Merchanter hadn't helped, she'd stayed in her cabin the whole way. She was scared to stick her nose out now. It was funny. She could see that. She could even laugh at herself. It didn't help. She sat on the bunk with Ailiki on her lap, singing nursery songs to her, trying to convince herself she didn't mind the stuffy darkness of the room.

The walls closed in on her; the cabin was turning into a coffin.

"I've got to do it sometime, Aili my Liki. And you have to stay here, my Lili. Watch my things for me, hmm?" She tapped Ailiki on her tailbone. "Shift yourself, luv. I've got to unpack my meeting-people suit."

She'd bought Temueng traveling gear, a padded jacket and loose trousers gathered at the ankle over knee-length leather boots, a veil that went over her head and extended in two broad panels that hung before and behind, brushing against her knees. The veil had embroidered eyeholes, a knotted fringe on the edges; it was heavy cotton, a dusty black, and she hated it. Bumping elbows, knees, buttocks every time she had to shift her body, she changed to her new clothes and pulled the veil over her head. She coughed; she couldn't breathe. She knew that was stupid, she was doing it to herself. She reached under the veil and pushed the cloth away from her face, groped for the door and went out.

When she climbed onto the deck the wind took hold of her; it nearly ripped the veil off her and used the loose cloth of her trousers as a sail. Blinded and more than a little frightened, she clung to the doorjamb and struggled to get control of her clothing. Hands closed on her arms; someone large and strong lifted her, carried her down the ladder and set her on her feet in the companionway.

"Get rid of that damn veil, woman; it's a deathtrap. You're no Temueng; what are you doing dressed up like one?"

Korimenei dragged the veil off and glared at the man. He was a big man, broad rather than tall, his eyes on a level with hers. His shoulders were wide enough for two, his bare arms heavily muscled, his hands large and square; she remembered the strength in them. A Panday sailor. His ear

dangle had three anchoring posts it was that heavy; it was
ovals of beaten gold set with pearcut emeralds; it swayed
with every movement of his head, the emeralds catching the
light, winking at her. He was grinning at her, his green eyes
glinting with an amusement that infuriated her even more.
"Who do you think you are and why's it any business of
yours what I do?"

"I think I'm Karoumang, Captain and Owner of this
vessel and it makes all kinds of trouble for me when a
passenger falls overboard because she's too lamebrained to
know what the hell she's doing."

"Oh." She passed her hand from her brow to her nape,
feeling the straggles and bunches dragged into her hair. A
mess. She must look terrible.

"Here. Let me have that thing." He took the veil from
her, hung it over a lamp hook. "You can retrieve it later.
You still want to go on deck?"

Hands pressing her hair down, she nodded. It seemed
safest not to say anything.

He followed her up the ladder, grabbed a handful of her
jacket as the wind caught her again. "Been on a riverboat
before?"

She hesitated, then shook her head.

"First thing to remember, when we're moving there's
wind, no wind, we stop."

She snorted, tried to pull away. "I'm not a child."

He ignored that, kept his hold on the back of her jacket
and moved her along, threading through the bales and barrels piled about the deck, roped in place or confined by
heavy nets. "Second thing, wind takes us upriver. Down,
the river takes us and we fight the wind. One way or
another there's always wind." He piloted her past the main-
mast, the noise of the sails and the singing of what seemed
hundreds of ropes was all around her; it was like air, always
there, so much so that in minutes she scarcely heard it,
underscoring what he'd just said to her. "Third thing, this is
a cargo boat. We take passengers, but not many of them.
The cargo comes first. Passengers, even cabin passengers,
should stay put when we're moving. If they think they need
air, they should get air when we're tied up at one of our
calls. Or they should join the deckers in the cage and stay
there."

He stopped her by a heavy ladder with a hand rail; it led
to a raised platform in the bow. "Up," he said.

She glared at him, considered telling him what she thought of him; she wasn't quite sure what she did think of him, so she kept silent, caught hold of the rail as he took his hand away. She went up those steps quickly; in spite of her irritation she was enjoying the brisk scour of the wind, the sounds and sights around her, everything new, everything strange and exciting. Even Karoumang, or perhaps especially Karoumang. Her body responded to him even as her mind said be careful, woman. As she stepped onto the narrow flat, she kept hold of the railing, made her way along it until she was looking down into the yellow water foaming about the bow. A small boy who was an exact miniature of Karoumang looked up from his perch in a bag net suspended from a stubby bowsprit; he waved a small grimy hand and went back to his watch, green eyes like Karoumang's intent on the water ahead. A tarnished silver horn hung on a thong about his neck, swaying with the movement of the boat.

Karoumang leaned over the rail. "Lijh't aja, i'klak?"

"Tijh, ahpa."

Korimenei looked from the boy to the man. "Your son?"

"One of them. I was asking about snags and he was saying there aren't any. So far." His eyes laughed at her as he turned to face her. He set his left arm on the rail, leaned on it. "Enigma," he said.

"The river?"

"You."

"Certainly not. Nothing difficult about me, I'm simply going home."

"Not up this river."

"Why?"

"Nobody like you north of here. Croaldhu, I wouldn't be surprised, Yuntipek I am. Married?"

"None of your business."

He inspected her, paying no attention to her words. "I don't think so. No man worth the name would let you run around alone. Virgin?"

"Definitely none of your business." She thought about leaving; this conversation was getting out of hand. She didn't want to leave. She glanced at him, looked quickly away.

"Hmm. I'll let that one hang. Twenty one, two . . . no, I'd say twenty-nine."

"Twenty-four." She snapped it out before she thought, glared at him when she realized what she'd done.

He stopped smiling, narrowed his eyes at her. "Over age, alone, no guards, no chaperone. Not someone's daughter coming from a visit or going to a wedding. Not wed, not courtesan, not player, not trader. Priestess or acolyte? No, the attitude's all wrong. You're no holy she. Holy terror, maybe. Student?"

She thought that over for a moment, then she nodded. "Was."

"Croaldhu? No. You have the look, but your accent's wrong. And there's that attitude. You're a little shy, but there's fire under it. You're edgy, but you're not afraid of me or anyone else. Not womanfear. You think . . . no, you're sure you can back me off. I outweigh you and out-reach you. If I took a notion, I could pull you limb from limb in about thirty seconds. Or tear those idiot clothes off you, throw you down and do the usual. I don't see anything you could do to stop me. You're looking at me now like I'm the idiot."

"Your word, not mine."

"I see your shyness is starting to wear thin. Silili?"

She thought that over, shrugged. "Why not. Yes."

"Which school?"

"Does it matter?"

"Curiosity. I'd like to know."

"The Waymeri Manawha, Head Shahntien Shere."

"Sponsor?"

"How do you know about that?"

"I have a son with Talent."

"Ah. He's in school?"

"Will be, come spring. The Mage Barim Saraja has agreed to sponsor him. For a fee big enough to buy an emperor, though as a favor don't repeat that. Yours?"

"Why should I tell you?"

"Why not?"

"Why not. The Sorceror Settsimaksimin."

"One of the Four Primes, eh? I am impressed."

"So I see."

"I am." He moved away from the rail, bowed at the waist, his hands pressed palm to palm before his nose. He straightened, chuckled. "No lie."

"Curiosity satisfied?"

"Whetted." He arched a brow at her. "With questions I'm not going to ask. Where you came from and what your story is." He waited a moment to see if she was going to respond; when she didn't, he rested both arms on the rail and gazed ahead at the river which was a broad empty stretch of ocher fluid; there was no other traffic in view, only this boat riding the wind upstream. "How you came to the notice of a Prime, what there was about you that interested him." He looked along his shoulder at her, letting his appreciation show. Odd. She liked it. It was essentially the same as the looks she'd got from men in Jade Halimm and those made her sick. The looks that saw her as prey for the taking. In those long narrow eyes, green as the stones in his ear dangle, it had a different flavor somehow. Definitely she liked it.

"What your rank is now," he murmured, "and what it's apt to be when you come to full strength. What you are." He counted types, tapping his fingers on the rail. "Charm spinner, diviner, dowser, shaman, necromancer, witch, thaumaturge, wizard, magus, sorceror. Do I have them all? Probably not." His brow shot up again. He seemed to be enjoying this, playing his little wordy game with her, then his pleasure faded. "Where you're going and why, what you're doing here, now." He looked away, the exaggerated Panday curves of his wide mouth straightening to a grim line. "A favor, Saöri. Keep it off my boat."

"There's nothing to keep," she said. "On or off. I'm just traveling. That's the truth, Karoumang Captain. I'm going somewhere, but where's a long long way from here and nothing to do with you." She put her hands on the rail beside his; they looked anemic, sickly almost, next to his rich coppery brown; her arms were thinner than his, much thinner, despite the bulk of the quilted sleeves, and pale like her hands with pale pale pinkish brown freckles scattered through the fine colorless hairs, blitchy blotchy like a red and white cow. She was glad they were hidden. She felt anemic all over, spirit as well as body; her irritation at his prowling round her, sniffing at her, which had armored her so feebly against him, had gone away altogether and left her stranded. She wanted to touch his arm, to see if it was as hard and sleek as it looked. She tried not to think of her initiation, of the golden, glorious chthone who'd made her every nerve a river of fire, but her body was remembering. When she sneaked a look at Karoumang from the corners of her eyes, it seemed to her he was outlined in shimmering gold light, that he was as beautiful as the god had been. She wanted to see him naked like the god; she pictured him

naked, lying beside her, his hands on her, his strong hands
moving on her. The breath caught in her throat; she tightened her fingers on the rail.

He was frowning at the water ahead. Abruptly, he leaned
over the rail and spoke to his son. "Aja 'tu, i'klak? Mela'
istan." He pointed to a line and some dots on the water
around a half mile or more ahead of them, a long, dark
thing with several stubby outthrusts that was rapidly coming
to meet them. "Angch t'tant." He waved his hand at the
horn. "Lekaleka!"

"Eeya, ahpa." The boy steadied himself, eyed the object
for a few beats until he was sure he know its course, then he
put the horn to his lips and blew a pattern of staccato notes.

Karoumang swung around, hurried to the rail, his eyes
moving swiftly about the ship, following his crew as they
went to work with a minimum of effort and a maximum of
effect while the echoes of the horn notes still hung in the
air; he watched the sail panels change conformation, watched
the helmsmen on the overhang shift the tiller the proper
number of marks to take them from the path of the snag.
He relaxed, came back to Korimenei, smiling. "A good
crew; they save me sweating." He leaned over the rail.
"Baik, i'klak."

The boy laughed. "Babaik, ahpa."

"He's a clever boy," Korimenei said. "Reminds me of my
brother. How old is he?"

"Nine. The only one of the bunch with a call to the
water." He took her hand, spread it on his palm. "What
small hands you have for such a tall girl."

"Not so small, it's as long as yours almost."

"But narrow. Bird bones, light as air." He turned the
hand over, drew his forefinger across her palm. "Do you
read these lines?"

Her breath turned treacherous on her again. She called
on the discipline the Shahntien had hammered into her and
when she spoke her voice was light, laughing. "I play at it.
It's only a game."

"What other games do you play?" He stroked her palm
absently, as if he'd forgot what he was doing.

"Girl's games," she said, deliberately misunderstanding
him, "but not many of those. There wasn't time. The
Shahntien kept us at it."

"And now?"

"And now I follow my own inclinations."

"And what are those?"

"What do you want them to be?"

"What shall I say?"

"That I'll be a student again, a day, a week, to Yuntipek, perhaps."

"You think I could teach you?"

"I think you are an expert on a subject I know little about. I think you enjoy such teaching and I like that. When the teacher enjoys, it's likely the student will."

"Sometimes there are consequences to this exchange."

"Not for a fledgling sorceror from the Waymeri Manawha who has urgent claims on her time and energy." She chuckled. "Though distant ones." She was pleased with herself, enjoying the suggestive obliquities.

He laughed, placed a kiss on her palm. "Shall we begin the lessons after supper tonight?"

A tiny gasp escaped before she could swallow it.

He squeezed her hand. "Would you like to stay here or go below?" A glance at the bank gave him time and place. "We'll make a call in a couple hours. We have cargo to unload, probably pick some up, so we'll be there a while. You can go ashore, if you want to walk around. I wouldn't advise it. It's a chern village, you might see things you won't like. These country chernlords are an ugly bunch. Even a fledgling sorceror should watch what she says and does around them."

"Karoumang teacher, it's not lectures I need from you," she smoothed her fingers across the back of his hand, ". . . but demonstrations."

"You need a whole skin to appreciate them, ketji. Stay on board at Muldurida. The next call up the river is a freetown and friendlier. Saffron Moru. We'll tie up for the night there."

"I think I'd like to go below for a while. Do you mind my being a bit afraid?"

He threw back his head and laughed, a big booming sound that came from his toes. "Noooo," he said. He took a handful of her jacket. "Let's hit the wind, ketji."

3

Korimenei stepped from her trousers and kicked them across the narrow cabin; she sat on the bunk and began working a boot off her foot; the boots fit close to her legs and took some maneuvering to put on and take off. "Aili

my Liki, I've got myself into something and I don't know
how it's going to turn out." She dropped that boot, started
on the other. "Consequences, he said. He meant pregnant,
but there's a lot more to think about, isn't there, Lili. Every
act has consequences and most of them surprise the hell out
of you. Back at school they kept hammering that into us: *Be
careful what you do; the more powerful the act, the more
unpredictable the outcome. Don't do what you can't live
with. Undo is a word without real meaning.* They didn't have
to tell me any of that, I knew it already, especially the last.
Look at Maksim, look at where he is now, look where I am.
Tré and I summoned the Drinker of Souls because we
thought we could get the soldiers out of the Vales and things
would go back the way they were before Amortis got greedy;
we thought she'd cancel what Maksim was doing to us.
Undo it. They're right, they're right, they're right, you can't
undo anything." She dropped the second boot, dug under
the blankets for the pillow and tossed it against the headwall.
"I want to do this, Lili. My body screams do it." She swung
her feet up and half sat, half lay, staring at the scraped and
oiled calfhide stretched across the porthole. "What if I don't
want to stop when I get to Yuntipek? Gods, the minute I
saw him, I wanted him. He's got kids, a wife. A life he
likes, no, loves. I'm a kind of trophy, aren't I, Lili. No,
maybe not. But he does like power. Probably never had a
sorceror before." She giggled, snapped her fingers. Ailiki
jumped from the seat beside the porthole and landed on her
stomach, driving a grunt out of her. Stroking her hand down
and down and again down the mahsar's small firm body,
she went on talking to herself. "Most of them are men, you
know. I wonder if you do know, I wonder what you are, my
Aili, my Liki. No men for our Karoumang. He's single-
minded that way, you can smell it on him. I lay with a god
of sorts and got you out of it, Lili. I've never been with a
man. I wonder if I'm spoiled for mortal sex. I'll know by
tomorrow morning, won't I. Oh Gods."

Ailiki purred like the cat she wasn't, her body vibrating
and warm.

"Words. All words. No illusions and scared to my toe-
nails, but I'm going to do it." She lifted Ailiki, held her so
the mahsar's body dangled and they were looking eye to
eye. "Lili my love, you watch my back, hmm?" She laughed,
set the mahsar on her stomach and lay stroking her and
watching the light change.

4

Night followed day and day followed night; the world turned on the spindle of time. It was a curious time for Korimenei, a happy time. A respite.

Nights she spent in the Captain's bed. Days she sat on the forehang and watched the land flow past, the little villages with their mud walls carved and decorated with the local totems, their wharves and storetowers; she watched horses run in clover fields, cattle and sheep graze in sun-yellowed pastures; she watched serfs and small farmers finish up the fall harvest and line up at flour mills and slaughter grounds; she watched the creaking wheels that were set thicker than trees on both banks send water and power to the fields and the two and three family manufactures in the villages. She watched the day passengers going from village to village, carrying things they wanted to sell, or visiting relatives; one time a wedding party came on board and celebrated the whole distance with music and wine and dancing; one time a band of acrobats came on board and earned their way with leaps and ladders. These sights were endlessly interesting, partly because it was a place she hadn't seen before, a people she didn't know; partly because it reminded her of the life she'd left behind when Maksim discovered her Talent and flung her two thousand miles away from everything she knew.

Life was on hold for her, as if responsibilities and dangers were standing back and waiting for the trip to finish. Even Tré's eidolon stayed away. She called him once, curious about his absence, but he didn't answer. She was annoyed for about five minutes, then she shrugged off her irritation. She didn't really want him around. The thought of him watching her with Karoumang made her itch all over.

She was enjoying her bi-nightly lessons as much as she thought she might. Karoumang was a man of wide and varied experience and it was a matter of pride with him that she got as much pleasure from their coupling as he did. He could be maddening at times, especially when he treated her like some brain-damaged infant, but he liked her. He really liked her. Part of that was because he simply liked women, all women. Part of it belonged to her. She stopped worrying about what was going to happen at Kapi Yuntipek. Her infatuation was settling into something less exciting but a lot more lasting.

##

Twelve days after the Miyachungay left Jade Halimm, she
came to the hill country and passed through the first series
of locks; there were three more sets she'd have to negotiate
before she reached the high desert plateau of Ambijan and
the run for Kapi Yuntipek.

5

Something hard and cold slapped against Korimenei's buttock, then was gone; small hands and feet with sharp nails
ran along her back. Something cold and hard slid along her
shoulder and stopped against her neck. Long whiskers tickled her face. She muttered something, even she didn't know
what, opened her eyes. There was just enough light from
the nightglim over the door to show her she was nose to
nose with Ailiki. "Wha. . . ."

Ailiki backed off. When she reached Karoumang's pillow,
she sat up, her handfeet pressed into the soft white ruff that
flowed from neck to navel.

"Something wrong? Karou. . . ." Korimenei shivered; the
nights this time of the year were chill and damp, each one
colder than the last, and someone—probably Ailiki—had
pulled the quilts and blankets off her. Twisting around, she
reached for the covers. Something rolled off her shoulder
and thumped down on the sheet. She blinked. The Old
Man's bowl? Wha. . . .

Ailiki darted at her, picked up the bowl and scampered
back to the pillow. Sitting on her haunches, holding the
battered pewter object against her stomach, she stared fix-
edly at Korimenei. Her ears were pressed flat against her
head. The guard hairs on her shoulders were erect and
quivering. Her lips were drawn back, exposing her small
sharp fangs.

Korimenei rubbed at her eyes, tried to get her brain in
order. "Lili? What's happening? What are you. . . . Karoumang?" She touched the sheet where he'd been. It was cold.
Is it . . . Gods. His being gone hadn't bothered her before;
he always got up some time during the night and took a
walk around the boat, checking things out, making sure his
Second was doing a proper job and his night crew wasn't
sacked out on some of the softer bales. She slid out of bed,
began groping for her clothes.

Ailiki beat on the bowl with her fingernails, a tiny, scratchy,

tinging sound. Korimenei straightened, stared at her. Somehow, without crossing the intervening space, the mahsar had
got over by the porthole and was squatting on the table
where Karoumang worked on his books. She took the bowl's
rim in her little black hands and hammered at the table,
producing a series of resonant clangs. Then she sat on her
tail and fixed her round golden eyes on Korimenei.

"Not Karoumang?"

Ailiki shook her head and patted the bowl.

Puzzled, Korimenei tossed aside the trousers she was
holding and pulled on her dressing gown. "I wish you could
talk, Lili. It'd make things so much easier on both of us."

Ailiki hissed at her; in spite of her relatively immobile
features, she managed to look disgusted. She waited until
Korimenei reached for the bowl, then she went elsewhere.
She returned a moment later with a two-handled crystal cup
filled with very clear water. She set it in front of Korimenei
and stood back, expectation quivering in every line.

"Ah." Korimenei kicked the chair away from the table,
sat and poured the water into her bowl. "Farlooking?"

Ailiki wiggled her whiskers.

"Danger ahead?"

Ailiki scratched at the table.

"For me?"

Two scratches.

"For me and Karoumang?"

Three scratches.

"For everyone on the boat?"

Ailiki's ears came up and her whiskers relaxed. She
stretched out on her stomach, her chin resting on her folded
forearms.

Karoumang came in. When he saw Korimenei at the
table, his brows lifted. "What's doing?"

"You see anything to worry about?"

He crossed to stand behind her, slid his hand into her
robe and stroked her neck. "No, should I have?"

She leaned into his arm as his hand worked down to play
with her breast. "No. . . ." Ailiki lifted her head and scratched
at the table again, her nails digging minute furrows in the
wood. Korimenei sighed. She put her hand over Karoumang's,
stilling it. "Go to bed, Karou. You distract me."

"From what?" His voice was sharper than usual; he wasn't
used to being told to go away. He freed his hand, cupped it

under her chin and lifted it so he could see her face. "What are you doing?"

She caught hold of his wrist, pulled his hand away. "I don't like that, Karoumang. I won't be handled like that."

He walked to the end of the table, faced her. "And I won't be sent to bed like a naughty boy. What are you doing?" It was the Captain speaking, wanting to know everything about what went on aboard his boat. She wasn't lover anymore, she was an unhandy combination of crew and passenger.

Korimenei relaxed. "Pastipasti, Captain Saö. Remember my profession." She flattened her hands on the table, the bowl between them. "I had a warning. I was about to take a look and see what it meant. Now, will you please go sit on the bed and let me get on with it?"

He frowned, fisted a hand and rubbed the other over and around it. She could see that he'd forgot what she was since he'd taken her to bed; anyway, he never thought of women as having professions apart from their families; he wasn't hostile to the idea, it simply wasn't real to him. "Do it with me here," he said. "I want to see it."

"Hoik over that hassock and sit down then, you make me nervous, looming over me like that."

She waited until he was settled, then she leaned over the bowl and began to establish her focus. She banished Karoumang, banished Ailiki, banished the boat, the noises around her, everything but her breathing and the soft brilliance of the water. She began a murmured chant, using archaic words from her birthtongue, words she'd learned from the rhymes her cousins and AuntNurse had sung to her when she was a baby. "Yso.yso.ypo.poh," she softsang. "Ai.gley.idou.pan.tou.toh. Pro.ten.ou.kin.tor.or.thoh, nun.yda.ydou.ydoh."

She blew across the water, creating a web of ripples that rebounded from the sides of the bowl, canceling and reinforcing each other until they faded and the water was smooth as glass. An image appeared, a narrow valley, heavily wooded, shadowed by the peaks that loomed over it. A cluster of houses inside a weathered palisade. A two-story building with a four-story tower beside the river, fortified, the second floor extending beyond the first. A lock gate with heavy tackle bolted to massive stone bulwarks and huge, heavy planks.

Karoumang whispered, "The locks at Kol Sutong."

The scene fluttered and nearly vanished. She hissed through her teeth at him and he subsided. With some difficulty she retrieved her concentration and brought stability to the image.

The point of view had changed when the picture cleared. She was looking inside the Lock House. There were bodies scattered about, some sprawling like discarded rag dolls, some bound and gagged. All dead. Small dark men dressed in leather and rags and heavily armed were sitting at a table playing a game of stone-and-bone on a grid one of them had scratched in the wood. The view shifted again, showed the inside of the watchtower. One of the raiders was standing at the south window, looking down along the river. The sun was just coming up, staining the water red; the fog lingering under the trees was pink with dawnlight. A boat appeared, the Miyachungay.

Karoumang growled, lurched onto his feet.

"Sit down!" Korimenei pushed him away, keeping her eyes fixed on the image, willing it to hold as it wavered and threatened to break up.

The image boat slowed, moved past the gates and hove to. Some of the men in the Lock House ran to the tackle and began winching the gates closed. As soon as the bars clunked home, other men came trotting from behind the House, carrying canoes; they dealt competently with the eddies and the undertows and went racing for the boat. In minutes they were swarming over the rail, hacking and clubbing the crew, killing everyone they came across; Karoumang and the crew fought back, but there were too many attackers. When the killing was done, the raiders tore into the bales and barrels, spoiling what they didn't want. When they were finished, they set fire to the boat. They opened the lock before they left, sat on their shaggy ponies cheering and waving bits of cargo as the charred timbers and the dead went floating away.

The image vanished.

Korimenei watched her fingers twitch, then flattened her hands on the table. "Well," she said. "You know the river. When will we get to . . . what was it . . . Kol Sutong?

Karoumang was frowning at the water; when she spoke, he turned the frown on her. "It didn't show you. Why?"

"It never does. The seeker is always outside the scene. Um." She ran her finger around the rim of the bowl; unlike glass, the pewter was silent. "You needn't take these things as chipped in stone, Karou."

His fingers drum-rolling on the table, he examined her face. "I've been to seers before, Kori Heart-in-Waiting. I've seen the water pictures summoned before. Always the seers tell me, that IS what will be."

"They lie, Karou. Well, maybe not lie, just make things simple for a simple man."

"Tchah! I'll give you simple, ibli ketji." He wrapped a hand around her wrist. "Stop being perverse and explain."

"If I'm a devil, why should I?"

"Come to bed and let me show you."

"Shame-shame. Bribery. I accept. Seriously, Karou, what you've seen here is something that's set up to happen, that will happen unless we act to stop it." She tapped the back of his hand and he opened his fingers, freeing her wrist. "So, tell me. How soon?"

"It was almost moonset when I came down, dawn's about three hours off. We should be seeing the tower roof a little after first light." He stared past her, unseeing eyes fixed on the porthole. "Unless I go back and pass a few more days at Maul Pak."

"Any point in that? Would the local chernlord send troops to rout out those raiders?"

"The Pak Slij huim Pak?" He made a spitting sound without actually spitting, it being his boat and his table. "I don't have the gold it'd take to stir that tub of lard into action. The Jade King himself doesn't have that much gold."

"Mmf. What if you did tie up for two, three days? The hillmen wouldn't stay put that long, would they?"

"Turn tail like a pariah dog. Turn once, I have to keep turning. No." He frowned at her. "With a sorceror on board? No."

"Fledgling sorceror, Karou; I left school less than a month ago. I have no staff, I haven't pledged to a Master, I haven't . . . oh, so many things, it'd take too long to list them. I don't know what I can do . . . should do," she rushed the last words, "I have to think." Her hands were shaking again and she pressed them hard against the wood, finding a kind of comfort in the resistance of the seasoned oak. "Is there a place along here where you could tie up for an hour or so? I'd better not try anything difficult on water, I'm not good with water, I need to have earth under me."

"That's water." He waggled a thumb at the bowl.

"That's different. What you need, it costs more; it takes . . . well, if I manage anything, it'll take a solider base."

"It's your business, ketji. I suppose you know what you're doing." He got to his feet. "I'll give you two hours; if you can't come up with a plan by then, I'll take the crew and burn the bastards out."

6

A worn broom under one arm, a lantern in her free hand, Korimenei turned slowly in an open space where an ancient had fallen in some long-ago storm. Woodcutters had carried it off, leaving only the hollow where the roots had been. The cedars ringing the glade were young, their lower branches sweeping the ground, lusty healthy trees with no limbs gone. She held the lantern high; there was no down-wood anywhere, not even chunks of bark. "Cht!" she breathed. "Pak Slij. No doubt he'd sell air if he could figure out a way to bottle it."

She set the lantern down on a relatively level spot and began sweeping away the loose earth and other debris. Working with meticulous care, she removed everything movable from a circular patch of ground, ignoring insects, worms and other small-lives because she couldn't do anything about them anyway. When she was finished, she took a fragment of stone and drew a pentacle with the same finicky care, humming absently one of the nursery songs her dead mother sang to her. After the drawing was done, she took off her sandals and laid them beside the lantern, shucked off her outer robe, folded it and set it on the sandals. She took a deep breath, smoothed down the white linen shift that was all she was wearing, then stepped into the pentacle, carefully avoiding the lines. The night was old, near its finish, the air was chill and damp; frost hadn't settled yet, but it would before the sun came up. Shivering, eyes closed, she stood at the heart of the drawing. By will and by skill she smothered the fire in the wick; the lantern went dark.

By will and by skill, chanting the syllables that focused patterning and re-patterning, she redrew the lines, changing earth and air to moonsilver until the circled star shone pale and perfect about her.

She opened her eyes, smiled with pleasure as she viewed her work. It was one of the simpler exercises, but there were an infinite number of ways it could misfire. She dropped to her knees, then sat with her legs in a lotus knot, her hands resting palm up on her thighs, heat flowing through her, around her.

Minute melted into minute, passing uncounted as she sat unthinking.

The Moonstone emerged from her navel, oozed through her shift and rolled into her lap. Moving slowly, ponderously, as if she were under water, she lifted the stone and looked into the heart of it.

She saw the village. It was dead. The palisade gate sagged open; the streets were filled with bodies, men, women, children. Mutilated, eviscerated. She looked into the houses. They were filled with the dead. Ghosts wandered through the rooms, reliving what had been.

She saw the Lock House. The raider deadpriest had chased the ghosts away so they wouldn't alarm the crew on the boat they expected, but the dead were there, sprawled or bound. She saw again the game of stones-and-bones, she saw hillmen curled up, sleeping, she saw hillmen gnawing at plugs of tjank, eyes red and unfocused, she saw hillmen with three girls from the village, passing them around like the tjank.

She considered what she'd seen.

There were fifty-five raiders, fifty-three fighters, a warleader and a deadpriest. She thought about the fighters. Patterns. The original band must have been five groups of twelve. The villagers had gotten at least seven of them. That pleased her.

The Moonstone moved in her hands. She pressed it against her navel and it melted into her.

"Every act has consequences." Her voice was soft as the wind whispering through the cedar fronds; she spoke with a formality that was almost chanting, using memories from school to give her the confidence she needed. She was young and untried. Serious and a bit pedantic. She could not afford to doubt herself once the search began if she expected to emerge from it alive and intact. "Every refusal to act has consequences." Her voice comforted her, grounded her; ten years' study spoke through her. "Consider them. Look beyond the moment. If I kill them all, will their kin kill more folk to avenge them? The people of Kol Sutong are dead. They can't be hurt. What about other villages? Karoumang and his crew? There are other boats. Will they be more at risk?" She smiled as she saw fireflies flickering among the trees and heard an early bird twitter close by, life balancing death, a small beauty balancing a great horror. "No. Raiders raid; it is their purpose. Raiders kill for loot more often than vengeance. The death of those men will help more than hurt those who live by the river and on it." She mourned a little for them; she owed that to herself. They were brutal bloody murderers, but they were also men. "Fifty-five men dead because I willed it. I don't know them. I don't know anything about their lives. I don't know why they do what they do. I reach out and they cease. What am I? Maksim fed a child a month to BinYAHtii for fifty years because he considered it a small evil compared to the good he was doing. Am I going to walk that road? I don't know." She mourned for herself, for her loss of innocence; this virginity cost more in blood and pain than the first had and there was no pleasure in its loss. "Do what you must," she sang softly, "but do it without pride, without anger, knowing they are simple, stupid men, helpless before you."

Centered and ready, she sank into silence, letting the sounds of the waking forest flow through her. Hands on thighs, she sat not-thinking, not-waiting, open to whatever came to her.

Presently she was swimming among the realities as she had on the third night of her Ordeal. At first she wandered without direction, then she felt a tug. She flashed faster and faster past the layered realities, the infinite, uncountable elsewheres, faster and faster until she burst into one of them, a universe of heat and light where salamandri swam in oceans of sunfire.

She drifted, pushed here and there by the lightwinds.

Salamandri swam to her, hovered about her.

She contemplated them. Pulsing slippery shapes, constantly changing, growing extra limbs, absorbing them, growing denser, attenuating, shortening, lengthening, they were vaguely like the rock skinks she played with when she was a child. She caught one in a mindseine because once upon a time she'd caught a skink in a net she'd knotted for herself. It lay passive, eyespots fixed on her though she doubted it actually saw her. She caught another and another with no more reason than the first, went on catching them until their weight began to strain the meshes of her mind.

She drifted with her captives. They glowed like coals at the heart of a fire, redgold-whitegold, flickers of blue. She was reluctant to release them though she had no thought of using them. It took no effort to hold them, they were not struggling, they seemed content to stay with her. They warmed her, pleased her eyes and oddly enough her palate.

She felt a sudden twinge and started to move.

She came to the membrane at the edge of the reality.

The salamandri stirred, gracefully undulant.

She thought about releasing them. She thought about taking them with her. Vaguely she understood the danger in that. She knew it in her mind but not in her bones. Yes, she thought. Yes. I can, I must, I will.

Dragging the netted salamandri behind her, she broke through the membrane. Faster and faster she fled, running for her homeplace. Faster and faster until she was sitting within the pentacle, the salamandri swooping in swift orbits about its outer rim, turning the moonsilver red with their fires; around and around they raced, keening their anger and their triumph in a high, terrible whine.

They fought her. They were wiry, wild, leaping against her hold, their bodies were hard and strong, bumping, bumping, bumping against her. They'd lain passive all this time to catch her napping; they knew what she was, they knew she'd come for them, knew it before she did; they knew there was a world they could plunder and burn. They fought her and nearly won free before she hardened her hold on them.

She hadn't actually handled demons before, that was meant to happen when she had a Master backing her, but she drew on analogs from her training and descriptions of the process from her teachers; she cast lines at them, sank hooks into them, seven lines for seven salamandri. They lunged at the cedars with their enticing explosive resins. She jerked them back. The tips of several fronds sizzled, filling the air with an acrid green fragrance. That was all they got, the trees stood intact, untouched.

She laughed. "I've done it. I've really done it," she shouted to the night. "I have summoned demons." She was sweating though, and underneath the laughter she was shaking. She refused to acknowledge that and broke the demons to her hand. They swung round and round her, keening, sad. Round and round until she rode their senses and reined their bodies. Round and round until they answered her will as swiftly and surely as her own body did.

She sent them arcing up over the trees, out along the river, racing faster than the wind, pulsing eerie unsteady fireforms flitting over the water.

They came to the Lock House. The windows were shuttered against them, the door was barred. They burned through a wall. The deadpriest tried to turn them. The lead salamander shot out a long red tongue and licked his face off the bone. The warleader slashed at one and saw his blade melt. The salamander wrapped itself about the man and a moment later dropped a chalky skeleton and swooped on.

What Korimenei received through their senses was strange beyond anything she could have imagined, but she learned to read it and kept them from the House, its furniture, everything but the men. Only the men, she droned at them, over and over, only the men. She kept them from the captive girls, though a quick hot death might have been more merciful than life after what the raiders had done to them. She counted the kills and when the number was fifty-five, she jerked on the leashes and called the salamandri back to her.

They didn't want to come. They wanted to burn and burn until the world burned with them, hot and glorious and wholly theirs. They fought her; they turned and twisted and contorted themselves, trying to throw out the hooks. They flung all their weight and strength against the lines again and again and again, they never seemed to tire. Every inch she won from them was contested with a fury that seemed to increase as her own strength decreased.

She faltered. A salamander leaped away; it almost broke free. The jerk tore something inside her. She struggled to enfold and smother the pain and at the same time keep her hold on the demons. If they got loose. . . . She didn't dare admit even the possibility of failure. She pulled the demons to her and they came, slowly, painfully, but surely, they came. They brushed against tree tops and the trees burned. They cawed their pleasure, jarring shrieks that started high and squeezed to a thready wail as the sound soared out of hearing; they swung at the ends of the lines, back and forth, back and forth, working at her, changing the direction, the force, the intensity of the pull. She trembled. She was so weary. She couldn't think. She held on and held on. Inch by slow, torturous inch, she dragged them back to her. Strength oozed out of her. So tired. So tired. Her muscles were mush. Every nerve in her was vibrating raggedly. She was going to give way. There is a point beyond which will cannot drive body. She was reaching it, but she held on, she held. . . .

Coolness spread over her like a second skin, the waves of shivering slowed and smoothed out, a flow of energy came like water into her. She lifted her head and whipped the

salamandri across the final stretch, brought them to her
whimpering and cowed. She wasted no time with them, she
squeezed them into a clot of fire and flung them back where
she'd found them, sealing the aperture behind them.

Coolness peeled off her and pooled in her lap, weariness
flooded back. The pool sublimed to mist, the mist swirled
and billowed, took a familiar form. Ailiki.

When Ailiki was solid again, her plush fur neatly in place,
her catmouth open in her mocking catgrin, Korimenei lifted
her, held her eye to eye. "Once upon a time I said watch my
back, Aili my Liki. You make one fine bodyguard, Lili."
She settled the mahsar in her lap, smoothed her hand again
and again down Ailiki's spine. Breathed the syllables that
banished the moonsilver, erased the pentacle. Earth was
earth again, air was air. "Ahhhh, I'm tired, my Liki. Consequences, gods! I could have burned the world to ash. One
salamander was enough to handle that pitiful bloody bunch.
Shuh! More than enough. So I bring in seven? Pride, my
Liki. Carelessness. Jah'takash must've been beating her pig
bladder about my fool head, dubbing me idiot, fatuity su-
preme. I won't try anything like that again soon. I won't be
awake enough, I'm going to sleep for a year."

A laugh. She looked up. A lantern swinging by his knee,
Karoumang came from under the trees. "I've known women
like that. I take it you managed to come up with something.
What were those streaks?"

"Salamandri. You don't have to worry about the raiders
any more." She yawned, thought about rubbing gritty eyes,
but her arms were too heavy, too mushy to lift that far.

"You going to sit there the rest of the night?"

"Probably. Unless someone feels like carrying me."

"That bad, huh?"

"Tired, terrified, and frozen."

He lifted his lantern, turned the lightbeam on her face.
"Preemalau's fins! If you were dead, you'd look better."

"Thanks for telling me, huh." She giggled, then sobered.
"I came close, Karou. Came close to killing you and everything. I nearly lost control of them." She yawned again,
slumped over Ailiki, her head swimming.

He swore, took a step toward her, stopped. "I'll be back.
One minute."

She was barely conscious when he returned with one of
his sailors, a man name Prifuan. Karoumang scooped her up

and started for the ship; Prifuan came along behind them
with the lanterns and the rest of her gear.

7

Karoumang took the Miyachungay cautiously up the river,
moored her between the bulwarks and sent Prifuan and four
more ashore to work the gates. The girls from the village
saw this and crept from the trees; they were bloody, bruised,
dressed in clothing salvaged from the dead and deep in
shock. Women among the deck passengers took charge of
them, got them cleaned up, fed, wrapped them in blankets;
they petted the story out of the girls, gasped and sympa-
thized in the proper places, got the names of kin in the next
Lock village and carried the information to Karoumang.

Korimenei slept through all this. She slept through the stir
at the next lock as the girls went ashore and Karoumang
consulted with the village elders. She was deep, deep asleep
as Prifuan and his four arrived; they'd been left behind to
open the gates once the Miyachungay was far enough upriver.
She slept for three more days, woke to find the Miyachungay
past the locks and moving through a dun and dreary
landscape.

When she stepped onto the deck, wind beat at her, the
dust it carried scoured every inch of bare flesh. She went
back and dug out the despised veil, belted the hanging
panels so they wouldn't flap about too badly and tried the
deck again. She picked her way through shrouded bales and
climbed to Karoumang's favorite perch. He was there now,
wearing a Temueng headcloth, the ends wrapped about his
face, leaving only his eyes free.

"Well," he said. "You found a use for it after all." He
rubbed his thumb over the veil where it snugged against her
cheek. "How you doing otherwise?"

"Well enough. One of these days I might even be hungry
again." She stood at the rail and looked around. "This is
lovely stuff, Karou. Hunh. Where are we?"

"Ambijan. Nine days to Kapi Yuntipek." He turned his
back to the wind, pulled her closer, sheltering her with his
body.

"All of them like this?" She leaned against him, smiling
under her veil, drowsy and comfortable.

"Long as we're in Ambijan. Five days, six if there's more
cargo than I expect at Limni Sacca'l."

"I'm surprised you get anything. Who'd live here?"

"Ambijaks. They're all a little crazy."

She slapped at her breasts, raising a dust cloud of her own. "I believe it. Mind my asking, what DO you get here?"

"Canvas. Jaxin do some of the tightest weaving you can find anywhere. Need to, I suppose. Keep the dust out. I use it whenever I need new sails. Jaks make colorfast dyes, there's always a good market for those, especially new colors. Drugs. Opals. There are mines in the back country somewhere. I don't ask." She felt rather than heard his soft laugh. "Ambijaks spend words like blood. Their own blood, not yours, they're generous with yours. Crazy. But they know me so they keep it down some."

"Mmm." Despite the veil her eyes were watering and the skin of her face was starting to burn. She looked past his head, tried to see the sun. All she saw was a dull tan sky. "What time is it?"

"Coming on third watch. Want lunch?"

"Getting that way. I think I'll go back down, this wind is peeling the skin off me flake by flake. Any chance of a bath?"

"If you'll work for it."

"Scrub your back, huh?"

"You got it."

She rubbed her shoulder against him. "Anything, Captain Saö, I'll do anything to get clean."

"I'll keep that in mind. We might even manage some hot water."

"Ah, bliss to be alive and in your presence." She giggled, eased out of the circle of his arm and bent into the wind as she started down.

8

The Miyachungay traveled upstream day on dreary day. The Wansheeri was sluggish here, winding around broad bends and serried oxbows. It carried a load of silt and occasional animal carcasses, but few snags; in Ambijan trees were an exotic species, any floaters that got so far from the mountains were seized by the Jaks and hauled ashore as soon as they were spotted. The wind blew steadily out of the east, cold dry wind, engendering melancholy and distraction. The sound of it never stopped, it muted everything, reduced the comfortable small noises of the boat to whimpers; words were unintelligible a few paces away from the

speaker; crew and passengers alike communicated with grunts
or single shouted words, no more. The pressure of it never
stopped; it drove west, west, west without letup. When the
river turned east, they fought to shove the boat forward
against the wind; when it turned west, if they lost their
concentration a single moment and let the wind take her, it
could jam her into the bank before they had a chance to
recover; getting her around some of those bends took sweat
and prayer and curses in nearly equal amounts. It was
almost worse when she pointed straight north; then the wind
threatened to blow her sideways. Karoumang got little sleep,
a few hours of sweaty nightmare filled with snatches of
horror. He was wild and rough when he took Korimenei
those nights, using her to ease his wind-frayed nerves, the
grinding tension built up during the day. He didn't care who
she was, only that she was there. She should have resented
that; other times, other circumstances she would have been
furious, she would have given him a scar or three to remember her by, but she wasn't thinking these days, the wind was
getting at her too; she was rough and wild as he was, she
used him for needs that would have terrified and shamed
her a month or two ago, and slept like she was slugged when
it was over.

When they slid through a tattered ghostring into the lee of
Kapi Yuntipek, even the Miyachungay seemed to sigh with
relief.

9

A pseudopod of the ghost stuff ringing Kapi Yuntipek
stayed with Korimenei as she rode away from the city a
week later, a clotted white finger set firmly on her, unable
to touch her; she ignored it, kept her pony pacified and
moving along at a steady walk. Behind her, Ailiki perched
on the pack pony, calming the little gelding and holding him
in place. Abruptly the pseudopod snapped back and they
were moving through a bright chill day; the air was so clear
the mountains seemed close enough to touch.

The Silk Road was not much of a road despite its fame. It
was a dusty path marked by stone cairns spread so that the
pile ahead came into view as the pile behind sank below the
horizon. At the moment it was winding in lazy curves through
the thin rind of small farms north of the city, going across
bridges like hiccups over narrow ditches, thumbnail scratches
filled with water from the river. Temu serfs working in the

fields straightened and watched her, their dark eyes wary and hostile. The land they stood on belonged to the Kangi Pohgin, the Headman of Kapi Yuntipek; they were worked until they dropped, two-thirds of every harvest was taken from them, they were exposed to depredations from stray raiders out of the Temueng grassclans and bandits sweeping down from the mountains; they expected nothing but harassment from everyone outside their own families. They reminded her of the lowlanders in Cheonea; they had the same hard, knotty look, the same secret stares, the same sense they were rooted to the landheart, mobile manshaped extensions of the soil they stood on. If she gave them any opening they would swarm over her and leave nothing but bones behind; that was in their eyes and the set of their bodies.

When she came out of the farms she rode between walls of Temu grass that reached past her stirrups, swaying in the eternal east wind, the individual rustles of stalk rubbing against stalk sunk into a vast murmuring whole. It was a hypnotic sound. She swam in it, breathed it; after an hour or so she seemed to hear voices in it whispering secrets she couldn't quite make out. North and east of the city the grass stretched out and out, to the horizon and past, an ocean of yellow and silver-dun, rippling, constantly changing color, subtle changes, barely distinguishable shades of the base colors. An ocean of grass wide as any water ocean.

The piercing, aching loneliness she'd felt in the city fell gradually away from her as she shed the sense of pressure, of neediness, the hurry-hurry, get-on-with-it that afflicted her within those walls; she settled into the long slow rhythms of the land, birth, growth, death, rebirth, inevitable, unchanging, eternal. She was an infinitesimal mote in that immense landscape, but she didn't feel diminished, no, it was almost as if her skin had been peeled back so she was no longer closed within it but was intimately a part of that vast extravagant sky, that shimmering ocean of grass.

After about three hours she stopped, watered the ponies at one of the Road Wells and let them graze. She leaned against a cairn, crossed her ankles. Ailiki jumped on her stomach; she laughed and began scratching the mahsar behind her twitching ears.

"What are you doing, Kori?" Tré's eidolon hung above her, his voice cut through her drowse. "Why are you just sitting there? Get moving. You have to beat the snow."

"So you're back." She continued to stroke the mahsar. "How nice."

As he always did, he ignored questions expressed or implied. "You can't waste a minute, you have to cross the Dautas as soon as possible."

"Tré. . . ." She sighed. "You know what riding stock is like, you push too hard and they quit on you, you can't have forgot that, what's wrong with you?"

"You know what's wrong." The crystal vibrated though the mouse-sized figure of the boy inside changed neither expression nor position. "I want out of this."

"Why do you think I'm here?" She sighed. "If I push the ponies too hard, this jaunt stops before the day's out. Quit niggling at me, Tré, I know what I'm doing." She lifted Ailiki off her. "Go fetch them, Lili; they've had enough rest for now. Tré, what about the weather? From here, it looks clear enough, but that's a lot of mountains."

"No blizzards yet. There are some washouts from rain, a lot of rain has been falling, no snow, I'm not sure why. There's black ice in the passes; it makes treacherous going. You should try to hit the steepest slopes in the afternoon, when the sun's been at the ice long enough to clear some of it out. If there is any sun."

"Lovely. Look, Tré, you seem to show up when you want to stick pins in me and ignore me otherwise. I'm trying to remember you're my brother; don't leave me hanging out to dry, help me. Talk to me even if there's nothing else you can do."

The eidolon flickered, faded, appeared again like a washed-out watercolor painted on the air, vanished completely.

Korimenei sighed, got to her feet. The ponies were standing on the Road, foam dripping from their mouths as they chewed at a last clump of grass. She smiled wryly as Ailiki ran up the packer's side and perched on its withers. "Aili my Liki, I'm beginning to wonder what the hell's going on here."

The mahsar folded her arms across her narrow chest and took on the aspect of Sessa who looked after lost trinkets, one of the little gods who scampered like mice from person to person, coming unasked, leaving without warning, a capricious, treacherous, much courted clutch of godlings. She nodded gravely, but what she meant by it was impossible to guess.

"You're a big help." Korimenei shook her head, swung into the saddle and nudged the pony into a plodding walk.

10

Two weeks slid past. Korimenei rode and walked, walked and rode, nibbled at trailbars and apples during the day, usually while the ponies grazed, cooked up stew and panbread when she camped for the night, washing these down with strong tea and a bowl of the rough red wine she'd picked up in Kapi Yuntipek. Water wasn't a problem, there were wells and troughs at intervals along the road. The sky stayed clear, there wasn't any frost in the morning, the air was too dry, but even long after the sun came up, the days were crackling cold. Despite that, she passed up the Waystop Inns as she came to them, riding on to camp at one of the wells. As if he were trying to make up for a fault he wasn't about to admit, Tré came each night with a weather report and stayed to chat a little, mostly about what had been happening to Korimenei, he said it was because he was sealed in crystal, stuck in the cave; since nothing was happening to him, there was nothing to talk about unless they went over and over past times which he didn't want to do. She grew easier in her mind; she wanted to believe that the closeness they'd shared was still there, waiting to be resumed when he was free.

In the third week she left behind the last sparse clumps of Temu grass and moved into the foothills of the Dhia Dautas. The waves of land had a flat wispy ground cover, gray-brown, limp; there seemed to be no vigor in it, but the ponies relished it when she let them graze. The thorn-studded brush had small leaves that a series of hard frosts had turned into stiff rounds of maroon leather, and copper-colored crooked branches that wove in and out of each other to form a dense prickly ball that only changed size as it aged, not conformation. It grew in tangled clumps in and around dumps of boulders like the droppings of some immense and incontinent beast.

In the fourth week she was on the lower slopes of the mountains winding upward toward the first LowPass, moving through thick stands of trees and a different ground cover, broad-leafed vines that were crimson and gold, crawling across red earth that crumbled into a fine dust which settled on every surface and worked its way into every crevice. The slopes were steeper, the air thinner and colder.

It cut her throat like knives when she was winded near the top of a rise and breathing through her mouth. She saw deer and narru herds, wolves trotting in ragged lines, sangas and mountain cats sunning on boulders or in trees, squirrels and rabbits and other small scuttlers, birds hopping along the ground, feeding on seeds and insects. There was a sense of waiting in the air, a feeling that the season was changing, but not yet. Not quite yet. Most mornings there were only a few wisps of cloud scrawled across the sky; as each day wore on, though, the clouds thickened and darkened, the light took on a pewter tinge, colors were darker, richer. She saw no one, the road was open, empty, but she was aware several times of eyes watching her. She ignored them. Let them watch.

At the end of the week she ran into rain and black ice.

11

When she crawled from her blankets the sky was clear and cold as the water in the stream, the world was a glitter of ice and frost flowers. Her skin tingled, she was intensely alive; when she started along the Road again she wore seven league boots and could stride across the mountains like a giant.

A patch of black ice reminded her she was merely mortal. Her feet slid from under her and she landed on hands and knees hard enough to jar her back teeth. She got painfully to her feet and inspected her hands; the palms were scraped raw, smeared with dirt. With slow stiff movements she rubbed them on her jacket; when the dirt was off, she pulled her gloves from her pocket and put them on. She made a face at Ailiki who was being Sessa again, sitting plump and sedate on the saddle, smirking at her. "Laugh and I start thinking Liki stew."

On the far side of the ridge was a long narrow valley, smoky with steam from hotsprings, steam that wove in and out of dark ominous conifers and went trickling up to a white-blue sky bare of clouds. About a half mile from the Road, she saw a huddled village; there were no people visible, no stock in sight; the harvest was already in, the fields were mud and stubble. A ghost drifted across the mud, circled her, then fled without saying anything. She could sense hostile eyes watching her and had a strong feeling she'd better not stay around for any length of time.

Half an hour later, she came on a small scraggly meadow;

she stopped there, fed the ponies the last of the feedcake
and let them graze.

When Ailiki brought them in, they were mud to the belly.
Korimenei swore, dug out a stiff brush and went over their
legs and feet, cleaning away the mud and the small round
leeches they'd collected off infested brush. She worked up a
sweat that damped her underclothes and ripened her smell
until even she was aware she stank. She knocked the brush
against the trunk of a conifer and straightened. "Lili, if it
takes till midnight, we keep going until we reach an Inn."

They plodded on, winding up the next ridge in long slow
loops that gained height with the tempered speed of a slug
in winter, passing other xenophobic settlements nested on
small mountain flats, blank-walled, secret places that turned
their shoulders to the Road and refused to acknowledge its
existence. By late afternoon more clouds were blowing off
the peaks, blocking what small warmth the pallid sun had
been providing; a chill, dank wind rolled down the Road.
She pushed on, riding and walking, walking and riding. The
day grew darker and darker. The sun finally sneaked down,
no display of color this night, only an imperceptible harden-
ing of the dark. Finally, near midnight, she reached the
Waystop Inn at the throat of HighPass.

The doors were barred, the windows shuttered, the Inn
was dark and silent. Korimenei was in no mood to tolerate
obstacles or delicately weigh consequences. She sent the bar
flying from its brackets, kicked the door open and went
stalking in. She crafted a will-o, hung it by the thick ceiling
beams and stood waiting in the eerie, bluish light, Ailiki on
her shoulder, the ponies huddled close outside the gaping
door. "Hey the house," she shouted. "You have clients. Stir
your stumps or I'll turn this dikkhush into kindling."

The Host came down the stairs, his nightshirt tucked into
trousers pulled hastily on, the lacings untied, ends dangling.
He carried a lamp, set it on the counter when he saw the
will-o and Korimenei standing under it. "It's late," he said.
"We closed for the night."

"Looks like I just opened you. I want a hot bath, a hot
meal, and a bed. And stabling for my ponies. We can debate
the metaphysics of open and closed all you want come the
morning. Right now I'm tired and I haven't a lot of patience."

"Sorceror." It wasn't a compliment the way he said it. He
shrugged. "Bath's no problem, we're sitting on a hotspring.
Meal, that'll take some time and it'll cost. M' wife works

hard and she needs her sleep, you're not the only one tired this night. Ponies, take 'em round yourself, get 'em settled. You had no trouble getting in here, do the same to the stables if you can't wake the boy up. I'd take it kindly if you didn't scare a year's growth out of him. He's m' wife's cousin and worth hot spit on a summer day, but kin's kin."

She laughed. "You're a clever man, Hram. You could milk the poison from a reared-back cobra. I expect to pay, but control your appetite, Hram Host; double is enough, more than that is sin and punishable by wart, eh?" She listened. "It's starting to rain, I'd better get the ponies under cover." She beckoned the will-o to her. "And let you shut your door so all the heat doesn't leak away."

Warm, replete and clean for the first time in days, she crawled between fresh, sweet-smelling sheets and sighed with pleasure. "Well, Aili my Liki, this is something else. Why oh why am I putting myself through this muck? Ah I know, oh I know; poor Tré, he didn't deserve having his life taken away from him like that, just so Old Maks would have a hold on me. It's my fault he's there, my fault I'm here. I owe him. Sometimes though. . . ." She yawned, turned on her side and pulled the quilts up to her nose. Ailiki was a hotspot curled up against her stomach; the mahsar was already asleep and snoring with that tiny eeping that was a comforting nightsong. The rain was slashing down outside, a steady thrum against the shutters. A cold draft wandered past her nose. She murmured with pleasure, dreaming she was home again, a girl in her narrow bed, safe in the arms of her kin and kind, then she dropped deeper into sleep and left even dreams behind.

In the morning she half-fell out of bed and barely made the slop basin before the nausea erupted and she emptied her stomach.

When the spasms stopped, she dipped a corner of the towel in the pitcher and washed her face, then sat on her heels, eyes closed, while she waited for the upheaval in her body to die down. Ailiki came trotting over to her, pressed against her leg. She lifted the mahsar, held her against her breasts, her warmth helping to soothe away the ache. "Well, Lili, I'm going to have to look, aren't I."

Sitting in the middle of the bed, rain dribbling down outside, a dull dreary drizzle, she turned inward and explored her body.

There was no mistake, no way of avoiding the truth. She was pregnant. The wind had worn away more than her nerves those days in Ambijan. She sat there in the quiet warm room, thinking: What do I want? What am I going to do? In the end, it was all words. She wanted the baby and she was going to have it. She needed it. Karoumang's child. No. Mine. The thought warmed her. My daughter. She knew it was going to be a daughter. She wasn't going to be alone any more. It didn't matter what her brother did. Didn't matter if Maksim wouldn't have her as apprentice. She folded her arms across her body, hugging herself and what she bore. I'm not going to worry, she thought. There's plenty of time to finish this thing before there's enough child to worry about. Tell Tré if he bothers to show up again? No! No way. It's none of his business.

She crossed HighPass and went through the serried ridges of the western flanks of the Dhia Dautas, daughters of the dawning sun, though there was little sun in evidence, dawn or dusk or anything between. It snowed twice in the first week, light snows, two inches one storm, six the next. Then it rained and that was worse. Each morning she woke and vomited. Then she rode on. Day after day, walk and ride, ride and walk until she was down in the grass again and twenty days out of Dil Jorpashil.

12

Korimenei looked at the tuber stew. The cook's heavy hand with the spice jars couldn't disguise the sweetish sick smell from the shreds of anonymous meat. I can't eat this, she thought, there's no way I can eat this.

She finished the dusty tea and the bread, got quietly to her feet and went outside. She leaned against the tie-rail and breathed in the clean cold air off the grass, thinking about the gaunt little girl who'd carried her gear to the sleeping loft with its scatter of husker mattresses and tattered privacy curtains. Ten years going on a hundred and running the Waystop alone; most likely her father was in the hedgetavern built onto the back of the hostel, playing host to the local drunks, a drunk himself if she read the signs right. From the smell that wafted up to the loft, he stilled his own sookpa. Must taste worse than that rancid meat. I've got to do something about food, she thought. She smiled into the darkness, patted her stomach. Well-fed cows make healthy calves. Old cow, I'd better see about keeping you properly fed.

She went exploring and found the girl in the kitchen, washing up. "Where's your father, child?"

The girl's eyes darted to the back door, flicked away. She shrugged, said nothing. She stood hunched over the wash-tub, her hands quiet in the greasy water, her body saying: go away and leave me alone.

"I see. Your mother?"

"She dead."

"You do the cooking?"

"You din' eat ye stew. We don't give coin back f' what ye don' eat."

"A starving sanga wouldn't eat that stew. It's not the cooking, child. It's the meat. I take it you don't raise your own?"

The girl shook her head, began scratching at a bit of crust in a loafpan.

"Your father doesn't hunt?"

"An't no game close enough. T' Road scare 'em." Her voice was muffled, defensive; once again her dark eyes went to the door, turned away.

"Hmm. If I brought you meat, would you cook it for me? I'll leave you what's left over in payment."

"What kinda meat?"

"Geyker."

"Ah-yah. When?"

"Soon. An hour, perhaps a little more."

"I wanna see t' hide." Her shoulders were hunched over, her hands shaking; she wouldn't look at Korimenei. She was terrified, but determined.

Korimenei laughed. "Yes yes. You're a good sonya. I wouldn't give you forbidden fare. You'll see hide, hooves, and all. Tell me something. Would Waystops down the Road take meat instead of coin?"

"I couldna say f' sure. I think so. Dada woulda if ye'd asked."

"Thank you. Good e'en, sonya." Korimenei left the

kitchen, paused in the middle of the common room to
consider site options. There was the sleeping loft, but she
didn't like the feel or the smell of the place. The stable. No.
The hostler was nested inside there like a rat in a wall and
not even the sookpa stoups in the tavern were going to
entice him out. She didn't want anyone looking over her
shoulder while she went dipping for a demon to hunt some
meat for her. She pushed away the fears that kept recurring
about attracting notice and even a challenge from a local
sorceror. She had to do this, she had no choice. She moved
to the door; it wasn't barred yet; the sun was barely down; a
few rosy streaks on the western horizon lingered from a
pallid sunset. The Wounded Moon was breaking free of the
horizon in the east, nearly full, the moonhare-crouching
plainly writ in streaks of blue-gray on the yellowish ground.
The night was clear and brilliant with almost no wind to
blow the grass about or stir the naked branches of the three
gnarly olive trees growing beside the well. The well . . . ah,
the well. Wells are powerpoints and sanctuaries or so Master Kushundallian claimed. I'll know the truth of that before
the night's much older.

She pulled the door shut behind her. "Lili, I need you,"
she called. The mahsar was out hunting her dinner; she
turned her nose up at anything cooked or dead before she
made it so; in emergencies she'd share Korimenei's meals,
but not without expressing her opinion of such slop with
some full-body grimaces. "Aili my Liki," she called again,
then went to sit on the well-coping and wait for her backup,
smiling at herself, amused by her new-won prudence.

Ailiki materialized in Korimenei's lap, sat washing her
whiskers with tongue-damped forefeet. Korimenei laughed,
scratched behind her tulip petal ears, then lifted her and
carried her to the bare earth where horses, mules, four-
footed beasts of all kinds had milled about waiting their turn
to drink from the troughs, their hooves cutting up the grass,
grinding it into the earth, beating the earth into a hard
crusty floor. She set Ailiki down and began drawing a pentacle. "What I'm going to do, Lili . . . I need a hunter who
will go and get me a geyker. Hmm. I need fruit too, maybe
I can do something about that." She inspected the pentacle.
"That's done. Come here, babe."

She silvered and activated the pentacle, insinuated herself
into the realities and drifted, waiting for the call. There was
no urgency, only a quiet need; it took longer she couldn't

tell how long her time-sense was useless here it might have been seconds or parts of a single second but finally the pull came and she eased through into an immensity that would have frightened her if she stopped to think, but she went swimming so swiftly that the darkness and the cold was only a mountain pond, she swanned through the dark and floated over the face of a world turning and turning in the light of a yellow sun. Sand and more sand, sand and brush and sand-colored cats prowling after herds of sand-colored deer. She dipped lower. Mancats with snakes for hands and four legs padding pacing loping over the sand. Mancats with eyes that *knew*. She called one and he came to her, he came rushing at her, she hadn't realized how big he was, how powerful. She smelled him. He reeked but it was an attractive stink, sensual, sexual. *Hunt for me,* she called to him. *Hunt for yourself and hunt for me.*

He shook himself, considered her. She felt his consent given and threw a mindseine about him. In some way, he leaned into her, helping with the shift. He was amused at the whole thing, curious, intensely immensely curious. Pleased at having the chance to travel away from his sandhills. He landed on the ground outside the pentacle and settled on his haunches, his massive head turning and turning, his black nostrils flaring as he tasted the air. She thought a geyker at him. He rumbled his assent, went loping off into the grass.

She flowed away again, floated aimlessly awhile, until a sweet-tart smell invaded her. She followed it into richness, a world lush with fruit, ripe fruit, oozing with juice. She drifted among the trees, choosing, dropping the fruit into a mindnet woven tighter than before. When she had as much as she could eat that night and the next day, she drifted back, carrying her gleanings with her. She juggled that fruit as the mindnet came apart when she touched down, dropped pieces that cracked open but were otherwise still edible. She piled it all by her knee and looked around. The mancat was close, she could smell him on the wind.

A moment later the grass parted and he came carrying a dead geyker. He laid it on the ground beside the pentacle and trotted off again. She looked at it. Lyre-shaped horns like polished jet. Black nose with blood coming from it like threads of ink. Rough, brindled coat in its winter growth, the guard hairs longer than her hand. Silken white ruff about the long neck, spattered and matted with more blood. Split hooves, black and sharp as knives. Tail like a flag, black above, white below. A good plump beast with its winter fat in place. She sighed and sang the old tributesong her people in the Vale sang over their butchered stock, giving its beastsoul rest and rebirth. Then she settled herself to wait until the mancat was finished with his own business and ready to go home with his prizes.

16

She *progressed* across the plain. There was no other word for it. She was a rolling storm of magic accompanied by demons, delivering fresh meat to the hostels, fruit and fish; she was a cornucopia of good things and generous with them, trading meat for stable space and sleeping room, leaving more always than she bargained with. One mancat after another came to her, hunted for her and himself, played with her, teased her, took pleasure in this *other place,* gave way to the next mancat and that one to the next, each one of them grinning that terrifying tender toothy grin, each one of them full of good humor and delight.

Tré came. "What are you doing?" he shouted at her. "What are you doing? Stop it. You're asking for trouble. You're asking to be challenged. Stop it. What are you doing?"

She waited until he ran down. "I'm saving coin and staying healthy. You want me to stop? Fund me, Tré. I'm spending my Passage gift for you, I've probably lost my chance to apprentice to Maksim. Either bring me some coin or leave me to do this my way."

The eidolon shivered, anger flared around her, brushing against her skin like nettle leaves, burning. Then with an almost tangible, almost audible *pop,* her brother's eidolon vanished. She trembled. After a few moments of nausea that had nothing to do with morning sickness, she started crying. There was an aching emptiness inside where her love for her brother had been. She hadn't stopped loving the boy she knew once, but he was gone. Whoever it was caught in crystal was not her brother. Not any more.

17

Dil Jorpashil.
Korimenei stopped to buy tea and trailfood and look around the city, relishing the Market with its noise, its cacophany of color and smell; it reminded her of the Market at Silili and she was brushed with a pleasant melancholy at

the thought. Already her days at school seemed as if they'd happened to someone else in another lifetime and they'd taken on the golden patina of nostalgia.

The day she left, while she waited on a ferry landing for a riverboat to pass, heading south, she saw a woman standing at the rail looking back at the city, a widow in black robes with a small M'darjin page at her side. Drinker of Souls, Korimenei thought, startled. I wonder what she's doing here? She didn't know how she knew who the woman was—her hair was black, her face was different—but she did. She watched the boat glide away and thought she'd know the feel of that woman anywhere, whatever face or shape she wore. Drinker of Souls. Hmm.

The ferryman wound his cable from the water, rang his bell. Along with some noisy grassclanners from the south who were heading home after a hectic time in the city, she led her ponies onto the flat. She stood between the two beasts, trying to ignore the nomads; they were young and randy, on the loose and apt to see a stray female as fair game.

When the ferry reached the far side, she let them ride off ahead of her. When she came off, they were waiting. She put on an ASPECT, was suddenly twelve feet tall with world-class warts and fangs that curved down past her chin. They took off, screaming. Amused and rather pleased with herself, she led the ponies past the stubby pillars that marked the resumption of the Silk Road, mounted and rode toward the Dhia Asatas, the daughters of the setting sun, invisible now behind a shroud of the thick gray clouds.

IV: DANNY BLUE

Having been trapped by a cabal of Dirge Arsuiders, injected with poison and ordered to bring back the Talisman Klukesharna in return for the antidote to the poison, Danny Blue and the back-up help (two thieves and a courtesan) provided by the Arsuid Ystaffel climbed aboard the riverboat Pisgaloy and started for Hennkensikee.

1

At sunrise on the fifth day after she left Dirge Arsuid, the riverboat Pisgaloy rounded a long low knoll that was thick with mighty millenarian oaks and pointed her nose at Hennkensikee on the island cluster half a mile out in Lake Patinkaya. The sun was gilding the pointed roofs and the walls dissolved in glitters reflecting off water hard and bright as knife blades. The Pisgaloy leaned into the uncertain wind and clawed her way up the last stretch of free water.

Hennkensikee was tall and toothy, built of red brick fired from clay taken eons ago from the banks of the north rim of the lake. The ovens that fired the bricks were abandoned when the job was done; these days they were pits like pocks with snag-tooth beams poking through thistles and nettles and ragweed; the city witches went hunting herbs around there because they had ten times the potency of those picked elsewhere. In the days when the pits were roaring with the kiln fires, the god Coquoquin took the bricks and laid the walls of Hennkensikee, the towering curtain wall and the needle towers within, weaving the courses into complex, continually changing patterns, a subtle dance of design across all the surfaces, invisible at any great distance, meant to please eyes and fingertips simultaneously. She built and watched over a city of subtleties, of fountains playing in hidden courtyards, glimpsed through a confusion of arches or heard but not seen, of faces behind screens of wood and ivory, of layered fragrances from incense burned at every door. A city of patterns but no color, the brick was dull, the wood stained dark; the figures moving unhurriedly though the narrow winding streets wore black wrappings, rectangles of cloth wound about and about their bodies, a second, shorter rectangle rope-anchored to the Lewinkob long heads, male and female alike, falling like shrouds about squat Lewinkob bodies.

The Pisgaloy circled carefully wide about the island group and crept up to the end of a pier that extended like a finger into the Lake. A motley collection, all sizes, shapes and genders, the passengers went streaming off with their packs of tradegoods or sacks of coin. Danny Blue and his associates came ashore in the middle of the flood, joined the line formed up at the gate and waited for the Wokolinka's inspectors to let them into the city.

Trithil Esmoon was draped in the robes and embroidered veil of a Phrasi courtesan, not all that different from what she wore in Arsuid. Simms was nondescript in a new way, hair brushed back flat against his skull, his clothing a mix of dark grays and black; the colors suited him better than the reds and pinks he favored when not working, but nothing could make him handsome.

Felsrawg was enjoying herself. She looked fierce enough to slaughter a regiment of rapists. Her black hair was pulled up tight to the top of her head except for three earlocks on each side of her face; it was twisted into a spiral knot that added several inches to her height. Twin gold skewers with animal heads for knobs were driven through that knot and rose like horns above it. She'd replaced her earstuds with long gold arrowpoints on gold rings; they danced with every move of her head. A black leather tunic was laced tight to her slim body over a white silk blouse with long loose sleeves that hid her knives; with this she wore a narrow black leather skirt slit to the hip on the left side and black leather boots with razor-edged spurs strapped to them.

"Tirpa Lazul, Trader, out of Bandrabahr, come for the silk sale," Danny told the beard behind the table. "My associates," he waved a hand at the others. "The hanoum Haya, also Phrasi, companion. Hok Werpiaka, trader's son, out of Silili, traveling to learn the markets."

"He's not Hina."

"No. Croaldhese. His family moved to Silili for . . . hmm . . . political reasons some generations back. The other is Second Daughter Azgin kab'la Savash, Matamulli up from the Southland to earn her dowry."

"Looks like she's wearing part of it."

"You got it."

"One taqin each, any silver coin will do, provided it weighs at least five tunts. Drop them in the pan. Good." He emptied the coins from the balance pan into a leather box, pushed four wooden plaques across the table. "Keep these on you at all times. Be quick to show them if a S'sup asks to see them. Curb all uncouth behavior in the streets or elsewhere, except in the taverns. We are not barbarians, we realize our visitors need relaxation. However, this must be kept within limits and inside where it will not offend our eyes. Exceed those limits or provide reason for a complaint against you, and you will be warned first, then fined, then ejected. There is no appeal from a Tsi-tolok's judgment. Have you questions? No? Good. You may pass."

2

For two days and two nights they poked about in Hennkensikee, the walls constraining them, the only interiors open to them the great warehouses where dour old women spread silks on padded tables and squeezed the last tiny copper from the circling bidders. Trithil Esmoon reclaimed her hithery and the old women leaned toward her as if they smelled her sweetness, sniffed it in to compare with ancient memories the scent rewakened in them, tumbling over themselves to answer her questions.

While Danny Blue and Trithil Esmoon played their cover games in the fragrant dimness of the warehouses, Felsrawg explored the city, insofar as she could, plotting thieftracks on its walls, climbing and entering in her mind the needle towers and tall square houses with their high-peaked roofs and ogeed windows. Shuttered windows, unglazed, outsider eyes blocked by wood-and-ivory screens carved in intricate serpentines pierced and repierced, the wood age-dark and tougher than iron. Fingers and mind both itched as she read the chances; she wanted to climb those walls and work her way past the screens, to puff in the sleep powders and prowl in darkness hunting for the treasures she knew lay inside. She watched the colored liquids of her skry ring shift and coil beneath the crystal as they registered and reacted to the wards and traps; a glance was all she needed to know how weak and careless the ward-setter had been. She could slide through slick as a serpent slipping down a mousehole. She kept moving, ignoring the Lewinkob who turned to look at her and follow her with their eyes. Twice she was stopped by one of the armored S'supal, the Wokolinka's amazon guards. She played Second Daughter with zest, exulting as she fooled them; the cockiness might have sunk her, but they knew Matimulli and discounted it. By evening on the second day she'd got all she could and was beginning to repeat. She went to the meeting that night filled with impatience, irritation and anxiety. The sooner the job was done, the sooner she could claim the antidote.

Simms drifted about, his hair damped and darkened, his gray and black clothing and his stocky shape much like the other Lewinkob men walking around him, though he lacked the billowing beards they favored. He went into pocket parks, havens of greenery open to the public, and made himself available to the ghosts who blew about the streets, courts and public spaces, looking wistfully after the locals who more or less ignored them. He let them tell their stories and listened to their complaints, slipping in a word now and then to nudge them in directions he wanted them to go. When he wasn't talking to ghosts or doing his own thieftracks, he was leaning against walls, staring vacantly at the sky, listening to the ancient bricks tell their long creaky tales. By the evening of the second day, he too was beginning to hear things twice.

3

Danny Blue strolled around the room, checking the wards he'd woven about the windows and set into the threshold of the door; there was almost dust on them, they were so untouched. Carelessness on the guardians' part, but he wasn't about to fault them for it. He opened the door a crack and set the ward to admit three, then snap closed again. Witches made him nervous, he liked them best when they were tired or lazy. Against possible overlooking, which they could do through anything belonging to the city, he'd brought an old sheet from Arsuid. To keep it from being contaminated when he wasn't using it, he left it rolled within a warded leather sack which he hung from a peg beside the wardrobe. He took the sheet from the sack, snapped it open and spread it on the floor. He stepped onto it and lowered himself until he was sitting cross-legged. The others were elsewhere at the moment, though they were due to join him soon. He was content to sit and wait, to enjoy these few blessed moments alone. Because she was supposed to be his concubine, Trithil Esmoon was sharing his room and his bed. She was always there, always. . . . Last night she'd turned to him, all warm and enticing and he told her to shut it off; he didn't trust her an inch and wasn't about to give her that kind of hold on him.

He thought about that, grimaced. It'd been a long dry spell. Last time he'd had a chance at sex, he'd been with Brann and got knocked cold because he was too rough with her; it was enough to put anyone off his stroke to get half the life sucked out of him in medias res as it were. He thought about that now, uneasy because he wasn't reacting to Trithil as he'd expected to. Even when she turned on the hithery. He worried it around and around, then decided he could live with it. He decided he needed the sense that there was at least some reciprocity involved, more than mingled sweat, spittle and other fluids. She was a splendid fake, but fake she was, and he couldn't forget that no matter how skillfully she counterfeited her responses. He couldn't forget how cold and uninterested she was when she dropped the mask. He thought about Felsrawg and smiled as he pictured her. Her passions burned from the bone out; she prided herself on her gambler's face, but a child could read what she was feeling. She'd make a scratchy armful, but she wouldn't be boring. She was making signs like she'd be willing to try it out and see what happened. He rubbed at his chin, shook his head. Remember, old Dan, she might look frank and frisky and forthcoming, but she has orders to off you and take the talisman; if you doubt she'd do it, you're playing head games with yourself.

Felsrawg pushed the door open, stalked in with the coiled energy of a hungry puma. She dropped onto the sheet and sat fidgeting with one of her knives. She kept glancing at the door, frowned impatiently when Simms came strolling in and settled beside her on the sheet. She turned the frown on Danny Blue. "Where's the hoor?"

Danny shrugged.

Felsrawg took a bit of soft leather from one of her pockets, began polishing the blade. "Leader, hunh! Old cow would do more."

"Take over, do it better."

"Don't think I wouldn't if I could handle wards and witches."

"Then shut up till you can."

"Hah." She stopped her hands, stared pointedly at the mussed bed. "I can see where you've got your mind on other things, but couldn't we get this klatch moving? If the hoor wants to know what's happening, we can catch her up when she gets here."

"We wait. The ward is open till she crosses the threshold."

Felsrawg made a spitting sound, went back to polishing the blade.

Twenty minutes later Trithil came undulating in. She stripped off her veil, tossed it on the bed and took her place on the sheet.

Danny waited until he felt the ward click shut, then he flattened his hands on his thighs and looked at each of the others. "Any ideas about getting across those bridges to the Henanolee Heart?"

Simms pursed his mouth, shook his head. "I went an' leaned 'gainst one of the gate piers this end the firs' bridge. Bridge be trapped. " 'Larums an' sinks. Either the S'sulan drop on you, or y' get dropped to the eels that live in the straits 'tween the islands. What I know 'bout the S'sulan, better the eels. Ghosts say this: the S'wai, that the witches, they lower'n the belly of a starvin' snake. What they mean, the S'wai they tired. Burnt out. Been a long, hard season an' it coming up on Closeout so they lettin' down, doin' the min, y' know."

Felsrawg slid the knife back in its bootsheath. "Yeh. You'd expect them to have tightasses here where they let foreigners in, knowing how these Lewks see us all, but t'ain't so, Laz old Sorce. You pick a wall, any wall, I'll go up it like it was flat and clean out everything behind it without a peep from the 'larms. The wards are in pitiful shape. Creamcheese here, everywhere."

"Perhaps not creamcheese." Trithil slid a fingertip over and over the dome of the star sapphire in her thumbring. "But not far from it. The Maskab Kutskab spent the afternoon complaining about her S'sulan, she says they're spending more time in taverns than on the street. Half the time they're drunk out of their skulls on sourmash wukik or sucking the ton off some male whore. The other half, they're slicing pieces off each other in knife duels. When she wasn't

carping, she was drooling over the hell she's going to put
them through come Closeout. She didn't say much about
the other islands, except some mutters about Maskabi too
lazy to do their own breathing, Wokolinka's kin who got
their places through toelicking or worse. I believe that con-
firms what our tame thieves are telling us." She gave Felsrawg
a mocking smile, looked coldly at Simms, then lowered her eyes
to the thumbring and contemplated the pulsing of the star.

"So," Danny lifted his legs. "We go round the traps and
climb the walls. I thought it might come out like that. My
first thought was a boat. Any ideas?"

Simms shrugged. "Ne'er been on a boat 'n m' life till
Pisgaloy."

Felsrawg clicked her tongue, the sound expressing her
disgust. "Nor me."

Trithil lifted her eyes briefly, shook her head went back
to watching the star.

Danny shook his head. "And you're all island born. Well,
we fall back on something I did a while ago. It'll make
things easier, but it's noisy as . . . well, never mind that,
we'll just hope there's no sorceror around to hear me working. Trithil, I need the room, find some other place to wait.
You've all had supper? Good. Get some sleep. We go two
hours after midnight."

4

Midnight.
Danny Blue waggled a finger at the wick. The spark
caught and the oil-soaked braid began to burn and smoke.
He cranked it down until the flame seemed to spout from
the brass tube. As soon as the smoke cleared away, he fitted
on the glass chimney and clipped the lamp into its brackets.
He frowned at the leather sack, shook his head. No point in
it since he was planning to use local materials to build his
boat. Airboat. He grinned as he peeled the blankets off the
bed, dragged the lumpy mattress onto the floor, doubling
it over so it was thicker and half the width. What I did
before, I can do again. He pushed at the pallet with the toe
of his boot, walked around it, inspecting it. After a moment
he dug through the bedclothes, found one of the thin pillows
and tossed it down at the end of the pallet. Unless the damn
god wakes and sticks her long nose in my business, or one of
the S'wai gets a twinge. The way his luck was running,
either one could happen or worse. Tungjii my friend, I

could use a smile from you right now. He stepped into the middle of the pallet, knelt as comfortably as he could in front of the pillow and pulled a shield tight about him except for a tiny hole he hoped no one would notice.

He thought a moment, then began gathering his forces, putting bridles on his half-sires, whipping them into a momentary subservience and opening himself to both sets of memory; when he was ready, he adapted his half-sire Daniel's energy cables to his half-sire Ahzurdan's fire-handling and wove a lead; he drove the lead through the pinhole into the violent reality of the salamandri. He couldn't project himself into that reality, he couldn't draw demons from it, but he could tap into it and use its raving energies to power his Shaping and Transforms. When he had a steady flow coming through the lead into the accumulator cells he'd formed inside his body, he brushed his fingers across the pillow, back across the coarse canvas of the pallet cover. Murmuring a minor Transform, he turned a roll of cloth into a marker that drew coarse black lines. He narrowed his eyes, focused will and attention, and began blocking in the areas where he needed to make the major Transforms that could convert the pallet and pillow into a liftsled like the one he'd made once from a kitchen table, like the sled Daniel knew so well from his home reality.

Sketching with the marker he shuffled backward on his knees, sweeping lines across the flat in broad X's; he hobbled to the front again and began drawing honeycomb braces around the edge of the pallet. He finished, straightened his aching back, and inspected his work. "Good," he muttered. "Now the hard stuff."

He knelt before the pillow, touched it. As it happened before, it happened now. Chant poured out of him with a rightness that seemed to come from bone rather than brain, as if the rightness and the elegance of the design once more commanded him, mind and body and spirit, as if the liftsled was using him to be born. He Reshaped the flocking and canvas into glass and ceramic, metal and plastic. Sucking great gulps of fire from the salamandrin reality, he poured it into the Patterns his will created, pressing and shaping that fire into the esoteric crystals that were the heart and brain of the liftfield. He laid down layer on layer of them, embedding them in intricate polymers, wove more polymers into honeycomb braces that stiffened the floppy mattress into something like solidity. He Reshaped the pillow into sensors and readouts, a canted control plate that would let him regulate start-up, velocity, direction and altitude; he drew a pair of powerlines from it to the rear of the palletsled. Dropping the lines for a moment, he sculpted twin energy sinks in the tail; he reclaimed the lines and joined them to the sinks. Then he rested a short while, until the shaking went out of his hands.

Holding the tap quiescent, he inspected his work inch by inch, making small changes here and there to improve the conformation. When he was done with that, he knelt by the sinks, put a hand flat on each and began feeding power into them until they were topped off, humming to the touch like a hive of angry bees.

He let the tap fade, let the shield dissolve about him. He got up and stepped away from the liftsled, triumphant but too drained to crow or preen—for the moment, anyway. He tossed the blankets back on the bed, spread them over the interwoven ropes that had served to support the mattress. It wasn't particularly comfortable, but he was too tired to care. It was a transient thing he'd made, fairygold, apt to vanish if you kept it around too long, but it'd last the night and it was so alien to this reality it wouldn't trigger alarms for the witches; even the god Coquoquin might not notice what was happening under her nose. Too bad it wouldn't last. He lay staring at the ceiling, imagining the look on Pawbool's face if the four of them came swooping in, waving Klukesharna and demanding the antidote. He lifted a heavy hand, checked his ringchron. Nearly two hours gone. No wonder I'm tired.

His muscles were sore, even his bones ached; too tired to sleep, he lay brooding over his limitations. Fused through all Ahzurdan's memories was the sense of ease, the exhilarating ease with which the sorceror handled the power that leaped to his hands, the getting drunk with that power, riding a high like no other. . . . And Ahzurdan was second rank at his best. Settsimaksimin was something else. His mind drifted to that last battle. Maks alone against all of them, him and the changers and Brann. Funny that . . . in a way . . . Maksim depending on a talisman like BinYAHtii to capture and store power for him when he had a thousand thousand realities laid out for plundering. I don't know, Danny thought, wrong mindset, I suppose. There's nothing like forcefields and directed energy flows in this universe, they don't even have something simple like electricity. That's

it, probably. They don't have the physical analogs to show
them how to handle the hot stuff. If you don't know something exists, kind of hard to use it. Hmm. Wonder why Old
Garbagegut didn't think of that? H/it's been sucked in, I
suppose. Thinks like everyone else here. Computer, mmf.
An't it the way, they have all the data but can't jump the
ruts. Just as well, I hate to think what life would be like for
ordinary folks here if h/it knew how to get h/its tentacles on
that much power. Maksim now, he could handle anything
the realities put out, if he happened to think of it. Look
what he can do without the tap, transfer himself anywhere
in the world he wants, wards're cobwebs he brushes aside,
hardly noticing them. At least, that's how Ahzurdan re-
members him, larger than life and more powerful than a
god.

Danny drifted awhile through Ahzurdan's memory, melancholy at the loss between then and now. When Ahzurdan
was on his own and at his peak, he could jump the horizon
to any place he'd been before, he could snatch unwarded
items half a world away. Me, I'm lucky if I can do a simple
line-of-sight snap. To save my life, I couldn't round a corner
ten feet off. Too bad. Too toooo bad. If I could look into
the heart, If I could make the exchange without going in
. . . Klukesharna's copy in the warded sack under the sheet
. . . for Klukesharna in the Heart . . . no use regretting
what I can't do . . . so much simpler, though. . . . He drifted
into a light sleep.

He started awake, heart pounding, as some idiot pounded
on the door. He sat up. "Come," he said. "Door's not
locked."

Trithil Esmoon slipped in; she stood at the foot of the bed
and inspected him critically. "You look like you've spent
the whole time sniffing dust."

He yawned, dragged a hand across his eyes. "I've been
working."

"On that? What is it?"

"Skyboat." He swung his legs over the edge of the bed,
groaned himself onto his feet. "The others awake?"

"I heard Felsrawg slamming about in her room. Simms,
who knows? It's raining out."

"Heavy?" He crossed to the door that led onto the balcony, unbarred it and swung it open. Enjoying the cool bite of the mist blowing in under the overhang, he stood in the doorway, listening to the rain, watching the gray lines slant through the patch of light from the lamp behind him. Across the garden court on the third floor of the other wing, he could see strips of yellow light tracing out shutters and balcony doors. A few patrons must be still up or sleeping with nightlights. "It doesn't look that bad."

"Does rain make a difference?"

"Short of a cloudburst, no problem, except we'll end up wet as the Godalau. If the S'sulan are as wiped out as you all think, the rain and the chill will keep them inside, make it easier for us. The S'wai?" A shrug. "The little I know about witches doesn't help much. Can't expect everybody to be sleeping sound, but rain does tend to wash away alertness. Something we'd better keep in mind too." He pulled the door shut, looked at his chron. "Go see if the others are ready, it's time to move."

5

Since she'd be a drain, not an asset, in this part of their plan, Trithil Esmoon stayed behind; she'd keep busy packing the gear and shifting it into Danny's room and covering for them if the S'sulan, the Inn's Host, or anyone else developed an unhandy curiosity. Felsrawg and Simms stepped onto Danny's peculiar version of a flying carpet and crouched uneasily behind him as it rose and hovered in the thick damp darkness inside the room; it swung round, hovered some more, then it glided forward, sliding through the balcony door with a hair's clearance on both sides. Trithil pulled the door closed and barred it again as the mattress curved up and around, then darted for the island called the Henanolee Heart.

The rain battered at them, the sled danced and shivered, dropped with sickening jerks and surged up again as the wind bucked under it, snatched at it, sucked air from around it, under it. The darkness was smothering, no stars, no moon, no lights anywhere around them. Danny crouched over the console, flying by the numbers; he was uneasy about the uncertainties involved, but there was nothing else he could do. When the counters showed the readings he'd been watching for, he slowed the sled until it inched along, hardly moving. Still he saw nothing, only the lines of rain a handspan in front of him, faintly visible in the flickering lights of the console. Wary of snags he crept closer and closer to the Henanolee, peering into the darkness ahead of him, straining to see the walls and the towers. Finally he made out the thickening in the darkness he was expecting; he took the sled up a meter and slid across the top of the curtain wall.

He brushed against the side of one of the towers, a few of its bricks shimmering ghostlike at the edges of the glimmer from the console, eased around that tower, slid past another and took the sled down until it hovered an armlength above the grass in the Meditation Garden at the center of the Henanolee. After another handful of minutes inching along past trees and shrubs and less identifiable obstacles, he found what he'd been looking for, a small open hermitage in a group of willows. He nudged the sled inside and relaxed when he saw that the rain didn't penetrate the thick vines growing up the lath walls; he wasn't too sure how well the liftsled would operate if it were sodden, his Reshaped circuits and crystals swimming in rainwater. He lowered the sled to the flags, shut down all drain from the powersinks except for the trickle required to keep the console lit. He wanted to see their faces, to make sure they knew what his limitations were; reminders never hurt, no matter how well your co-workers knew the drill. "We're shielded," he said, "Don't move more than five paces from me unless I tell you to."

Felsrawg snorted.

On the other hand, worrying at things could be counterproductive. "All right, forget it. Let's go." He touched off the console lights, got to his feet and followed the two thieves as they moved quickly and surely through the darkness; he was impressed, more than impressed as he tried to imitate them but kept getting switched across the face by wet branches and stumbling over unseen rocks and roots.

Felsrawg and Simms waited for him by the door they'd chosen as the best way into the Heart itself. When he joined them under the stubby overhang that kept the rain off the top steps, Felsrawg thrust her left hand at him; the skry rings were glowing faintly. "Wards. The knots are here, here and here." She pointed to places on the wall, one on each side of the door, one below it; as she moved her hands, the rings pulsed rhythmically. "Sloppy, Laz. Old stuff. Want me to shut them down?" She patted her belt pouch. "I've got some smothers I've used ten years now without a smell of trouble."

Danny Blue read the knots; Felsrawg was right, the wards were old and ragged, fading even as they stood there. He could untie and reset them between one breath and the next; the trouble was, he couldn't know how they were linked into the witchtraps inside, if they were. "Simms? Any complications?"

"No."

Terse, Danny thought. Hmm. Smothers are neutral things. Why not. "All right, Felsa, go ahead."

She ran her hand carefully over the bricks and the stone threshold, pinning down the exact location of the knots. When she knew what she had to know, she formed three nubs of clay, slapped them in place, shoved a tiny crackle-sphere like a cooked glass marble into the soft clay; she worked so swiftly the three smothers were in with no discernible gap between the sets, zap, zap, zap. She ran her rings around the door, nodded with satisfaction when the stones didn't even flicker.

Simms flattened his hand against the bricks. "Good job," he murmured, "you want to take the lock or shall I?"

Felsrawg grinned at him. "Make yourself useful, little man."

6

The empty corridor had no traps in it until they reached the first turn. No traps but ghosts like ragged bedsheets drifting around, oozing up through the floor and vanishing through the ceiling, or dropping down to sink like spilled milk into the elaborate parquet, or sweeping back and forth across the hall before and behind the intruders, passing through the darkwood wall panels like fog slipping through unglazed windows. Watchghosts supposed to warn the watchwitches if they saw a wrongness in the halls.

Simms sang:

Swingle, tingle ghostee bayyy beee,
dance y' shroudee, mama mine oh,
timber time-bar, aren't y' prettee,
round around the troudee tree oh,
swingle mingle pattartateee,
diddle doo dih dee dee dee. . . .

His droning endless song was an insect buzz in the gray

light, a crooning tenor buzz that was irresistible, it seemed, to all those ghosts.

He sang:

Pittaree pattaree prettee ghostee,
prithee dance a shingaree
round and round in silkee laces
dance the laughee lovee thee. . . .

Words, Talent, song, a mix of all three, whatever it was, it worked. Simms charmed the ghosts into a complex dance and kept them so occupied with his nonsense they forgot to issue the warnings they were meant to give.

At the corner, Felsrawg lifted her hand to stop them, rings flickering.

Simms leaned against the wall, closed his eyes, his face blank, cheeks drawn in, mouth pursed. His hands drifted through small circular movements, unfocused, apparently uncoordinated. The ghosts drifted around him; now and then they nuzzled against him like cats bumping their heads against him, begging for a scratch behind the ears, but he'd tamed them so thoroughly he could take his attention away and still keep them focused on them, fascinated by him. He sighed, opened his eyes and moved away from the wall. Holding his voice to a murmur that fell dead two paces off, he said, "Triple trap. Firs' part, five steps on, the floor melt under you, jus' 'nough to let y' sink up to y' nuts, then she get solid and you stuck. Second part. Rack of scythe blades taller'n a man they swing down fro the ceilin', set s' close together it take a snake standin' on his tail to pass 'em, sharp 'nough to mince a bull. They come at you the min y' start sinkin', no time t' jump back and if y' did, you jump into the points of those blades. An' y' canna jump for'ard. f'r one thing, you couldna get a hold and you wouldna go anywhere 'cause you'd hit the third part. There some kind of pipe there shoots out fire from down where the islands was born; the firemountains come up underwater. Down where Coquoquin sleeps, y' know. If y' wan' a worse-case event, the roarin' of the fire wake the god. The fire it crisp what left after the scythes finish. Fifteen feet, you past it all, Laz. Count four lamp down, halfway to the next. Anythin' else?"

"Solid beyond?"

"Yeh, for three-four feet. That's far as I can reach."

"Got it. You know the drill, grab on." Danny grunted as

Felsrawg wrapped one arm about his biceps and shoved her
other hand down behind his belt. Simms attached himself
less impetuously but as firmly. Danny concentrated, tapped
into the power stored in the flesh-accumulators, then snapped
himself and the two thieves to the fifth lamp down. They
landed heavily, Danny staggered, stood trembling as the
other two unwrapped themselves and started on, both of
them as matter-of-fact as if they did this kind of thing every
day. It was a minute before he could follow them; he hadn't
been all that sure he could handle the weight and the complications of transporting them all together while he kept
the shield intact. He'd half expected to fall short and end
fried by that earthfire. He wiped the sweat off his face,
caught up with that pair of idiots before they left the protection of the shield and hissed anathemas at them for their
carelessness. Felsrawg laughed silently at him, patted his
arm, then went back to work.

They moved on in a flickering grayness, the nightlamps
burning at intervals too wide to do more than dent the dark,
down and down in a jagged spiral with witchtraps in every
flat, some double, some triple, all lethal to any intruder
without the resources of the team. Danny Blue was surprised at how well it was working. Felsrawg and Simms were
like hostile cats circling each other and neither of them had
much opinion of him and he was not all that fond of them,
who could be? They were primed to kill him once things
calmed down and the job was done, but now they clicked,
they were amazing; every step he took, he felt better about
this project. Down and down they went, down and down to
the earth-chamber of the Henanolee Heart.

Felsrawg was first again, senses taut, knives ready, dustpipe
charged and clipped to her belt, her ring hand swaying in
broad arcs before her. She was fierce, intent, silent. In an
ordinary house she'd be unstoppable. Not here. Single traps
she had no problems with, but her rings weren't subtle
enough to detect doubles and triples twisted inextricably
together.

Simms followed close behind her, fingers brushing the
paneling, reading the flow as he moved, his tenor buzz going
on and on, nonsense to amuse and distract any ghost that
might take a notion to flash ahead and alert the watchwitches
that intruders were wandering the hallways. Though Felsrawg's
rings were more sensitive than his natural talent, warning of
traps and hidden alarums long before Simms was aware of

them, once they reached whatever it was, he was able to read the nature and extent of the trap from the walls and floor; even the ambient air breathed information into him when he was working at peak. The bumbling idiocy he wore as an everyday mask had dropped away, the lazy amiability had vanished; he was a deadly and efficient predator.

Danny Blue kept close behind, holding the shield tight about them, containing the psychic noise of their progress, lifting them again and again across the witchtraps he could not see. Again and again, sweating each time over his limitations. If he had all of Ahzurdan's old skills he could jump straight to the Heart, bypassing all the nasty surprises. He didn't have them; what he had was a team of two thieves whose natural talents and hard-earned skill and, yes, some handy tools here and there, acted as a blind man's white canes, showing him what he couldn't see. What a team, he chanted to himself, what a team, too bad we can't stand each other. What a team. What a team.

Down and down they went, around the great spiral that screwed itself deep into the earthen center of the island, down and around until they stood at the end of the corridor looking into the Henanolee Heart.

7

The Heart was a six-sided brick-walled chamber with a domed roof. It was sunk in an opening carved into the living stone with the space between the chamber and the stone packed with tons of fine hard clay; in that clay, huge serpentine entities not-quite and not-quite-not elementals lay wrapped around the chamber, drowsing in a rest-state that was not-quite sleep. Each of the chamber walls had three arches in it, all but one with that off-white earth filling the bared space, openings where the serpents could emerge if they chose to, where they would emerge to crush any unwary intruder. The floor was white marble veined with gold, a Hexa of ruddy gold inlaid in it, a six-pointed star drawn around one circle and within another. In the inner circle was a low four-sided dais of white marble with three shallow steps on each side; on the dais was a black marble cube, its sides mirror smooth, reflecting the light from the gold-and-crystal lamps on each post of the brick arches. There was another lamp, larger; it hung in a webbing of gold chains from the apex of the dome, a crystal sphere with a sourceless gold flame burning in its heart.

Klukesharna lay on the unadorned top of the cube, small, unobtrusive, an irregular strip of black iron no longer than a man's hand.

Felsrawg looked at her rings, shuddered. She held up her hand; the stones were on fire with warning.

Simms touched his temple, squeezed his brows together; his eyes were filled with pain. Like Felsrawg, he said nothing. He'd stopped his song a few turns back, the ghosts had abandoned him, they didn't like it down here.

Danny nodded. He waved them back into the shadows of the HeartWay and stood in the arch looking across the chamber at the cube. The air was thick with wards; to his mindeye it was like reflections off seawater cast on a white wall, pulsing angular loops of light. He contemplated the chaos, trying to decide what to do. He could wipe them away, it wouldn't be hard. Trouble was he had a notion that was all it'd take to wake the serpents. He didn't want to do that.

In the end it was simple. Tiring, yes, tedious, yes, but simple. The Ahzurdan phasma shivered with a mix of tension and fear; at first the Daniel phasma resisted everything he saw, then he got interested as he associated the wards with the control systems he knew better than the configuration of his own palms; he had an intuitive understanding of interactive systems, it was one of the talents that made him among the best of the stardrive engineers, and when he got bored with that, one of the best com-offs around. Daniel Akamarino's talent and training melded with Ahzurdan's encyclopedic knowledge of wardforms told Danny Blue in exhaustive detail exactly what he had to do. He picked up the wards one by one and eased them aside, clearing a path to the cube; he didn't untie them or alter them in any essential way, he simply unhooked them from each other, rehooked them into another configuration. Like playing jakstraws with exploding straws. Simple. And oh so tedious.

Heat built up under the shield; it was trapped there; he didn't dare let it dissipate and wake the serpents. He might be able to handle them, but the battle to do it would most likely wake Coquoquin and a newly wakened god was bound to be cranky, a newly wakened god who found intruders messing around with one of her toys would escalate from crankiness to downright irritation. His voice went hoarse under the strain, his hands wanted to tremble, but that too he couldn't afford, the gestures had to be smooth and controlled or he'd blow a ward which would be a lot worse than leaking a little heat. He ground his teeth together, blinked as perspiration dripped into his eyes. Felsrawg startled him dangerously when she swabbed at his forehead, but he managed to spare her a smile, then went back to work.

An hour slid past. The clear passage drove deeper and deeper into the chamber. The serpents moved, he could feel them shifting, they were drifting up out of their vast placid slumber, drifting into dreamstate and uneasiness, crumbs of dirt broke from the earthfaces in the archways, there was a deep grumble in the earth around them, almost too low for his ears to hear it. Time and danger pressed down on him. Hurry, hurry, hurry. . . .

He resisted. The steady tedious untangling went on and on. Hurry hurry hurry . . . heads turned in the earth, blind eyes turned toward him, they weren't awake yet, but they were beginning to dream of him. Hurry hurry hurry. . . .

The path was clear. Eyes fixed on Klukesharna, Danny thrust out his left hand. Simms put the false Klukesharna in it. Cold and heavy, black iron copy. Dead iron. He looked at Felsrawg, waited while she wiped his face dry again. Arm held stiffly straight, he brought the false Klukesharna around in front of him. Lips drawn back in a feral grin, he bled the waste heat under the shield into the copy, giving it a false life. When the heat was sucked into the iron, he jerked his head toward the shadowy darkness up the HeartWay and waited until Simms and Felsrawg had retreated as far as they dared.

He let energy build up in his hands, then let the chant roll through his mind, though he didn't dare speak it aloud. The words poured silently out of him, wrote themselves in black and red in front of him. He opened his hand, holding the false Klukesharna in the crease between thumb and palm, the bitt hooked over his thumb. The words roared in his head, built to a mighty shout like a spill of black ink thrown across in front of him. The "key" jolted against his palm so hard he almost dropped it. He closed his fingers and felt Klukesharna recognize him, accept him. The exchange was made.

He swung round, two pairs of eyes were watching him avidly. He put Klukesharna in a doubly shielded leather pouch, hung it around his neck and tucked it inside his vest. With an impatient gesture, he urged the two thieves up the Way. Behind him he heard creaks and groans as the serpents stirred again. Felsrawg shivered, glanced at her rings, wheeled and started up the ramp. Simms was slower to look away, but even more than Felsrawg he felt the building danger. He caught up with her, walked half a pace behind her, ready to read the traps again because there was a good chance they'd be asymmetric, entirely different when approached from the other side.

Danny tightened down the shield until his own senses were tied in and he had to depend almost entirely on his companions.

Asymmetry. They couldn't trust anything they'd learned on the way down. Safe areas were no longer safe, the walls, the ceiling were set to erupt, they moved slower and slower until they were barely crawling. There was only one easing in the strain as they circled past the second coil of the HeartWay, the serpents were sinking back to sleep; that lessened the odds on Coquoquin waking and destroying whatever chance they had of getting away. Again and again and again Danny snapped himself and the others across the traps; again and again and again he Transformed air into a solid dome over them so they wouldn't trigger the walls and the ceiling; again and again he poured energy out of his stores until they were empty and he was feeding on himself.

Up and around they went until they reached the ground floor and moved through the hallways toward the door into the garden. Danny kept a wary eye on his companions; they weren't going to do anything yet, not until they were out of this place, they weren't fools, but afterward . . . he'd better not play the fool either. Gods, he was tired.

A man came from one of the rooms, a servant of some kind, yawning, unhurried. His eyes opened wide as he saw them, his mouth opened to yell. A knife hilt bloomed in his throat. Felsrawg stooped as she came up with him, pulled the knife loose, avoiding the gush of blood with a minimum of effort. She wiped the blade on the dead man's tunic, straightened and slid the knife into an arm sheath. She barely broke stride as she did all this.

Danny Blue watched grimly; in less than twenty minutes he was going to be sitting on the liftsled with that at his back.

They reached the door without further trouble. The man Felsrawg killed was the only person they saw during the whole time they were in the Henanolee. Once they were outside, Felsrawg collected her smothers, threw the clay out

into the garden where the drizzle would melt it into the
grass, then moved at a quick trot through the dark, heading
for the hermitage. Simms loped after her, content to let her
take the lead. Danny followed more slowly, loosening the
shield a little to choke off some of the drain on his strength.
He ached to stretch out and sleep for a year. In a while, he
told himself, don't let down yet, you've got what you wanted,
now you have to keep it. He fashioned a cherry-sized will-o,
dropped it down near his feet so he could see where he was
walking; he was in no mood to flop on his face or stub his
toes on roots or rocks. He trudged after them, muttering
curses at the drizzle soaking into his clothes and trickling
down his neck.

At the entrance to the hermitage, Danny kicked the will-o
up and into the darkness ahead, held his left hand canted
before his face, palm out. "VRESH," he shouted, the command shunting aside the spurt of dust aimed at his eyes; he
continued the shunting gesture with an outsnap of his arm.
"SOV," he chanted, curling his fingers tight against his
palm, all but one which he pointed at Felsrawg who was
leaping at him, knives ready. She dropped, unconscious. He
turned his glare on Simms who was leaning against the
lathwork, arms crossed, no apparent interest in what was
happening.

Simms unfolded his arms, held his hands level with his
shoulders, palm out. "Nothin' to do with me."

"Keep it that way. Load her on the sled."

"Y' got it." He gathered up Felsrawg, laid her on the
pallet, started to straighten.

Danny curled his fingers again, snapped out the forefinger, pointing at the middle of Simms' back. "Sov," he
murmured. He smiled as Simms collapsed across Felsrawg.
"There it is," he said aloud. "I should leave the pair of you
right here. Let the Wokolinka play with you. Ah hell, I
wouldn't leave a rabid rat to face torture. Shut up, Sorceror,"
he told the Ahzurdan phasma, who started protesting vehe-
mently as Danny rearranged the unconscious pair so he'd
have room to sit at the console. "I don't give a handful of
hot shit what you want." The Daniel phasma watched with
amiable satisfaction and more than a touch of self-con-
gratulation at seeing his semi-son adopt his ethics over those
of his rival and co-sire. Angry at both of them, Danny fed
power into the lift field. "Let's get out of here."

8

Danny Blue set the raft down on the balcony outside the door to his room. Before he could knock, it swung open and Trithil Esmoon came out. She raised her brows, mimed a question.

"We got it," he said. "Any trouble here?"

"Not even an insomniac roach." She looked past him at Felsrawg and Simms. "They dead?"

"Them?" He shook his head. "Sleeping." He glanced at his chron. "Be dawn in an hour or so, we won't wait. I think I can nurse this thing as far as the horses. Once the Wokolinka wakes up to what happened, she's going to shut this city down and shake it hard."

\#\#

Working quickly, they loaded the gear onto the pallet, stowing it about the recumbent figures of the two thieves. Trithil Esmoon produced a reel of silk cord and helped Danny rope the pouches in place. She started to tie Felsrawg's ankles, but Danny stopped her. "No need," he said. "They'll both be out till around mid-morning."

She straightened, gave him a small tight smile. "Me?"

"Keep your hands to yourself."

She twiddled her fingers and laughed at him, her eyes flirted at him, very blue even in the dim fringes of the lamplight. "A promise, I swear it. Until you ask, Laz."

"Take off your rings."

"What?"

"Take them off or join Felsrawg and Simms."

"I gave you my word."

"Fine. Now, put the rings away."

She looked at him a moment, looked away. "If I must." She folded back her left sleeve, stripped the rings off her fingers and thumb, dropping them into the hem-pocket and turned the sleeve back to fall in graceful points about her knuckles. "Are you satisfied?"

He grunted. "You'll sit on my left, that arm away from me."

The door was still open, the pale yellow light streaming out to lose itself in the drizzle. She stood in the light, her body outlined by it, her fine hair shining like silver silk. The yellow light slid off her elegant cheek, put a liquid glimmer between her lashes, gilded her upper lip, her chin. She was unreal, beauty like that was unreal. He stared at her; he was tired, so tired he was looking at her through a haze. He had no desire for her, no need to touch to take her. He simply looked and kept on looking because he couldn't turn away. Her hands were lifted, unmoving yet indescribably graceful in their stillness. She dropped them to her sides and the spell was broken.

"Climb on," he said. "Be with you in a minute." He turned his back on her and went to the end of the sled. As she settled herself in front of the pouches, he squatted beside the energy sinks. Despite having to wrestle stormwinds during the trips to and from the Henanolee Heart, the sled hadn't used much power; the sinks were still two-thirds full. He was the empty one, exhausted in both senses of the word. He flattened his hands over the cells, drew power from them into his own accumulators; he'd bleed it off later, use it to wash out some of the fatigue poisons clogging his mind and body. He had to stay awake; he had to watch the trau Esmoon. He trusted Trithil Esmoon less than the thieves, though her weapons were easier to combat—as long as he kept away from those venomous rings. He broke the contact and stood.

The rain had diminished in force until it was hardly more than a heavy mist. The towers rising around the Inn were dark; he couldn't see the streets, but he knew from the silence that they too were dark and empty; the island was sunk in its end-of-season weariness. There were no lights anywhere—except in his bedroom. He scowled, snapped his fingers, muttered a *word*; the lamps went out, making the dark complete. He wiped fog off his face, walked briskly to the front of the sled and settled himself behind the console.

9

The sled broke through into a silver-gray world of moonlight and starlight and boiling cloud floor. It was cold up there above the rain. Danny shivered, sneezed, swore. He released energy into his body, flushing out some of his fatigue, reinforcing his immunities. It was no time to catch a cold, he had enough problems with that poison eating at him. And three efficiently murderous companions.

It was as quiet as it was cold, as if they flew in a reality all their own, as if they were the only beings alive in it. His eyelids grew heavy, it was harder and harder to stay awake

though he knew if he slept with Trithil there, sitting loose
and ready, he'd wake up hitting the water below. He blinked
at the direction-finder, made a small adjustment to the
course and sat scowling at his hands because he didn't want
to scowl at Trithil and let her guess what he was thinking.

"Lazul." Fingers touched his arm.

He looked down, then at her. "Hands in your lap, if you
don't mind."

She dropped her eyes, looked momentarily distressed—
which he didn't believe at all. "Do you know the attributes
of Klukesharna?"

"Why?"

"She cleanses and heals. She unlocks possibility. If you
use her properly, she will leach the poison out of you."

"And you, of course."

"Oh no, for me there's no need. I came into this under
other pressures."

"Oh?"

"Which I do not plan to enumerate."

"Then why'd you say that?"

"I don't want to go back to Arsuid." She bit her lip,
stared unhappily at a heap of clouds rising like whipped
cream in front of them, a little off to one side. He watched
her, appreciating the performance. It was flawless, but he
didn't believe a word or a nuance. "I want Klukesharna."
Her voice was low and musing, liquid lovely tones blending
with the nearly inaudible hum of the liftfield. "I think it will
be easier to take it from you than from the Ystaffel. I'll do
whatever I can to get us beyond Coquoquin's reach, you can
trust that, Lazul or whatever your name is. I don't play
games with gods, they make up the rules as they go and the
rules always favor them." She smiled at him, her blue eyes
even bluer in the light from the console. "Like the Ystaffel,
in their despicable way. There isn't any antidote, did you
know that?"

"I suspected it."

"I'm a fool." She shook her silver head. "You planned all
along to use Klukesharna." She brooded a moment, then
looked startled. "Even the fight over the horses? Twisty
man." A trill of laughter, another shake of her head. "You
conned them. Got them to set up relay mounts at five stages
along the river. You aren't going to use any but the ones at
Kuitse-ots, are you. The rest are dust in the eyes."

He shrugged. "Whatever happened, I'd need transport.

Horses can go where you point them, a river sticks to its bed. What are you?"

"Why do you say that?"

"A Great Talisman is useless to most people, except for its symbolic value. And when I say symbolic value, I do not mean gold; you haven't a hope of selling it. And you'd have to be witch, wizard, magus or sorceror to milk its power. You're none of those. We know our own kind. We smell the Talent on those that have it. And none of the Talented would follow your particular profession or, to be blunt, be any good at it. You're very good."

"I don't see why you say that. I'm no good with you."

"Circumstances, trau Esmoon. The discipline of my craft. You did some fancy footwork round my question. What are you?"

"Call me a visitor who wants to go home."

"Demon?"

"It's a matter of definition, isn't it. I prefer visitor."

"No doubt." He spoke absently. There was a new note in the field hum, a whine that appeared and disappeared, appeared again. His Reshaping was starting to unravel. He scowled at the counter; the reading said they'd come about twenty kilometers, which meant Waystop Kuitse-ots was still about ten kilometers off. It'd be a long walk if he had to set the sled down now, though at least they were finally over land not water. The whine started again, louder this time; it was like a circular saw chewing through hardwood.

"What's happening?"

"Nothing much, trau Esmoon. It's just we're about to be sitting on a flocking mattress with the flying characteristics of a rock." He put the sled into a long slant, took it down through the clouds, down and down, laboring, making horrible noises, down and down until it lurched along five feet off the ground. The rain had stopped, the air was chill and damp and gray with dawn. He leveled the sled and sent it forward at its maximum speed. "Keep watch for me. I can't leave this. Yell if we're going to hit something solid. Can you see in this murk?"

"I can see. Yell what?"

"How the hell do I know? Think of something."

"What about a road?"

"You see one?"

"No."

"Don't bother me then. Keep your mouth shut till you

got something to say." A crack crept in jags across the face
of the console, moving between gauges and readouts. He
smelled burning feathers, swore at the sled, willing it to
keep its shape. As he fought the dissolution, he gave an ear
to Trithil's murmurs.

"Tree, swing right. Good. Missed it. Another tree . . .
wait . . . wait . . . swing left . . . now! Missed it. Brush
ahead, don't bother turning, we'll scrape over it, no problem . . . I think. . . ." The sled lurched and there was a
loud crackling as they sheared the top inch off several bushes.
Then they were clear. "Oh. There is a road, Laz. Angle
about thirty degrees to your right. Good, you've got it. This
must be the post road, it's graveled and ditched."

Danny Blue was too busy to answer her. He drew power
from the sinks and sent it coursing through the frame to
hold the Reshaping as long as he could; on and on the sled
went, slowing as the crystals deteriorated, dropping lower
and lower until they barely cleared the gravel. Two kilometers, five, seven, eight . . . then they were crawling along,
moving as fast as a man could walk with arthritis and a
broken leg. He held it together and held it . . . nine . . .
nine and a half. . . . With a flare of light as the remaining
energy stored in the sinks was released, the sled turned to
mush under him; the rags of the Transforms vanished like
dry ice sublimating. The sled jolted to the ground, throwing
him onto a console that dissolved into charred cloth and
smoldering feathers.

Danny got to his feet, brushing bits of feather off his vest.
The pallet was a sodden mess. Simms had rolled over onto
Felsrawg and was snoring heavily. Felsrawg lay with limbs
sprawling, head rolled back, breathing through her mouth;
she was alive but not lovely. Slimy with rain and mud, the
silk cord had slipped off several of the pouches; they'd
tumbled over the two thieves and spilled into the ditch at
the side of the road. Elegant and immaculate, silver slippers
unsmutched by the mud and the gelid dew coating every
surface, Trithil Esmoon was standing on the gravel, sniffing
fastidiously at the unsavory scene.

The sky was heavily overcast, but the rain had stopped—
for the moment at least. The east was bloody with sunrise
and there was enough light to see for some distance around.

Low brush grew in mangy patches on the far side of the ditch. A scatter of wild plum trees with naked branches poked from the brush. There were other patches of trees dotted about the rolling grasslands, dull trees with a few mudbrown leaves still clinging to their branches. Across the road there was a low stone wall, a field of withered yellow-brown grass with a herd of dun cattle grazing in the distance. There were no houses or other buildings anywhere in sight, though the Waystop should be less than half a mile south along the road.

Danny rubbed the back of his neck as he looked round at the dreary land. Empty land. "Stay here. I'll bring the horses back."

"No. I don't think so."

"What?"

"You understand me. Where the talisman goes, I go."

"You think I wouldn't come back?"

"Lazul, ah Laz."

"Hmm." He squatted beside the pallet, opened one of the pouches, looked inside, dropped that one and picked up another. When he found his own, he began pulling things out, transferring and discarding until he had what he wanted in one pouch. He tied on a blanket roll, frowned. He undid the straps on another roll and shook out the blankets. He started to drop them over Felsrawg and Simms, changed his mind and got to his feet. "Help me shift them onto the pallet, straighten them out some."

"Why?"

"Do it."

"Needn't be so prickly, Laz, I was just asking what you intended for them." She waited while he dumped the gear off the pallet and spread out the blankets in its place; wrinkling her nose with distaste, she grasped Felsrawg's ankles and helped move her onto the blankets, then straightened and watched with avid curiosity as Danny fussed with the thief's clothing, opening her shirt at the neck, pulling loose awkward twists and catches. He folded her hands over her ribs, put a wadded shirt under her head. "You're laying her out like a corpse, you expect her to be one?"

"Sooner or later, we're all corpses."

"Speak for yourself, mortal man."

He grunted. "Help me move Simms."

When Danny had Simms straightened out and positioned, he covered them both, shoulder to feet, with more blankets, tucked the edges under them. He collected their gear and piled it around them.

"This is a waste of time, you know," Trithil said. "They'll be after us as soon as they wake."

"Take a walk, I'll catch up with you."

"Haven't you something to do first?"

"What?"

"Klukesharna. The poison."

"Klukesharna stays where she is as long as I'm in Lewinkob lands. The moment I take her from the shielding, Coquoquin will be here. You want that?"

She shuddered. "No indeed." She collected her own gear, slid the pouch strap over her shoulder. "No, that would be a very bad thing." She looked down at the sleepers. "You said mid-morning."

"Take a walk. Now."

"It's stupid not to kill them now."

"You want to join them?"

"You think you could handle me like that?"

"You want to find out?"

"Don't be a fool, I'm on your side, man."

"Nice to know. You've got two seconds to start walking or I drop you."

She shrugged. "You could try, but that'd likely bring Coquoquin and I'd lose a lot more. All right. Be sure you do come. I can get very unpleasant when I'm disappointed."

He watched her walk away. I bet you can, he thought. He looked down at Felsrawg and Simms. She's right, you'll be after me, you've got no choice, but I'm not a murderer and I don't plan to become one. I'll play the game my own way and take my chances. However, there's no point being a total fool. He shut his eyes, thought a moment, then began weaving a stasis web about them, once again melding the experience of his two half-sires, crafting a dome over them that would hold them unmoving and untouchable for the next several days. He wasn't all that sure exactly how long the stasis would last, two days or a week, it didn't matter, he was buying himself time to get out of Lewinkob lands and free the talisman to his uses. After that, let them try.

The sun had cleared the peaks of the Dhia Asatas, the wind was shredding the clouds and exposing patches of sky; the day wasn't brightening so much as pushing the horizon back. The land around him was brown and gray and blanched, even the naked sky looked dingy. Danny shouldered his

gear, breathed in that chill air and felt suddenly lighter than
those vanishing clouds. Klukesharna was his and in a day or
so the poison would be out of him, he was free, finally free
of the Chained God's hook and on the way to reclaiming his
Talent. Whistling a tune from one of Daniel's more ancient
memories, he started after Trithil.

THE REBIRTHING: PHASE THREE
The stones are moving.

I: BRANN/JARIL

> Having run full out into the geniod trap, Brann and Jaril are on their way to Havi Kudush to steal Churrikyoo from the Great Temple of Amortis so they can ransom Yaril from the grip of Palami Kumindri and her coterie.

1

The Mutri-mab went skipping about the deck of the pilgrim barge, holy fool in whiteface and fluttering ribbons. He leaped to the forerail and capered perilously back and forth on that narrow slippery pole, then struck a pose. When he was satisfied with the attention he had drawn to himself, he began beating two hardwood rods together, making a staccato melodious background to his chant. "Hone your wit," he sang in a powerful tenor:

Hone your wit with alacrity
Romp and revel, gaiety
Wait for thee, for us
In Havi
Kudush
Ah sing Amortis
More ah more ah more than this
Ecstasy, amour and bliss
Ah, ah Amortis, she
Waits for thee, for us
In Havi
Kudush

Don your slippers, dance for me
Tipsy wanton jubilee
Waits for thee, for us
In Havi
Kudush
Ah sing Amortis
More ah more a more than this
Ecstasy, amour and bliss. . . .

Brann pulled the heavy black veil tighter about her and wondered how stupid she was, coming here into Amortis' heartland. The two times she'd run into Amortis, she and the Blues, Yaril and Jaril had combined to whip the tail of the god. Her only hope was evading Amortis' notice. Unfortunately, the way things had worked out, it was near the end of the pilgrimage season and she didn't have masses of people to vanish into. Jaril stirred against her leg; since pilgrims didn't travel with watchpets, he couldn't be a hound again, nor could he continue as her M'darjin page, servants weren't permitted in Havi Kudush—not as servants, though they could come as pilgrims. So he was being her invalid son; the disguise concealed his oddities and provided an excuse for her.

She stroked his soft hair, smiled down at him, understanding all too well his impatience, his restlessness. He wanted Yaril freed as soon as possible. He wanted to fly in, take the talisman and rush back to trade it for his sister. He knew he couldn't do that, but the need was always there, an itch under his skin. And there were other strains, things she felt in him but couldn't find a way to ask about. There was an uneasiness in him now, needs that were growing toward explosion. She remembered his outburst in the cave and was furious at her helplessness. There was nothing she could do to ease him. She listened with half an ear to the chant swelling about her, the chorus of the paean to Amortis the Mutri-mab was singing. She joined in that chorus after a few minutes because she didn't want to be conspicuous in her silence. Not just worry about Yaril. Puberty, he said, a kind of puberty. He needs his people, he's ripe for mating, but Yaril's the only female of his kind in this reality. His more than sister, his twin. It's a recipe for disaster, she thought, one might even say tragedy. No more procrastination, I have to see them home. Even thinking about it hurt so much, she knew she'd bleed until she was empty when that knot was broken; two hundred years, more, they'd been her children, her nurslings, bonded to her mind and body. But what choice had she? Children leave you. That's the way things are.

Jaril sensed something of her trouble, nestled closer, trying to comfort her without words.

"Not much longer," she said. Her voice was lost in the singing of the other passengers, but even if one of them heard her, it'd mean nothing; it was the kind of thing anyone would say.

Have you figured out how, Bramble? There was a tinge of bitterness in the mindvoice; he trusted her, but he was afraid of Amortis and deeply angry at Maksim for letting them down.

"Don't," she murmured. "There are ears who can hear that shouldn't." She sighed. "No, I haven't. I don't know enough. Look ahead, Jay, there's the Holy Rock, we'll be there by dawn. We'll look around and see what's what."

The Rock rose like a broaching whale out of the stony plain—the Tark—that stretched from the misty reedmarsh where three rivers met to the southern reaches of the Dhia Asatas. At the highest point of the Rock, the three-tiered Sihbaraburj thrust up black and massive against the sunset. Above it the sky was still dark blue with poufs of cloud dotted across it, clouds that ranged from a pale coral overhead to vermilion in the west where the sun floated in a sea of molten gold. Havi Kudush the holy city. Harmony-tongued Kudush where pious hands hauled in tons and tons of warm gold bricks and laid them in a thousand thousand courses, brick on brick, slanted inward to make the three-step, truncated pyramid that was the Sihbaraburj, Temple to Amortis, that was the Heart of Phras, a made-mountain honeycombed with twenty thousand chambers where the Priest-Servants lived, where the Holy Harlots made worship, where healers and seers made promises that were sometimes kept, where dancers and singers, song makers and music makers lived and worked, where there were artisans of all sorts, goldsmiths and silversmiths, workers in bronze and copper, gem cutters and stone cutters, potters and weavers, painters, embroiderers, lace makers and so on, all of them creating marvels for the honor of Amortis—and the coin they got from selling their work to pilgrims as offerings or souvenirs. Havi Kudush the holy city. Its feasts flow with fat and milk, its storehouses bring rejoicing. Fill your belly, the hymns

command, day and night make merry, let every day be full
of joy, dance and make music, this is the pure bright land
where all things are celebrant and celebrated, dance and
make music, praise Amortis bringer of joy, praise her in
pleasure and delight.

The barge halted when the sun dropped out of sight,
changed teams and went on. The draft oxen plodded steadily along the towpath, used to the dark as was the drover
boy riding the offside ox, flicking his limber stick at the
bobbing rumps when the plodding slowed too much. On the
barge the pilgrims settled to sleep behind canvas wind-
breaks. The Mutri-mab sat on the forerail and played sleepy
tunes on his flute. The river whispered along the sides,
tinkling, shimmering murmurs that lied about the heaviness
of the silt-laden water which in the daylight ran thick and
red with the mud of three rivers and the marsh. Jaril lay
wrapped in a blanket he neither needed nor wanted but
wore like a mask to keep off the eyes of the other travelers.
He was sunk in that coma he called sleep, a shutting down
of his systems, a hoarding of the sunlight he drank during
the day. Brann lay beside him, but she couldn't sleep.

Head down, she told herself. I'm a poor lorn widow with
an invalid son; who am I to attract the notice of a god. I
wish we were out of here. Too much land to cover. What
happens if she feels it when we lope off with Churrikyoo?
What happens if she comes after us? We haven't got
Ahzurdan to shield us. What happened to Maksi? I wish he
were here. I'd feel a lot better about this business. He must
have put his foot in something. Idiot man, he's too soft for
his own good. That skinny whore he's so fond of leads him
around by the nose, well, not the nose . . . Slya! I'm jealous
of that little . . . that . . . damn damn damn all gods, why
does this happen to me on top of everything else? I thought
I was over wanting him. She luxuriated a moment in her
misery, squeezing tears from tight-closed eyes, then she
sighed and let it go; there was no point in scraping her
insides raw yearning for what she couldn't have. She'd got
over having to leave Sammang, she'd got over Chandro, it
just took time.

She lay brooding for some time longer until, eventually,
she drifted into a restless sweating sleep.

2

Havi Kudush the Lower was reed and mud and narrow

waterway, with clouds of black biters to chasten the proud and try the tempers of the intemperate. According to their natures and the choice available, the pilgrims spent the week they were allowed to stay in longhouse dormitories constructed from the ubiquitous reeds or in individual cells, also woven from the reeds; this late in the season there were many empty cells for those who preferred privacy.

The pilgrims were ferried to and from the Temple Landing by small shallow boats that scooted about the reeds like bright colored waterbeetles, poled by small and wiry marshboys whistling like birds when they weren't exchanging insults, nothing solemn about them however solemn and pious their passengers; they were the only way to get about and reaped coin like their elders reaped corn though the Temple taxed half of it away from them.

The barge landing was a stone platform at the edge of the marsh. The marsh elders had a tall reedhouse there, its front woven into intricate and elaborate patterns; morning light slid softly across the wall in an enigmatic calligraphy of shifting shadow and shades of yellow. In season, the elders sat at a table placed before the high, arching doorway, writing with reed pens on sheets of papyrus as they enrolled the pilgrims and passed out the clay creedeens that gave them the freedom of the city for seven days.

There was only one old man at the table when Brann's barge tied up at the landing. He looked half-asleep, sour and dirty; his fingernails were black with dried muck, there was dirt ground into the lines of his hands, a yellow-gray patina of sweat and rancid oil over every inch of visible skin and there was a lot of skin visible since all he wore was a light brown wrap-skirt of reedcloth, bracelets of knotted reedcord, a complicated pectoral of palm-sized rounds of reedcord, knotted and woven in sacred signs. When Brann finally reached him after standing in line for over an hour, she almost gasped at the stench blowing into her face; for the first time since she'd donned it, she was grateful for the protection of the veil.

"The Baiar-chich Kisli Thok," she murmured, answering the questions he'd dumped on her in his drawling indifferent voice. "Of Dil Jorpashil. My son Cimmih Thok ya Tarral. We come to seek healing for him." Jaril sagged against her, looking wan and drawn, all eyes and bones, the essence of sickly, pampered youth. She set seven takks on the table before the elders, the fee for a private cell plus the fee for the creedeen. It wasn't cheap, visiting the Temple at Havi Kudush.

Moving slow and slow and slower, the old man scratched her answers on the scroll; when he was finished he wiped the pen's nib on a smeared bit of cloth and inspected it, unhooked a small curved blade from his belt and shaved off a few slivers, repointing the pen to his exacting standards. He set it down, pulled over the stacks of silver coins and weighed each on a small balance. Satisfied he had the full measure of what was due, he set the coins in a box and blew a shrill summons on a small pipe. Behind her Brann could hear soft whuffs of relief; the harried weary pilgrims knew better than to complain about how long he was taking, but they fidgeted and sighed and otherwise made their discomfort known. He showed no sign he heard or saw any of that, simply pulled his inkpot closer and beckoned to the next in line.

A marshboy came trotting up, loaded Brann and Jaril and their gear into his poleboat; she was afraid the shallow boat was going to founder under their weight, but by some peculiarity of its construction it merely shuddered and seemed to squat marginally lower in the water. The marshboy hopped onto the platform at the stern, dug in his pole and pushed off.

Between one breath and the next he had the bright red shell flying across the open water where the river emerged from the marsh; then he took them scooting precariously through the winding waterways of the reed islands, sliding on thick red water moving sluggishly among shaggy reed clumps with their spiky leaves and finger-sized stems. Half new green growth stiff as bone and twice as high as a standing man, half dead, broken leaves and stems slowly collapsing into the muck they'd emerged from, the reed clumps creaked and rustled in the morning wind, a wind that Brann wished she could feel. Down near the water, in spite of the speed of their passage, the air was still and lifeless and far too warm. Swarms of marshbiters rose as they moved along the ways; most of them were left behind before they had a chance to settle; the marshboy seemed to know the route so well he could follow it in his sleep and keep flying too fast for the bugs, though Brann couldn't understand how he did it. One clump of reeds looked much like the next, the narrow channels were indistinguishable; she was lost before they'd gone through a handful of turns.

After twenty minutes the poleboat emerged into a more open area, a flat sheet of water dotted with hundreds of small islands gathered in tight clusters about a much larger one; when they got closer she saw that the islands were reed mats mixed with mud, pinned in place by pilings made of bundled nai reeds; each island had a small cell built on it. A lacework of suspension foot-bridges linked the islands within the clusters and the clusters with each other. On the big island there were several longhouses like the house at the Landing.

To build a longhouse: Take tapering bundles of towering nai reeds and wrap reed cords about them until they look like fifty foot spikes, their butts three feet across at the base. Drive them into the mud an armstretch apart in two rows of ten spikes, angled out like massive awns from some gigantic ear of wheat. Bend the spike ends over and bind them together, each to each, to make ten parallel pointed arches. Lay thin reed bundles across the arches to act as stringers. Sew on overlapping split reed mats for siding. Move in.

To build a cell: Do likewise, only in less degree.

The marshboy took them to one of the outer islands, basing his decision on some obscure calculation involving sex, age, and dress. After Brann counted out the coins he demanded, he pointed at the longhouses. "Wan' t' eat, t's tha," he said. He was a little monkey of a boy, black eyes like licorice candy, a snub nose and a cheerful grin that bared teeth like small sharp chisels and turned his eyes to black-lined slits. "Need else, t's tha." He hopped back on the boat, pushed off and in seconds had vanished into the reeds.

The cell was raised waist-high off the cracking mud; there was an odd sort of contrivance that led from the flat up to a narrow platform built onto the front end of the structure; it was like a cross between the foot-bridges and a staircase and was just wide enough for one person at a time. It groaned and darted sideways as Brann stepped onto the first segment; she grabbed at the handrope before the rampladder threw her and climbed cautiously to the platform.

When she opened the door, she smelled every pilgrim who'd lived there that season and maybe a dozen before. "Slya's Armpits." She groaned, wedged the door open and lifted the shutter mats from the windowholes, propping them up with the sticks she found thrust into loops beside the holes. "Favor, Jay?"

He was leaning in the doorway, the nose erased from his face. "What about it maybe alerting you know who?"

"Hah! You're just lazy, luv. If she hasn't smelled you yet,

she won't notice you crisping a few bugs and firewashing this sty. At least I hope not. How can you go looking for you-know-what if you can't change? Think of it as a test run."

3

Mid-afternoon. Veiled in opaque black, swathed in black robes, Brann trudged up the long ramp to the top of the Rock. Beside her Jaril was stretched out on a litter carried by two adult marshmen; wrapped in blankets, pale and beautiful with little flesh on elegant bones (a carefully crafted image since he had nothing remotely resembling bones), he lay like a fallen angel, crystal eyes closed to hide their strangeness, controlling his impatience with some difficulty. Brann felt the strain in him, took his hand. He relaxed a little, gave her a slight smile. And held her hand so tightly she knew she'd have bruises on her fingers. The link between them was tightening more and more as the days passed since Yaril was taken; it was as if he were trying to make her take Yaril's place. She refused to think about that or what would happen to Jay and her if they failed here; it was too troubling, she couldn't afford the distraction.

The ramp they were moving up was a broad roadway paved with the same warm yellow-ocher brick that the Sihbaraburj was made of; it was cut into the Rock, slanting up the entire length of its northern face, a slope of one in seven, steep enough to make the pilgrims sweat but not enough to exhaust them. No doubt it was an impressive sight at the height of the season when a hoard of incense waving, torch-bearing worshipers climbed that long slant with Mutri-mabs weaving through them, capering and singing, playing flutes and whirling round and round, round and round in a complex spiral dance up that holy road. In this late autumn afternoon, she was alone on the roadway with the litter bearers; she didn't like the exposure, she'd planned to wait for morning and the rest of the pilgrims, but Jaril was drawn too taut. He said nothing, but she knew he'd go without her if she forced him to a longer idleness. He'd go in a wild, reckless mood, risking everything on a chance of finding and taking the talisman. It was better to take the lesser risk of Amortis noticing them.

They reached the top after half an hour's climb and turned in through a towering stone gate carved to resemble the reed arches of the longhouses. They passed into a green and

lovely garden with fountains playing everywhere, palms casting pointed shadows over lawns like priceless carpets and
flowering plants in low broad jars glazed red and yellow and
blue. The walkway curved between two wrought iron fences
with razor-edged spearpoints set at close intervals along the
top rail: Look and enjoy but don't touch.

The bearers stopped just outside the Grand Entrance to
the Sihbaraburj. They set the litter down and squatted beside it to wait until it was time to go back down. The widow
helped her ailing son onto his feet and stripped away the
blankets wrapped around him. He wore fine silks and jewels
and arrogance, an exquisite, emaciated mama's darling.

With Jaril leaning on Brann's arm, they went inside.

Light streamed in through weep-holes, was caught and
magnified in hundreds of mirrors. There were mirrors everywhere inside that brick mountain, light danced like water
from surface to surface, images were caught and repeated,
tossed like the light from mirror to mirror until what was
real and what was not-real acquired an equal validity. Brann
wandered bemused in that warren of corridors and small
plazas, walked through shimmering light and cool drifts of
incense-laden air and marveled that she had no sense of
being enclosed in tons of earth and brick; like image and
reality there was a confusion between inside and out, a
sense she was in a place not quite either. They moved past
shops and forges, small chapels and waiting rooms; they
were stopped when they poked into the living sections,
escorted back to the shops when they claimed they were
lost. The place was so big that in the three hours they spent
probing the interior they saw only a minute fraction of it. As
the day latened, the light inside the Sihbaraburj dimmed and
filled with shadow, the shopkeepers worked more frantically
to woo coin from the straggling pilgrims, the Servants in the
Grand Chambers were bringing their ceremonies to a close.

Brann and Jaril stopped in front of a room filled with
shadow; fugitive gleams of gold, silver and gemstones come
from the glass shelves that lined the walls from floor to
ceiling.

A Servant was sitting at a table just inside the open archway,
a scroll, several pens and an inkpot at his elbow. He lifted
kohl-lined dark eyes and smiled just enough to tilt the ends
of his narrow mustache as she stepped in. "Yes, khatra?"

"May I ask, Holy One, what is this?" She moved her
hand in a small arc, indicating the objects on the shelves.

"They are gifts, khatra. Beauty to honor her who is beauty's self."

"Is it permitted to see them closer?"

"Certainly, khatra. However, it is so near to Evendown, it would be better to return on the morrow."

As soon as he said the last word, a gong sounded, a deep booming note that shuddered in the bone. He stood. "That is Evendown, khatra, you must leave."

She bowed her head, turned, and left.

4

Jaril moved impatiently about the cell as Brann unpacked the supper basket she'd brought from the big island longhouse that sold food to the pilgrims. "I'm going back tonight," he said suddenly. "It has to be in one of those giftrooms, don't you think, Bramble?"

"No has-to-be, Jay. But you're probably right." Brann pulled up the three-legged stool and sat down to eat. She wanted to tell him he was a fool to take the chance, but she knew he wouldn't listen and she didn't want to irritate him into a greater recklessness. "How you going?"

"Wings, then four-feet. I'll be careful, Bramble. I won't go till late and I won't touch it if I find it. All right?"

"Thanks, Jay."

"I been thinking. . . ." He dropped onto the pallet, lay watching her eat. "We need something to keep it in, Bramble. To hide it from her."

"I know. I can't see any way we can do it. I'm afraid we'll have to fight our way to Waragapur and count on Tak WakKerrcarr to hold her off his Truceground."

"We might still have to, but I've thought of something. I can make a pocket inside myself and insulate the talisman from everything outside."

"Even from the god?"

"I think so."

"That helps. We've got seven days here, Jay. I think we ought to stay in character, leave with who we came with. Can you wait that long? It's six more days if you find the thing tonight."

"I can, once I know. I said it before and it's true. It's not knowing that eats at me, Bramble. But I don't think we ought to wait to take the talisman on the last night before we leave. If she notices it's gone, she'll hit the outgoers hard."

"And the stayers just as hard, be sure of that."

"Well. . . ." He turned onto his back, lay staring up at the cobwebs under the roof. "Damned if we do, damned if we don't. Maybe we should just toss a coin and let old Tungjii decide. Heads, early. Tails, late."

"Why not. Now?"

"No. Wait till I find the thing, Bramble. Till I know."

5

Brann sat on the bed, a blanket wrapped about her, chasing biters away from her face and arms with a reed whisk; the Wounded Moon was down, but the darkness was broken by stars glittering diamond-hard diamond-bright through the thin, high-desert air. She shivered and pulled the blankets tighter; that air was chill and dank here in the marsh; a curdled mist clung to the reed clumps and the floorposts of the cell; tendrils of mist drifted through the windowholes and melted in the heat from the banked peat fire in the mud stove. Outside, the big orange grasshoppers the marshfolk called jaspars had already begun their pre-dawn creakings and a sleepy mashimurgh was practicing its song. There was almost no wind; the stillness was eerie, frightening, as if the marsh and the Rock and even the air were waiting with her for something to happen, something terrible. What an anticlimax, she thought, if Jay comes sliding in and says he hasn't found the thing. I don't know how I could get through another night of waiting. Slya! I hate feeling so helpless. It should be me in there, not my baby, my nursling. She contemplated herself and laughed silently at what she saw. She was nervous about Jaril, but mostly she was irritated because she had no part to play in this, she was baggage. It was harder than she'd thought to reconcile herself to being baggage.

A large horned owl came through a windowhole, snapped out its wings and landed neatly on the reed mat. As soon as its talons touched, it changed to Jaril. He dropped onto the second cot and grinned at her.

"Well?" Brann scowled at him. "Did you or didn't you?"

"Did."

"Giftroom?"

"No, I was wrong about that. It was in a storeroom, the kind where they throw broken things and whatever they don't think has much value."

"A Great Talisman in a junk room?"

"What it looks like, Bramble. Dust everywhere, broken everything, cheap trinkets, the kind your sailor friends bought their whores when they hit port. Wornout mats rolled up, cushions with the stuffing leaking out. And the old frog looking right at home sitting up on a shelf smothered in gray dust. Maybe it's been there since the Sihbaraburj was built." He crossed his legs, rubbed his thumb over and over his ankle. "Funny, I'd 've never gone in there, but a Servant came along the corridor I was in and I thought I'd better duck. There was a door handy; it was locked so I oozed in and while I was waiting I took a look round. I was being firesphere so I wouldn't leave footprints or other marks in case someone came in there hunting something. I about went nova when I saw the thing way up on the top shelf, pushed into a corner and like I said covered with dust. I managed to ride the blow out, I don't know how. I nosed about some more, there was no sign Amortis was around and I've got pretty good at spotting gods. I guess we sit it out the next six days."

"Can you?"

"Oh yes. Um, I should get all the sun I can."

"Morning be enough?"

"Unless it's raining."

"We've got to go to the Temple. Hmm. We went up mid-afternoon today, I suppose that could be enough precedent. You need to be outside?"

"No. Your bed gets the morning sun, enough anyway, we can trade and if anyone comes snooping I just pull a blanket over me and pretend to be asleep."

"Good enough." Brann yawned. "Let's switch blankets." She yawned again. "Just as well we're not going up in the morning. I need sleep."

6

Night.

A gale wind blowing across the marshes, a dry chill wind that cut to the bone.

The Wounded Moon was down, a smear of high cloud dimmed the star-glitter and a thick fog boiled up from the marshwater.

Brann sat wrapped in blankets, staring at the faint red glow from the dying fire, waiting for Jaril to return.

A great horned owl fought the wind, laboring in large sweeps toward the top of the Rock; he angled across the wind, was blown past his point of aim, clawed his way back, gained a few more feet, was blown back, dipped below the rim of the Rock into the ragged eddies around the friable sandstone, climbed again and finally found a perch on the lee side of the Sihbaraburj.

Jaril shifted to a small lemur form with dexterous hands and handfeet and a prehensile tail. Driven by all the needs that churned in him, he crawled into a weep-hole and went skittering through the maze of holes that drained the place, provided ventilation and housed the mirrors that lit the interior of the made-mountain. He shifted again to something like a plated centipede, and went scuttling at top speed through the wall tubes to the junkroom where he'd seen the little glass frog. He hadn't been back since that first day, no point in alerting Amortis if she wasn't aware of what she had. He tried not to wonder if the thing was still there, but his nerves were strung so taut he felt like exploding. On and on he trotted, his claws tick-ticking on the brick.

He thrust his head into the room. The gloom inside was thicker than the dust, he couldn't see a thing. He closed his foreclaws on the edge of the hole, fought for control of the tides coursing through him. Preoccupied with his internal difficulties, for several minutes he didn't notice an appreciable lightening in that gloom. When he looked round again, he saw a faint glow coming from the shelf where he'd seen Churrikyoo. He shifted hastily to his glowsphere form and drifted over to it.

Having rid itself of dust, the talisman was pulsing softly, as if it said: come to me, take me. Jaril hung in midair, all his senses alert. He felt for the presence of a god. Nothing. He drifted closer. Nothing. Closer. Warmth enfolded him. Welcome. The little glass frog seemed to be grinning at him. He extruded two pseudopods and lifted it from the shelf. It seemed to nestle against him as if it were coming home. He didn't understand. He glanced at the shelf and nearly dropped the frog.

A patch of light was shifting and shaping itself into something . . . something . . . yes, a duplicate of the thing he held.

Jaril looked down. Churrikyoo nestled in the hollows of his pseudopods and he seemed to hear silent laughter from it that went vibrating through his body. He looked at the shelf. The object was dull and lifeless, covered with a coat of dust. He gave a mental shrug, slipped the frog into the pouch he'd built for it and flitted for the hole.

He shifted form and went skittering up the worm holes, a pregnant pseudocentipede. Now and then he stopped and scanned, every sense straining, searching for any sign of alarm. Nothing, except the frog chuckling inside him, nestling in a womblike warmth.

He wriggled out of a weep-hole and shifted again as he fell into the wind. Broad wings scooping, he fought the downdraft that flowed like water along the brick; there was a moment when he thought he was going to impale himself on the spearpoints of the walkway fence, but a sudden gust of wind caught him and sent him soaring upward, carrying him over the outer wall. He regained control and went slipping swiftly to the cell where Brann was waiting.

Brann looked up as Jaril landed with a thud, changed. "Did you?"

He patted his stomach, gave her an angelic smile. "I'd show you but . . ."

"Right." She rubbed at her neck. "I'm going to get some sleep. Barge leaves at first light. Wake me, will you, luv?"

7

The barge slid smoothly, ponderously down the river, considerably faster than it came up, riding the current, not towed behind eight plodding oxen. The deck passengers were quiet as they left Havi Kudush, tired, drained, even a little depressed—because they hadn't got what they wanted, or because they had. There were two Mutri-mabs aboard, but they huddled in blankets, as morose as the most exhausted pilgrim.

Brann and Jaril had a place near the middle of the deck where they were surrounded by pilgrims; it was a fragile shield, probably useless if Amortis came looking, but the best they could do. Brann held aloof from the rest, concerning herself with her invalid son. That concern wasn't only acting; she was worried about Jaril. He'd lost all his tensions. She didn't understand that. Some, yes. They had what they'd come to get. Keeping it was something else. Nothing was sure until the exchange was actually made. He was relaxed, drowsy, limp as a contented cat; it was as if the talisman were a drug pumping through his body, nulling out everything but itself. His dreamy lassitude became more pronounced as the days passed.

Late in the afternoon of the third day, a gasp blew across the deck.

Golden Amortis came striding across the Tark with a flutter of filmy draperies, her hair blowing in a wind imperceptible down among the mortal folk. A thousand feet of voluptuous womanflesh glowing in the golden afternoon.

Brann huddled in her robes and veil, grinding her teeth in frustration. It was obvious Amortis had missed her talisman and was coming for it; no doubt the copy it'd made of itself had melted into the light and air it had come from. Jaril slipped his hand into hers; he leaned into her side, whispered, "Don't worry, mama."

Don't worry! Brann strangled on the burst of laughter she had to swallow. Not real laughter, more like hysteria. She closed her eyes and tried not to think. But she couldn't stand not seeing what was happening, even if it was disaster coming straight for her, so she opened them again. Bending down to Jaril, she muttered, "Could you build that bridge without Yaro?" The first time they'd clashed with Amortis, Yaril and Jaril had merged into a sort of siphon linking Brann with the god; once the connection was established, Brann sucked away a good portion of the god's substance and vented it into the clouds; they'd scared Amortis so badly she'd run like a rat with its tail on fire.

Jaril laughed, a soft contended sound like a cat purring. "Sure," he said. "But I won't need to."

That tranquillity was beginning to get irritating. She straightened, tensed as Amortis changed direction and came striding toward them.

The god bent over the river, cupped her immense hands ahead of the barge. Up close her fingers were tapering columns of golden light, insubstantial as smoke but exquisitely detailed, pores and prints, a hint of nail before the tips dipped below the water—which continued undisturbed as if there were no substance to the fingers.

The barge plowed into the fingers, passed through them.

Brann felt a brief frisson as she slid through one of them; it was so faint she might have imagined it.

She heard what she thought was a snort of disgust, unfroze enough to turn her head and look behind her. Amortis had straightened up. She was stalking off without even a look at the barge.

"Told you," Jaril murmured. "It doesn't want to be with her any more. It's taking care of us." He yawned, stretched out on his blanket and sank into his sleep coma.

Brann frowned down at him. If she wanted to play her role, she'd pull the other blanket over him; she chewed her lip a moment, glanced at the sun. Take a chance, she thought, let him draw in as much energy as he can, he's going to need it, poor baby.

8

For three more days the barge swung through the extravagant bends of the broad Kaddaroud. Twice more Amortis came sweeping by, ignoring the river and those on it, her anger monumentally visible. The pilgrims huddled in their blankets, terrified. When she was angry, the god had a habit of striking out at anything that caught her attention. If the force of that anger rose too high in her, she struck out at random; anything could set her off, a change in the wind, a gnat on her toe, a fugitive thought too vague to describe. Anyone who got in the way of her fury was ashes on the wind. All they could do was pray she didn't notice them.

She didn't. After she stalked by the second time, she didn't return.

##

The Bargemaster unloaded his passengers at the Waystop where the Kaddaroud met the Sharroud, took on a new load of pilgrims, hitched up the draft oxen and started back upriver.

The Inn Izadinamm was a huge place, capable of housing several hundred in a fair degree of comfort. This late in the season, there were scarce fifty there, three scant bargeloads come back from Kudush to wait for the riverboats that would carry them north or south to their ordinary lives.

Five days after they came to the Izadinamm, a northbound riverboat moored for the night at the Waystop landing. In the morning it left with a score of passengers, Brann and Jaril among them.

9

Waragapur, green and lovely, jewel of peace and fruitfulness.

Truceground and oasis, a place of rest among stony barren mountains jagged enough to chew the sky.

Warmed by the firemountain Mun Gapur, steamed by hotsprings, hugged inside hundred-foot cliffs, Waragapur knew only two seasons, summer during the hottest months and spring for the rest of the year. When Brann arrived it was the edge of winter elsewhere, but there were plum trees in bloom at Waragapur, peach trees heavy with ripe fruit, almonds with sprays of delicate white flowers and ripe nuts on the same tree.

Tak WakKerrcarr came down from his Hold and stood on the landing, leaning on an ebony and ivory staff, waiting for the riverboat. He was an ancient ageless man, his origins enigmatic, his skin the color and consistency of old leather drawn tight over his bones, long shapely bones; he was an elegant old man despite being a home to an astonishing variety of insect life and despite the strength and complexity of the stink that wafted from him—apparently he bathed every five years or so. He ignored the stares and nudges of those who came to gape at him (very careful not to annoy him by coming too close or whispering or giggling), ignored the nervous agitation of the boatmen who'd never seen him but had no doubt whom they were looking at. When Brann came off the ship with the passengers stopping here, he reached with his staff, tapped her on the shoulder. "Come with me," he said, turned and stalked off.

Brann blinked, looked after him. His voice told her who he had to be. It was a wonderful voice, a degree or two lighter than Maksim's, with much the same range and flexibility. "Jay," she glanced over her shoulder at the changer, frowned as she saw him curled up on the landing beside their gear, "look after things here." She hesitated, went on. "Be careful, will you? Don't trust that thing too much."

Jaril nodded, gave her a drowsy smile, and got to his feet.

She didn't want to leave him, but she hadn't much choice. She walked slowly after Tak WakKerrcarr, chewing on her lip, disturbed by the changes in the boy; after a few steps she shook her head and tried to concentrate on WakKerrcarr. She didn't know what he wanted with her or how much he knew about why she was here. He'd be dangerous if he took against her; Maksi wouldn't admit it, but even he was a little afraid of the man. Tak WakKerrcarr. First among the Primes, older than time. Brann straightened her back, squared her shoulders and followed him.

WakKerrcarr waited for her in a water-garden at the side of the Inn, sitting beside a fountain, one fed from the hotsprings, its cascades of water leaping through its own cloud of steam. She caught a whiff of his aroma and edged cautiously around so he was downwind of her.

He pounded the butt of the staff on the earth by his feet, bent forward until his cheek was touching the tough black ebony. He gazed at her as she stood waiting for him to speak. "Take off that kujjin veil, woman. You're no Temu priss."

With an impatient jerk, she pulled off the opaque black headcloth; she was happy to get it off, warmth poured more amply than water from that fountain. She smoothed mussed hair off her face, draped the veil over her arms. "So?"

"Got a message for you." He straightened up, laid his staff across his bony knees. "Fireheart come to see me. Said to tell you watch your feet, but don't worry too much, you're her Little Nothin and she won't let any god do you hurt."

"God?"

"I'm not telling you what you don't know." He crossed his legs at the ankles, wiggled toes longer than some people's fingers. "That bunch tryin to run you, they're fools dancin to strings they can't see."

"What god?"

He got to his feet. "Said what I planned. Not goin to say more. Well, this. Tell that demon, she don't play fair, I'll feed her to the Mountain." His eyes traveled down her body, up again, lingered briefly on her breasts. "When this's over, come see me, Drinker of Souls." A wide flashing smile, one to warm the bones. "I'll even take a bath." Chuckling and repeating himself, take a bath sho sho, even take a bath, hee hee, he strode out of the garden and vanished into the orchard behind.

Brann shook the veil out, whipped it over her head and adjusted it so she could see through the eyeholes—and started worrying about Slya's offer of protection. The god wasn't all that bright, she had a tendency to stomp around and squash anything that chanced to fall under her feet which could include those she meant to help. Nothing Brann could do about it, except stay as nimble as she could and hope she'd be deft enough to avoid any danger that might provoke Slya into storming to her rescue. She went back to the landing.

She collected Jaril and their gear and marched into the Inn. The Host came running, treating her with exaggerated deference; guests and servants stared or peeped at her from the

corner of their eyes; she heard a gale of whispers rise behind
her as the Host led her to the finest suite in the house and murmured of baths and dinner and wine and groveled until she
wanted to hit him. Tak WakKerrcarr was the reason, of course;
his notice had stripped away any anonymity she might claim.

When the Host stopped hovering and left the room, she
started unbuckling straps. "Serve that toe-licker right if I
skipped without paying."

Stretched out on the bed, Jaril watched Brann unpack the
pouches and hang up her clothes. "What did WakKerrcarr have
to say?"

She finished what she was doing, went to stand by the
window, looking down into the garden where she'd talked
to the sorceror. "Message from Slya," she said. "That I'm
not to worry, she's going to watch over us."

"Us?"

"All right, me. Same thing."

"Not really."

"You think I'd let her. . . ."

"Thorns down, Bramble. Course not."

She sighed, settled onto the windowseat. "So now we
wait. Until the letter is delivered, until the smiglar get here,
if they get here, until, until. . . ."

"If they get here?" Jaril lay blinking slowly, without the energy
to pretend to yawn. "Relax, Bramble. They want the thing.
They'll come."

She made a face at him. "Seems to me we've changed
positions, Jay. I'm the impatient one now."

He chuckled. "Tell you what, Bramble. Go paddle around
the bathhouse awhile. Should be plenty of hot water. You'll
feel better. You know you will."

"Run away and paddle, mmm? Like a fractious infant,
mmm? Jay, that wasn't a very nice thing to say to me."

He came up off the bed and ran to her, his sleepiness
forgotten, his tranquillity wiped away. Trembling with dry
sobs, he wrapped his arms about her, pushed his head
against her. "I . . . I . . . I," he stopped, dragged in the air
he needed for speaking, "I was just teasing, Bramble. I didn't
mean it like that, you know I didn't mean it like that."

She stroked his white-gold hair. "I know, luv. I've tripped
on my tongue a time or two myself. Just don't do it again."

10

Two days passed.

Jaril slept much of the time; Brann wandered about the Waystop gardens until the feel of eyes constantly watching her drove her away from the Inn and into the parklike forest at the base of Mun Gapur.

An hour past midday on the third day, she took a foodbasket the Inn's cook prepared for her and went into the forest to a place of flattish boulders beside the noisy little stream that burbled past the Inn and tumbled into the river. She spread out a blanket, filled a water jug and settled herself to enjoy a peaceful picnic lunch.

When Tak WakKerrcarr strolled from under the trees, she was sitting with her feet in the water, eating a peach. He settled himself beside her, dipped a napkin in the stream and handed it to her so she could wipe her sticky face and stickier fingers.

She glanced at him, opened her eyes wide. "You've parked your livestock."

He laughed. "So I have. They're accommodatin little critters."

His voice sent shivers along her spine. The Grand Voice of a Sorceror Prime. A single word from Maksim could stir her to the marrow of her bones, that WakKerrcarr could do the same when she didn't even know him . . . it wasn't fair. He'd got rid of the stench too. He was tall and lean and powerfully male; she could feel his interest in her, the most effective aphrodisiac there was. "Why?" she said, more breathlessly than she intended, then reminded herself she was a grown woman with more than a little experience in these things.

"The critters? Backs off people I don't want to talk to. Besides, I like 'em. You got some time to spare, heh?"

"Seems so," She frowned as something occurred to her. "Heard from Maks?"

"Not to speak of," he murmured; he took her hand, moved his thumb across her palm. "Why?"

"I'm worried about him." She looked down at the hand caressing hers; his skin was a smooth olive, baby fine, there was almost no flesh between it and the slender hand bones.

"There's reason to be." He set her hand on her thigh and began stroking the curve of her neck, his long fingers playing in her hair. "And reason not to be. Maks is formidable when the occasion requires it."

She leaned into his hand, her eyes drooping half-shut, her breath slowing and deepening. "What are you talking about? Tell me."

"There's things I can't say."

"*You* can't?"

"When the gods are at play, a wise man keeps his head down. Or it gets bit off."

She pulled away from him, jumped to her feet. "Great advice, Tik-tok, I'm sure I'll follow it."

"It don't count when it's your strings they're pullin." He rose with the liquid grace of a man a fraction of his great age, clasped his hands behind his back. "All you can do is dance fast and try keeping your feet." He smiled at her, his yellow eyes glowing. "You're formidable yourself, Drinker of Souls."

"Does he need help? Can you tell me that?"

"He's doing well enough; don't worry your head, Brann. You're fond of him." He raised his brows. "More than fond, I think."

"For my sins."

He moved closer, wary and focused, predator stalking skittish prey, and set his hands on her shoulders, close to her neck, his long thumbs tucked up under her jaw. "For my sins, I want you."

"Will you help me?"

"No. Not beyond maintaining the Truce." He moved his thumbs delicately up and down her neck, just brushing the skin. "Must I buy?"

"No."

"I thought not."

"You plan to take?"

He curved his hand along her cheek. "I wouldn't dare. Besides, the sweetest fruit is that which comes freely to the hand. I'm not a rutting teener, Bramble-all-thorns. I can wait. If not now, then later."

Brann laughed, turned her head, brushed her lips across the palm of his hand. "Rutting ancient. Let it be now."

"And later?"

"I lay no mortgages on tomorrow."

"It doesn't hurt to dream."

"If you remember that reality is often disappointing."

"One can always adjust the dream. Come see my house."

"You mean your bed?"

"That too. Though I've never made a practice of confining myself to a bed. Shows a dearth of imagination."

11

"Bramble. Brann."

Someone was shaking her; she groped around, touched Tak's shoulder. He mumbled something indecipherable, snuggled closer against her. The shaking started again. "Wha. . . ."

"Shuh!" Sound of water running. Cold wet slap.

Brann jerked up, clawed the wet cloth from her face and flung it away. "What do you think you're doing!"

"Bramble, they're here. You have to get back."

"Jay?"

"Pull yourself together, Bramble. The smiglar. They're here. They didn't wait for a riverboat to bring them. They want you now."

Brann felt the bed shift as Tak lifted onto his elbow; she shivered with pleasure as his strong slender fingers smoothed along her spine. "Go back," he told Jaril. "I'll bring her in a few minutes."

Jaril snarled at him, hostile, angry; he was close to losing control.

Brann could feel the tides pulsing in him. She caught hold of his hands, held them tightly. "Jay, listen. Listen, luv. You've got to be calm. You're giving them an edge. Listen. Go down and watch them. I'll be there as fast as I can, I've got to get dressed. Do you hear me?"

Jaril shuddered, then slowly stabilized. With a last glare at Tak, he shifted to glowsphere and darted away.

Brann sighed. "I have to see him home somehow. Tak. . . ."

"Mmmh?" His hands were on her breasts, his tongue in her ear.

She relaxed against him for a moment, then pulled away. "No more time, Tik-tok." She slid off the bed, stood a minute running her fingers through her tangled hair.

"You'll come here after?" He lay back on the pillows, his fingers laced behind his head, his eyes caressing her.

She padded over to the basin, poured some water in it and began washing herself. Will I come back? I don't know. Once we ransom Yaril . . . there's Maks, I have to find out about him. . . . She began working the knots out of her long white hair. After a moment she chuckled. "First seacaptains, now sorcerors. I wonder if that means my taste in men is improving or worsening."

"Don't ask me, m' dear. You can see I'd be biased."

Brush in hand, she set her fists on her hips and contemplated him. "What I see, hah! You wash up lovely, old man."

"I like you too, old woman. You coming back?"

"I want to. Tak. . . ."

"Mm?"

"This isn't a condition, it's just a favor I'm asking."

He sat up. "Such diffidence, Thornlet. Ask, ask, I promise I won't let thoughts of past orgies influence me." He chuckled, slid off the bed and strode to the window. As she began pulling on her heavy widow's robes, he chirruped and chirred, calling his little critters to come back and crawl on him.

"The children have to be sent home. As far as I know, Slya is the only one can do that. Would you talk to her for us? They need their own kind, Tik-tok."

He opened the door to a closet, took out his ancient greasy leathers. "You realize how much more vulnerable you'd be without them?"

"That doesn't matter."

"It does to your friends, Thornlet. Slya is very fond of you, more than you know, I think." He took out his staff, leaned it against the windowsill.

"They'll either die or go rogue before much longer, Tik-tok, what use are they then?"

"You're sure of that?"

"I'm painfully sure of that."

"I'll talk with the Fireheart, I can't promise anything."

"I know. She goes her own way and Tungjii help us all." She folded the veil over her arm. "It's time."

"Come back."

"When I can."

"Maks?"

"I've got to see about him. Do you understand? He's a dear man."

"I think I'm jealous."

"Why? You know where Maksim's fancies lie."

"Sex is a delight, love's a treasure."

"Aphorisms, old man?"

"Distilled experience, old woman."

"You've had a lot of that, eh?"

"But never enough. Take my hand."

12

The Chuttar Palami Kumindri sat in the largest armchair in the suite's salon with a velvet wrapped bundle in her lap, Cammam Callam behind her, arms crossed, lively as a rock.

Palami Kumindri raised an elegant brow as Brann walked from the bedroom followed by Tak WakKerrcarr. "Are you interfering in this, WakKerrcarr?"

"Only to see the Truce is kept." He moved to the suite's main door, stood leaning on his staff, his face blank.

The Chuttar looked skeptical but didn't question what he said; she turned to Brann. "You wrote you had the ransom."

"We do. You have our friend?"

Palami Kumindri unfolded the black velvet, exposing the fractured crystal. "As you see."

"Give her to me."

"Give me the talisman."

"I'll let you see it." She went to the window, swung the shutters wide. "Jay, come in."

The great horned owl dropped like a missile through the unglazed window; he spread his talons, snapped his wings out and landed on the braided rug. As soon as he touched down, he changed and was a slender handsome youth. Eyes fixed on the Yaril crystal, he reached inside his shirt and brought out the little glass frog. "Churrikyoo," he said.

"Bring it here."

"Give my sister to the Drinker of Souls first."

"Why should I trust you?"

"Tak WakKerrcarr's Truce. I would rather not face his anger."

She shrugged. "Why not. Come here, woman." She indicated the crystal without touching it. "Take it."

As soon as Brann touched the crystal, she knew that it was Yaril and that the changer was still alive. "Give her the talisman, Jay."

Jaril flung Churrikyoo at Palami Kumindri and rushed to Brann's side; he took the crystal from her and fed sunfire into it until it throbbed with light; he crooned at it in a high keening that rose beyond Brann's hearing threshold. The pulsing grew fiercer, the edges of the stone melted into light and air. Silently but so suddenly Brann later swore she heard a *pop!*, the stone was gone and a glowsphere floated in front of Jaril. It darted at him, merged with him. He changed and there were two spheres dashing about the room in a wild dance of joy and celebration.

Brann laughed and spread her arms. A moment later she was hugging two slender forms, one a pale gold boy, the other a moonsilver girl.

And then darkness swallowed her. Swallowed them all. Swallowed Brann, Yaril, Jaril—and Tak WakKerrcarr.

She heard Tak WakKerrcarr scream with rage.

She heard Palami Kumindri laugh.

And then there was nothing.

II: KORIMENEI/DANNY BLUE

After her long journey, Korimenei has finally caught up with the Rushgaramuv and is waiting for a chance to steal Frunzacoache from the shaman. After that she can race south along the Mountains to the Cheonene peninsula and at last—at long, long last—can release her brother from the spell and put the Talisman in his hands.

1

Korimenei lay on her stomach at the edge of the cliff, her chin resting on her crossed forearms; she watched the rites and revelry below and felt exhausted; the autumnal fertility celebrations had been going on all day and all night for a week now. It's enough to put one off sex, beer and food for years, she thought. Maybe forever. It was boring. And it was frustrating. Until the Rushgaramuv settled and started sleeping at night, there was no way she could get at the shaman.

She watched until sunset, sighed when she saw the bonfires and torches lit once more, new white sand strewn about the dance floor. How they can, she thought. She wriggled back from the cliff edge, got to her feet, and brushed the grit off her front. She shivered. The wind had teeth in it. Any day now those fattening clouds were going to drop a load of snow on her; she was surprised it'd held off this long. She pulled the blanket tighter about her and went trudging back to the camp, thinking she hadn't been warm in days.

Nine days ago, before the Rushgaramuv reached the wintering grounds with their diminished herds, she'd come up here on the mountain and found a hollow in a nest of boulders. She'd caulked the holes between the stones with mud and leaves to shut out the icy drafts and stretched her tent canvas over the top, covered that with more mud and twigs and sods she'd cut from patches of tough mountain grass. A man could walk by a bodylength away and not suspect what he was passing.

Ailiki had killed and dressed some squirrels for her and nosed out some tubers. Korimenei smiled as she saw the neat little carcasses laid out on a platter of overlapping leaves. The first time she'd seen the mahsar dressing meat, she'd gaped like a fool, unable to believe what her eyes were showing her—Ailiki using a small sharp knife, its hilt molded to fit her hand, the blade a sliver of steel shaped like a crescent moon. Where Ailiki got it, how she knew how to use it. . . .

Korimenei looked down at the squirrel carcasses, shook her head and went to gather wood to cook them.

2

A persistent tickle woke her, something brushing again and again against her face. Shining like a ghost in the darkness, Ailiki scampered away as Korimenei sat up. The air was so cold it was knives in her lungs; the silence was spectral. She could hear her heart beating; Ailiki moved a foot and she could hear the faint scratch of the mahsar's claws in the dirt. "What is it, Aili?"

The mahsar flicked her tail and pushed past the piece of canvas used as an inadequate seal to the shelter, a door of sorts; Korimenei hastily crafted a tiny will-o, set it up against the roof canvas so she could see what she was doing. Not relishing the thought of going outside, she pulled on her bootliners, boots, gloves, a sweater and her coat, wrapped a scarf about her neck and head and crawled reluctantly after Ailiki.

The wind had quit. Snow fell like feathers. There was already half an inch on the ground. "I suppose this means the festival is over," she said aloud.

Ailiki clattered her teeth and lolloped off, looking over her shoulder now and then to see if Korimenei was following her.

When they reached the cliff edge, Korimenei dropped onto her knees and looked down. The canyon was as dark and silent as the slopes behind her. "How many hours till dawn?"

Ailiki drew three scratches in the snow, contemplated them a moment, then added a fourth, half the length of the others.

"Three and a half. Good. That's time enough. Aili, I'm going to start down, you fetch the fake, will you?"

3

Following the glimmering Ailiki, Korimenei groped through the scattered corrals and barns, then past the line of long-houses, making her way to the small sod hut off by itself where the Rushgaramuv shaman had gone to sing over his sacred fires, where he'd slept the past several nights, dreamwalking for the clan. She'd watched several women bring him his meals there, wives or female kin, she supposed. None of them went inside. The Siradar and his Elders made a ceremonial visit to the hut on the first day of the rites; his headwife and the clan matrons went the next day. Now that the rites were finished . . . Gods! maybe he'd already moved back, it was snowing, the longhouses would be a lot warmer. . . .

The snow fell thick and silent, soft as down against her skin until it melted, turning in an instant chill and harsh, leaching the warmth out of her. She followed Ailiki past the dance floor to the giant oak where the hut was; it was very much like the dance ground in Owlyn Vale where she'd pranced the seasons in and out with her cousins under the guidance of the Chained God's priest and AuntNurse Polatéa, though the Valer's celebrations were a lot more decorous than those she'd just witnessed. She frowned. Like all the other children she'd been sent to bed at sundown, maybe the decorum vanished with them. She shook her head. This wasn't the time for such things. Hold hard, woman, she told herself. Stray thoughts mean straying emanations, you don't want the old man waking.

She crept closer to the hut and listened at the leather flap that closed off the low, square entrance hole. Snores. He was inside, all right, and very much asleep from the sound of it. She leaned against the sods and did a cautious bodyread of the man inside.

He was drugged out of his mind; a herd of boghans could stomp across him and he wouldn't notice.

"Liki," she murmured, "brighten up a bit, mmh?"

She lifted the flap and followed the mahsar inside. The air was hot and soupy with a mix of herbs and sweat and ancient

urine; there was a small peat fire in a brazier putting out
more smoke than heat; half that smoke was incense and the
other half came from the remnants of the dried herbs that
sent the shaman into his stupor. He was curled up on a pile
of greasy leathers, snoring. He had some Talent, she'd
smelled that on him from the cliff, but not much. Even if he
woke and found her here, he was no threat.

In spite of that, she was wary as she crawled over to him,
shields up and as much I'm-not-here as she could smear
over herself. Her precautions would've been pathetic if she'd
been moving on Maksim, or even on the Shahntien, but it
was good enough for this man.

He wore his torbaoz on a thong about his neck, an oiled
leather pouch the length of her forearm. She touched it,
pulled her hand back when his snore broke in the middle.
She touched it again. He seemed uneasy, but he didn't
wake. Right, she thought, if I'm going to do it, better do it
fast.

She memorized the knot, got it untied. After spreading
the neck of the torbaoz, she dipped two fingers into the
mess inside, felt the cool nubbiness of the silver chain. She
got a finger hooked through it and began drawing it and
what it held out of the pouch. The snores went on, more
sputter to them now; there was a restlessness in the old
man's sleep that warned her she'd better hurry. He groaned
but still didn't wake as she freed Frunzacoache from a dried
bat wing and some stalks of an anonymous plant; the exhaustion from six nights' rituals were like chains on him.

She hung Frunzacoache around her neck, slipping it down
inside her shirt to rest like a warm hand between her breasts,
surprised at the temperature because the talisman was silver
and crystal, neither of them welcoming to naked flesh. She
took the copy she and Ailiki had made and eased it into the
torbaoz, pushing it well down among the rest of the ritual
objects. When she was satisfied with its set, she pulled the
cords tight and worked the ends into as close a match to the
original knot as she could manage. Waving Ailiki before
her, she crawled from the hut.

The cold outside stunned her. A wind was rising, blowing
snow into her face. Her elbows and her knees were like
iced-over hinges; they'd break if she bent them. Ailiki came
back to her, nuzzled her, sent a surge of fire through her
that woke Frunzacoache from its passivity. The talisman
spread warmth along her body, heated her joints enough to

help her creak onto her feet. Walking eased her yet more.
She followed Ailiki's spriteglow through the blowing snow,
stumbling past longhouses still dark and sodden with sleep,
past corrals filled with white humps where sheep and oxen,
geykers and boghan lay, down the treeless flats to the mouth
of the canyon.

The climb to her camp was easier than she expected. The
wind was at her back instead of blowing in her face, Ailiki
shone like a small yellow sun so she could see where to put
her feet and Frunzacoache radiated warmth through her
body. She had little time for thinking as she struggled up the
treacherous slopes, only enough to wonder at the bonding
between her and the talisman; as soon as it settled against
her it was as if it had always been there.

Tré's eidolon appeared before her as she crawled into the
shelter. "Well?"

She crouched on the groundsheet and stared at him. "I
have it," she said finally. "How long is this snow going to
last?"

When he spoke, his mindvoice was flat and dull, scraped
down to bone. He was answering her for one reason only,
his report would get her to him faster. No, not her, the
talisman. "It will be finished around sunup. The wind will
blow hard after the snow stops falling, but you can ride in it;
you had better ride in it, it will cover your tracks. It will
drop after an hour or so, but there will be gusts of cold
damp air, the kind that eat to the heart. You need to watch
the ponies, do not override them. There is a road of sorts
going south through the foothills, the Vanner Rukks use it
in spring and summer, but they have settled for the winter
so you will not see them. If you follow the road and make
fair time you should reach a Gsany Rukk village by sundown. You can shelter for the night in the CommonHouse
and buy more grain and tea there, they keep a supply for
winter travelers. After that, you will have a week of clear,
cold weather, then the next storm hits. You had better find
shelter for that one, it is going to be a three-day blizzard;
there are several Gsany villages close together, so you will
have a choice of where to spend the waiting time. Come as
quickly as you can, sister, I am very weary of this state."
The eidolon shimmered and was gone.

Korimenei sighed. "Well, Aili my Liki, looks like nothing's changed. I'll be happier'n he is when this is over.
Every time I see him, I feel like he's clawed me." She

smoothed her hand down the front of her coat, then scratched behind the mahsar's ears. "We'll go somewhere warm and friendly, my Aili, and wait for my daughter to be born."

##

In the morning, as the eidolon had predicted, there were six inches of snow on the ground but none falling and a wind that cut like knives. Ailiki brought the ponies in, fed them grain she'd stolen from the Rushgar stores. The little mahsar was changing as every day passed, becoming less a beast than a furry person, even her face was flattening—slowly, imperceptibly, but steadily until Korimenei was sure she saw a human face emerging from the fur. If the change continued, maybe someday Ailiki would be able to talk to her. She stowed her gear in pouches that were beginning to show the strains of this long journey and took apart the shelter, rolling the several pieces of canvas into a neat packet.

By midmorning she'd found the Vanner Road; the stiff winds earlier had swept parts of it clear of snow, so she made better time, but the ponies refused to be pushed. They were shaggy with their winter coats, but not nearly so fat as they should have been. Despite the care she'd taken of them, they were as worn as the leather on her pouches, as worn as she felt some days though the morning sickness had left her before she reached the mountains. She walked and rode, rode and walked, slipped, trudged, cursed the mountains and the cold and her brother for sending her out in this weather.

As dusk settled over the slopes she rounded a bulge and found herself on the outskirts of a small neat village that reminded her very much of her home vale. She stopped her pony, whistled with pleasure. Even in the shadowy dimness she could see how bright the colors were, how clean and simple the lines were. The houses were smaller than the multifamily dwellings she knew as a child, they were like beads on a string, elbowing their neighbors, instead of standing solitary in a Housegarden, but they had the same high-peaked roofs with cedar shakes oiled until they were almost black, the same whitewashed walls with painted straps and beams, the same heavy shutters carved in deep relief. She couldn't see the designs, no doubt they were quite different, the thing was, they were there in the same place as the ones she knew. She felt her souls expand, her metaphorical el-

bows come away from her sides. She understood for the first
time how much she missed her family, her people. She'd
joked with Frit about going home; now she was indeed
going home and she was suddenly very happy about that.
Smiling fondly, perhaps foolishly, she nudged the pony into
a weary walk and headed for the CommonHouse on the
west side of the Square. Behind her, Ailiki made the little
hissing sound Kori thought of as mahsar laughter and clucked
the pack pony into moving after her.

4

Three days later she rode from a thick stand of conifers
and saw a dead man sprawled facedown on the snow, three
stubby arrows like black quills protruding from his back and
his left leg. Blood was a splash of crimson on the snow.
Crimson? It was still leaking out of the man. He had to be
alive.

She slid off the pony, ran to him and knelt beside him,
fingers searching under his jaw; she couldn't feel a pulse,
but bodyread told her, yes, he was alive. "Aili, come here."
She scooped up the mahsar and set her on the man's back.
"Do what you can to warm him, my Liki, while I figure how
to move him off this snow." Without realizing what she was
doing, she closed her hand about Frunzacoache; the talisman felt eager, as if it had suffered frustration from being
unused all the years it sat in the shaman's pouch. It was a
focus of renewal, that's what the books said anyway. The
Great Talismans weren't living creatures in any sense of that
word, but Kushundallian said they sometimes showed a kind
of willfulness, as if they recognized in some nonthinking way
what they wanted and used whatever hands that came their
way to get it.

She sat on her heels and rubbed at her back. It was late
afternoon, the sky was boiling with clouds though the air
down near the earth was barely stirring; it was several
degrees above freezing, but that was not much help to the
man stretched out beside her. If he wasn't to die on her, she
had to get those shafts out of him and move him under
cover . . . she touched his long black hair, drew her fingers
along his cheekbones, down his nose, trying to remember
where she'd seen him before. There was something . . .
something about him . . . she couldn't catch hold of it, not
yet. He was warmer; Ailiki's cuddle was starting to work on

him. He was also bleeding faster. She jumped to her feet
and ran to her stores.

She tugged him into the road and onto a piece of canvas,
bunched blankets about him to hold in the warmth Ailiki
was feeding him, then she sat on her heels scowling at the
arrows. She had to get them out without killing him. Cut
them out? She shuddered at the thought. Inanimate Transfer? Might as well grab hold of them and drag them out of
him. She could burn the shafts, but that would leave the
points sunk in him. Inanimate Transform? Hmm. Might
work. With a little help. Leg arrow first; if I blow it, I'll do
less damage there. She pulled Frunzacoache from under her
shirt and pressed her left hand over it as she got ready for
the act of transforming. She started to reach for the shafts,
stopped her hand. Are the points iron or bone or stone or
what? She grasped the shaft and read down it. Iron, yes.

"Meta mephi mephist mi," she chanted, hand tight about
the shaft, feeling it vibrate against her palm as currents of
change stirred in it. "Syda ses sydoor es es. Meta mephi
mephist mi. Xula xla es eitheri."

The wood sublimated into the air; a thread of clear water
oozed from the wound.

She smiled, shook herself, and eased Frunzacoache's chain
over her head. Pressing the flat crystal enclosing the death-
less leaf over the puncture wound, she held it there though
the heat it generated grew so intense it was painful, held it
and held it until the heat dropped out of it. She lifted the
talisman and inspected the place where the wound had
been. The puncture was closed; there wasn't even a scar to
mark where it had been.

She rocked on her knees along his body until she could
reach another of the arrows; it jerked rhythmically, a movement so tiny it was hard to see unless she looked closely at
the flights. It had to be lodged tight against the man's heart.
Tricky. If it had penetrated something vital, getting it out
might be as dangerous as leaving it in, he might bleed to
death before . . . She opened her hand and gazed thoughtfully at Frunzacoache for a minute, then closed her fingers
about it and chanted: Meta mephi mephist mi . . . and as
soon as the chant was done, slapped the talisman over the
wound and held it. . . .

Contented with the results, she moved to the arrow high
in the shoulder and began the chant for the third time. . . .

When she lifted Frunzacoache, it felt swollen, tumescent,

as if it drew power into itself by expending power. It was so heavy it seemed to jump from her fingers to land on the man's back, driving a grunt out of him though he didn't seem to be waking up.

"Sounds like you're going to live, whoever you are." She felt under his jaw. A strong steady throb pulsed against her fingertips and his skin was warm, but not too warm. "Yes indeed." She started to straighten, but stopped as Ailiki chittered anxiously and put a small black hand on her arm. "You want me to do something more? Obviously you do." She moved closer to the man so she could kneel on the canvas; the cold from the sodden earth was striking up through her trousers and worrying at her bodyheat. Frowning, she focused on the man, scanning him in a full bodyread. "Poison, tchah! He's rotten with it. I wonder . . . mmh! no time for that. Back to business." Reluctantly, because her fingers were aching and stiff with cold, she cupped her hands about Frunzacoache and called on its gift of renewal to help her flush the poison from the man and heal its ravages.

When the work was complete, she lifted the talisman. Heavy, dark, swollen, it frightened her; though she didn't want to, she slid the chain over her head and tucked Frunzacoache under her shirt. It was hotter than she'd expected, the heat burned into her but vanished almost as soon as she felt it. She tucked her trembling hands into her armpits and looked around. The ponies were kicking through the snow and tearing up clumps of withered grass. A deer came to the edge of the trees, gazed out at her a long minute then retreated into the shadows. Otherwise the narrow winding flat and the stony slopes were devoid of life; sunk inches below the level of the flat by generations of hooves and high-wheeled wagons, the Road was the only sign that people had passed this way. Overhead, there was a high thin film of cloud, gray and cold. A chill wet wind was gathering strength around her; it blew across her face and insinuated itself into every crevice in her clothing. She shivered and wondered what she should do next. She couldn't just leave the man lying beside the Road. I have seen him before. I know it. Somewhere. Silili? Doesn't feel right. Where . . . where. . . .

The wind blew a strand of black hair forward over his face; it tickled his nose and he sneezed. And opened his eyes.

He rolled over, dislodging Ailiki.

She gave an explosive treble snort and lalloped across to the ponies; she jumped onto the saddle and sat watching the man with vast disapproval as he pushed himself up and ran his eyes over Korimenei.

"I know you. At least. . . ." He moved his shoulders, felt at his leg, looked round at the splatters of blood and forgot what he'd been saying. "I owe you one, Saöri."

Korimenei laughed. "Three."

"Huh? Ah! Your point." He narrowed his very blue eyes, inspected her more closely. "Kori?"

"It's Korimenei these days."

"Does that mean you've taken a husband?"

"No husband. I travel alone." She stood, fumbled in the pocket of her coat for her gloves. He knows me as Kori, she thought, I haven't been called Kori for ten years, ten . . . god's blood, I DO know him. She glanced at him again. I think I know him.

He struggled onto his feet, grimacing at his weakness; it would take time to replace the flesh he'd lost in healing and the blood that'd leaked out of him. "I see you didn't stay home and marry one of your cousins. How's your brother? Don't tell me he got taken in the Lot?"

"Daniel?" She stared at the thick wavy hair; it was part of him, she'd stripped poison from those strands. "But you were. . . ."

"Bald? That I was. And you were a child?"

"Ten years ago. One ceases to be a child in the ordinary course of time. Bald heads don't grow new crops."

A brow shot up, giving him a quizzical look. "And one turns a hair pedantic, it seems."

She sighed. "So I've been told. If you're stuck in a school ten years, it can do that to you. Even school doesn't grow hair."

"A sorceror can grow hair anywhere he wants, didn't you know?"

"But you weren't. . . ." She stepped close to him, flattened her hand against his chest. "But you are." She stepped back, disturbed. "Why didn't I smell it before when I was working on you? And now. . . ."

"Long story." Waves of shudders were passing through his body; she could see the muscles knotting beside his mouth as he fought to control the shaking of his jaw. She glanced at the sky, located the watery blur that was the sun. At least three hours of light left. On the one hand, she didn't want to waste that much travel time; on the other, Daniel was in no condition to go anywhere. No coat, nothing but that odd vest she remembered more vividly than she did the man, now that she thought of it. A vest with two new holes in it, which wouldn't help it turn the wind.

"You can tell it later." She walked to the ponies, her irritation audible in the staccato crunch of her feet. "We'll stay here until tomorrow morning. While I'm getting camp set up, you cut find some wood for the fire. The work'll warm you up a bit." Her hand on the saddle, she looked over her shoulder at him. "If you're up to it."

"If you've got an axe, my teeth just won't do it." His voice sounded strained, but he finished with a quick twitch of a smile.

"Fool." She relaxed, reminded of the days in the cart, him telling stories, listening to her chatter, playing his flute for her and the other children. "No axe, just a hatchet which you can curse all you want with my blessing." She began working on the straps that held it, doing some of her own cursing at the stiff, reluctant leather and the clumsiness of her gloved fingers. "I saw plenty of downwood as I came through the trees. Ah!" She caught the hatchet as it fell, held it out to him. "Better you than me. I put an edge on this thing last night. That should last about three cuts."

He took the haft between thumb and forefinger, gave her another of those twitchy smiles and marched off, vanishing under the trees.

"Right. Aili, I'll get the canvas. You chase the ponies to a place where we can camp."

5

The fire crackled vigorously, hissing now and then as the heat from it loosened a fall of snow from the branches high overhead. "Settsimaksimin decided I had Talent so he flipped me over to Silili, sponsored me at a school and made sure I stayed put until I Passed Out." Korimenei pulled the blanket closer about her, sipped at the cooling tea in her mug. "Why I'm here, now, I'm going home. You?"

"Things happen, I get booted about." He was using her spare mug; he cradled it between his hands, frowned down at the inch of cooling tea it held. "Why not." He lifted his head. "Remember Ahzurdan?" You met him at the Blue Seamaid when you went to see the Drinker of Souls."

She stared at him. Inky shadows cast by the fire emphasized the jut of his nose, his high angular cheekbones. His face changed and changed again with every shift of shadow. It was like looking at one of those trick drawings where background and foreground continually shift, where a vase becomes two profiles then a vase again. "I remember," she murmured. "Who are you?"

"Daniel Akamarino. Ahzurdan. Both and neither. Call me Danny Blue."

"I don't understand."

"Like I said, it's a long story."

"Well, what have we got but time?"

"All right. Chained God . . . remember him?"

"How could I forget?"

"Right. He wanted a weapon to aim at Settsimaksimin. He made one. He took a sorceror and a starman and hammered the two men into one. Me. You might call Daniel and Ahzurdan my sires. In a way."

"That's not long, just weird." She wrapped her hand in the blanket, took the kettle from the coals at the edge of the fire and filled her mug. "Want more?"

"Better not if I intend to sleep tonight."

She sipped at the tea and thought about what he'd just told her. No wonder Tré was frightened of the god and wanted Frunzacoache to protect him. Does he know about this? She sneaked a look at Danny Blue. This abomination? He didn't say anything, but then he wouldn't, not where the god could hear him. She clung to a moment's hope, maybe her brother wasn't the way he sounded, maybe . . . no, don't be a fool, woman. She took too sudden a mouthful, spat it out, her tongue felt singed. "Did you know you were rotten with poison?"

"I know." He lifted a brow. "The past tense is the proper tense, I hope?"

"Very proper. I can't abide a half-done job. Blackmail?"

"Mmm-hmm. Bring us the talisman Klukesharna and we give you the antidote, that's what they said."

She looked quickly at him, looked away. Another Great One being snatched. She slid her hand inside her shirt, touched Frunzacoache. It felt warm, it seemed to seek her fingers as if it wanted to be stroked. I wonder, she thought Kushundallian told us They get restless sometimes, They go through a period of dormancy, then They start moving, going from hand to hand until They feel like settling down again. Hmm. "You don't have Klukesharna."

"Not now."

"I see. Hence the feathering."

"You got it."

"You can't have been lying there more than an hour before I found you, you'd be dead otherwise. You could go after whoever took it. Will you?"

"No. That's trouble I don't need. Or want."

"Hmm." She looked down; she'd been playing with Frunzacoache all this time without noticing what she was doing. Either he wasn't the chosen or the person who took it had enough gnom to overpower a fresh link. She thought about asking, decided better not. "Have you decided what you're going to do now?"

He didn't answer for several minutes; finally, he tossed down the rest of his tea, set the mug by his foot. "She left my coin, all she took was Klukesharna. I need a horse and winter gear. Where's the nearest settlement?"

She, Korimenei thought. He knows who shot him. I suppose that's his business. "There's a Gsany village a day's ride south of here."

"You said you're for Cheonea?"

"The Vales. My Vale. Owlyn Vale." She spoke slowly, tasting the words, finding pleasure in the feel of them in her mouth. I'm going home, she thought. Home.

Danny Blue yawned, went back to brooding at the fire. His face was drawn and weary. Khorimenei watched him a while, wondering what he was thinking about; it wasn't pleasant if she read him rightly. His eyelids fluttered; he forced them up again, but he said nothing. She smiled. No doubt he thought he was being courteous, letting her state the conditions of their cohabitation, because cohabitation it was going to be. She had no intention of forgoing the comforts, such as they were, of her tent and her blankets and he certainly wasn't strong enough yet to survive the night outside even with a fire. Gods, it's one of those tales Frit was always reading, twisting and turning to get the hero innocently into bed with the heroine and give him a chance to show just how heroic he was. How noble. Put a sword between them and grit the teeth. Silly. He was in no shape to . . . damn, she didn't want him thinking he had to . . . how do you say . . . hah! just say it. In a while. Not now.

She pushed the blanket off her shoulders and got to her

feet, checked the pot she'd washed after supper and hung
upside down over the top of one of the young conifers
huddled in an arc around the rim of the glade, an adequate
windbreak if the wind kept coming from the north as it had
the past several days. The pot was dry enough to put away.
She moved busily around the camp space, collecting items
scattered about and stowing them in the pouches; when she
was finished she took a last tour of the camp, came back to
the fire.

"We'd best turn in now, I want to get started with first
light." She picked up the blanket she'd been wearing, shook
it out and draped it over her arm. "We'll be sharing tent
and blankets, Danny Blue. You're tired. I'm tired. I'm sure
neither of us is interested in dalliance."

"Kori my Thiné, Amortis her very self couldn't get a rise
out of me tonight." He stood, staggering a little as he
unfolded.

"I like to have things clear," she said. "You go in first,
I'll follow."

6

Morning. Early. Frost crunching underfoot, whitening every surface.

Ready to start, saddle and packs in place, the ponies are
huddled next to the fire, lipping up piles of corn set out for
them, tails switching at half dormant blackflies. When the
two people speak, they puff out white plumes of frozen
breath.

Bulky with her layers of clothing, tendrils of soft brown
hair curling from under her knitted hat, the girl stood with
her fists on her hips, glaring at Danny Blue. "I don't give
spit for your blasted vanity, man. Either climb in that saddle
or get the hell out of here. I don't care where."

The Daniel phasma being off somewhere or still asleep,
the Ahzurdan phasma seized control of the body; hating his
weakness, hating her for her strength, resenting her because
she'd saved all their lives and laid that burden of gratitude
on them, Danny Blue found himself wanting to smash that
imperious young face. He wanted to beat her and by beating
her, batter in her all the other women who'd dominated and
rejected Ahzurdan, his whining mother and Brann chief
among them. Lips pressed together, he swung into the saddle. He felt like a fool; even with the stirrups lowered as far
as they'd go, his knees stuck out ridiculously, he thought he

looked like a clown in a child's chair. He pulled the blanket about his shoulders and looked around. The odd little beast that traveled with Korimenei went running past and scrambled onto the packs; Korimenei tossed the lead rein into the small black paws.

She strode past him without looking at him and set off along the Road. He toed his pony into a brisk walk, heard the pack pony snort, then start after him.

They passed the whole day in silence; even when they stopped to rest the ponies and let them graze, neither acknowledged the other's presence with so much as a grunt.

Danny Blue was exhausted before half the day was gone, but Korimenei kept on, walking with steady, ground-eating strides, never looking back. She was no doubt partly putting it on to annoy him, but there was an impatience about her he couldn't discount; he knew she was eager to see her home again and he'd cost her time and was still slowing her down, something he found sourly satisfying for a while, until he was too tired and sick to sustain any kind of emotion so even the Ahzurdan phasma who'd been ruling him was forced to give way.

Though the pony had an easy rolling walk, he had to concentrate to stay on its back. At the last stop only the impatient jerk of Korimenei's shoulders gave him the strength to pull himself into the saddle. He sat there fumbling with his feet, unable to find the stirrups. She didn't say anything; grimly controlled, she caught hold of one boot, shoved it in place, circled the pony, dealt with the other foot, then started off along the Road.

In his head the Ahzurdan phasma sneered at the girl, at Danny Blue, and the Daniel phasma watched both with sardonic appreciation. Wearily, Danny Blue did his best to reclaim his body. Every step of the pony juddered through him, jolting his brain, shattering his sequences of thought so he had to begin over and over before he finished one. He stared at the striding girl and wondered who the hell he was and where his life was going. He couldn't get a hold on himself, he came to pieces when he tried, though he was getting a glimpse of something, a feel of potential; fatigue had stripped away his defenses, he couldn't hide any more. Or slide any more. A woman, a lover, had asked Daniel

Akamarino once don't you want to do something with your life and he said no and left her behind. Now Danny Blue was being forced to ask the question of himself. And forced to realize he had no idea what the answer was. There was another thing. Puppet, he thought, playtoy, the god's still jerking my strings and making me dance. Bored. H/it wants to amuse h/itself. I know it. Running me in a circle. I go with her I go back to h/it. Round and round. Not a puppet, no, a rat in a running wheel. Round and round. Back to the place I started from. Kori's going home. I want to go home. I want to get out of this madhouse reality.

More and more he was drawn to the rationality of Daniel's world, the reality where gods were products of the mind and necessarily reticent about interfering in the lives of common men. Where the forces that worked on those lives were perhaps as powerful, but much less personal. The Ahzurdan phasma resisted this with all his strength though that was little enough; he was fading, his painfully cultivated Talent slipping away from him into the unappreciative hands of his semi-son. All he could do was try keeping his part of Danny Blue's double memory shut away from that semison, frustrating Danny's attempt to find a way to transfer himself to the Daniel reality. Danny had no doubt that was one of the constraints that kept him out of the realities, that blocked him from regaining this part of Ahzurdan's skill.

As the sun went down, the idea came to him. Settsimaksimin. If he can't do it, no one can. Yes. If he knows where my reality lies, if he can reach it. I'm sure of it. He can do it. All I have to do it is find him. And find out what price he wants for doing it. Kori knows him, maybe . . . can't think. God, I don't know. Is this my own idea? Or is that Compost Heap messing with my head again? Pulling my strings? Jump little puppet, run little rat?

The jolting stopped. When he realized that, he lifted his head. They'd been moving through huge old conifers for several hours, he'd noticed that without being particularly conscious of it; now they were on the edge of a broad clearing with a small village rising up the slopes of both sides of the track, its bright colors muted by the twilight and a dusting of snow; they'd ridden beyond the heart of the blizzard that laid the deeper snow to the north. Gsany Rukkers were moving about the slopes and the broad mainstreet, coming in from the night-milking and other chores, gossiping over the last loaves from the communal oven, going in and out of a notions shop and the tavern built into the largest building, the village CommonHouse. It was a busy, cheerful scene, all the more so in its contrast to the dark, brooding conifers that surrounded it.

Kori slapped him on the leg, waking him from his daze. He looked down. "What?"

"I said do you have enough coin to pay the shot at the CommonHouse? I'm close to flat."

He thought that over. "How much will it take?"

"A handful of coppers, around twenty. Thirty if you're willing to spring for grain for the ponies."

"Thirty?" He rubbed his fist across his brow. "Yes. All right. Ah. . . ." Seeing she was still waiting, he frowned at her, shut his eyes. "Yes. I see." He tugged a zipper open. His hand was shaking with cold and exhaustion. He scooped up a fistful of the coins in the pocket, gave them to her. "If it's not enough, tell me."

She inspected the miscellany she held. "It's enough. Look . . . ah . . . Danny, they've got hotsprings and a bathhouse here. I think you ought to soak awhile before you sleep."

He blinked then smiled at her. "You telling me I stink?"

"Don't be an idiot, man. You're cold to the bone, you should get warmed up."

He brooded on that a moment, then nodded. "I need you with me."

"What?"

"Not that." Again he shoved the back of his fist across his brow; he was beginning to feel more alive, but he wasn't sure whether that was good or not since he was also feeling every ache and pull of his muscles. "If I soak alone, I'll go to sleep and drown."

"All right." She took hold of the halter's nose-strap. "Let's do it."

7

She was a seal in water, agile and slippery; she cast off whatever burden it was that kept her short-tempered and turned playful. Danny drifted in a corner of the bath, smiling a little as he watched her splash and sputter, dive under and come shooting up with Ailiki in her arms, sending waves of herb-scented water washing at him. She seemed hardly older than the child he remembered. The water rocked him gently, warming away his aches and much of his weariness without sinking him into lethargy; it was the efferves-

cence that did it, the clouds of tiny bubbles that went
rushing past his body like pinhead fists kneading and ener-
gizing him. He found it extraordinarily pleasant, the more
so since he'd reached a temporary peace with himself. His
mind was at rest, leaving his body to tend itself.

Kori came paddling over to him, hooked her arms over
the bathsill; her freckles shimmered in the lanternlight, her
eyes were the color of the water, her hair was slicked back
though tiny curls had escaped the mass to make a frizzy halo
about her thin face. "Feeling better?"

"Mmm." He reached out, brushed a fingertip across a
dimple. "You don't look a day older than that girl in the
cart."

"Am." With an urchin grin, she skimmed her hand lightly
up his chest, then flicked water into his face.

Before he could react, a voice like icewind cut through
the tendrils of steam. "Look up, you l'hy'foor!"

8

Korimenei levered herself up and over the bathsill, sprang
to her feet. And froze.

A woman stood at the end of the pool, a taut, dark figure
wreathed in steam with a short recurve bow held at stretch,
one arrow nocked, a second held by the notch end between
two fingers. She vibrated like a tuning fork with a rage that
was on the raw edge of erupting.

Danny floated in his corner without trying to move.
"Felsrawg," he said softly, "I should have known."

A stocky man came from the dressing room. "It's not in
his clothes or hers." He inspected Korimenei. "What's that
she's got round her neck?"

"Simms," Danny said, "that's nothing to do with you.
You can see it's not Klukesharna."

Felsrawg drew in a breath; it sounded like the hiss of a
snake about to strike. "Where?" she spat at him.

Danny didn't waste time pretending not to understand
her. "Trithil."

"I don't believe you."

"Wasn't it you shot me? How'd you miss her?"

The bow shook. Danny's hands began to move under the
water, gestures to support and shape the spell he was weaving; Korimenei saw that and took a half step away from
him.

"You! Hoor! Don't you move."

Again Korimenei froze.

"You! Laz! Get your hands out of the water. Put them on the sill where I can see them. I swear if you move one finger you're dead."

Danny hesitated.

"Do it," Korimenei whispered, just loud enough for him to hear. "Don't be a fool. Remember what I am."

"I hear," he murmured.

Korimenei slid a hand up to touch Frunzacoache; the woman he'd called Felsrawg was glaring at him, watching him like a cat before a mousehole. She took advantage of Felsrawg's distraction to ease another step away, but forced herself to relax and go back to watching Danny when she saw the one called Simms watching her.

Moving slowly so he wouldn't trigger Felsrawg's precarious temper, Danny eased around so his shoulders were tucked in the corner, his arms outstretched along the sill. "Satisfied?" he said.

"Simms! Scrape your eyeballs off that hoor and get over there with him. Laz, you know what we want. You know how far we'll go to get it." She eased up on the bow though she could still get that arrow off before he could move. "Be sensible, man. What's the point?"

"I can't give you what I don't have. The Esmoon went off with it. See her anywhere about?"

"That silka limp? You expect me to believe she's any good off her back?"

"She's not a woman, she's a demon."

Demon, Korimenei thought. Salamander? No. Too damp in here. It'd likely panic and go out of control. A mancat. Yes. . . . Keep her distracted, Danny, give me time to reach. . . . She moved uneasily at a bark of laughter from the stocky man. Standing beside Danny, a skinning knife in his hand, Simms was watching her with cool speculation; Felsrawg might think he was looking at her breasts, but Korimenei knew better. It was Frunzacoache that attracted him, not her.

"You're lying. Simms!"

"Let him talk, Felsa. There's plenty of time for the knife."

Danny snorted. "Much good it'll do you, knife or talk." He waited for Felsrawg to stop quivering, then said, "You got me good three times, Felsa. What happened after that? The Esmoon was there, why didn't you get her? Think about it."

"You know." She growled the words. "You know. Sorceror! You blasted us. Laid us out and went off leaving us to freeze."

"I was facedown in the snow, leaking blood from three holes, woman. You had to see me down. Use your head. You came within a hair of skewering my heart and you know it. I was in no shape to do anything to anybody."

"No!" Felsrawg was getting agitated again. "No! Liar! If it was true she had it, you'd be nose to the ground after her. You'd have to be."

"For one, who says I'm not, eh? Think of that?"

"You're saying she came this way?"

"No. Far as I'm concerned, I'd be delighted if I never saw the creature again. Come on, Felsa, put the bow down. The poison's out of me. My friend here, she did that when she healed my punctures. She's got a Talent for that sort of thing."

Felsrawg stretched her mouth into a mirthless feral grin. "Good for her," she said, "she can enjoy herself putting you together again. Simms."

Gods, Korimenei thought. She dropped to her knees, hugged her arms across her breasts and slipped dangerously unprotected into the trance that took her across the realities.

Sand and more sand, sand and brush and sand-colored mancats prowling after herds of sand-colored deer. She saw a mancat she knew and called to him. *Help me,* she said to him, *name your price and help me.*

He came trotting up to her, considered her. After a minute he opened his formidable mouth in a broad grin. She understood from him that he was fond of her as a man would be fond of a favorite pet and would help her for the fun of it.

Korimenei lifted her head and smiled.

The mancat dropped from nothing behind Felsrawg, wrapped thick muscular tentacles about her and breathed hot, meat-tainted breath in her ears. She screamed her rage and tried to kick and claw, but his front legs were spread too wide for her to reach and her arms were locked against her sides; she was as about as helpless as she'd ever been since she started walking. She went quiet and lay against the mancat's powerful chest, glaring at Korimenei and cursing bitterly.

The instant the beast came through the membrane, Danny Blue acted; using his elbows to power himself up, he slapped his hands about the wrist on Simms' knife hand and toppled him into the water; he set his feet against the thief's floundering body and kicked, using the resistance to help him roll out of the pool. He was over the sill and on his feet before Simms surfaced sputtering. Panting a little, Danny smiled at Korimenei, waved a hand at the mancat. "A friend, I hope?"

She chuckled. "My demon's better than yours."

"No argument there."

The mancat interrupted with an apologetic coughing rumble. He was uncomfortable in the damp and thought it was time he left.

"Right," she said. "Danny, you take care of him, I'll do her." She nodded at Simms who was holding on to the edge of the pool, watching them warily, then padded around to face Felsrawg. "Are you intelligent enough to know the truth when you hear it?" She inspected the woman, sniffed. "I wonder." Over her shoulder, she said, "Where'd you meet this pair, Danny?"

"They were my backup getting Klukesharna." He smiled lazily at Felsrawg. "And sent along to slide a knife between my ribs once we got her."

"Shuh! I don't think much of your taste."

"Not mine."

"Mmh." She tapped the mancat on his shoulder. *Lower your um arms a little, my friend; I need to get at the woman's neck.* After he readjusted his tentacles, she put pressure on the carotid until Felsrawg was unconscious. *Put her down, thanks. Anything I can do for you? No? Well, let's send you home.* She pulled her mindseine about him and snapped him back to his sandhills, promising in transit to visit him, them, again when things weren't so hectic.

When she looked around, Danny Blue was watching her, a hungry look on his face. She didn't understand. He was a sorceror and a ripely Talented one if her nose wasn't fooling her. Gods of Fate and Time as Maks would say—why am I thinking of Maksi—that's his business not mine, Tungjii's blessing on us both for that.

He shook off whatever it was on his mind. "You going to wash the poison out of them, Kori? I wish you would. I don't owe this pair anything, but poison!" He dredged up a wry grin. "Besides, the only way I know of to get rid of them is kill them or cure them."

"Right," she said. "I'm just about to do that. Aili, where are you? Good. Watch my back. Danny, if you don't mind, fetch my clothes, hmm? This is no season for parading about as Primavera." Without waiting to see what he did, she dragged the chain over her head, dropped Frunzacoache on Felsrawg's leather bosom and began the cleansing.

9

"Frunzacoache the Undying," Danny said aloud, though he was speaking to himself, not Simms. "First Kluke-sharna, now Frunzacoache. Coincidence, maybe? Coincidence, hell."

Careful not to move too suddenly, Simms pulled himself onto the sill and sat with his legs dangling in the heated water. He watched Korimenei work, nodded. "I c'n feel it," he said. "You wahn't havin' us on."

"What? Oh. Yeh." Danny dragged himself away from the pulses of power throbbing out from the girl; the part of him born of Ahzurdan found the effect intoxicating. He ran a hand through his hair, frowned down at Simms. "You're not stupid."

"C'n see where you might think I was. Young for 't, an't she."

Danny yawned. As the tension drained out of him, his weariness came flooding back. "If she weren't still tender, you'd be ash and gone. Give me your hand." When Simms was on his feet, Danny tapped him on the shoulder, pointed toward the dressing room. "Come on, she wants her clothes and I'm tired of prancing around stark."

"What was that thing?"

"Don't ask me, it's not one of mine."

##

Simms hauled off a boot, upended it and shook out the water. "Sling me one of those tow'ls, eh Laz?"

"Make it Danny, Lazul was for the duration only."

"Sure. Why not." He pulled off the other boot, dried his

feet and legs, then the inside of the boots. "Us'ly I don' bath with m' clothes on."

"Better I dump you than I fry you. I could've, you know."

"I 'spect you could. I 'spect you din't 'cause you'd fry yourself with me."

"Maybe so." Danny stomped his feet down in his boots, ran a towel over his hair, scooped up Korimenei's clothing. "On your feet, Simmo. She should be ready for you by now."

In the Bath Room he tossed the shirt and trousers to Kori. There was a pile of knives, poison rings and other weapons on the tiles. Felsrawg stood on the far side of the pool, glowering at nothing in particular, hands thrust in her trouser pockets. She turned that scowl on Danny a moment, then looked away.

"Gracefully grateful, I see," he said.

Kori grinned at him. "Yes, oh man, you did it much better. You, Simms, if you roll up that towel, you can stick it under your head and be a bit more comfortable. Stretch out where she was and I'll get to work on you."

Danny dropped to a squat, began examining the collection of weapons, trying the balance of the knives, testing the mechanisms in the rings. He felt eyes on him and lifted his head. Felsrawg was glaring at him, indignant at the insult he was offering her. He looked down at the ring he was fingering, then at her; he got the feeling he might as well have been fingering her naked body. He set the ring down and got to his feet, embarrassed at his boorishness, annoyed at the woman for challenging him. Muttering under his breath he moved to stand behind Kori; once again the waves of power she was outputting swept through him, pleasuring him. He drifted in that borrowed glow for a few moments, felt a wistful deprivation when the power abruptly cut off. Kori continued to kneel for a short time longer, head bent. Slowly, with visible reluctance, she reached for Frunzacoache and lifted it off Simms. The way she handled the talisman, it was far heavier than it looked. And hotter. She slid the chain over her head, slipped the pendant under her shirt.

"Want a hand, Kori?"

"I could use one." She swiveled round on her knees, held up her arms and let him pull her onto her feet. "What are we going to do with this pair?"

He swung her against him, her back to his chest, folded his arms under her breasts. "If they don't behave," he murmured into her ear, "you can send them to join your feline pet."

"Certainly not, he's a friend, I wouldn't do that to him."

Simms sat up, grimaced at his unexpected weakness. "A thought I wish you'd keep firmly in mind, Angyd Sorcelain. Why do I feel like the end of a long fast?"

Danny felt her relax against him; her ribs moved as she took a deep breath, let it out. "The poison has been working in you," she said. "I stripped fat and muscle from your bones to heal that damage. You'll get it back with a few good meals and some sleep."

"Sleep, sounds good." He got heavily to his feet. "You going to boot us out of here?"

"And waste my work? No."

Felsrawg snorted and came strolling around the end of the pool; she was pale and drawn, there were dark smudges under her eyes, but she refused to give in to her weakness. "Laz, where do you go, come the morning?"

"Where do I go, Kori?" He slid his hand down her side, rested it on her hip.

"Where you want. Why ask me?"

He chuckled. "I wouldn't touch that if you paid me." He eyed Felsrawg. "South," he said. "We go south all the way to water. Why?"

"We can't go back to Arsuid, not for a while anyway." She turned to Simms; he nodded. "This isn't a good time for traveling, the wolves are out, four legs and two. I want to come with you. Simms? Yes. We're not begging, Laz. We'll pay our way." She ran her eyes with slow insolence from Danny's bare feet to his stubble-shadowed face. "You look a fool on that pony. We can mount you. Her too, if she wants."

"The horses we had?"

"No, the ones from Soholkai-ots, the next stage on. You left us on foot, remember? We had to steal a fishboat to get to Soholkai. The Esmoon must have gone off with yours. Look," she said, "we were a good team before, we could do it again and four will scare off trouble better than two. I'm not saying you couldn't handle anything that came up, just that it'd be easier if it didn't. Come up, I mean."

Kori pulled loose, started for the door. "See me in the morning. I'm too tired to think. Danny, where you want. Read me?" She didn't wait for an answer.

"Not too early in the morning," Danny told Felsrawg and left.

10

Danny pushed the sweaty hair off Kori's brow. "Why'd you change your mind?"

"I don't know." She moved her head as he started nibbling on an ear. "All those bubbles, maybe."

"Mmmm."

"Stop that." She wriggling away from him. "Gods, man, I thought you'd be used up after. . . ."

"All those bubbles."

"They should bottle them and sell them to tired old men." She giggled, then sobered. "That pretty pair. You didn't tell me about them."

"Didn't know they were anywhere around."

"Mmm-hmmm."

"Don't believe me?"

"I melted three reasons out of your body."

"Ah, well. I said, *know*."

"What do you think, do we let them come?"

After tugging a fold of blanket from under him, he eased onto his back and pulled her against him, her head pillowed on his shoulder. When he was comfortable, he thought about the question. "It's your call," he said finally. "We could use the horses."

"Yeh, the poor ponies, they've walked a long way. Why does Felsrawg want to come? I don't think Simms does, not really."

"Felsa looks round corners that aren't there."

"Huh?" She tilted her head to look up at him.

He brushed fine flyaway hair away from his mouth. "She's decided to believe me about the Esmoon, but she doesn't think I'd let Klukesharna get away. She intends to be there when I find it. It's her key to Dirge Arsuid, if you'll pardon the pun. She wants to go home."

"Don't we all."

"Mmh."

"What's that mean?"

"If I answered that I'd feel like a damn whore."

"Huh?"

"Selling my services. Or should I say servicings?"

"Do and you'll lose your asset."

"Challenging me, Angyd Sorcelain?"

"Never, Addryd Sorcesieur. Offering my knee."

"And a dainty one it is, if somewhat angular." He rolled over swiftly, pinning her to the rustling mattress, shutting off her protest with mouth and hands. After several minutes of this, he lifted his head. "May I move where I need to be, love, or should I fear that militant knee of yours? I'll take care to avoid it if you'll just tell me which it is."

"You talk too much."

"Never say it. Ah, I'm crushed."

"Hah! You stand tall for such a humble man."

"You can bring me low quickly enough."

"Talking again. It's deeds I demand."

"Command me, Angyd Sorcelain."

"Hear me, Addryd Sorcesieur. Do again what you did before. If you can."

"Be ready, Angyd Sorcelain. Here I come."

"So soon? Ah! that tickles."

"Good. Come has another meaning, love, you have a one-rut mind."

"No, a rutting friend, pra . . . aise be t . . . to Tungjiiii!"

11

Korimenei left the ponies behind, paying a stablemaster for their care with money she borrowed from Danny, adding a gloss on the coins by summoning a salamander and holding him overhead to show the man what would happen to him if he mistreated or neglected them. They were affectionate, hardworking little beasts and they'd been part of her life so long it was like tearing an arm off to leave them behind, but they were exhausted by the rough going and would have a much easier winter in the Gsany village Fal Fenyott, dining on grain and rich mountain hay.

Always a breath ahead of storms as if the northwinds and the snow were chasing them, the mismated quartet rode south on the wave of power pouring from the melded sorcerors, unwilled as breathing and copious as an artesian spring, sustaining humans and horses both, injecting into them the strength for enormous effort, letting them flee from dark into dark without stopping to rest or breaking down.

Simms withdrew into himself as the days passed. With the poison out of him, he didn't see any point in chasing the talisman; he had no real wish to return to Dirge Arsuid, in fact there were a lot of reasons he'd prefer not to, his lover

had betrayed him to the Ystaffel when the guards came
searching for him, his family had cast him out long before
that, he was bored, he saw no challenges left in his profession or personal life. Lots of reasons. He watched Felsrawg
nosing about Danny Blue and found the sight distasteful;
the bond forged between the two thieves as they fought
desperately to survive dissolved as soon as the danger was
removed. On the tenth morning of that precipitous journey,
he lost patience and left the group, riding east, bound for
the river Sharroud and transport south to Bandrabahr. There
he'd have a wide choice of destinations. Remembering what
Danny had said about Croaldhu he had a vague notion of
visiting that island, but mostly he wanted to escape the cold,
the constant exhaustion and the disturbing urgency of that
charge southward. He didn't understand what was happening and he didn't want to.

Korimenei drove Danny and Felsrawg south and south
and yet south; she was more and more aware of the child
growing in her, of the need to find a place where she could
rest and feel safe. She wanted this hideous journey over, she
wanted to be done with her brother's demands. The eidolon
came every night to quiver over her after Danny had gone
to sleep; Tré said nothing, but she felt him pushing at her to
hurry, hurry, hurry. The passionate playful exchanges between her and Danny Blue, begun in Fal Fenyott and continued through the first few days of travel had turned brutish
and wordless, greedy and needy, like the time in Ambijan.
After Simms left she felt odd, lying with Danny while Felsrawg
was rolled in her blankets outside the tent, listening . . .
maybe not listening, but hearing it all; she was uncomfortable, it was too much like a public performance, but she
couldn't stop, or let him stop. It was as if something was
generated between them that was necessary to the journey
and until that journey was finished she could neither understand it or do without it.

Danny Blue rode beside Korimenei, watching her, worrying about her. His half-sire Daniel grew up in a vast and
fecund family, Family Azure on Rainbow's End in another
reality altogether, but a woman here was no different from a
woman there so the Daniel phasma was soon aware of
Kori's pregnancy and passed the word to his semi-son. The
Ahzurdan phasma hung about, gibbering his fear and distaste, his growing resentment of Kori, sneering at Danny for
being so protective of another man's child. The Daniel

phasma snarled back, scornful of such intolerance. In Family Azure all children were treasured, all mothers were the responsibility of the Family, not merely the particular male who'd got the woman pregnant; the Daniel phasma's protectiveness was automatic and all the more powerful because of that and it was transferred almost intact to Danny Blue.

There was another reason for the sharpening conflict between the two phasmas and the headache they were giving Danny Blue. Korimenei could send him home—or rather into Daniel's reality, a place Danny was more and more thinking of as home. He didn't have to hunt up Settsimaksimin, he had his transport; after seeing how easily she handled the massive mancat, he was sure she could do it once she was free to put her mind to the problem. He was determined to stay with her and give her what protection he could until that moment came.

Felsrawg's hopes eroded as the days passed. By the time they reached the Gallindar Plains, she was forced to concede she'd make a mistake. Danny Blue wasn't going after Klukesharna, he was tied to the heels of that woman. He trotted after her like a dog after a bitch in heat. It wasn't an edifying sight, Felsrawg thought, and burned with a jealousy she wouldn't admit even to herself. Especially to herself. She thought about leaving like Simms had, but she stayed. I've nowhere else to go and I want to see what happens when we reach the end of this journey, maybe I can wring some profit out of it, the woman's got a reason for half killing us like this, I want to know what it is. She refused to countenance what she considered her silly yearning for the man, it was too demeaning. She wasn't some sickly teener bitch, she'd survived a two decades against the odds, been wholly on her own for the second of those decades. But she couldn't help going soft in the middle whenever she looked at him. And she couldn't stop wanting to skin that sorcelain who had her claws in him.

South and south and south they raced, outrunning hostile Gallinasi bands, flattening Gallinasi youths out to win their coup-studs with foreign ears and noses, south and south until they reached the shore of the Notoea Tha, and even there Korimenei wouldn't stop, barely paused, terrifying a misfortunate smuggler (who'd come slipping through the Shoals to trade Matamulli brandy for Gallindar pearls) into carrying them yet farther south, down the Fingercoast of Cheonea.

On a cold blustery morning, gray with a storm not yet broken, the smuggler landed Korimenei, Danny Blue and Felsrawg Lawdrawn at the mouth of a smallish creek, then hoisted sail again and got out of there fast as the wind would take him.

12

Korimenei lifted the lantern; nothing much had changed in the Chain Room. Ten years. It might have been ten minutes. She looked at the platform, looked quickly away. The crystal was there with Tré curled up in it, but she found she was reluctant to go near the thing. All she had to do was put her hand on the crystal, then Tré would be free, she could give him Frunzacoache and that would be the end of it. Instead, she turned in a slow circle, the light from the lantern spreading and contracting with the irregular circumference of the cave chamber. Chains hung in graceful curves, one end bolted to a ceiling so high it was lost in the darkness beyond the reach of the lantern, the other end to the sidewall a man's height off the floor. Chains crossed and recrossed the space above her head, chains of iron forged on a smithpriest's anvil and hung in here so long ago all but the lowest links were coated with stone, chains of wood whittled by the woodworker priests knives, chains of crystal and saltmarble chiseled by the stonecutter priests, centuries of labor given to the cave, taken by the cave to itself, a layer of stone slowly slowly crawling over all of it. No, there was no change she could see; if the stone had crept a fingerwidth lower, it would take a better eye than hers to measure it. She finished the turn facing the Chained God's altar, a square platform of polished wood sitting on stone blocks that lifted it a foot off the stone floor, above it, held up by carved wooden posts, a canopy of white jade, thin and translucent as the finest porcelain. In the center of the platform the crystal lay beside the kedron chest where Tré had found Harra's Eye and given it to her so she could use it to locate the Drinker of Souls. "Be careful what you do," she said aloud. "The more powerful the act, the more unpredictable the outcome."

Danny touched her shoulder. "You feel like telling us why we're here?"

"Take this, will you?" She handed him the lantern. "You see that thing?"

"Hard to miss."

"That's my brother in there. You said you remembered him."

"Ah. Who. . . ."

"Settsimaksimin. He wanted to make sure I stayed in school."

"You're out now."

Felsrawg shivered. "It's colder'n a fetch's finger in here. Whatever you got to do, do it."

"Stay out of this, Felsa," Danny said, "you're along for the ride, she doesn't need your ignorance yapping at her."

"T'ss! Don't need yours either, seems to me. All she needs from you is your. . . ."

"Shut up, both of you." Korimenei striped her gloves off, shoved them into a coat pocket, lifted Ailiki from her shoulder and gave her to Danny. "Stay there, Aili my Liki. Wait." She took a deep breath, let it out slowly. Scratchy little thief was right, what you got to do, do it. Don't stand around dithering. She walked to the altar, took hold of a post and pulled herself onto the platform. She took another breath, reached out and flattened her hand on the warm silky crystal.

It quivered like something alive, then she was touching nothing. She could still see it, but she was touching nothing.

Like water emptying down a drain, it flowed away from Trago, lowering him gently to the polished planks.

When it was all gone, her brother straightened his arms and legs, yawned and opened his eyes. He was on his side, his back to Korimenei. He didn't look round, he just got to his feet and went to the chest, opened it and took the crystal out, Harra's Eye. He turned finally and saw her. "Who are you?"

"I'm Kori, Tré."

"You can't be Kori, you're old."

"You don't remember?"

"I remember . . . I remember being at the Lot. Kori got the blue, I got nothing. They took her away. I went back to the Hostel with the others. AuntNurse gave me a drink to make me sleep. That was yesterday. . . ." He frowned as he saw Danny and Felsrawg standing silent under the chains. "You shouldn't have brought strangers in here." When he realized what he'd said, he looked frightened. "What am I doing here? How'd I get here?"

"That wasn't yesterday, Tré. You've been spelled, brother, you've slept ten years away without knowing it. I thought

. . . I thought you did know it, I thought you found a way to talk to me." She saw the confusion in his eyes and knew finally how completely she'd been fooled. "It wasn't you, was it?" At first she was relieved, the eidolon she'd grown to resent so bitterly wasn't her brother; then she was angry and afraid. She reached out to touch him; he shied away, frightened of her, then at last he seemed to accept her. He didn't say anything, but he let her pull him close and put her arm about his shoulder. "I am Kori, Tré, I am your sister. Really. I came to wake you and give you . . ." she touched the face of the talisman, slid her fingers over it and over it, drawing a measure of calm from the way it nestled against her. "Let me take you home, Tré. I want to go home too. I've been away at a school. A long, long way from here."

"Kori?"

"Come on, I'll tell you all about it. You going to keep the Eye with you?"

He looked down; he was clutching the crystal sphere against him, holding it in both hands. "I NEED to," he said.

"All right," She lifted him down. "Danny, Felsa, let's. . . ."

Darkness swallowed them.

She heard Danny curse, she heard Felsrawg scream with rage, Ailiki leapt at her, she felt the mahsar's claws dig through her coat into her flesh.

The darkness swallowed them all.

III: SETTSIMAKSIMIN

Driving south to steal Shaddalakh from the Grand Magus
of Tok Kinsa in order to re-
deem his souls from the geniod
who'd trapped him, Maksim
was caught in a blizzard and
blown across the path of Simms
the thief who had taken shelter from that storm in an abandoned farmstead.

1

On his third day out of the mountains, Simms ran into
the front end of a Plains blizzard. A few snowflakes blew
past, at the moment more of a promise than a threat; wet
winds brittle with cold snatched at him and whipped up the
mane and tail of his horse; the beast sidled uneasily, fought
the bit, snorted and tried to run from the storm. "Hey
Neddio, ho Neddio, slow, babe, go slow," he sang to the
horse, "soft, Neddio, steady, Neddio, it's a long way we got
to go, Neddio."

Calling on his Talent, reading earth and air, Simms sniffed
out a vague promise of shelter and rode toward it, angling
across the wind. "Here we go, Neddio, just a lit-t-t-tle way,
Neddio, you'll be warm, Neddio, out of the wind, out of the
storm, Neddio." He loosened his hold on the reins, letting
the horse stretch to a long easy lope.

Around noon, though it might as well have been midnight, the gloom had thickened until it was nearly impenetrable, he saw a scatter of dark shapes that turned into trees
and blocky buildings as he got closer. A shoulder-high wall
loomed ahead of him. Neddio the horse squealed and shied;
when Simms had him steady again, he followed the wall to a
gap. There should have been a gate, but he didn't see any.
He turned through the gap and felt a lessening of the wind's
pressure as the wall broke its sweep. He couldn't see much,

so he let the horse find the driveway and move along it toward what had to be the house.

No lights. Nothing.

"Hallooo," he yelled, raising his voice so he could be heard above the wind. "Hey the house! You got a visitor. Mind if I come in?"

Nothing.

"Well, Neddio, seems to me silence is good as a formal invite." He slid from the saddle, hunted about for the tie-rail; he found it by backing into it and nearly impaling himself on the end. He secured the reins around it in a quick half-hitch and went groping for the door, expecting to find it closed and barred.

It was open a crack, but resisted when he pushed against it. He pushed harder. The leather hinges tore across and the door crashed down. He heard some quick scuttlings in the darkness as vermin fled from the noise. Nothing else. The stead was deserted; from the dilapidation he could feel and smell it'd been that way for a long time. He leaned against the wall and listened to the slow, rumbling complaints of the rammed dirt, ancient memories of blood and screaming, present groans about the years and years since the wall had a coat of sealer brushed over it. Even the dirt knew it was decaying. He didn't listen long, it didn't matter that much why the folk had left, all that mattered was getting shelter before the storm hit.

He left Neddio at the tie-rail and groped his way around to the barn. It was in much worse shape than the house, two of the walls had melted away, the roof was lying in pieces about stalls and bins also broken and half burnt. It's house for old Neddio, he thought, and I best get as much wood in today as I can. When that blow hits full force, we're not going anywhere. Wonder if there's something about I can use as a drag so I won't have to make so many trips? Mellth'g bod, can't see a thing. Raaht, Simmo, one step at a time. Fire first, then see what I can locate. He gathered an armload of the wood scraps and felt his way back to the front door.

##

The house proved to be in better condition than he'd expected. There were two stories, the roof was reasonably intact and whatever leaked through the shakes was generally soaked up by the cross laid double floor of the second story. He decided to camp in the kitchen; there was a fireplace, a brick oven, several benches and a table that must have been built where it stood since it was far too big to fit through any of the doors. There was a washstand at the far end, close to the fireplace; that part of the kitchen was built over an artesian spring that was still gurgling forth a copious flow of cold pure water, the overflow caught and carried away by a tiled waste channel that split in two parts as it dipped under the back wall. One part flowed under the room next door and emptied into what had once been a large and flourishing vegetable garden—Simms found some tubers and herbs there that made a welcome addition to the stores he was carrying; the other part went to the barn; he found that ditch by falling into it when he poked about in the store sheds and corrals behind the house. In one of those sheds, a low, thickwalled, sod-roofed cube, he found a dozen ceramic jars almost as tall as he was, the tops sealed with a mixture of clay and wax. He put a hand on each of them, red beans, peas, lentils, flour, barley and wheat, old but untouched by rot or mildew. He tried shifting one of the jars; if he put his shoulder to it, he could tilt it and rock it across the floor, but getting it all the way to the house was something else. He'd have to use Neddio to haul them, something the horse wasn't going to like much. Wood first, though. He stepped outside, got a flurry of snow in the face; in the gusts and between them, the snow was coming down harder. He didn't have all that much time left before nightfall when even the dim gray twilight would vanish.

He cobbled together harness and collar with bits of rope and the saddle blanket, tied the ends of the harness rope to the front corners of a piece of canvas he'd found rolled up in a closet in the kitchen and began hauling wood back to the house, everything he could scavenge. He worked steadily for the next several hours, back and forth, rails, posts, bits of barn roof, rafters, stall timbers, anything he could chop loose and pile on the canvas, back and forth, the wind battering them, the snow coming down harder and harder, smothering them. Until, at last, there was no wood left worth the effort of hauling it.

He cut the canvas loose and left it in the small foyer, took Neddio around to the shed and hitched him to one of the jars. Hauling proved slow, awkward work; Neddio balked again and again, he detested those ropes cutting into him, that weight dragging back on him. Simms patted him, coaxed him, sang him into one more effort and then one more and again one more.

Heading out of the house for the last of the jars, he heard a mule bray and a moment later, a second one.

"Visitors? Yah yah, Neddio, you can stand down a while till I see what's what." He stripped off his heavy outer gloves, tossed them inside, slapped the horse on the shoulder and waited until the beast had retreated into the semi-warmth of the parlor, then he followed the sound of the braying. He groped his way to the wall, found the gap. He could see about a foot from his nose, after that nothing but the flickering white haze so he was very wary of leaving the shelter of the wall, it would be all too easy to get so turned around and confused he couldn't find his way back to the house. He stood in the gap, leaning into the wind and listening. The mules were off to his left, not far from the wall though he couldn't see them. He whistled, whistled again. The sound died before it reached them, sucked into the keening of the wind. That was no good. He began to sing, a calling song he'd learned from his outlander grandmer when he was a child. She died when he was six, but he still remembered her songs and the things she'd taught him. He sang across the wind, willed the mules to hear him and come. He sang until he was hoarse—until two dark shapes came out of the snow and stopped before him.

They were hitched to a light two-wheel dulic, the reins loose, dragging on the ground. The driver was a large lump mounded along the driver's bench, unconscious or dead. Didn't matter, the mules were alive, he had to get them into shelter.

Still singing, he teased them closer and closer until he could take hold of a halter and retrieve the reins.

He led them along the driveway and took them into the parlor, stripped off their harness and chased them into the corner where he'd spread some straw he'd retrieved from under a section of barnroof and piled up for bedding. After a minute's thought, he pulled the improvised harness off Neddio and sent him after them; the last jar could stay in the shed until they needed it. If they did.

Now for the driver, he thought. Dead or alive? Well, we'll see.

He shivered as he plunged into the wind and snow, groped over to the dulic and climbed into it. He burrowed through

layers of scarves and cloaks until he could get his fingers on
the man's neck, poked about until he discovered the artery
and rested his fingertips on it. The man's heart was beating
strongly, but he was very very cold. Something not wholly
natural about the chilly flesh, he didn't know what it was,
but it bothered him. Still, he couldn't leave him out here to
freeze. Offing someone when the blood was hot, well, that
was a thing could happen to anyone, cold blood was different, and by damn his blood and everything else was cold.
He pried up the massive torso, gritted his teeth under the
weight and length of the man, got as much of him as he
could wrapped around his shoulders and began the labori-
ous process of getting back to the ground without injuring
his load or doing serious damage to himself.

Ten sweaty staggering minutes later, he laid the stranger
out on the tiles in front of the kitchen fire. He left him there
and went to fetch in the gear and other supplies from the
dulic, piled the pouches and blanket roll on the table and
went back for a second load. There was more baggage
than he'd expected, this was no wandering beggar, whatever
else he was.

When the last load was in and piled on the table, he went
to look at his patient. The man hadn't changed position and
wasn't showing any signs of waking. Simms touched his
brow. No fever. He was still cold but not quite so deathly
chill. You'll do for a while. I sh'd get those wet clothes off,
but that can wait. Dulic first, then I deal with the door an'
take care of the stock, then it's your turn, friend. Plenty of
time for you. I be glad, though, when you wake and tell me
what in u'ffren you're doin' out here. Wonderin' makes me
itch.

After he pulled the dulic back of the house and rolled it
into a shed, he inspected the door he'd knocked down; he
and Neddio had tramped back and forth across it dozens of
times but even Neddio's iron shoes had done little to mark
the massive planks of mountain oak, glued together and
further reinforced by horizontal and diagonal two-by-fours
of the same oak nailed onto the planks with hand-forged
iron nails. He muscled the door into the opening, propped it
against the jamb, walked one of the jars against it to keep
the wind from blowing it down again.

The two mules were tail switching and fratchetty, they
kicked at Neddio if he went too close to them, nipped at
Simms when he shifted some of the straw into another

corner for his horse, even followed him, long yellow teeth reaching for arms and legs or a handy buttock, when he went to lay a fire in the parlor fireplace, though they didn't like the fire much and retreated to their corner when it started crackling briskly. Keeping a wary eye on them, he dragged one of the parlor benches to the hearth and spread corn along it from a corn jar in the foyer. He rolled an ancient crock from the kitchen, filled it with water, took a look round and was satisfied he'd done what he could to make the beasts comfortable.

In the kitchen, he filled the tin tank in the brick stove and kindled a fire under it so he'd have hot water to bathe his patient; he laid another fire in the stoke hole, filled one of the stranger's pots from the spring, dropped in dried meat from his own stores and lentils and barley from jars in the parlor, along with some of the tubers and herbs from the garden and set it simmering on the grate. He put teawater to heating beside the stew and went to inspect the stranger.

He was a long man, six foot five, six, maybe even seven with shoulders of a size to match his length. He had been a heavy man, big muscles with a layer of fat; he'd lost the fat and some of the muscle, his skin hung loose around him. He w'd make a han'some skel'ton. Simms smiled at the thought and drew his fingers over the prominent bones of the man's face. Beautiful man. Thick coarse gray hair in a braid that vanished down the cloak. Brows dark, with only a hair or two gone gray. Eyelashes long and sooty, resting in a graceful arc on the dark poreless skin stretched over his cheekbones. Big, powerful man, but Simms got a feeling of fragility from him, as if the size and strength were illusions painted over emptiness. Beautiful shell, but only a shell.

He turned the stranger onto his stomach, eased his head around so his damp hair was turned to the fire and began stripping the sodden clothing off him, boots first, boot liners, knitted stockings, two pairs, wool and silk with the silk next to the silk. Gloves, fur lined. Silk glove liners. Fur-lined cloak. Silk-lined woolen undercloak. Wool robe, heavily embroidered over the chest, around the hem and sleeve cuffs. Silk under-robe. Wool trousers. Silk underwear. Whoever he was, he was a man of wealth and importance. What he was doing crossing the Grass in winter, alone . . . itch itch, wake up an' talk t' me, man, 'fore my head explode.

He fetched the water from the tank and began bathing the stranger, concentrating at first on his hands and feet, check-

ing carefully for any signs of frostbite, pleased to see there
were none. He didn't understand why the man didn't wake
up, worried about it and was frustrated by his own ignorance. If his family hadn't been so opposed to anything that
smelled of witchery, if he'd had the drive and intelligence to
go out and get training, beyond the little he picked up from
his grandmer, if and if and if. . . . Beautiful beautiful man,
if he die, it's my fault, my ignorance that kill 'im. He dried
the man, rubbing and rubbing with the soft nubby towel
he'd found in one of the pouches, and still he didn't wake,
he yielded to Simms' manipulations like a big cat to a
stroking hand, it was almost as if his body recognized Simms
and cooperated as much as an unminded body could.

He folded the towel, put it under the man's head. I need
clothes for you. I hope you don' mind, I been goin' through
your stuff. He touched the man's face, drew his forefinger
along the elegant lips. Wake up, wake up, wake. . . . He
sighed and got to his feet.

The table was spread with the pouches and things he'd
already pulled from them. He unbuckled the pouch that
held the man's spare clothing. Robes, rolled in neat, tight
cylinders. He shook them out, chose one and set it aside.
The blankets, I'd better have them. Another pouch. Meat,
apples, trailbars wrapped in oiled silk—he set those aside as
he came on them. A large leather wallet with papers inside.
He tossed that down without exploring it, none of his business, at the moment anyway. A plump, clunk-clanking purse.
He opened it. Jaraufs and takks, Jorpashil coin. Another
towel, in an oiled silk sac along with bars of soap and a
squeeze tube with an herb-scented lotion inside.

He gave over his explorations, carried the robe and lotion
back to the man. Kneeling beside him, he rubbed the lotion
all over him, enjoying the feel of him, the brisk green smell
of the lotion. Y' walk in circles I can't even sniff at, everythin'
say it. He felt a pleasant melancholy as he contemplated the
probable impossibility of what he wanted. When he was
finished with the rubdown, he rolled the sleeper over, spread
one of the blankets on the hearth; after sweat and swearing
and frustration, he finally got the dry robe on him and
shifted him bit by bit onto the blanket.

Weary beyond exhaustion, weary to the bone, Simms got
heavily to his feet. The soup was sending out a pleasant
smell, filling the kitchen with it, making it feel homier than
any place he'd been in for years. He stirred the thick,

gummy liquid, tasted it, smiled and shifted it from the grate
to the sand bed where it could simmer away without burning. The tea water was boiling; he dropped in a big pinch of
tea leaves, stirred them with a whisk and set the pot on the
sand to let the leaves settle out. He picked up the wet,
discarded clothing, hung it on pegs beside the fireplace to
dry out and went into the parlor to check on the horses. The
water in the crock was low; he emptied what was left onto
the floor and fetched more from the kitchen. Neddio was
sleeping in one corner, the mules were dozing in another.
The truce seemed to be holding. He put out more grain,
thinking: feed 'em well while I got it and hope the storm
blow out before we in trouble for food. He checked the fire,
threw a chunk of fence post on and left it to catch on its
own.

Back in the kitchen he stripped and straddled the waste
channel, scooped up water and poured it over himself, shuddering at the bite of that icemelt, feeling a temporary burst
of vigor as he rubbed himself dry on his visitor's towel. He
hung it on a peg, pulled on his trousers, turned to pick up
his shirt and saw the man watching him.

"Well, welc'm to th' world, breyn stranger." He pushed
his arms into the sleeves and began buttoning his shirt.
"Was wonderin' when y'd wake." He went to check the
soup, tasted it and turned, holding up the ladle. "Hungry?"

"What is this place?"

"I'm as temp'ry as you, blown here by the wind. Whoever
lived here left long time ago." He started ladling soup in a
pannikin. "Name's Simms Nadaw, out of Dirge Arsuid."

"Long way from home."

"Way it goes."

"Maks. Passing through everywhere, lighting nowhere.
Recently at least."

"Right. Feel good enough to sit up?" He took the pannikin and a spoon to the hearth and set it on the tiles, went
back to the stove. "Get some of that down you. Start
warming your insides well as your out."

"Give it a try." After a small struggle Maks managed to
raise himself high enough to fold his long legs and get
himself balanced with his shoulder to the fire. "Weaker 'n I
thought. Soup smells good." He tasted it. "Is good."

"Hot anyway." Simms spread a square of cheesecloth
over his mug, poured himself some tea, rinsed the cheesecloth and repeated with another mug, then filled another

pannikin with soup. Over his shoulder he said, "You want
some tea? It's yours, I poke through y' things, they over
there." He nodded at the table.

Maks looked amused. "See you found my mug."

"That I did. Take it that mean yes."

"Take it right." He set the pannikin down. "The mules?"

"Parlor. With Neddio. M' horse. Bad tempered mabs,
an't they."

"Not fond of freezing, that's all."

"Mmh. Shu'n't keep 'em so hungry then, they were doin'
their best to eat ol' Neddio. Me too. Got toothmarks on my
butt. Want some more soup?"

"Just the tea for now. I don't want to overload the body."

"Odd way o puttin' it." Simms took the tea to him,
collected the empty pannikin and rinsed it in the channel.
He turned it upside down over the tank and went back to
leaning on the wall beside the stove, enjoying the warmth
radiating from the bricks while he ate his soup. He was
immersed in flickering shadows while his visitor was centered in the glow of such light as there was in the kitchen.
The firelight loved Maks' bones, it slid along them like
melted butter, waking amber and copper lights in his dark
skin, face and hands and the hollow where his collar bones
met.

"Listen to that wind howl. Bless ol' Tungjii, I wouldn't
want to be out there now." He had a rich deep voice,
flexible, musical, Simms thrilled each time the man spoke;
he had trouble concealing his response to the sound, but he
worked at it, he didn't want to disgust him or turn him
hostile.

"Blessings be, on heesh an' we." Simms finished his soup,
rinsed his pannikin and spoon in the channel, set them on
the stove. "We were both luckier'n we deserve running
across a place like this." He gave himself some more tea.
"Too bad the steader were chase out, a spring like this 'n is
flowin' gold."

"Chased out?"

" 'M a Reader, Maks; walls remember, walls talk. Blood
and screams, 's what they tol' me. But it was all a long long
time ago. Ne'er been this way b'fore. You know how long
Grass storms us'ly last?"

"It's still early winter. This one should blow out around
three days on."

"I put the dulic in a shed out back. I don' know how

much good it's gonna do you if there's a couple feet of snow
on the ground."

"We'll see what we see." He chuckled, a deep rumbling
that came up from his heels. "There's no horse foaled that'd
carry me." He yawned, screwed up his face. "My bladder's
singing help," he said, "you have any preference where I
empty it?"

"You see the spring here, they led a channel off from it
under the tiles the next room over, what we call straffill in
Arsuid, there a catch basin, for baths I s'pose. Got a hole in
the floor, a spash-chute on th' wall, leadin' to the hole. You
wanna shoulder t' lean on?"

Maks bent and straightened his legs, rubbed at his knees.
"Give a hand getting on my feet, if you don't mind, breyn
Nadaw."

"Simms, y' don' mind." He offered his hands, braced
himself and let Maks do most of the work. When the big
man was on his feet, standing shaky and uncertain, he
moved in closer, clasped Maks about his thick, muscular
waist, grunted as long fingers dug into his shoulder and the
man's weight came down on him, not all of it, but enough to
remind him vividly of the effort it took to haul him inside.

"Not too much?"

He could feel the bass tones rumble in the center of his
being as well as in his head, he felt the in-out of Maks's
breathing, the vibrations of his voice, the slide of muscles
wasted but still bigger than most and firm. "It's not something I'd do for the fun of it," he said, almost breathless,
though that definitely didn't come from fatigue.

"Let's go then."

2

He lay listening to the wind howl outside and the steady
breathing of the man he shared the hearth with. Now and
then he heard Neddio or the mules moving about in the
parlor, the clop of iron shoe on wood floor. He turned his
head. The fire was low, but he could leave it for a while yet.
He closed his eyes and went back to listening to Maks.
Maks . . . it was his name . . . it fit in his mouth with a
familiar easiness . . . it wasn't the whole name. He thinks
I'd recognize the whole name. Maybe so maybe not. He
wanted to touch Maks, but he didn't dare, not now, not
when he might wake and know he was being touched. Not
yet. Simms drew his hands down his own chest. What was

wrong with him? He was lively enough when he came out of
that trance or whatever it was, unperturbed by his condition, but there was that . . . that something. . . . The man's
spirit was so vital, so . . . absorbing, entrancing . . . Simms
smiled into the fire-broken darkness . . . it obscured that
other thing. Almost. Part of him wanted Korimenei here so
she could work her magic on Maks. Part of him didn't want
to share Maks with anyone, anything. Even if their enforced
cohabitation came to nothing, there would be at least three
days alone with him, time out from the world.

Round and round in his head, was he sick with something? Will he love me will he hate me will he look through
me like I'm nothing? Round and round until he had to
move, do something. He slipped out of his blankets and
added wood to the fire, chunks of tough hard fence post
that'd burn all night. He bent over Maks before rolling into
his blankets again, touched his fingertips light, light, feather-
light to the man's brow.

It took him almost an hour to get to sleep.

3

The house rumbled and rattled and shook under the blast
of the wind as the blizzard settled around them.

Maks slept heavily while Simms fed the mules and Neddio,
used an old cedar shake to scoop up their droppings and
carry them into the straffill where he dumped them down
the hole. He brewed tea, ate one of Maks' trailbars and put
a new pot of soup to simmering on the stove. He washed his
shirt, trousers, socks and underclothing in the waste channel, looked over Maks' clothing, brushed the mud and debris off the outercloak, washed the undercloak and the
other things, hung them all to drip dry on a cord he'd
stretched between two pegs in the straffill. It helped the
morning pass. Now and then he went over to Maks, squatted beside him, worried about the long sleep, but there was
no sign of fever or other distress, so he went away again and
let him sleep on.

Maks woke an hour past noon. He stretched, yawned,
looked relaxed and lazy as a cat in the sun. He turned to
Simms, gave him a wide glowing smile that sent flutters
running round Simms' interior. "What's the time?"

"You couldn't tell it from out there," he nodded at the
shuttered window, "but it's a little after noon."

"Ahhhh. Perfect. I hate mornings. Best way to greet the sun is sound asleep."

Simms chuckled. "So I see."

"Don't tell me you're one of those pests who leaps out of bed at dawn caroling blithely. They should be swatted like flies."

Another chuckle. "Ne'er uh blithe, but up, yeh. When I wan't workin'."

Maks raised his brows at that, but didn't ask for explanations. He closed his eyes, turned his head from side to side. After a minute, he said. "Today, tomorrow, I think. Day after that we can move." He pushed the blankets off and got to his feet. He was steadier, visibly stronger.

Simms finished sewing a button on his shirt, tied off the thread and cut it with one of his sleeve knives. "Tea on the stove. More soup, should be ready by now." He rolled a knot in the end of the thread, turned the shirt inside out and started examining the seams.

Maks wandered out. Simms could hear him talking to the mules. He came back in the kitchen, looked through his packs, found a currycomb and a stone and went out again. A little later as Simms was putting a new edge on the frayed hems of his trousers, he heard splashing in the straffill, Maks whistling a cheerful tune. Maks came in, glanced at him, went to the stove and filled his mug. He looked at the tea. "You sure this isn't going to crawl out and jump me?"

"Wake y' up."

"One way or another. You've had a busy morning."

"Help the time pass, keeping y' hands busy. 'Sides, I been puttin' off a lotta this, might's well catch up while we stuck here."

Maks nodded. "Not a bad idea." He ladled out a pannikin of soup, glanced at Simms. "Want some?"

"After I finish this, I think. I'll take some tea, if you don't mind."

Maksim brought him the tea, fetched the pannikin and ate his soup while he squatted beside Simms and watched him set small neat stitches.

Simms was quietly happy; he said nothing because he felt no need to talk, and he was pleased that Maks seemed equally comfortable with the silence. He finished one cuff and began on the other. Maks set the pannikin down and sipped at the tea. The fire flickered and shadows swayed around them in a slow hypnotic dance, the wind howled and

icemelt drafts whispered through the room. Maks set the
mug down and gave Simms' shoulder a squeeze, got to his
feet and wandered out again.

He was back a moment later with the mules' harness,
some rags and a bottle of oil. After some maneuvering, he
settled at the edge of the hearth, pulled a blanket round his
shoulders and began working oil into the leather, cleaning it
and working supple the places where the damp had stiffened
it. Filled with the small peaceful sounds of their labor, the
hiss and snap of the fire with the muted noised of the storm
as background, the silence wrapped like a blanket about the
two men as they went on with their work. Finally Maks
spoke, his voice lazy and undemanding. "Arsuid's a long
way south of here."

Simms chuckled, a small soft sound. "Y' mean I got rocks
in m' head ridin' into this kinda weather." He glanced at
Maks, met his eyes and looked away from the laughter in
them, not because he didn't like it, he liked it far too much.
"C'd say the same, don' y' think?"

"So you could. Never visited Arsuid. What's it like?"

"Yesta'day. Ev'ry yesta'day."

Maks thought about that a minute. "I see what you mean.
It can get boring if nothing changes."

" 'Pends where y' sit."

"More so on whether you're a sitter or sat on."

"Y' know 't."

"Spite of that, Arsuiders seem to stay put."

"T's so. Arfon, he like to keep his folk hoverin' round.
Way I got loose, well, y' might say I was flung out."

"Feel like telling it, or is it none of my business?"

Simms tucked the needle into the cloth, dropped his hands
and frowned at the fire. "Don' know the whole, 's more
confusin' than entertainin'." He snapped thumb against middle finger, shook his head. "Here tis. Arfon got a itch for a
talisman of 'is own. He a jeaaalous god, yehhh. An' there
was this sorceror came by, call hisself Lazul. Turn out,
wan't so."

"Sorceror, hmm. Did you ever find out what his name
was?"

"After, yeh. Danny. Laz was for th' duration, what he
said."

"Danny. Danny Blue?"

"Dunno. Might be. 'Staffel trap him, me, a couple more,

fill us fulla poison. Say go get Klukesharna, we wipe you clean when y' give her to us."

"Not nice."

"Nah, that tisn't." Simms grinned at Maks, went back to watching the fire. "You know 'im? Danny?"

"I know one Danny Blue. A student of mine once. In a way."

"You a Sorceror?"

"For my sins. And you're a Witch."

"Nah." Simms sighed, shook his head. "Ne'er got the training."

"You have the Talent, you could still train."

"I don' think so."

"Well, you have to want it. You got Klukesharna?"

"Yeh, we made one gwychcher team, in and out, slick's a trick."

"So Arfon has Klukesharna now."

"Nah. We got her yeh, but after that, things got outta hand."

"Danny?"

"Part. There was this putch the 'Staffel land on us. Din' need her, don' know why they bring her in. Their mistake, for sure. Her 'n Danny, they dump Felsa 'n me, run for the Asatas. We wake up, go after 'em. Had to. Poison. We catch up to 'em this side the Asatas. Felsa nails Danny. He fall out facedown in the snow. I go for the Esmoon. Think I hit her. What happens next I don' know till later. Felsa and me, we went out, whoosh, blowin' a candle. We wake up next day half-froze with heads like y' get after a three-day drunk. We still got no choice, so we take after Danny again. We catch him up. He with this woman, not the Esmoon, don' know where she come from. No Klukesharna. Felsa gonna to skin him, she don' believe nothing he says. He says the Esmoon went off with Klukesharna. He says the Esmoon's no woman, she a demon."

"Demon? Tell me what she looks like," Maks's voice was suddenly taut, compelling, for the first time he was putting the power on Simms.

Simms blinked. "Fahhn silver hair, way she wear it, it go to her waist in long waves, shiny. Blue eyes. Velvet skin. Beautiful and she know it. I 'spect mos' men go crazy for her. I 'spect Danny right 'bout her, I thought sure I put one shaft, maybe two in 'er. You know 'er?"

"Probably not her. But something like her. Go on. What happened next?"

"It was in this Gsany village, in a bathhouse. We caught 'em pants down, you'd think we had 'em flat. Wan't so. The woman drop a demon on Felsa an' Danny drop me. Blessings be, old Tungjii stirring the waters, it turn out that the woman has this talisman, Frunzacoache, she use it to leach the poison outta us. Korimenei. Goin' home and goin' fast. Takin' Danny with her. Felsa taggin' along, she don' believe Danny don' wanna see Klukesharna or the Esmoon ever again. I go along until I get tired a hurryin'. I leave and that's how I end up here."

"Korimenei." Affection and amusement rumbled in the word. "How'd she look?"

"Like you damn well better not get in her way when she goin' somewhere." Simms rubbed his thumb along the seam of the trousers he'd been working on. "She a student too?"

"More like adopted daughter. Apprentice if I survive and she wants it."

Simms blinked at him. "Cheonea," he said. "Settsimaksimin. Sorceror Prime." He folded his arms across his chest and hugged himself as he watched hope and possibility wither and wash away; that was all he could see for the moment, then he realized what Maks had just said. "Survive?"

"It's a web they're weaving, Simms, the demons, the gods and the Great Ones. Arfon and the Ystaffel pumped you full of poison, my set of demons robbed me of my souls, temporarily I hope. They pointed me at Shaddalakh, either I get it or I die. I'm dying now. When the body's empty, it begins to fall apart. No healer or herb doctor can stop the decay." He shook his head. "They send me out and at the same time rob me of my best tools. Without my earthsoul I have no Shamruz body to journey for me, I can't walk the realities or summon demons."

Simms nodded, thinking he knew what Maks was saying. "Yeh. Y' c'd fetch a demon an' send it t' get th' talisman."

Maks laughed, a happy shout that embraced Simms and invited him to share the joke. "Nooooo, no," he said, "never let a demon near that much power, you could end up dancing to the demon's tune rather than the other way about."

"I s'pose. Yeh, thinkin' 'bout Esmoon, yeh." Simms scowled at the fire, wrestling with himself; he hated the thought of messing with demons again, but his impulse

toward spending himself for the man who attracted him so
fiercely won out over his fears. He turned to Maks. "Take
me with you. I c'n maybe help. Reason the 'Staffel land on
me an' Felsa, we the best thieves in Arsuid. Tol' y' I c'd
read walls, stones, dirt. I c'n see witchtraps, help y' 'void
'em. I c'n sing ghosts t' sleep. Tickle locks. Lots more."

"Simms. . . ."

"Y' don' want me, a' right."

"It's not that. The Magus knows that someone is coming.
He's one of those who reads could-be nodes like other men
read print. You could get swallowed up and spat out, it's
not worth it, my friend."

"Y' don' know, Addryd Sorcecieur." He gazed at his
hand, stroked his fingertips up and down his thigh. "Goin'
in the Henanolee, that was dangerous too. It was the bes'
time in m' whole life. I was workin' on top of it, ne'er felt so
full so strong so gooood. I was scared t' bone but e'en that
felt good. An' what's it matter if I die? What am I? Jus' a
thief. No one give a shit."

"No Addryd. Maks." He leaned toward Simms, touched
his face. "What's this nonsense? Not just a thief, I have
your word for it, best in Arsuid." His hand was warm and
smooth, Simms leaned into the curve of it, it was comforting
and exciting. "You'd best keep out of this, little witch."

Simms turned his head, kissed Maks' palm. He smiled
dreamily at the big man. "No," he said. "No . . . command
me . . . anythin' but go 'way."

"And if I commanded you to climb to the roof here and
jump into the wind?" The voice was darkness and light,
caressing him, stirring him to the seat of his souls. It was
fully there, the compelling, seducing Voice of the Prime.

Simms drew away a little, steadied his breathing before he
spoke. "I w'd prob'ly do 't. But I sh'd wanna know why
first."

Maks threw back his head and laughed, the sound filling
the room, overpowering the storm and everything else.
"Good, good. Never jump without knowing why. And if I
said love me, would you want to know why you should do
such a thing?"

"No. I don' need t' ask 'bout what already is."

4

On the fourth morning they dug out and found the blizzard
had been more blow than snow. Maks hitched up his frisky,

rambunctious mules, Simms saddled Neddio and they started south toward the spur of the Asatas where Tok Kinsa was, walled city walled in by snag-tooth mountains, secret city, the ways in warded and hidden from all but the select. There was about six inches of snow on the ground and no road, so the going was difficult even for the huge-wheeled dulic, but they made fair time and by the end of the week had reached the end of the grass. Maks left the dulic in a dry wash and turned one of the mules loose, loaded his gear on the other and prepared to walk into the mountains. Simms followed, leading Neddio.

The trek was hard on Maks; he faded visibly as each day passed.

Simms ached for him; he was filled with frustration and fury at the gods, the demons, everyone, everything responsible for Maks' hurting. In Arsuid, Simms had pretended to be loose and easy, that was what people expected from him, what his lovers wanted; he lost them again and again because he cared too much and it frightened them. So much passion, so much need demanded a response they were unwilling or incapable of giving. He was feeling his way warily with Maks; he knew so little that was real about the man, only legends and legends lie. Maks seemed to like him, that was a wonderful thing, but Simms saw it as fragile as a soapbubble, a careless touch could destroy it. Maks was willing to love him, though not always able, especially after a hard day's climbing. But he'd hold Simms anyway, caress him; he made Simms fell wanted, needed. Loved.

The way Maks chose was narrow, steep, treacherous. Snow above was loose, always falling, avalanche a constant danger. Underfoot there were patches of ice and always more snow. They struggled on and on; once again Simms was traveling with a driven person. The only thing that bothered him this time was his inability to help; he'd never been in snow before he crossed the Dhia Asatas, he knew almost nothing about mountain traveling. He told himself he was useful around the camps, doing most of the work so Maks could rest. It was something.

On the third day they came on a small stream wandering through a ravine choked with aspen and waist-deep snow. They made camp on the rim of that ravine in a thick stand of conifers. Around the bulge of the mountain there was a windswept cliff that looked down into the bowlshaped valley where Tok Kinsa drowsed in the watery winter sunlight. They lay there staring down at the city.

Tok Kinsa, Home Ground of the Magus Prime. Power Ground of Erdoj'vak, Patron of the Rukka Nagh, Vanner and Gsany both. Like most local gods, he slept a lot, he was sleeping now.

No Outer Rukks allowed within the walls outside the pilgrim season and the season had finished weeks ago. No strangers allowed within the walls, with the minor exception of a few well-known scholars who were specifically invited to visit the Magus.

A bright city, full of saturated color, reds, yellows, blues, greens shining like jewels against the equally brilliant white of the snow, a paisley city with every surface decorated, even both sides of the immense curtain wall, in the geometrics of Rukk design. Inside the walls the streets were paved with alternating black and white flags; they were laid out like the spokes of a wheel, radiating from the round tower with the spiraling ramp curling up around it, the Zivtorony.

The streets were busy with Kinseers dressed in dramatic mixes of black and white, even the children. The city was busy, brightly alive, but the massive gates were closed and stayed closed. There were no footprints in the snow around Tok Kinsa.

Lying on folded blankets with blankets over them, Maks and Simms watched the whole of the day and by the sundown certain things had become obvious.

They couldn't go in openly or disguised. No one was entering the city and even if they were, there was no way Maks would pass as a Rukk. A six-foot seven M'darjin mix would stand out in any crowd.

It'd be impossible to slip over the walls without the Magus perceiving them and brushing them off like pesky flies. Maks was in no shape for a protracted challenge-battle—especially with a Magus Prime supported by one of the Great Talismans.

The attack would have to be quick, leap in, seize Shaddalakh, leap out the next second, nothing else would work.

##

"The longer we hang around up here, the more certain it is the Magus will locate us and attack." The fire threw black shadows into the lines and creases in Maks' face, underlining the fatigue in his voice. "I have no doubt he's probing for us right now, reading the could-be nodes over and over and plotting the changes."

Simms was watching his face, paying little attention to what he said; he didn't understand could-be nodes or any of that higher magic, he knew tones of voice and new lines in the face he loved. And he knew how to get into impossible places, though he'd never tried something so impossible as that snow-sealed city on the other side of the mountain. "Danny jump us over traps in the Henanolee Heart. C'd you jump us into the Zivtorony?"

"In, yes. Out, I don't know. If we have to tear things apart searching for Shaddalakh, it gives the Magus time to throw a noose round us and squeeze." He opened the wallet and pulled out a handful of parchment sheets, looked through them, pulled out a plan of the city, discarded that an useless, took up a sheet with diagrams of the tower. He passed it over to Simms. "Any ideas?"

Simms spread the sheet across his lap, bent over it, guessing at what the lines meant; he couldn't read the writing, he could barely read Arsuider and this was something else. His fingertips felt itchy, tingling. "Do y' b'lieve the Magus know it's you coming?" He thought a minute. "Or someone like you?"

"Sorceror? Yes. He'd know that."

"Then I tell you one thing, he got Shaddalakh where he c'n reach out an' touch him." He smoothed his hand across the parchment. "Gotta jump direct." There was a vertical view, the tower sliced down the middle to show how the levels were arranged. He brushed his fingers up the center of the view, stopped where the tingling grew intense, almost painful. He closed his eyes. No image, but he smelled roast geyker and his mouth watered. He was startled. He moved his fingers on up the tower. The tingle faded, the taste went away. He looked up, frowning.

"What is it?"

"Smell anythin', like meat cookin'?"

"No."

Simms touched the diagram again, he didn't close his eyes this time, but there it was, the rich, mouth-watering aroma of red meat swimming in its own gravy. "Magus eatin' dinner," he said.

Maks looked at Simms' fingers resting lightly on the parchment, trembling a little. "Dowsing?"

Simms blinked. "I . . ." He looked down at his hand, lifted it off the drawing as if the parchment had suddenly gotten hot. "I never did that before." He was delighted with the discovery, it was a gift he could give his lover, a wanted gift, a needed gift.

Maks smiled. "Told you, little witch, there's Talent wasting in you; you should train it. Try for Shaddalakh."

"Do m' best." He rubbed his thumb across his fingertips, he was nervous, both hands were shaking. He looked at the vertical drawing, rejected it and moved to the floor plans of the different levels. One by one he brushed his fingers across them. When he touched the third level, he smelled the roast again, located it in a long narrow wedge of a room. That was the Magus, he got no sense of Shaddalakh. He moved on, level to level until he'd touched all seven levels. Nothing more. He shook his head. "All I read is Magus." He grinned suddenly. "Or maybe t's m' belly yearnin' for roast geyker."

Maks scowled at the fire. "I'd rather avoid a confrontation with him, but it looks like we have to remove the Magus before we start hunting." He rubbed his hand along his thigh as if the palm were suddenly sweaty. "Tonight," he said. "I go tonight. If I wait, I get weaker while he gets stronger."

Simms set the parchment aside, slipped a sleeve knife from its sheath and began working on the edge with a small hone. "What time?"

"Simmo. . . ."

"No, Maks. If y' have any feelin' for me, no."

"It's because I do. . . ."

"Turn things round an' think 'bout it, y' see?"

"Ahhh! Why do I always love contrarians! Brann who never lets me get away with anything and little Kori who has to be tied down to keep her out of trouble and you, stubborn man, if something happens to you, I die a bit."

"Do I hurt less if you go down? Am I s' useless, all I am 's a bedmate?"

"Being right all the time, it's as bad as a taste for getting up early."

Simms smiled happily at Maks, knowing he'd won his point. "What time?"

"Two hours after midnight."

"You get some sleep, Maksa, you the one gonna do all the work. I'll clean up here and wake y'."

"Simmo, don't hobble Mule or Neddio and set out the grain we have left."

"Yeh. Give 'em a chance, we don' be back. Pass me the wallet, Maksa, I'll put this away." He picked up the plan. "No use leavin' it out."

"Keep it by you, you'll have to dowse again before we go. The Magus won't be sitting at the dinner table then, no telling where he'll be. Tungjii bless, Simmo, I don' know how I could have managed this without you."

Simms' mouth tightened as he struggled to control his surging emotions; he was afraid of scaring Maks off like he'd driven away so many others. He set the hone aside, took a bit of leather and began polishing the steel. "Maybe he don' know 'bout me. Think of that?" He held out the knife. "Maybe steel c'n cut spell."

"No no, not steel. Take him out if you can, but don't kill him, there's no reason to kill the man, he's only trying to protect what's his."

"A' right, gimme a sock." Simms tapped his foot. "I got no spares." He laughed at the look on Maks' face. "Sock an' sand, whap, whiff 'em, out like blowing out y' candle."

6

Simms brushed his fingertips up the vertical diagram, stopped at the top. The seventh level. "Here," he said. He closed his eyes, but he got nothing more than the location, no smells, no sounds, just an itch so intense it was painful. "I don' know what he doin', but he there." He scratched at the parchment, his fingernail moving across the highest level in the tower. He left the vertical and drifted his fingers across the floor plan of that level. He touched each of the rooms indicated, stopped at one that looked south toward the serried mountain peaks beyond the valley. "Here," he said. "This room."

Maks took the plan, read the glyphs. "His bedroom. Do you get the sense he's sleeping?"

"I . . . hmm . . ." Simms closed his eyes, focused inward, slid his thumb over and over his fingertips. "No . . . I don't . . . I can' . . .'f I hadda guess, he awake an' waitin'."

Maks slid the sheet into the wallet, tied the strings, got to his feet. "Let's not keep him waiting."

7

The Magus struck at Maks before they touched foot to

floor, exploding time-energy around him, ripping reality
into wheeling chaos that manifested as blinding color and
extreme form-distortion—and a discarnate hunger that sucked
at him, struggling to dissolve him into that chaos.

The attack ignored Simms. He came down behind Maks,
his aura masked by the sorceror's lifeglow, a fire that spread
nova strong, nova bright, about Maks, made visible by the
whirling forces that filled the room. Simms dropped to his
hands and knees. He relaxed, smiled; the floor was familiar,
comfortable to his reading-touch. Polished wood, then a
velvety carpet. He didn't try to comprehend what his eyes
were showing him, he simply ignored it and took his direction from the carpet. He began edging toward the Magus.

Instead of trying to block that chaos, Maks sucked it into
himself, stripped away the force in it and slowly, painfully
recreated an area of normality about himself, gaining strength
as the Magus expended his.

Still unnoticed as the two Primes hammered at each other,
Simms circled wide and came round behind the wavering
distorted figure. Reality twisted and tore about him, time-nodes
exploded, but none of it was directed at him, it battered at
him but the blows were glancing, he was rocked but not
seriously hurt. He kept crawling. He came up behind the
Magus, a dark column broken into puzzle pieces as if there
were a glass of disturbed water between them.

Simms slipped the knotted sock from his coat pocket and
sat on his heels peering at the column, trying to resolve it
enough to find his target. Black and white, blurs of pinkish
brown swaying swinging, changing rhythm suddenly, never
still. Hands, he thought after a moment. He got to his feet.
He could have reached out and touched the shifting uncertain figure, but he was careful not to. Finally he caught a
glimpse of pinkish brown higher on the column, only a
glimpse, it was swallowed a moment later by an amorphous
blob of black. Must be the face, has to be the face. He set
himself, swung the sock with carefully restrained force. He
felt it slam against something, heard a faint tunk.

The confusion vanished instantly.

A man lay on the carpet at his feet, white and black robes
spread around his sprawled body, an angular black and
white striped headdress knocked half off his bald head. He
was tall and lean, with a strong hooked nose and a flowing
white beard.

Maks wiped sweat off a gray face. He found a chair and dropped into it. "Lovely tap, Simmo."

Simms looked at him, dazed. There was something throbbing in him that distracted him, even in his anguish at Maks' distress. He licked his lips, tried to say something, but he couldn't. He dropped the sock, turned slowly so slowly, until the string tied to his gut whipped tight and began reeling him in.

Step by slow step he went to the head of great four-poster bed, touched the post on the left side. It was at least six inches square, deeply carved with the interlacing geometrics of Rukk reliefwork. He stroked his fingertips up and down the different faces of the post. There was a click. A part of the post slammed against the side of his hand. A shallow drawer. He pulled it open and looked into it. Shaddalakh lay there, dull white, sandpapery sand dollar. He lifted it out. It was like touching a lover, warm, accepting. He held it, tears gathered in his eyes, though he didn't cry. He smiled instead.

Maks' hand closed on his shoulder. "May I have it?"

It was the most difficult thing he'd done in his twenty some years of life. He turned slowly, held out the talisman.

Maks took it, there was a sadness in his face that told Simms his lover understood the gift he'd just received, but at the moment that didn't help lessen the ache from the loss.

"Time to go," Maks said. "We. . . ."

Darkness swallowed them.

Simms heard Maks cursing, something was wrong, he didn't understand. . . .

THE REBIRTHING: END PHASE
The stones assemble

SHADDALAKH

FRUNZACOACHE — MASSULIT

BinYAHtii

HARRA'S EYE — CHURRIKYOO

KLUKESHARNA

Roaring with rage, Settsimaksimin landed on one point of a Hexa star; Simms came down at his feet. Maks clutched at Shaddalakh and gathered himself to snap out of this place wherever it was.

He was frozen there, Shaddalakh vibrated in his grip, but something blocked his access to the talisman. He gathered the remnants of his strength—threw all he knew and all he was into a bind-shatter Chant. His Voice was there. It made the dust jump. Nothing changed. The confusion of hums and whistles and other small ugly noises went steadily on around him. He'd never seen anything like this place. He understood nothing he saw, even less what he heard.

The dull gray light shuddered. Sparks came pouring into that dusty gray hell, shrieking as he'd shrieked. Geniod. He remembered them from the cavern.

Something caught them, something prisoned them in a glitternet of force lines above the dusty gray throne chair beside the Hexa. They quieted, he thought they were doing what he'd done, looking around, weighing their chances, deciding how to attack and free themselves.

The light shuddered again.

Palami Kumindri, her Housemaster Callam Cammam, another female figure. Simms gasped. "Esmoon," he whispered. Finally the simulacrum of Musteba Xa, holding Massulit clutched against his bony chest.

Something snatched Massulit away from him, brought it swooping around to hover over Maksim's head. His souls spun from the stone and fled back into him, swirling round and round in him, turning him dizzy with the euphoria of the Return.

When he recovered, the four of them were gone and the sack above the throne was jerking and jolting and brighter than before.

The light in that decaying dreadful room shuddered.

Brann appeared on the Hexa-point at his right, Tak WakKerrcarr standing behind her, his staff in one hand, his other hand resting on her shoulder. Massulit swept away from Maksim and rushed to her. She looked startled, caught it, stood holding it. "Maksi," she said, "so this is why you didn't answer the *call-me*'s."

"That's it. Tak."

"Maksim."

"Surprised to see you here."

"Not half so surprised as I am." He touched Brann's cheek, returned his hand to her shoulder. "Seems to be one of the drawbacks when you grow fond of a certain turbulent young lass."

"Fond, hah!" Brann said. "You're just a horny old goat."

"That too."

Maksim started to speak, shut his mouth as the light shuddered again.

Yaril and Jaril appeared at the next Hexa-point. They stood side by side, each with one arm about the other's waist. Jaril held his free hand chest-high with Churrikyoo sitting on it. Two pairs of crystal eyes turned to Maksim, turned away; they chose not to greet him.

The light shuddered.

Korimenei appeared at the Hexa-point at Maksim's left, a long-tailed beast on her shoulder. She wore Frunzacoache around her neck, the leaf within shining a brilliant green. She glanced quickly around, nodded as if she recognized what she was seeing, then she smiled at Maksim. "I missed you," she said, "I thought you'd lost interest in me."

"No, daughter mine, never that. Just unavailable as you see."

"Take me as an apprentice?"

He laughed, a shout that filled the room with life and vigor and made its deadness even deader. "Kori, you don't waste your opportunities, do you?"

"Doesn't Tungjii say take your Luck where you find it? Well?"

"Of course I will. As you propose, so I accept. If we

manage to get clear of this." He looked round. "What is this place, anyone know?"

Brann sighed. "I forgot you hadn't seen it, Maksi. Chained God. We're in his body."

The light shuddered.

Trago appeared on the Hexa-point beside Korimenei, frightened and uncertain. He held Harra's Eye clutched tight against his chest and looked wildly around, started to speak to Korimenei, but didn't; instead he bowed his head and stood staring intently into the flawless crystal sphere.

The light shuddered.

Danny Blue appeared with Felsrawg crouching at his feet. He flung out a hand and Klukesharna slammed into it. He stared at the talisman a moment, then looked round. "Family reunion," he said. "Brann, Kori, Maksim, Changers. I was beginning to wonder if I'd see you all. It's like trail stew, drop in the ingredients as before and stir vigorously. Simms, sorry to see you, man. Where's the Esmoon? She ought to be here, seeing I'm infested with this thing again." He held Klukesharna between thumb and forefinger and waved it about.

Simms chuckled, he was amused but there was an edge to his enjoyment. "Sucked up there," he said and pointed at the glittersack; he was content to sit where he was at Maksim's feet and didn't try to stand. "I don't think she's enjoying it either."

"Should hope not." He reached a hand down to Felsrawg. "You gonna sit there or what?"

She moved her shoulders, looked disgusted. "I can't get up," she said. "I'm stuck here. Let me alone, fool."

"Your call. Hey, Garbage Guts," he yelled, startling Maksim and drawing a grimace from Brann. He was scowling at the broad sheet of milky glass spread across the front of the room. "What the hell's going on?"

For several breaths nothing happened. Lights flickered, threads of god-stuff danced and darted, minor lightnings struck and rebounded. The noises got louder; though they weren't music in any other sense, none of the euphony Maksim expected, there was a rhythm in those noises, a pulse not quite a heartbeat but similar; as they got louder, more demanding, their effect on him and the others intensified. There was a sense of something ominous getting closer and closer.

Maksim set himself to resist. He fought to tie into

Shaddalakh, fought to resist unnamed, shapeless demands the noises made on him. He fought the god.

##

Korimenei saw Maks stiffen, begin to gesture and chant. She couldn't hear him. As if she were sealed off from him, a wall between them. She dropped and sat cross-legged with Ailiki in her lap, closed one hand about Frunzacoache, rested the other on the curve of the mahsar's back. Frunzacoache shook. She thought she could hear it screaming with rage as it tried to touch her. When reaching for the realities didn't work, she flipped through her choices and began trying everything she could think of to attack the forces holding her. She fought the god with everything inside her.

##

Brann leaned against Tak WakKerrcarr and struggled to draw energy from Massulit. Nothing. She reached for Yaril and Jaril. They were sealed off from her. Tak said losing them would put her in danger; she understood that now. She was powerless against anything she couldn't touch; whatever stayed beyond the reach of her arms was safe from her. She ignored the pressure from the Chained God and concentrated on reaching the Changers. If they could make that bridge again, the Chained God would find his metaphorical fingers singed. She denied the god, denied his hold on her, refused to let him shape her acts. She fought the god with everything in her.

##

Danny Blue's half-sires forgot their differences and fought the god. They were shadows of what they were, but they had their skills and their stubbornness. They poured all that into Danny; he fought the god with Daniel Akamarino's will to freedom and Ahzurdan's learning and his own rage. Danny clutched at Klukesharna, felt her quiver as she tried to break through to him and help him. He fought to reach her, he fought the god.

##

Jaril and Yaril raged as one; they struggled to reach

Churrikyoo, but could not, together they punched at the force holding them on the Hexa-point, they struggled to reach out to Brann, they could see her, they knew she was trying to reach them. Wordlessly, they merged into a single glowsphere with Churrikyoo floating in their core. Wordlessly, furiously, they fought to break free and suck the life out of the god.

##

Trago clutched at Harra's Eye. He fought against being swallowed, but he knew so little about what was going on, he was, after all, only a six-year-old boy, the ten years he'd passed in spell might have been ten minutes. All he could do was deny and deny and deny. He could not relate to the woman who said she was his sister, she was a stranger. He didn't want any of this, he was terrified and angry, the god made him feel sick when he looked at it, it was ugly, rotten. No, he shouted into the crystal, no and no and no.

##

The noises changed, the noises were a chant.

The Chained God chanted, gathering his forces, thrusting his will at them, a wordless spell or if there were words, they were sunk so deep in computer symbology and machine noise they were wholly unintelligible to mortal ears, even Danny Blue's.

BinYAHtii appeared, hovered over the Hexa-center.

The glittersack opened, poured out the geniod.

BinYAHtii quivered, hummed with power, put out a pulsing red aura, calling, calling the geniod to it: hungry hungry hungry: Hunger Incarnate. A HUNGER greater than even the geniod's. Demanding. Compelling.

The geniod struggled, screamed—and streamed in a river of light into the heart of the talisman.

BinYAHtii ate and ate, ate them all, its power song sinking into subsonics.

The river vibrated, distorted, took on one shape, then another, then was Palami Kumindri half submerged in the liquid light. "The Promise," she screamed. "We obeyed in all things. The Promise. Pay us what you promised."

The God spoke, h/its multiple voices like a swarm of locusts buzzing. "This is MY reality. What made you think I'd let you eat it bare? You've lived well enough. I owe you nothing. I used you and now I purge you. Consider it the price you pay for the worlds you have destroyed." H/it sounded prim and complacent. H/it drove the geniod into the Hunger of BinYAHtii until every fleck of light had vanished and the talisman glowed like a small red sun.

H/its power enormously increased, the god reached out and PUT H/ITS HANDS on them: *Settsimaksimin/Simms* *Brann/WakKerrcarr* *Yaril/Jaril* *Danny Blue/Felsrawg* *Trago* *Korimenei* H/it seized hold of them, turned them to face BinYAHtii. H/it seized hold of the Great Talismans and pulled at them, drawing the stone bearers with them into the heart of the Hexa, drawing them closer and closer to BinYAHtii, chanting all the time in its harsh insectile voices, faster and faster, the force in the machine words (if they were words) increasing, the rhythm more and more compelling.

They fought.

They struggled to join against him.

They could not touch, physically or psychically. The god held them separate, held them that way until h/it managed to bring them to the Hexa-center.

Maksim's grand basso broke free suddenly, battered at the humming clicking tweeting chant, joined a moment later by the grand baritone of Tak WakKerrcarr, the Voices of Sorceror Primes at their most powerful, most urgent. They slowed the inward creep, they couldn't stop it.

Closer and closer to BinYAHtii h/it forced them.

Maksim's arm jerked out, out of his control, he held Shaddalakh before him like an offering.

Danny's arm jerked out, out of his control, he held Klukesharna before him like an offering.

Brann's arm jerked out, out of her control, she held Massulit cupped in the palm of her hand, held it like an offering.

Trago's arms jerked out, out of his control, he held Harra's Eye between his two hands, held it like an offering.

Frunzacoache flew out from Korimenei's breast, dragging her with it as it sought the middle, offering itself.

Yaril and Jaril dissolved from their sphere into twin bipedal shapes, moved side by side, each with an arm about the other's waist, moved with staggering, reluctant steps toward the middle. Jaril's arm stretched straight before him, Churrikyoo cupped in the palm of his hand, held like an offering to that demanding red Hunger throbbing at the Hexa-center.

Slowly, inexorably, resisting h/it all the way anyway they could, the stone bearers and their companions drew closer and closer to the HUNGER.

They touched it.

At the same instant the six talismans touched the seventh.
reality dissolves
ego-centers hover in a blinding burning golden featureless nothingness
hang disembodied, self-aware in only the dimmest sense
wait
are aware of waiting without being aware of time
are aware of waiting without being aware of purpose
are finally aware of otherness otherwhereness
six point-nodes of power tremble in a burning featureless nothingness
they begin to move
they swim toward certain ego-centers
they touch certain ego-centers, merge with them
ego-centers sense imminent change which is a change in itself
no time has passed
an eternity has passed
nothingness EXPLODES

2

Danny Blue finished the step he'd started ten subjective years before and nearly tripped over Felsrawg who was crouching on the roadway in front of him. He took her hand, pulled her to her feet.

"What happened?" Felsrawg turned her head from side to side, startled by the strangeness around her. "Where are we?"

"Skinker world, from the look of it."

"What?"

"Another reality, Felsa, I doubt you're going to like it. No gods here."

"Hah, that so. I like it already." She shied as a skip went groaning past overhead. "What. . . ."

Danny looked from her to the skip vanishing in the distance. What am I going to do with you, he thought. You're a survivor, but it'll take some doing to catch up on a good ten millennia of technological development between one breath and the next. He started walking; Felsrawg was still lost in shock and let him get several steps ahead. She gave a sharp exclamation and trotted after him; when she caught up, she walked beside him staring round with interest and uneasiness at an array of vegetation odd enough to start her licking her lips and touching the knives hidden under her long loose sleeves.

She shied again as a ground vehicle clattered past, the Skinker in it turning to stare at them from bulging plum-colored eyes. "Demon!"

Danny scratched at his stubble, sighed. His immediate future looked a lot more interesting than comfortable. "No demon, Felsa. You start acting evil to these Skinkers and I'll thump you good. This is their world. You hear?"

She scowled at him, shrugged. "Demon," she said stubbornly, but relented enough to promise a minimal courtesy. "Just keep them away from me."

Gods, Danny thought, xenophobe on top of everything else. He ran a hand though his hair. Tungjii Luck, if I ever go back there, so help me, I swear I'll put matches to your toes. He jerked to a stop as a tiny Tungjii sitting on an airbubble floated past his nose. The god twiddled hisser fingers, winked and vanished. Danny glanced at Felsrawg, but she was kicking along staring at a pair of hitsatchee posts planted beside an U-tree in bud. He stopped, felt the buds. They still had the fuzz on. Either he was coming back in the same season, maybe the same day in the season, or the time spent in that other reality had gone past between one blip and the next in this. He frowned at the sun. Not quite that fast. It was morning then, it's near sundown now. If this is the same day, I bet La Kuninga is ready to snatch me . . . he grinned and smoothed his hand over his thick wavy hair . . . bald again.

The traffic got heavier; Felsrawg stopped twitching as the groundcars rumbled past, but she was still taut with a feeling half-fear, half-loathing. She kept snatching glances at him as if she expected him to turn into a slick skinned six-limbed lizardoid. When they reached the rim of the town, he stopped her. "Felsa, best thing for you is keep your mouth shut and do what I do. In a way it's too bad the jump here gave you interlingue, there's a lot to be said for dumbness covering ignorance."

She gave him a fulminating look, but dropped a step behind him, even followed him into a ribbajit without comment. He dropped on the tattered seat, shifted over when a broken spring gave him a half-hearted poke. "Port," he said and settled back as the jit trundled off.

Felsrawg spread her hand on her knee, exposing the skry rings, watching them from under her lashes.

Danny chuckled. "They won't read, Felsa. This is a machine, it runs on batteries, not magic. Nothing stranger than a . . . um . . . a loom or a waterwheel."

"There's nothing to make it move and there's no driver."

"It moves, doesn't it. Go with the flow, Fey."

She was silent for several minutes as the ribbajit clunked around the edge of the town. "Why am I here, Danny?"

"You want me to explain the multiverse?"

"Fool! You know what I mean. You belong in this place. I don't. "

He touched the pocket where Klukesharna had somehow inserted itself during the crossing between realities; he had a suspicion the thing had imagined some kind of link between him and Felsrawg just because she was standing beside him in that cave. Typical computer-think if you could even say a hunk of iron could think. "You do now. Better get used to it."

"Send me back."

"Can't. There's no magic here." He said that flatly, giving her no room for argument. He believed it mostly, told himself that Tungjii's wink was imagination, nothing more. The ribbajit clanked to a stop by the hitsatchee posts outside the linkfence that ran around the stretch of metacrete the locals called a starport. "We're here," he said. "Come on."

"What's here?"

"I don't know. Let's go see."

A tall bony blonde woman with a set angry face was snapping out orders to a collection of Skinkers using motorized assists to load crates and bundles on the roller ramp running into the belly of her battered freetrader; now and then she muttered furious asides to the short man beside her.

"No, no, not that one, the numbers are on them, you can read, can't you." Aside to her companion: "Mouse, if that scroov shows his face round my ship again, I'll skin him an inch at a time and feed it to him broiled."

The little gray man scratched his three fingers through a spongy growth that covered most of his upper body; he blinked several times, shrugged and said nothing.

"Sssaaah!" She darted to the loaders, cursed in half a dozen languages, waved her arms, made the workers reload the last cart. Still furious, she stalked back to where she'd been standing. "Danny Blue, you miserable druuj, I'll pull your masters rating this time, I swear I will, this is the last time you walk out on me or anyone else."

"Blue wants, Blue walks," the little man said. "Done it before, 'll do it again."

"Hah! Mouse, if you're so happy with him, you go help Sandy stow the cargo."

"I don't do boxes."

She glared at him, but throttled back the words that bulged in her throat, stalked off and stood inspecting the crates as they rolled past him.

Danny walked round a stack of crates, Felsrawg trailing reluctantly after her. "Hya, Kally, I'm back."

She wheeled. "Where the hell you been, druuj!" Her eyes went wide when she realized what she was seeing. "Huh? You're not Danny."

"Remember Inconterza? Matrize Lezdoa the scarifier? I can go on."

"Never mind. Someday you have to explain to me how you grew a head of hair and three extra inches and changed your face that much," she glanced at her ringchron, "in nine hours." She looked past him. "And where you got the baba there."

"Be polite, Kally, Felsa's no man's baba. Woman's either."

"Hmp. You not giving me any excuse for leaving me to do your job, are you."

"No. But I'll contract an extra year if you give Felsa space onboard."

"Guarantee no walking?"

"Guarantee. My word on it."

"Deal. She got anything but what she's carrying?"

"Nothing but a name. Felsa, I'll have you meet free trader and shipmaster Kally Kuninga. Kally, this is one Felsrawg Lawdrawn. She doesn't know what the hell's going on, but she'll learn."

"You finished? Right. Get your ass over there and do your job. Mouse he's been having vibrations which means we gotta get the hell out before the sluivasshi land on us."

She looked Felsrawg over, head to toe back again. "She's your problem, Danny. Keep her outta my hair and see she's fumigated before you bring her on board." She twitched her nose, swung round and stalked off.

Felsrawg snorted. "Bitch."

"Sure. And if you say it to her face, she'll laugh, then she'll slap you down so hard you bounce. Come on. I've got work to do."

##

Felsrawg found a quiet corner near a stack of empty crates where she'd be out of the way of the workers. Danny was right, she didn't understand any of this, maybe she never would. She thought about that a minute and decided it was blue funk and not worth the air it took to say it, she might not know how those clink-clank slim-slam things worked, but she could see what they did. That's all she needed. She looked at her skry rings, sniffed. *I don't know how they work either, but I got damn good at reading them.* The sun was going down in the west, she thought it was the west, it felt like west, just like it did back home and the Kuninga woman was a gasht all right, but she looked normal, at least there was that.

The clattering stopped, the demons rode their metal carts across the hard white stuff that covered the ground and vanished behind some odd looking buildings. The rollerramp was folding itself up, squeezing together into an impossibly small package; it might not be magic, but it surely looked like it. Danny loped around like a Temu herder chasing strays, getting everything folded up and tucked away in that thing. Ship? It reminded her of an old tom swampspider after twenty years of mating battles, battered and molting, missing a leg here and a mandible there, but tough as boiled bull leather. She heard her name and stepped out of the shadow to wait for Danny who was coming to get her. *It starts,* she thought. *Say one thing, it should be interesting.*

3

Yaril and Jaril went slipping down a long long slide and burst into brightness, glowspheres zagging across complex crystal lattices on a hot young world circling a sun in the heart of a hot young cluster. Aulis came zipping round them, cousins and strangers, seekers and linkers, greeting them swinging through wild exuberant loops yelling welcome come and see we thought a smiglar had eat you Yaroooh Jaroooh. Aetas came, younglings budded since they left, bursting with curiosity, wallowing in the explosion of joy, Afas came, trailing after Nurse Agaxes, laughing and singing their infant songs, absorbing the excitment, the joy, though they had no idea what created it. And Agaxes came, majestic and slow, swimming in on all sides, and, finally, finally, father-mother meld at last there shimmering, expanding, opening to absorb them, hold them within in a hot and loving embrace.

Churrikyoo *moved*.

Before the absorption was complete, it emerged from Jaril, fell into the lattice and went hopping away, matter become energy, stasis become motility, non-life become life.

Yaril and Jaril rest in the embrace of mother-father reading off memory into memory until the whole is transferred, then the embrace ends.

Father-mother go drifting off to digest and discuss the tale with their community-companions. Waves of joy flush pink and gold through them, their children who were dead are alive again, more than alive are triumphant and weighty with story, treasure beyond all other treasures, a meaty and complex narrative to be considered for meaning and style, taken bit by bit, balancing each bit by another, bit against whole, centuries worth of contemplation and dissection.

Surraht-Aulis whole and complete again, Yaril and Jaril emerge, go darting away to join a cluster of other aulis. They race through the lattices, chasing the radiant frog Churrikyoo, a new game for aulis, a wonderful game because no one can win, no one can touch the frog, only chase after it until he, she, they lose it. They play the old games too, merging and remerging, telling their tale into the auli legend horde. They are sad when they remember Brann, but they remember her less and less as the world turns on the spindle of time. They are home and valued, they are merging with their agemates, spinning a community of copulation and exploration, song and story, merging, emerging, remerging.

They are Home.

4

Knowing with all her body that the pocket reality was collapsing around her, Brann fell away from it and landed on her hands and knees in black sand. The Bay at Haven. Massulit lay on the sand beneath her. She closed her hand about it, pushed up until she was sitting on her heels with Massulit cuddled against her stomach.

Tak WakKerrcarr came over to her, reached a hand down to her and pulled her onto her feet. He pointed at Massulit. "I see you've got yourself a new playtoy."

She looked at the sapphire, watched the star pulse for a breath or two. "You want it?"

"It's not the kind of thing you can give away, m' dear."

She slipped the Stone into a pocket, rubbed at her eyes. "Yaro? Jay?" She remembered the Eating of the Geniod and was suddenly terrified, turned so quickly she stumbled and nearly fell; recovering, she continued to swing round, kicking sand into a storm about her knees, her arms flying out, her eyes wild. "Yaro? Jay?" Her voice cut through the twilight, agony in the syllables as she cried out again and again the names of her change-children. "Chained God," she shrieked, "If you ate my babies. . . ." She ran along the sand, past Trago who was kneeling in the wash of the outgoing tide ignoring them all, staring into the shinning heart of the Eye, past Simms and Korimenei who stood silent on the sand, watching the drama but outside it. "If you fed my children to that Abomination. . . ." She stopped, glared at the mountain rising dark against the gegenschein, Isspyrivo the Gate. "If you took them, you DIEEEE!!!" She turned and ran back. "I'll tear you," she screamed as she ran. "I'll feed you to rats, I'll . . . I'll. . . ." She stopped where she'd started, swung round and round, flinging words to the wind, helpless to do anything but shout yet almost demonic in her rage. "I'll DRAIN you. . . ." Round and round. "Dead, *dead!* DEAD!"

Tak WakKerrcarr came running and tried to hold her but she broke away, Maksim swore and plunged at her. He ignored her struggles, wrapped his arms about her and held her tight against his massive chest. She kicked and hit at him, clawed at him, she was blind with rage and grief and an overmastering terror, she didn't know him, she no longer knew where she was. He kept her pinned with one huge arm, caught her hands in his and pressed them against his ribs, all the time talking to her, his bass voice flowing over her, calm, quiet, caressing, until she stopped fighting him and lay against him, shaking and sobbing.

A vast red figure came down the Mountain, shrinking as she came until she was a mere fifty yards of four-armed, crimson female god. Slya Fireheart tapped Maksim on the shoulder, wrapped her upper right hand around Brann when he released her. She got to her feet, lifted Brann till they were more or less eye to eye. "T'SSSH, T'SSSH, LITTLE NOTHING. WHAT'S ALL THIS?" A huge fingernail moved along Brann's face, scraping away tearstreaks.

Brann blinked, tried to gather her shattered wits. "What happened to them? My babies. . . ."

"THOSE FUZZBALLS? EHHH, LITTLE NOTHING, THEY WENT HOME, THAT'S ALL. YOU WANTED THEM TO GO HOME, DIDN'T YOU. YOU HAD POOR OLD MAN OVER THERE SPRINKLING ITCH POWDER ON ME, SAYING SEND THEM HOME SEND THEM HOME."

"Home. . . ." Brann tugged a hand free, scrubbed at her eyes. "Yes . . . but I . . . not so soon, not without saying . . . not so suddenly. . . ."

Slya set her down on the sand. Like a huge and clumsy child playing with a doll, she brushed at Brann with her upper right hand, plucked at her clothing with her upper left hand, smoothed her hair with one huge forefinger. Though the god was being kind and affectionate and meant no harm, Brann was exhausted and more than a little battered when Slya left off her efforts. Brann edged cautiously away, backing into Tak. She tilted her head to look up at him, smiled at him, then held her hand out to Maksim. She started to speak, closed her mouth, startled by a loud shout from the boy.

Trago was on his feet, pointing at Isspyrivo's peak. "Look," he cried again. "Chained God. God-not-Chained."

A golden metal man a hundred meters tall stood upon Isspyrivo's glaciers, posing like a dancer. The setting sun glinted on hundreds of angular facets, the light off them so brilliant it was blinding. He moved. He was slow and clumsy at first, lurching, teetering on the verge of falling over, but he kept coming. Like Slya Fireheart he came striding down the Mountain toward them and with each step the awkward stiffness diminished until the metal moved with the elasticity

of flesh and the God-Not-Chained gleamed and shimmered
liquidly instead of glittering.

Paying no more attention to them than to the seagulls
gliding around him, he walked out across the water and
stopped in the middle of the bay. Slya Fireheart whistled,
stomped her feet and shouted her approval of this new male
god in the pantheon. He looked over his shoulder at her,
crooked a finger. She whooped and went running to him
across the water, each fleeting touch of her huge red feet
sending up spurts of steam.

There was a shine not the sun on the northern horizon.
Amortis came undulating across the water, her hair flowing
in her personal wind, her gauzy draperies molding her lush
body, her large blue eyes flirting with the God-Not-Chained.

Slya glared at her, Amortis glared back.

The god watched, preening like a cock two hens were
fighting over. A thought flowed sluggishly across his perfect
face. He left his companions, came striding back to the
beach. He scooped up Trago, set the boy on his shoulder
and went off with him.

Korimenei cried out, then fell silent as her beast came
running across the sand and jumped into her arms.

Slya and Amortis trotted after the god, Slya slid her top
right arm about his shoulders, her lower right arm about his
waist, bumped her solid hip against his. Amortis took his
other arm, brushed sensuously sinuously against him murmuring at him all the time, her voice like leaves rustling in a
lazy summer breeze.

There was silence on the beach until the unlikely quartet
vanished over the horizon.

Brann sighed. "So that was why," she said. "That was
what all this was about. All the terror and the dying and the
pain. To build a body to house that . . . that Monster."

"So it seems," Tak WakKerrcarr murmured in her ear.
"Do you mind?"

"Yes," she said fiercely, then she shook her head. "It's
futile, but I mind. Look what we've loosed on this miserable
world. I'd like to. . . ."

'It's god-business, Thornlet. We're out of it now and
lucky to be alive. Let's stay that way. You coming back with
me?"

She leaned against him and looked at Maksim. He was
over with Korimenei and a stocky red-haired man she didn't
know; she saw him touch the man's face with the affection

and tenderness he'd saved for her till now. I've lost him too, she thought, but I never had him, did I. He looks well. And happy. What kind of jealous bitch am I that I resent it? She smiled. Just your average sort of jealous bitch, I suppose. Nothing special. "Maksi," she called.

He looked round. "Bramble?"

"Going back to Jal Virri?"

"Yes, I've got an apprentice to teach." He threaded his big hand through Korimenei's flyaway hair, shook her gently. "Work her little tail off. You?"

"I'm for Mun Gapur. See you round. Tak?"

"Give the girl a rest, Maks, come see us some time. Bring your friend if you want. Ta."

5

The next morning, a bright clear cool morning with air that bubbled in the blood like wine, Brann stood beside one of the few coldsprings in Tak WakKerrcarr's watergarden at Mun Gapur. She held Massulit out away from her. "I don't want it, Tik-tok. I don't want it anywhere round me. It makes me nervous. It reminds me. . . ." She swallowed, the pain suddenly back, the loss raw in her.

"It goes where it will, Thornlet and that's not me. You want to lay a curse on me even I couldn't handle, try giving it to me." His mouth twitched in a smile part rueful, part calculating. "You might give it to Amortis."

Brann snorted, then she smiled too, a small reluctant lift of her mouth corners. "I will never ever forget that scene. I hope Slya sets her hair on fire." The smile went away. "And melts him into slag."

"Ah, m' dear."

"Hunh!" She contemplated Massulit a moment longer then tossed it into the spring and watched it sink through the clear cold water. It shone briefly but intensely blue, then settled dark and anonymous among the stones at the bottom of the pool. "There. I give it to nobody." She turned away, brushing her hands as if she brushed away the whole of the painful time just past. "This is a fire mountain," she said.

"True. Why?"

"Build me a kiln, Tik-tok."

"You need to rest a while, Thornlet. Relax."

She moved her shoulders, ran a hand through her long white hair. "I can't, luv. Not for a while yet. Do you understand? I need to be busy. I need to do something with my body, my hands, my mind. Something with meaning to me. When I was last in Kukurul I saw newware from Arth Slya. It gave me idea I want to try. Any clay deposits round here?"

"I don't know. I'll see what I can find out. You're sure?"

"They were my children, Tik-tok. I have to grieve for them a while. But only a while. We have time, luv. If nothing else, we do have time.